THE DNR TRILOGY

VOLUME 1: BACKING THE WRONG PRIMATE

DON W. HILL, M.D.

Copyright © 2022 by Don W. Hill, M.D.

ISBN   Softcover   978-1-950596-81-2
        Hardcover   978-1-950596-82-9
        eBook   978-1-950596-83-6

All rights reserved. No part of this book may be reproduced or transmitted in any form or by any means, electronic or mechanical, including photocopying, recording, or by any information storage and retrieval system without express written permission from the author, except in the case of brief quotations embodied in critical reviews and certain other non-commercial uses permitted by copyright law.

This is a work of fiction. All of the characters, names, incidents, organizations, and dialogue in this novel are either the products of the author's imagination or are used fictitiously.

KJV: Taken from the King James Bible

Printed in the United States of America.

To order additional copies of this book, contact:
Bookwhip
1-855-339-3589
https://www.bookwhip.com

TO FALLEN HEROES

Lieutenant Dick Dowling—As you are a true Lone Star hero, I have referred to a fictionalized university in this novel that was named in your honor. If at first you don't *secede*, try and try again.

Major General Robert Ross—I absolutely loved the urban renewal project you orchestrated in Washington, DC, a while back. Strong work! Some may consider what you had done to be nothing more than the expected brutality that may transpire within the context of a bloody war. On the other hand, others may believe what you had done was an act of malicious terrorism. I however, have a completely different perspective on this historical event. In retrospect, it would appear to me that you were simply trying to jump-start the "draining of the swamp" in which American politics are now so deeply mired. I was wondering if you and your boys weren't too busy, perhaps you could come back across the pond and reprise that singular act of love that you once showed for the American people. Remember the famous words immortalized by Magnificent Montague: "Burn, baby! *Burn!*"

Keller Stadig—I wept bitterly when I learned of your tragic passing. Your father told me that what you did for our country weighed heavy upon your heart and even heavier upon your soul. The patibulum that was thrust upon your shoulders must have been unbearable, and for that I am deeply grieved. Thank you eternally for your service to our country, and just in case you did not know, your father, Bryan, is one of the most decent human beings this author ever knew. I thought so much of your dad that I had actually named my own son in your father's honor. Keller, when you run into your fellow patriots who all had offered their very last and full measure of devotion, please bestow upon them all my warmest and heartfelt regards. They truly deserve America's gratitude and our prayers. May God bless and keep you, Keller, and may you forever rest in peace.

To the Guru of the Twelve-String Electric Rickenbacker

J. J. (Roger) McGuinn—A tenant within the realm of fundamentalist convictions is the steadfast faith that Adam was touched by the hand of God, as was portrayed by Michelangelo in his famous painting found on the ceiling of the Sistine Chapel. Although theologians may vociferously debate the veracity of that proclamation based upon one's persuasion as to whether the events that were accounted for in the very beginning were literal or allegorical, there can absolutely be no doubt that Roger McGuinn was touched by the hand of God the very first time he strapped on the mighty Ric and plugged it into an amplifier. If it was not for Roger McGuinn and his band, the Byrds, the vexing poetry of Robert Zimmerman may not have ever been put to *real* music. Thank you, Mr. McGuinn. There must be a special place in heaven reserved for you.

DISCLOSURE

This novel transects many genres, including historical fiction, medical drama, crime and punishment, and also sin, redemption, and perhaps even salvation. It has also unintentionally turned out to be a probe into the roots of evil that all too often embroil the human condition. Tribalism and racism, as perpetuated by modern progressive ideology, are also obvious undertones in this novel. Hopefully individuals who tackle this trilogy (black, white, brown, or otherwise) will have an opportunity to reflect on their own complex relationships with their fellow humans who occupy this small blue orb in the Milky Way galaxy. One may also find a teaspoon of mysticism sprinkled into the mix, with regard to the expressed conviction that everything in the universe seems to be connected somehow.

Although this work of fiction was not initially intended to be a tome that would fall directly into the realm of classic Judeo-Christian spirituality, the author would not be surprised if this novel were publicly received as such, as the strained relationship between humankind and God is addressed throughout this treatise (if indeed such a relationship still exists within the moral vagaries of the modern, post-theistic epoch in which humankind now largely finds itself). After all, does God still care, much less ever intercede anymore, in the various and sundry self-destructive activities perpetrated by humankind? If the end result of human behavior to date is evaluated as a surrogate barometer to ascertain the possible likelihood of whether divine intervention may occasionally occur, even in extremely remote circumstances, the answer to this philosophical and theological query may indeed be a resounding and unequivocal no! If that sadly is indeed the case, then we have nobody left to blame in the universe but ourselves.

As life and death are weighty subject matters, hyperbolic humorous anecdotes have been thrown in to occasionally lighten the somber nature of this novel. Another recurrent theme that readers may note is that this novel is peppered with overt political editorial comments. As such, the reader may try to infer that many of the evil and stupid antagonists portrayed in this book may perhaps seem reminiscent of evil and stupid contemporary public figures who profess evil and stupid ideology. If any public figures are offended by such satirical inferences, then they should carefully scrutinize their own images in a mirror.

The bulk of this fictional novel occurs over a compressed two-year time frame in the early 1980s, but the events portrayed in this story are largely inspired by clinical and historical occurrences that the author witnessed or was otherwise privy to over the course of half a century. Except for obvious exceptions regarding true public figures and factual historical events that have been woven into the fabric of this story, the other names, hospital settings, and precise clinical details that are mentioned in this novel have been thoroughly fictionalized to protect the true identities of the individuals and institutions portrayed, be they innocent, guilty, living, or dead.

The book is Orwellian in its scope and intent, and I hope the reader will be as deeply disturbed in reading this book as the author was in writing it. It is my fervent prayer that the horrific accounts portrayed in this novel were only the product of a bad dream that was induced by the consumption of a nasty, week-old fish taco that had been scraped out of the back of a refrigerator. No doubt the aforementioned unsavory taco was inadvertently contaminated with pathogenic microbial, coliform organisms. In and of itself, such an epicurean extravaganza would cause overwhelming nausea, vomiting, and diarrhea, but it would unlikely be an insult toxic enough to germinate such a nightmare. The above medical opinion is likely an accurate prognostication, unless, of course, the taco in question had been subsequently chased down with a glass of piss-warm stale beer that some delinquent miscreant dropped a cigar butt into.

This is not an attestation that the author who penned this novel ever had the pleasure of experiencing such a celebratory gastronomical event. However, if the above-noted gustatory drama had ever actually occurred to anybody at any time in the annals of recorded human history, the subsequent transcendental happenstance would have likely engendered a bona fide out-of-body experience that would no doubt be intrinsically associated with frightening visual and auditory hallucinations. Well, if that were only the case…

INTRODUCTION

As I sit down to compose this introduction, it is hard for me to believe that I graduated from medical school over one-third of a century ago. When I was a student, my colleagues and I would make derisive comments about the elderly faculty members at our institution of medical training. We would refer to these seasoned educators as "dinosaurs" or "old fossils." Well, somewhere along the way, I became a grizzled old bastard myself, and I never saw it coming. One day I just looked into the mirror and saw a crabby old crab picker with a lot of gray hair looking back at me. Once when I was asked to describe the distillation of my very essence as I approached the thirty-fifth anniversary of my being awarded a medical degree, I responded that I was simply a blue-collar guy who happened to practice medical oncology and hematology. Perhaps at best I have only been a glorified traffic cop trying to direct cancer patients in the right direction.

Over the course of my career, I have seen many strange and wondrous events that ran through the entire spectrum of the human experience. Sadly, I recall a great deal of brutal violence and crime that occurred around the Texas Medical Center during the time I received my doctoral education there. I witnessed disturbing events both while I was in medical school and later in my postgraduate training in New Mexico that left me somewhat dispirited and cynical for a great deal of my career. Perhaps all I experienced could one day be boiled down into a few interesting anecdotes or short stories. For quite a long time, however, I did not have enough material to truly warrant an attempt at a full-fledged novel.

All of that changed, however, through what I would call the rule of unintended consequences. In an effort to bottleneck and contract the expanding universe of the cost of health care that has been spiraling out of control now for many years, the federal government in its infinite stupidity has decided that the first amendment to the constitution no longer applies to medical personnel or the pharmaceutical industry. If a pharmaceutical representative discusses any "off-label" use of a chemotherapeutic agent, or even if there is a discussion about a new drug that may be coming down the pike, there will be hell to pay.

This warped thinking is the result of a misguided conviction that if a doctor doesn't know about some type of treatment that has not been given a green light by the FDA, then he or she is certainly not going to try to administer such a therapy in an unapproved fashion. This makes absolutely no sense however, as oncology clinics and hospitals cannot get reimbursement for the administration of chemotherapy drugs unless the employment of said therapeutic agents is preapproved by an insurance company or the medication has already met Medicare treatment guidelines. I know this from firsthand experience. I have had to eat huge pharmacological bills in the past when I made mistakes and treated cancer patients with chemotherapeutic agents outside of the realm of approved FDA guidelines.

These unfounded concepts, to which the FDA slavishly adheres, have actually permeated into medical/scientific symposiums. The American Society of Clinical Oncology, known by the acronym ASCO, holds a yearly spring conference where thousands of cancer specialists gather for confirmation of state-of-the-art cancer treatment and discussions about new therapeutic triumphs. At these major conferences, pharmaceutical companies are invited to set up display booths to have an opportunity to introduce their products to the conference attendees. Because of the aforementioned strange FDA rules and regulations and also careful self-policing in which drug firms are now fully engaged, pharmaceutical companies must often set up two separate presentation arenas at these international venues. One display is typically the bare-bones and rather pedestrian presentation that is specifically tailored for only the lowly American doctors. For all the other international attendees, the second type of product presentation may be completely different. Lavish, sumptuous, and gold star wing-dings for foreign oncologists may be going on just behind a guarded curtain.

American physicians are forbidden to find out anything that the non-American physicians are learning about if there is any mention of off-label treatments or any therapies that are not yet approved in the United States by the FDA. Please understand that I am talking about presentations for cancer specialists that occur at medical/scientific symposiums that are conducted right here inside the United States of America. There are truly data that American doctors are not allowed to learn about at these conferences that are hosted on American soil. Wow! I can't make this stuff up.

Well, it was at an ASCO meeting that occurred well over a decade ago where this rule of unintended consequences raised its ugly head, and it put me in a situation where I was truly in the wrong place at the wrong time. I overheard a conversation that was never intended for my ears. I learned about the details of a wicked event that occurred likely in the early to mid-1980s. The tale of evil that I learned about vexed me for many years until I finally decided to sit down and put together a coherent story in the form of a novel.

At the ASCO meeting in question, I decided to take a break in the formal medical/scientific presentations and go over into the exhibition hall, where the pharmaceutical representatives had set up display booths to educate the attendees about their various products. At one booth there was, as would be expected, a small, bland, uninformative display for the American doctors. However, this company had actually set up a large upstairs international display for the non-American conference attendees to discuss the new cancer treatment products that the company was promoting outside of the US market.

Now to me it seemed the upstairs display that was set up for the non-American (i.e., European) doctors was particularly alluring. This was especially true since the upstairs, non-American attendees were in the process of jamming down copious quantities of complimentary schnitzels, brats, and cold German beer. Are you kidding me? The American doctors weren't offered so much as a pen or a sticky pad. This situation was pure and unadulterated BS, rank with the highest order of malodorous, politically correct stench. Well, to hell with that load of crap. I was going upstairs into the non-American pharmaceutical display site with the express intention of sucking down a cold German brew and chomping down on a nice fat brat. Nobody better try to stop me, either.

At these large international medical/scientific seminars, it is not uncommon for pharmaceutical firms to hire local eye candy to draw in visitors. You know the type of person I'm talking about. They are generally twenty-five-year-old, nubile females who are essentially attractive models with little or no experience working in the pharmaceutical industry, much less having any firsthand knowledge about the sophisticated bio-therapeutics on display. At the presentation I intended to crash, the upstairs restricted area stairwell was guarded by such a person. She was essentially a gatekeeper to make certain that no lowlife, scumbag American doctors tried to sneak upstairs and sample the tasty treats reserved for the foreign attendees. Her job was simple. She had to look at the name badges to make certain that no homegrown American doctors were trying to make their way into the off-limits display zone.

It was time for me to make a move. I approached the booth babe and showed her my credentials. She furrowed her brow and gave me a curious look. "You know, sir, this display section upstairs is restricted to only non-American physicians. Where are you from?" she queried.

At that time, my practice was in Casa Grande, Arizona. My identification badge listed my name and where I was from. Underneath my name in bold print were the letters *AZ*. It was a make-or-break time for me, and I was going to try to bluff my way upstairs to taste the fruits of forbidden knowledge.

"Well, I'm from AZ. That is the international symbol for the Azores."

A broad smile had spread across her face, and she seemed genuinely interested. "You're from Azores? Oh, my goodness. How exciting! Where are the Azores?" she asked.

Well, this was just too easy. God forgive me, but I just could not help myself from turning into a deluxe asshole at that point. "Well, my country is an island nation. You can find it on the map, just south of Bumflock, Egypt."

With that, she gave me a nod and directed me up the stairwell. On my way up the stairs, she whispered into my ear and gave me a wink. "I didn't know the folks in the Azores had a Texan accent. I know the Azores are actually in the Atlantic Ocean, by the way. It's all okay, Doctor. I think it's absolutely wrong that they won't let American physicians into these restricted display booths. After all, this is an American medical seminar, and this is still our country, is it not?"

Wow! It had been a long time since I had gotten poned upside the head. This just goes to show you that you can't tell a book by its cover. I scampered upstairs and grabbed a fat white sausage, stuck it into a bun, squirted spicy mustard on it, and then buried it in kraut and a gentle sprinkle of diced onions. Should I add a little grated cheese? Why, certainly. There was a variety of German beers to choose from, the brands of which I was mostly totally unfamiliar with. I grabbed one that had a picture of a robust blond Fraulein on the label holding multiple beer steins. It was ice cold, and I proceeded to guzzle it down. I was delighted by the explosion of carbonated bubbles against the back of my throat. Perfect! Well, the Hun may have invented the concept of putting sausage and beer together, but I can assure you that the Texans were the ones who perfected the consumption of said items.

Suddenly, I felt a heavy hand on my shoulder. A large security agent spoke to me in a thick German accent. "I'm sorry, sir, but you are not allowed to be in here. You must put down your food and beverage items and leave immediately."

Now wait just a second, I thought. *You should back off right about now, Adolph.* I was not going to leave until I had at least finished my beer and brat. Well, the security agent was in no mood for any of my churlish behavior, and he escorted me unceremoniously down the back stairs and out into the rear section of the display area.

My embarrassing rear-exit departure was akin to an inebriated miscreant being strong-armed out of a bar and getting tossed into a dingy back alleyway. It was done to ensure that no henchman who may have been on patrol from the FDA would catch wind of my evil transgressions. I surmise now that if I was ever caught committing such a heinous and rebellious act in the time frame that I'm writing this novel, I would be severely punished. I might very well be sent to GITMO to get water-boarded. After all, eating a brat and drinking a German beer in a restricted display area would no doubt be considered a mortal sin. Such a crime would be an evil deed of such magnitude that it could very well shake the foundation on which our noble republic was established.

I found myself in no man's land. I was in an area about five feet wide, where two display booth rows faced each other in a back-toback fashion. This is where the pharmaceutical companies stored their educational brochures and other surplus display items. To vacate this long makeshift hallway, I had to walk to the very end of this very long and narrow row to make my exit. Needless to say, I felt humiliated.

However, this is where things got interesting. As I was working my way out of that unpleasant predicament, I overheard a conversation between two women on the other side of a draped partition that stopped me dead in my tracks. Clearly, I should not have been privy to this intimate discussion. I was only five feet or so away from the two women, but as they were on the other side of a draped wall, they had no idea I was eavesdropping on their little chat.

One of the women, by her mannerisms and expressions, spoke as if she may have just completed her fellowship training in hematology/oncology. It seemed to me that she was talking to an older mentor, probably somebody who was my contemporary. The older individual had a soft Southern drawl. I could not determine, however, from what part of Dixieland she may have originated. The younger physician lamented that she had been physically assaulted by family members of an elderly patient who was afflicted with terminal cancer. She stated that when she informed *Abuela* (Grandmother) that she had a lethal and incurable disease process, the patient's two adult granddaughters retaliated with violence. During the beat down the young female physician received, the two granddaughters stated that the revelation of truth regarding their abuela's illness had left the patient *sin fuerte* (without strength).

I found that story to be a sad and fascinating cautionary tale. After all, if a physician is at risk for being physically assaulted as a consequence of giving family members bad news, then any medical oncologist, such as myself, would definitely be at risk for being on the receiving end of a similar violent outburst. You see, oncologists tend to be messengers of bad news most of the time. However, what I heard next made the hair stand up on the back of my neck.

The mentor consoled the younger woman and then proceeded to inform her about another chilling circumstance that was worth noting. This matter was actually a lethal patient-on-nurse act of violence. Afterward, there was retribution manifested by a lethal physician-on-patient act of brutality. She recounted a disturbing tale that had apparently occurred several years earlier. The older physician spoke of an event where a patient, who was incarcerated within the penal system for various and sundry violent crimes, was admitted into the hospital with an acute case of pneumonia in conjunction with the underlying comorbid condition of an infection with the AIDS virus. During that hospital admission, the prisoner/ patient assaulted a nurse, and it resulted in her death.

Several months later, when the prisoner/patient was readmitted to the hospital under similar clinical circumstances, a small contingency of medical students and house staff members made certain that the prisoner/patient only left the hospital facility after his ravaged body had achieved ambient room temperature. When a body reaches room temperature, a one-way trip to the hospital morgue is generally warranted. When I left the ASCO meeting, this macabre tale that I overheard was stuck in my brain.

Oh my God! Could that story be true? The story was so compelling with passion and conviction that I have no doubt to this very day about the veracity of what I heard. Could such a vigilante act of clinical justice actually happen even today? Oh, yes. Yes, indeed. If after you've digested my tome of fiction, you might find that you've been plummeted into a dark and disturbing place. If that happens, then my mission as a wordsmith will have been accomplished. Take a hot shower and go forth into the bright sunlight after you've read this novel. It might make you feel better. Then again, it might not …

CONTENTS

I ♥
KONA Coffee

1

THE MAUSOLEUM

When Dr. J. D. Brewster woke up in the mausoleum, he opened the top drawer of his nightstand to yet again grasp a loaded .45-caliber automatic pistol in his right hand, chamber a live round, and then vigorously suck on the end of the barrel of the weapon until the silver dental fillings that were imbedded in his molars began to tingle. It was the dawn of another mediocre day in a cursed life of mediocrity, and a litany of ancient and unforgiven sins would again have to be shoved back into what the spiritually broken man referred to as his own personal bottle of moral decay. Rote behavior had established a particular ritual, and it all had to be done before the sun rose over the Gulf Coast.

The thirty-fifth anniversary from the year that Dr. Brewster's immortal soul had made an irrevocable plunge into darkness was now only a mere eight weeks away. The doctor was painfully aware that he had not only violated the Hippocratic oath, but he also committed a crime that was so heinous that the grist mill of justice would surely grind him into dust if he were ever arrested and convicted of the foul deed. Unrelenting guilt had driven him to the brink of suicide, and his perpetual loneliness only whetted his resolve to do so. With this pending anniversary, Brewster could not help but notice that the metallic taste of the gun barrel had worsened to the point that he actually felt nauseous most mornings from the very moment he rammed the muzzle of the pistol into his mouth. As beads of moisture dripped down his forehead, his eyes would sting from the ocular irritation induced by the profuse hyperactivity of his own sweat glands.

On this occasion, he developed the sudden onset of dry heaves as he gently inserted the tip of his tongue into the barrel-end of the deadly weapon. As always, Brewster lacked the fortitude to pull the trigger, so he sucked on the muzzle of the pistol in vain to coax the lead projectile to exit the end of the gun, as if of its own volition.

From an intellectual standpoint, Brewster had never fully comprehended the scientific facts as to why the act of placing a gun barrel into his mouth caused the exact same sensation he would get if he had chewed on a piece of aluminum foil. Perhaps an artificially engendered, micro-electrolytic environment was the answer—a consequence, no doubt, of the exchange of electrons that would occur between the two dissimilar metals in his mouth, with his own saliva acting as a catalyst. As always, whenever he felt the tingling in his mouth and the beads of cold sweat trickling down from his forehead, his daily penance had been dutifully completed, and it was time again for him to unload the weapon and then safely secure the gun back into the top drawer of his nightstand.

Perhaps no absolution could ever be rendered for his heinous great sin. Two millennia ago, Judas Iscariot must have certainly felt that way when he found himself at the end of a rope after he sold out the itinerant rabbi from Nazareth for a measly thirty pieces of silver. Brewster's late friend Arby Fuller Jr. must have certainly felt that way when he found himself at the business end of a sidearm and elected to end his own life by eating a bullet.

Arby Fuller Jr. and J. D. Brewster were but two of the five coconspirators who were guilty of the great sin they committed together way back in the spring of 1982. The aging physician had long thought that he would one day follow Arby Fuller's sterling example of committing suicide. Whether the commission of punching his very own time card in such a dramatic fashion would be seen by others as a supreme act of courage or conversely as a supreme act of despair, J. D. Brewster nonetheless had long felt compelled to take his own life. If Arby was brave enough to kill himself, the doctor should have been brave enough to follow suit. Brewster knew that all he had to do was to pull the trigger ...

J. D. Brewster contemplated a myriad of excuses as to why he was incapable of simply killing himself in an act of self-inflicted, yet perhaps justly deserved retribution. If there was indeed an answer to Dr. Brewster's own semi-rhetorical question, it would seem that there are some sins that are simply impossible to *live* with. However, on the other heavy end of the cosmic balance scales of good versus evil, it would seem that there are some sins that are simply impossible to *die* with.

Once his unrelenting and perpetual morning ritual of self-flagellation had been accomplished, Brewster would finally be able to at least briefly look at himself in a mirror. After all, for the time being at least, the mortal sin he committed had been temporarily shoved back into a bottle that was already brimming with moral decay. Perhaps someday Dr. Brewster would be brave enough to press his index finger against the trigger with enough pressure to discharge the weapon and end his own life. This particular morning, like all the others that had preceded it for the last thirty-five years, would not be that day.

Once he was dressed, Brewster stepped out of his garage with a trowel in his hand and a tray of small perennials that had been aligned in a shallow top-lid, previously salvaged from a small, recycled cardboard box. It was the third weekend of March, and it was time to put some new flowers in the hanging baskets suspended from the ceiling of his front porch entryway. It was the first spring weekend in the autumn of his life. In the latter years of his solitude, Dr. Brewster had become quite obsessive about symmetry and order.

Mrs. McCullough and her sister, Rosalyn, from the Dancing Maid janitorial service dropped by on their monthly scheduled visit to tidy up and dust his home. The doctor was brewing a pot of coffee in the kitchen, and he secretly had hoped the two housekeepers would stay and visit with him for a while after he completed his minor Saturday morning task of gardening.

Brewster climbed down from the ladder after he planted the last root ball in one of the hanging baskets, and he was a bit surprised to see a city of Bellaire police prowler pull up to the front curb. In the driver's seat was a uniformed police officer the doctor had not met before, but he readily recognized the plain-clothed detective in the passenger seat. The detective, who held the rank of lieutenant, exited from the car and walked up the pathway to talk to Dr. Brewster.

J. D. approached the man slowly and with some degree of apprehension as he certainly did not want to get into another shouting match with the man who used to be not only a friend but also the spouse of one of his cancer patients who had recently passed away.

J. D. Brewster and Detective Aaron Parsons had known each other since high school, but their long-standing relationship was now definitely strained.

Brewster forced a smile, albeit insincere. "Well, well, well, it looks like Aaron Parsons is coming by to pay me a most welcomed visit, as I live and breathe. How are you holding up, Aaron?"

"As well as can be expected," mused the police detective. "As you can see, I'm already on the job. It certainly would be nice right about now if I could simply run off to Mexico and disappear, but it seems to me that life is always getting in the way of living. If that's the case, it's time for me to get back into the saddle and ride, amigo."

Brewster quickly glanced over to the police cruiser to ascertain if any trouble was brewing. Perhaps the great sin that he had orchestrated in the remote past had finally been discovered, and now he would be at the mercy of the criminal justice system. Fortunately for the doctor, that was not the case.

"It would seem to me that this isn't a social call. I suspect that you're here on some kind of official business."

"A custodian got roughed up at the high school last night when he caught a couple of thugs in the act of spraying graffiti on the entry doors of the gymnasium," the detective explained. "I'm sure we'll pounce on these knuckleheads sooner or later. When we do, they'll be charged with assault and battery in addition to vandalism of public property. Anyhow, this case was dropped into my lap. As the investigation of this crime brought me past your house, I thought I'd just stop by and just have a little chat with you if you were at home."

As Lieutenant Parsons had only become a widower in early February, Dr. Brewster thought it was perhaps a bit premature for the detective to return to work at the police station so soon. "It's hard to believe that it has already been about six weeks since Elizabeth died. Let me see you, Aaron. Are you certain you're ready to get back to work at this time?"

Aaron took a rather firm and aggressive grip of Brewster's right hand. It was certainly not meant to be a warm and friendly handshake, but rather a very hard grasp to overtly convey the displeasure the detective had with the doctor over the medical services that had been rendered at the time of Elizabeth Parson's clinical deterioration and eventual demise from metastatic ovarian cancer.

Her disease had rapidly progressed after multiple lines of unsuccessful systemic chemotherapy that J. D. Brewster administered on an outpatient basis at his cancer clinic in Bellaire, Texas. If the truth be told, Aaron Parsons was attempting to intimidate J. D. Brewster into admitting that perhaps medical negligence occurred that had contributed to his wife's death.

After staring Dr. Brewster in the eyes for several tense moments in an effort to detect any forthcoming deception, the police lieutenant finally answered the doctor's initial question.

"I have to hump up now and just do it. My leave of absence bereavement benefits from the union will expire soon, and I have a ton of bills to pay. I've got no real choice in the matter. It's time for me to get back to work, whether I'm ready or not. Look, Brewster—I, well, I just wanted to tell you I'm not happy at all as to how things broke down at the end," Parsons explained.

Brewster attempted to free himself from the firm grasp of Aaron Parsons, but the police lieutenant only squeezed the doctor's hand with even greater resolve. With his free left hand, Brewster pointed an index finger at his uninvited guest and countered, "Wait just one moment, Aaron. What in the world are you talking about?"

"When her cancer came back, you told me you thought she had about six months of life left. As it turned out, she only had three weeks. I blame you for talking Elizabeth into her terminal decision to sign up for what you said was a DNR code status. After that, she just gave up. You took away any hope she had. That's on you." Parsons was a bit surprised that Brewster held his ground and simply stared back at him.

Once the accusation of malfeasance had been levied against the physician, the detective sharply broke away from his less-than-cordial handshake with J. D. Brewster. As if he were a man knocking on a portal entry, the detective proceeded to tap the doctor firmly on his sternum with the knuckle of the middle finger of his right hand.

"Three weeks, Brewster. Do you hear me? Three weeks. That is all the time that I had left with her when you told me that the chemotherapy was no longer working. If I had known that her time on the planet was going to be that short, I would have taken off from work at the very moment she entered the hospice program."

Brewster raked his tongue across his top teeth. "What did you want for me, Aaron—a notarized guarantee of survivorship, perhaps signed in blood?"

Aaron Parsons repeatedly pounded his fist into the palm of his hand. "Don't you get it? I wasn't there when she passed away. I promised that I would be right at her side until the very end, but it was the hospice nurses who called me to explain that she died. Do you know what they told me?"

Brewster shrugged his shoulders and replied, "How could I possibly be privy to that, Aaron?"

The detective put his face down into his hands, and he started to weep. "She was asking for me, but I was out working a case. I can never forgive myself over that mistake. I'm sorry, Doc, but I don't think that you were on your 'A' game at that time. I don't know what your problem might be, but it's quite obvious that even now you're preoccupied with other matters. From my point of view, I simply wish that you had stepped up to the plate. Face to face, I'm calling you out on this."

The physician extended his right arm and was about to touch Parsons on his shoulder in an act of compassion, but Brewster reflexively stiffened. When his arm recoiled, the doctor jammed his hands into the front pockets of his blue jeans. Surely, the sequestration of his hands would likely deter him from actually trying to touch another person in an act of empathy. No, Brewster could simply not let something like having physical contact outside of the realm of a simple handshake to actually occur with a fellow human being.

The detective was absolutely correct in his supposition that Brewster was preoccupied and likely not functioning at a high level of clinical proficiency at the time that Elizabeth Parsons passed away. With the pending thirty-fifth anniversary of Brewster's great sin, intrusive thoughts and painful memories were coming back to haunt him with much greater frequency than ever before. Nonetheless, Brewster became truly indignant at the detective's critique regarding the end-of-life medical intervention that had been bestowed upon Elizabeth, and the doctor's reactions to the cricisms rendered by Aaron Parsons were more than just defensive measures.

Brewster raised his voice and adopted an offensive tactic at that point. "Stop right there, Detective. As far as I know, the universe did not give me a promotion to become God almighty. I wouldn't want the gig, and if I had it, I would probably do a pretty lousy job at it. As best I can tell, it seems to me that you only heard what you wanted to hear when I told you that your wife's cancer was entering an accelerated growth phase. I specifically told you that once Elizabeth had entered hospice she *might* have only an additional six months of life left, but that was certainly no guarantee. A person afflicted with advanced cancer can die at any time and for a myriad of different catastrophic reasons."

Parson's cleared his throat and pressed for clarity. "I wasn't looking for a guarantee, but perhaps something else could have been done. Tell me the truth—did you really try everything?"

Brewster replied, "I can't believe that I'm hearing this yet again. Don't go there. We've been through this, and there's nothing more for me to say."

The acute situational grief that can overwhelm a surviving spouse is often manifested by a tidal wave of anger. A sense of guilt may also be in the equation, especially if there is a perception that something important was left unsaid or undone. "I regret that I didn't challenge Elizabeth's decision about signing the recommended *do not resuscitate* code status. When I agreed to the DNR decision, perhaps it meant that I was giving up on her too!"

Brewster lowered his voice at that point and replied, "I tried everything in the book. I even presented her case at the tumor board. I spoke to the gynecological oncology experts at the Tumor Institute about her situation. A specific criterion to enter the Bellaire Kind Care hospice program is that Elizabeth had to willingly declare herself to have a *do not resuscitate* code status. She was dying. I ran out of treatment for her. *Everybody* ran out of treatment for her. In the end, your wife had a performance status that was too poor to allow her the opportunity to enroll into an experimental clinical trial program. I've told you that on many occasions already."

"How can you be so certain?"

Brewster slowly shook his head from side to side. "Her terminal prognosis was based upon what is currently reported in modern published medical literature. In addition, her projected remaining lifespan when her cancer had finally progressed to a lethal tumor burden was also based on my thirty years of experience at this line of work. I stand by that. What I told you and Elizabeth regarding the little time that she may have had left on this earth was an educated guess on my part. When she entered the hospice program, our objective was to concentrate on comfort measures only."

Parsons was trying to process the information that was being explained to him. "So it was an educated guess. Is that what you are calling it now? You disgust me."

J. D. put his hands together and extended his palms to the heartbroken police lieutenant as if he was presenting a small token gift as a peace offering. "Can't you see? It was only a best-case scenario—nothing more and nothing less. I'm truly sorry that you did not have more time to spend with her before she died. As you may recall, I specifically told you to take advantage of the Family Leave Act that was clearly available to you through your employment at the police department. I talked to Captain Matsumoto at the police station about your situation, and he said that all you had to do was to finish filling out the damned forms!"

"I finally filled them out just before she died. The paperwork was in the hopper to be processed. I did my part."

Brewster countered, "Well, I did my part also. Maybe you should have been a bit quicker on getting the requisition filled out. All you had to do was to simply pull the trigger! Why couldn't you pull the trigger? Maybe it was denial on your part."

"I can't accept it even now."

"If you needed to have extra time off from your work when Elizabeth entered hospice, it was yours for the taking," Brewster explained. "Perhaps you need to take a long look at yourself in the mirror if you're feeling guilty about something. When you do take that long look, you need to forgive yourself. I know you attend the Methodist church on Rice Avenue, and I think it would be a good idea to go over there right now and talk to Reverend Martin, as spiritual counseling is outside of my strike zone. If you don't recall anything else that I'm telling you today, you need to remember this one fact: having guilt is like having cancer. Let it go, Aaron, or else it will eat you alive. Trust me on this, as I'm well versed on the matter. We're done here."

Thoroughly satisfied with the outcome of his aggressive tactical response to a most unpleasant situation, Brewster turned away and began to slowly and defiantly stroll back up the walkway to the front door of his home.

The detective took a deep breath, squinted at the rain clouds on the horizon, and uttered a painful sigh. As the police detective was trained to look at matters objectively, he reflected on the simple summary of the facts concerning the sad case of Elizabeth Parsons; the victim contracted cancer, received treatment that was largely unsuccessful, and then she died. There was no evidence of foul play. There was no crime scene that needed to be dusted for fingerprints. Move along, folks. There's nothing to see here. A natural death from cancer happens to human beings every day, all over the world. Aaron Parsons came to the realization that he had to make peace with that.

To defuse the confrontation he had with Dr. Brewster, the detective called out, "You're right, Doc, that's on my head. Look, I'll get out of your hair. I guess I was just looking for somebody to blame. Maybe I should just blame God instead. Even if it's not His fault, He's big enough to take the hit." The detective returned to the patrol car, where the uniformed policeman was busy working on a crossword puzzle from the Saturday morning newspaper.

Almost as an afterthought, the doctor turned to the police detective to make a petition. "Hey, Aaron, maybe I can come down to the station and chat with you about some things that have been on my mind for quite some time. I've got a problem I need to get off my chest."

As the prowl car fired up, the detective noted that the physician had a troubled look on his face. Parsons was able to offer a brief smile while he waved back from the cruiser. "No hard feelings. I've given your recommendations strong consideration, and I think it might be a good idea for me to talk to Reverend Martin after all. Since you know him, Brewster, perhaps you should do the same. In the meantime, if there's something bothering you, come by anytime. Maybe I'll be able to help you hammer it out. At this point in my career, I'll soon be transforming into just a glorified desk jockey anyhow, so you'll know where to find me."

As the Dancing Maids were completing their custodial duties, Dr. Brewster rushed back into the house and went straight into his kitchen. When Mrs. McCullough and her sister, Rosalyn, finished up their cleaning chores, they came down the stairwell with the intent to flee the gigantic and gloomy house as soon as possible. The domestics were definitely never comfortable inside the doctor's home.

The dark, split-face concrete block structure with a contrasting gray standing-seam metal roof was a prototype of futuristic architectural styling known as "industrial cube" design. The edifice was so devoid of ambiance that trick-or-treaters would not even come to visit the house on Halloween, even though Brewster would buy full-size candy bars yearly for the event.

The domestics tried to beat a path back to their van and escape the premises before Dr. Brewster attempted to corral them for a prolonged visit. Unfortunately for the maids, it was too late. In an exaggerated singsong cadence, Dr. Brewster attempted to entice the two women to stay by offering them not only coffee but specifically a cup of Kona Joe.

"Ladies, I have a treat for you. Kona coffee! I've been told that it is the best in the world. I want to reward you for the hard work that you do by offering you a fresh cup of hot java. Tell me, how you take it? Cream and sugar? You name it."

Roz looked at her sister briefly in an attempt to establish a united front to thwart Dr. Brewster's unwelcomed invitation. "We can't stay as we're on a tight schedule. Perhaps we can have a cup of coffee with you next month or some other time, Dr. Brewster."

J. D. thought he would try a different angle to entice the Dancing Maids to come by more often. "You know, I have been thinking. My place here gets awfully dusty in between your visits. I think I would like to have you gals come by more often. Perhaps I should have you ladies clean my place twice a month. Please stay awhile and have a cup of coffee with me. I made it especially for your visit today."

Simultaneously, the two sisters tightly focused their vision on the aging physician. It was Mrs. McCullough who first spoke. "Well thank you very much, Dr. Brewster, but as Roz just explained to you, we can't be late for our next cleaning service appointment over in Meyerland. I must tell you now, there is never anything out of order in your house, and it needs very little dusting. We won't need to come by here more frequently than once a month. It's just not necessary. We would only end up taking money from you without doing any extra real work. That just wouldn't be fair."

Dr. Brewster raised a hand in protest, as if he was a traffic cop in a busy intersection. "Now this is the third time in a row that you've come by to tidy up my place and you gals haven't been able to stay for a cup of coffee. That's just not right, I tell you. I'll let you slip away once more this time, but if necessary, I will hold you both at gunpoint for a visit when you come by to clean my house next month. I'm not joking."

Sensing that the physician was becoming a bit testy, Mrs. McCullough attempted to defuse the situation by patting Dr. Brewster on top of his hand and stating, "Have a pleasant Saturday. Roz and I will see you next month."

As the two women turned away to exit the cold and sterile domicile, Rosalyn stopped and turned back to address Brewster. "Hey, Doc, do you like dogs?"

Brewster was uncertain whether he should answer the question truthfully. "Why do you ask?"

Rosalyn thought it would be perfect opportunity to help relieve Dr. Brewster from his obviously miserable loneliness. "I have a boxer, and she just had a litter of puppies. I would very much like to give you one, free of charge. It would be a gift from me to you. I've named one of the puppies Jimmy, and I think he would be perfect for you. Have you ever had a dog?"

Brewster smiled and nodded. "Yeah, Roz, dogs are probably the greatest gift God ever bestowed upon human beings. The problem is that they don't live very long. A decade, maybe a decade and a half, and that's if you're lucky. Then they're gone. Poof! Just like that. I had a dog named Electra when I was a boy. A neighbor gave it to my brother and me when I was only three years old, and my brother was five at the time. My father had just passed away, and that dog filled a huge void in my life."

"Of course it did," Roz said. "After all, it was a dog. That's what dogs are supposed to do."

"She lived until I was well into high school," Brewster explained. "The dog contracted breast cancer, manifested by multiple ulcerated masses involving her chest wall, and she eventually developed paralysis of her hind legs. In retrospect, she probably had metastatic disease involving her spine and liver. It was a horrible situation and nothing I could do about it."

"Did you do the right thing?"

"My brother and I eventually had the unenviable task of taking the poor creature to the vet to have her put down," Brewster answered. "No, I don't think I could ever own another dog. I would surely become deeply attached to the animal. Although I'm not a young man now, I have no doubt I would end up outliving it. The dog would just end up dying on me one day. I just couldn't abide by that inevitable outcome."

While leaving through the front door, Mrs. McCullough furrowed her brow and scolded Dr. Brewster with a sharp rebuke. "All living things are hardwired to die someday, Doctor. You of all people should appreciate that fact. It is the awareness of our own mortality that gives our very lives any meaning at all. What do any of us have? If a person is lucky, maybe he or she will have about a number of four score or so spins around the sun. That's it. That's all we get."

"Yes!" Brewster said. "That's the point I'm trying to make."

"I can't help but be philosophical about all of this," Mrs. McCullough emphasized. "I believe that we are all called to find some tangible mission that's righteous and good. Once we recognize that this divine calling may be our destiny, it is then our duty to try to accomplish this calling to the best of our God-given abilities. This commission to such a purpose gives our lives a deeper meaning. This is my conviction. Should we not also surely strive to pursue love and happiness along the way of this mystical journey, no matter how fleeting? I suggest you consider the same."

Well, that was the truth, and Brewster had heard it all before. It was another peculiar episode of déjà vu. Frankly, it seemed to happen all the time. After all, everything in the universe is connected somehow. J.D. Brewster had been repetitively subjected to hearing the same idioms and expressions over and over for the last thirty-five years at different times, at different places, and from different people. It was an exact word-for-word recitation that had already been recorded deep in his memory banks. These déjà vu episodes occurred so frequently in J. D.'s life that it should have been intuitively obvious that God was trying to get his attention, and the message that He was trying to convey was not subtle in the least.

The trouble was that Dr. Brewster was rarely able to grasp the big picture, even if it smacked him in the groin like a carjacker who was wielding a lead pipe. He pursed his lips and looked down to the floor when he asked, "So, what you're saying is that you'll not be staying for any coffee, is that right?"

On their way out to the Dancing Maid company van, Rosalyn whispered to her sister, "Do think we should go back and have that cup of coffee with him?"

Mrs. McCullough shook her head and sadly replied, "No. He's a lost soul. Well, that's perhaps not quite correct. What would be a much more accurate assessment about our client is that Dr. Brewster is not a lost soul; he has simply lost his soul. You know, I believe there is a subtle but nonetheless big distinction between those two possible circumstances."

Rosalyn paused in her tracks and asked, "What do you mean?" Her older sister answered, "Check this out, Roz; he lives alone in this enormous house with small, narrow windows all by himself. It makes no sense to me. Five bedrooms, five and a half baths, formals, a library, an office, a billiard room, an in-home exercise gym that clearly has never been utilized, a breakfast nook, a gourmet kitchen that likely has never been employed except for making a pot of coffee, and he also has a hobby room. There is even a ten-by-ten-foot glass-walled smoking room, complete with sofa chairs. Did I leave anything out?"

Rosalyn thought for a moment before she answered. "Don't forget that he owns that fancy in-home theater that I will venture he has never even entered. It would seem so, because the big-screen TV and surround-sound speakers have never been hooked up in all of the time that we've been attending to his home. Oh, yeah, let's not forget that he even has a family room. That's truly weird. He has a family room, but he's never had a family to go along with it!"

It occurred to Mrs. McCullough that there was perhaps some kind of rational explanation as to Dr. Brewer's domestic circumstances. "He owns a house with seven thousand square feet of living space, and it's all for just one person. Maybe he's built such a monstrosity for himself, not because he was ever blessed to have a family but to spit in the eye of his own personal curse of solitude. Do you know what the neighbors call this abode of his?"

Roz knew the answer and quietly replied, "They call it the Mausoleum. It's all really quite sad."

••••○ ▶◼◀ ○••••

Although crestfallen, Dr. Brewster had one more opportunity for company on that March day. Sitting in his garage was a 1968 Mustang notchback coupe with a dead battery. The "Mister Mobile Mike" Fuller repair van was on its way over to his house to remedy that situation, and Mister Fuller had promised to be at Dr. Brewster's house before eleven o'clock that Saturday morning. The car was cosmetically a near-faithful reproduction of Mustang California Special. Brewster had actually owned an original Mutang C.S. GT while he was in college and during his medical school training.

He was painfully aware of the fact that if he actually still owned the real California Special from his youth, it would now be worth a small fortune. It was not so much that the California Special was a particularly rare Mustang edition, as over five thousand examples were produced by the Ford Motor Company during 1968. The fact that would have made his original old Mustang so valuable was that it had experimental Shelby factory componentry that was never available for public consumption.

When Brewster first acquired the original 1968 California Special, he was doing his undergraduate work at the Dick Dowling University in Orange, Texas. At that time, the first OPEC oil crisis was going on, and people could not get rid of their old 1960s muscle cars fast enough. Brewster had bought the vehicle for a mere $1,200. It was equipped with a 428 cubic inch Cobra jet engine and a fourspeed close ratio top-loader transmission. Soon, however, the car would take on a new life that would have never been approved by the Ford Motor Company.

While attending college, Brewster had befriended a man known as Tiny Tucker, who was the head of the school of automotive engineering. What was good about this relationship, from the selfish perspective of Brewster, was that the engineering class would occasionally be willing to take on custom hot rod projects for private individuals, and the school would provide free labor. All that the owner had to provide was all of the necessary componentry that was going to be installed in the project. Once Tucker met J.D. Brewster for the first time, the professor of engineering realized that the young college student had a 1968 Mustang California Special that was armed with the mighty 428 CID motor under the hood.

Tucker was determined to take J. D.'s car and transform it into a venerable rocket ship. Tucker knew the whereabouts of an original Conelec fuel-injected intake system that was complete. He also knew the location of an original experimental independent rear suspension set up that was located in the city of Dallas. Unfortunately however, it was an incomplete unit. It seemed the rear suspension kit was missing the all-important mounting cradle. Nonetheless, Tucker felt that he and his students were skilled enough at the art of tube welding that a whole new mounting cradle could be fabricated from scratch.

He convinced Brewster to cough up $1,500 to seal the deal. Although this was more than the student had originally paid to acquire the entire car just one year earlier, he trusted that Professor Tucker was an automotive wizard. Brewster agreed to go along with the automotive engineering project, which would include a rack and pinion steering gear harvested out of a wrecked late-model Mustang II.

Tiny Tucker was true to his word, and he was able to round up the missing exotic high-performance pieces. He took Brewster's car into surgery for major organ transplantations. Tucker and his students fabricated a welded tubular rear suspension cradle that was bolted directly into the original spring leaf perch on either side of the frame rail.

Before installing the restored rear suspension, Tucker and his crew discovered a very interesting anomaly: the rear gear was an extraordinarily tall 2.47 nine-inch limited slip set up. Although such a tall rear gear would turn the car into an absolute dead dog off the starting line, it would result in an automobile with a theoretical top end speed of about 160 miles per hour if it could be properly motivated by five hundred-plus horsepower, five hundred-plus pounds feet of torque, and a six thousand RPM redline. The horsepower and torque target figures were almost achieved when the engine was rebuilt and the block was stroked and bored.

As it turned out, there was a dangerous time when Brewster and his friend, who was known as Russian Bear, needed every horsepower under the hood and every single mile per hour top-end speed that the old vehicle could possibly muster. Brewster and his colleague stumbled upon serious trouble south of the border in Mexico, and they were both facing certain death. That beloved old Mustang was able to propel Brewster and his friend back across the border to the safety of a country that still had rules, regulations, and relative safety.

Brewster would later repay a deep obligation of debt that he had owed to Professor Tiny Tucker by making certain that the affable old automotive engineer received appropriate information regarding the dosages of analgesics that would be required to achieve a specific therapeutic goal when the professor was approaching his own finish line in the race known as life. Brewster pulled it off long before any state in the union legalized physician-assisted suicide. Although he was a man vexed by chronic guilt, what he did for Tiny Tucker was definitely one thing Brewster did not have any regrets about.

Try as he might, the current Mustang edition now sitting in Dr. Brewster's garage was but a mere shadow of the proud creation he had owned many years before. As with every one of his other personal possessions, this particular custom iteration of an old 1968 Mustang really had no functional purpose at all. Just like the magnificent edifice in which he dwelled, the car was but a symbol of something that was missing in his life.

Dr. Brewster erroneously believed that he would be able to find distraction from the track and field meet that was now well underway on the other side of the chain link fence that separated his home from Bellaire High School. As it was one of the most prestigious high schools in the whole state of Texas, many parents would have given their eye teeth to live in this school district in an effort to give their children a leg up on life. Brewster was aware of this fact, and that is why he moved into this neighborhood directly across from the high school. He did it specifically because he didn't have any children or any heirs. Brewster was giving a stiff middle finger to the universe for the cards that life had dealt to him. If the truth be told, Dr. Brewster was also giving a stiff middle finger at the reflection in the mirror for the cards that he had dealt to himself.

He poured himself a cup of Kona coffee and was about to amble out to the backyard to watch the spring track meet when his doorbell rang. Brewster realized that the mechanic was right on schedule. The person standing at front door was none other than Mister Mobile Mike Fuller arriving to resuscitate the Mustang. Dr. Brewster took the mechanic out to the garage, and in only a few moments, the battery was pulled out from underneath the hood. Mister Fuller professed his admiration for Dr. Brewster's vehicle, which automotive aficionados would consider to be a "resto-mod" creation.

"That's quite a hot rod you have there, Doc. I can tell it is not a real California Special, as you have an elongated after-market fiberglass Shelby reproduction hood. The original 1968 Special had a steel hood. It looks like you've made a lot of high-performance modifications to this thing. It must have cost you both of your gonads to pull off a project like this."

Ironically, J. D. had no gonads. He had undergone a therapeutic left orchiectomy to remove a precancerous testicle when he was a preadolescent, and then he subsequently lost his right testicle after a traumatic event that happened on June 19, 1981. Coincidentally, this happened to be the precise date that J. D. Brewster had become an overt racist. Brewster was not a racist because he was sterile. He became a racist as a consequence of *how* he became sterile. Sadly, the perpetual contempt that he had for people of color quietly stewed inside him for decades.

Mobile Mike's statement, although superficially innocuous, was actually quite inflammatory. Dr. Brewster was decidedly annoyed at the mechanic's unwitting comments, which brought back a flood of unpleasant memories from his medical school days. He had spent his entire career trying hard to suppress such intrusive recollections. No matter how lonely he felt, the doctor was not about to offer the mechanic any hospitality at that juncture.

"Now, I was going to be a gentleman and offer you a cup of coffee," Brewster harshly stated, "Kona coffee, to be precise. I've been told that it's the best coffee in the world. I now rescind this rather gracious consideration, as I surely take exception to the comment you made about this car costing me my cajones. You have no idea about what you've just said."

Mobile Mike was taken back by the sudden 180-degree change in Brewster's demeanor. He meant no offense and quickly apologized for what he knew to be an off-color statement. He just didn't think such a comment should have been such an insult. He pulled his right earlobe and responded, "I'm sorry, Doc. That was indeed a bit of a blue note that I tooted through my horn."

Mobile Mike loaded the dead battery onto the back of his truck to take it back to his shop and put it on the trickle charger. "If this thing holds a charge, I'll bring it back on Sunday and reinstall it in the Mustang. If it's completely dead, you're looking at buying a new battery. I need to ask you a question."

"What would that be?"

"I can tell that you rarely fire this thing up, much less actually drive it," Mike noted. "I know because of the condition of all of your tires. They're underinflated. When I come back tomorrow, I'll also bring the mobile compression tank and gas those babies up with pure nitrogen. That's far better for tires than atmospheric air. I want to know just thing. No offense, Doc, but do you simply have a car like this to try and recapture some of your lost youth?"

Dr. Brewster circled his head in a peculiar counterclockwise motion and finally replied, "Well, it may be something similar to that. I actually did have a high-performance 1968 California Special many years ago. I loved that original old car because it once saved my life when a friend of mine and I found ourselves in some badass trouble down in Mexico. Two very bad hombres were about to execute us in cold blood, but that old Mustang I owned was a rocket ship, and somehow it got my friend and I back to Texas in one piece. Perhaps what I'm actually trying to recapture is some of my lost manhood."

Mobile Mike found the physician's response to be a bit odd, but he did not pursue a clarification as to what was meant by it.

J. D. was curious about the ancestral lineage of the man who had come to render aid to his Mustang. "Now, Mike, I must ask you a question. Quid pro quo. Be honest with me. Are you any kin to a fellow I met years ago named, Arby Fuller?"

"Why do you ask?" It appeared to Brewster that the mechanic was a bit reticent to address a subject matter that was most likely a painful recollection.

"I need to know," Brewster explained. "Arby Fuller and I participated in an event that happened 35 years ago. There's not a day that goes by that I don't think about him."

"Is that so?" the mechanic replied. "Of course I'm related to Arby. In fact, both Senior and Junior were kin to me. Arby Fuller Sr. was my uncle. I inherited his car repair service, as he had no living heirs. He had only one son who passed away quite some time ago. He was my older cousin. When Junior died, he took a gun and, well—I guess that was just all of his own doing. To be honest, it has been a shameful embarrassment to our family all of these years, and we really don't like to talk about what happened to Junior anymore."

"I just knew you were related to Junior," Brewster said. "I can see the family resemblance in your face and body habitus."

"Well, if you mean to say that Junior had a big fat tire around his middle like I do, I'd guess that your powers of observation are quite astute. In any event, before Arby died, he said that he was guilty of committing some kind of great sin. You wouldn't happen to know anything about that, would you?" Mike asked.

Brewster simply looked at the ground and shrugged his shoulders.

"You said that you participated in an event with Junior that happened 35 years ago," Mike continued. "Now, you boys weren't in cahoots involving some kind of criminal enterprise that went sideways, now were you?"

It occurred to Dr. Brewster that it was a very small world indeed. Everything in the universe seemed to be connected somehow. "Well, I knew your cousin many years ago. He used to be a corrections officer, and I considered him to be one of the few friends that I ever had. I was deeply grieved when I learned that he had committed suicide after I graduated from medical school. I knew your uncle also. He was a WWII hero and all that. He fought at the Bulge in the Ardennes. It was truly an honor for me to have known them both. That's all I really want to say."

"It seems to me that you know a lot more about the trouble that Arby got into, Doc. Some seriously evil shit must have gone down. It must have been bad enough for Arby to feel that the only way out was for him take his own life," Mike added. "Am I right?"

"I don't know what you're talking about," Brewster replied with a bold face lie.

"I don't want to step out of line here," Mike pressed, "but it would seem to me that there's a lot more to this story than what you're now willing to share. I can't help but feel that there's something dark inside you, Dr. Brewster."

"Hold your horses," Brewster said. "I'm sorry if I got a bit cross with you. I would hope that the way I behaved with you is not a true reflection of my basic nature. Thanks for attending to my car. Please keep me up to date on my car battery situation. Now if you excuse me, I have matters I must attend to."

Mobile Mike commented as he departed, "Hey, Doc, it seems like you enjoy doing your own yard work, but if you ever get tired of it, I have a brother named Bobby Fuller, and he has his own yard service called, I Fought the Lawn. Do you get it?"

Brewster laughed as he immediately recognized the play on words. The name of the lawn care company paid direct homage to a 1966 rock-and-roll classic recorded by the Texas band named the Bobby Fuller Four, which had a hit song called, "I Fought the Law". As everything in the universe seems connected somehow, Brewster still had the original old 45 rpm issue of the song in question. The doctor also actually remembered that tune was recorded in El Paso, Texas, and was originally released on a now-defunct record label called, Mustang. Wow! That was just too weird, even for a man who used to be an active lightning rod.

Brewster said, "One of the few pleasant memories I actually have about my time in medical school was when I was briefly the front man for a 1960s rock-and-roll cover band that was called DNR. Our band got its peculiar name because the music that we made sounded so dreadful that on one occasion when we were performing at a block party, some stoned yahoo in the crowd loudly professed that we were collectively dying on the stage. To this very day, it makes me laugh to think that if one of my band members had dropped over dead, it was highly unlikely that any resuscitative efforts would be forthcoming!

In any event, I'll definitely keep your brother in mind if I ever need somebody to manage my lawn."

With that, Mobile Mike departed back to his shop.

Dr. Brewster suddenly felt sour above and beyond his usual depressed affect. Meeting Mr. Mobile Mike Fuller had triggered painful memories about the late Arby Fuller Jr. who was an old lost friend that had been swallowed up by the very same dark and intrusive demons that perpetually tormented Dr. Brewster. These recurrent hauntings from his past were suddenly resurrected in the physician's cerebral cortex and they quickly proceeded to vanquish any residual pleasantries that Brewster may have had about mid-1960s rock-and-roll music, or anything else for that matter.

The guilt that he had from the great sin he orchestrated years ago could be sequestered in the bottle of moral decay for only a short period of time, but it could never be completely exorcised. His guilt returned to torment him yet again, and it was not even the noon hour on that Saturday in the month of March. He had lost any interest that he thought he once had in watching the high school track meet. Although the athletic events could have easily been viewed from his backyard, he turned and shuffled back inside his home and headed directly to his office instead.

Once in his office, Dr. Brewster was distracted by a check still sitting on the back of his desk, which he had received quite a while back from the International Zoological Society. The physician actually looked upon this monetary instrument that was honorably bestowed to him with irony and disdain. He had never bothered to cash the check or deposit it.

Three years ago, Dr. Brewster was the toast of the town. He was even put on the cover of the *Gulf Coast Monthly Magazine* after he had captured a photograph of an adolescent jaguar in the dense semitropical forests of East Texas with a nocturnal trail camera. That's right—it was a jaguar! The predator was probably a transient visitor that had come up from Mexico along the coast, but the Zoological Society was hoping there may have been a small breeding population of these big cats getting established in the forests east of the city of Houston. The last official documentation of a wild jaguar that had been seen in the state of Texas was in the north-central part of the state around Brownwood back in the year 1950.

The check sent to Dr. Brewster was an attempt to entice him to reveal to the Zoological Society the exact location in East Texas where the photograph had been taken. Dr. Brewster was not about to cooperate with the Zoological Society with any specific information, except for revealing to them that the photograph was taken south of Dayton, Texas.

Brewster kept the information as to where the young jaguar had been captured on film a tightly held secret. He did it for two reasons. The first reason was quite simple as Brewster held the exact same convictions about the matter that his mentor professed years ago. What Dr. Sassman once said, Brewster recalled verbatim: *I'm a Texan, and I know very well the basic nature of some of my fellow Texans. Some idiot would likely take a gun and try to find the poor creature, if it is indeed still out there, and then blow it into smithereens just to have a pelt to put in front of a fireplace somewhere.*

The second reason was quite complex. What Brewster long hoped to find in the forest was some type of tangible explanation for the disappearance of his former mentor, Professor Denny Sassman, who went missing in April 1982. For all intents and purposes, he had simply disappeared from of the face of the earth. What J. D. was specifically looking for was photographic evidence of the possible existence of a giant, nonhuman, hairy bipedal primate that allegedly lived in North America.

Dr. Sassman had mysteriously vanished while searching for the mythical primate after he had long expressed a near-religious and obsessive belief to Brewster that such creatures actually existed. As a tribute to his former missing mentor, Brewster would dutifully make a pilgrimage out into the forests of East Texas once every spring and set up motion-triggered trail cameras. In the three-plus decades that he had been on this quixotic quest, the young jaguar was the only thing of interest he had ever captured on film.

While looking at his calendar, Brewster thought that the following weekend would be a good time to try to get back out into the forest and again set up the trail cameras. He intuitively knew it would likely be another cryptozoological mission that would again end in ultimate futility. It was once the opinion held by the missing Dr. Sassman that such creatures were both solitary and migratory. Decades ago, the professor revealed to Brewster modest circumstantial evidence that the beginning of spring was likely the very best time to try and capture photographic evidence of the existence of the elusive beast, at least in East Texas.

For many years, Dr. Brewster had hoped for fame, or at least peer recognition, in the field of medical science. When Brewster had entered medical school decades earlier, he had actually hoped to get a PhD in addition to his MD, but his original aspirations to become a bona fide medical research scientist had been dashed long ago. Alas, when some degree of notoriety finally came into his life, it was for the unintentional discoveries that he had made in the field of zoology. It was a simple blind-ass accident, nothing more and nothing less.

When he was interviewed by the *Gulf Coast Monthly Magazine* after he had captured the photograph of the predatory cat on his trail camera, Brewster had to feign warmth, humor, and intellectual insight about the third-largest predatory cat extant on the planet earth. He handled the task quite well, however. The Texas jaguar was something

Dr. Brewster was not looking for or a subject matter he even cared about.

If the truth be known, Brewster actually didn't care about much of anything anymore. It had come to the point that Dr. Brewster no longer looked upon the life that had been bestowed upon him as a sacred gift; Brewster sadly perceived that his very existence as a human being was now just another hurdle he had to get over.

After all, he had been faking that he was actually alive his entire life. The despondent man wondered if he even had the simple ability to fog up a mirror if it was held under his nostrils on a cold day. If perhaps he could not accomplish such a mundane task, it would simply confirm just how truly dead he was inside. Maybe somebody should just intercede with a preemptive strike and haul away his carcass now. An interment at Forest Lawn would suffice. Better yet, maybe his corpse should just be left in a dumpster somewhere. The doctor was certain that his heart had already reached ambient temperature. It surely was already in advanced stages of decomposition, although it was still beating strongly in the middle of his chest. All he needed was the rest of his major organs to follow suit. For all that Dr. Brewster knew, his very soul may have already parted company from his body long ago.

It was now the right occasion to end it all. Brewster went upstairs and retrieved the pistol he kept hidden away in his nightstand. It was finally time to draw the curtains to a close on his miserable existence. The doctor took several heavy-duty plastic trash bags from his garage and proceeded to tape the vinyl bags onto the floors and the walls of the half bath downstairs. In the end, if he was going to eat a bullet like his late friend Arby Fuller, Brewster wanted to be courteous to whoever was destined to take on the unenviable task of cleaning up the residual bloody mess. After all, Brewster presumed that his dead body would eventually be discovered by somebody. What better place to commit suicide than within the confines of his own home? After all, he was already entombed in a mausoleum.

As Brewster sat upon his toilet with the .45-caliber gun in his mouth, he carefully contemplated the trajectory of the bullet that would transverse his brain and exit through the occipital portion of his skull. Certain that a bullet of such a large caliber would easily penetrate the bathroom wall behind him, Brewster thought that the better part of valor would be to commit suicide while he was in the supine position on the bathroom floor. He recovered the heavy Yellow Pages and also the big telephone directory book from the kitchen. As he extended his frame across the cool tile of the bathroom floor, he propped the back of his head against the telephone directory books.

Brewster was relatively certain when he would pull the trigger that there was no way a bullet could completely blast through his skull and then blow past the thick pages of the telephone directory books the back of his head would be resting upon. After all, not only was his bathroom floor covered in tile, but it also happened to be a lovely gold travertine. It would certainly be a shame to damage such an attractive and expensive floor covering just because he was simply compelled to blow his own brains out.

While lost in his own spiritual exile, Dr. Brewster was surprised to hear his telephone ringing just before he had mustered up enough courage to finally pull the trigger. He promptly took the gun out of his mouth, ejected the cartridge that had been chambered, pulled out the magazine of bullets from the receiver in the handle of the weapon, and set the gun on top of the bathroom counter. God works in mysterious ways, and it was not Brewster's time to punch his own time card. His soul was not completely lost, but J. D. Brewster likely misplaced it somewhere. Perhaps the doctor had simply left it out in the shed near his lawnmower and other garden tools. Maybe there was still some way he could find redemption and perhaps even salvation. Although the doctor felt that he was no longer living, perhaps he just needed to be raised from the dead. A rather daunting task no doubt, but nonetheless possible.

As he was not on call, it was quite unusual for anybody to ever try and contact him. In fact, it never happened unless it was his brother, Bill. No, it couldn't be Brother Bill, Dr. Brewster thought. Bill was off the grid trying to resurrect a dead oil well somewhere near the state border with New Mexico way out in West Texas. *Maybe somebody wants to come by for a visit*, he optimistically considered.

He walked back into the kitchen, picked up his landline telephone receiver, and said, "Hello?"

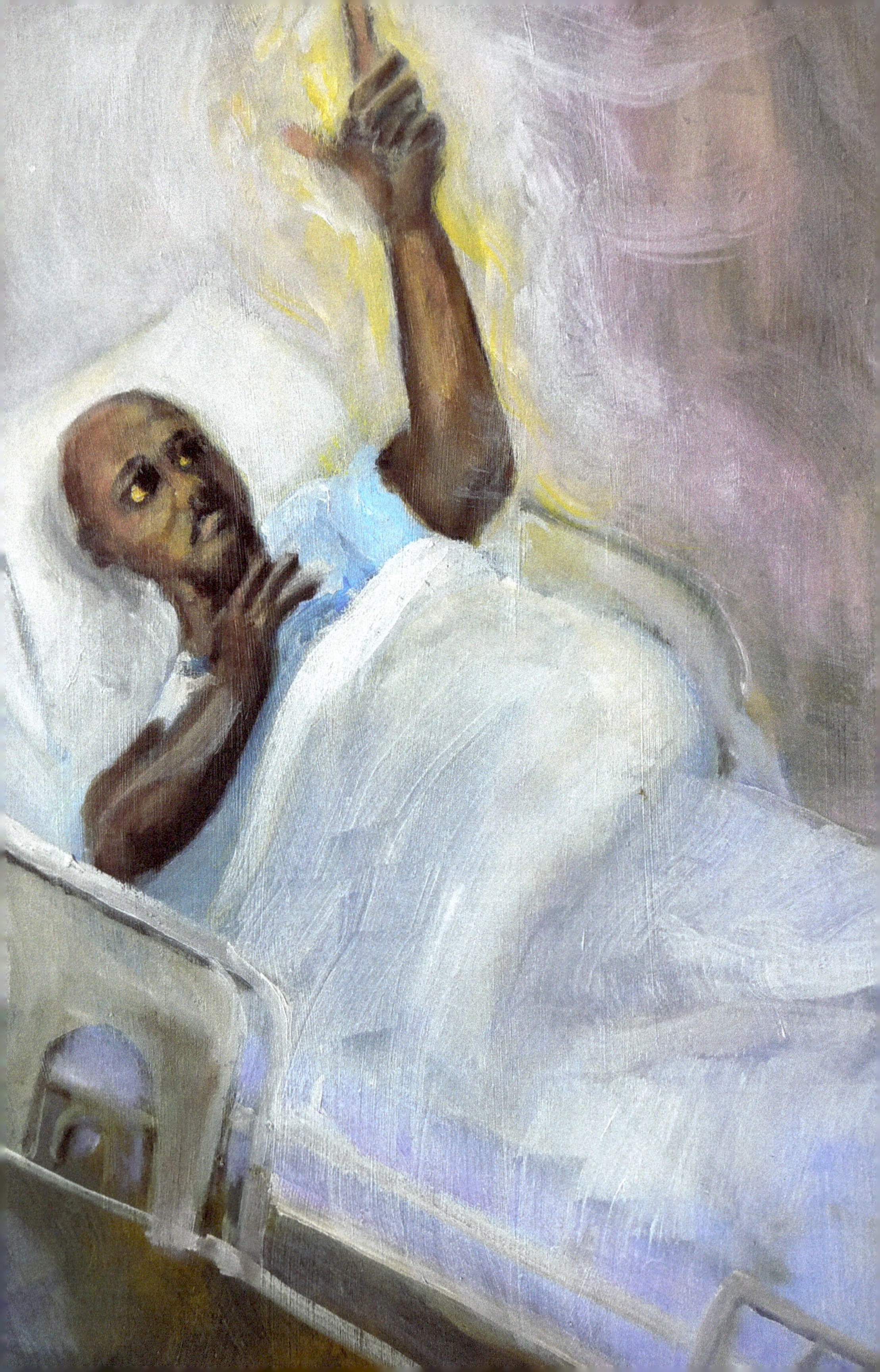

2

ETERNAL CARE UNIT

When the doctor answered the phone, he heard the voice of a very anxious young woman who identified her-self as Faith Mammon. She was the only daughter of Brew's former friends, "Feral Cheryl" Mammon and her late husband, Willy "Wooly Mammoth" Mammon. Although Brewster had not seen Faith or her mother, Cheryl, for many years, he had at least exchanged a Christmas card with them as recently as three months before.

Faith sounded distraught, and her voice quivered. "Dr. Brewster, my mom is very sick and is in the hospital. She wants to see you—right now. Can you—well, I know you and my mother have not been close for a very long time, but can you come right away?"

Not knowing the scope of Cheryl's illness, Dr. Brewster was ready to jump back into his superhero doctor persona. After all, it was the only thing that could still make him feel that he still was perhaps halfway alive. "Sure, I will, sweetie. Just tell me what's wrong and what hospital your mother has been admitted to and I'll be there right away."

Faith said, "Mother has triple-negative and widely metastatic inflammatory breast cancer. The cancer has spread everywhere. I am with her now. She's at Meyerland Memorial." The abrupt explanation of what was going on left Dr. Brewster slack-jawed and stunned. *Cheryl has breast cancer?* Inflammatory, triple-negative cancer had meant that his old, estranged friend was in deep trouble. Brewster thought Faith had called because Cheryl was requesting a second opinion consultation. The Meyerland Memorial Hospital was right past of the 610 Loop and was only a few minutes from Dr. Brewster's home in Bellaire.

Before J. D. left the house, he got on the internet and found the updated and published NCCN guidelines on the management of metastatic, inflammatory, triple-negative breast cancer. "Triple negative" implied that the cancer lacked estrogen receptors and progesterone receptors and there was also no amplification of what was scientifically referred to as the HER-2/neu oncogene. In layman's terms, this meant the cancer was extraordinarily aggressive and resistant to anti-hormonal treatment. It was also implicit that immunotherapy management with a magnificent anticancer drug that was called Herceptin would also be futile.

The physician printed a copy of the guidelines to take directly to Cheryl in case she had questions about therapeutic intervention. Brewster knew already that she had a terminal malignant process, but perhaps he could recommend a treatment plan that could buy her some time. As Cheryl was a registered nurse, she would certainly appreciate the most modern and up-to-date chemotherapy protocols.

Traffic was light until Brewster passed the Plaza, where the locals were pulling into the mall to do some spring shopping or perhaps grab a Saturday brunch. Once he got past the mall traffic, Dr. Brewster pulled into the Meyerland Memorial Hospital, and he used his identification badge to electronically open the security gate to the enter the staff parking lot just past the 610 Loop.

As he was hoping to wind down his career, Meyerland Memorial was the only hospital left where Dr. Brewster still had full staff privileges. In his haste to get to the hospital, he had neglected to ask Faith what room her mother was in. That mattered little, however, as cancer patients could almost always be found in the Oncology Unit located on the fourth floor in the South Tower.

Brewster popped out of the elevator on the fourth floor, and he immediately ran into the charge nurse, Ms. Ida Mae Pagan, who was from the Philippines. Over time, Dr. Brewster learned to love the Filipino nurses. They always seemed to be such cheerful, hardworking, God-fearing, and spiritual people. He was often invited to attend their potluck dinners in the nurses' lounge when one or more of the nurses would bring a big covered casserole dish of pansit noodles with shrimp or pork.

The only complaint about the Filipino nurses that Dr. Brewster ever had was the fact that many of them spoke very rapidly in a staccato fashion, without any modulation in their speech pattern. Brewster often thought that their diction was an assault rifle on full automatic mode. Now that Brewster was on the threshold of becoming obsolete, he was starting to have distinct difficulty in discerning the information the Filipino nurses tried to convey when they spoke to him.

As he walked up to the charge nurse, Ms. Pagan playfully tugged on Dr. Brewster's gray beard. "What's the matter with you today, old man? You look more depressed today above and beyond your usual sour demeanor."

Brewster generated an insincere smile and replied, "Now, Ida Mae, I have had a pretty decent day thus far, so don't go off and spoil it for me. I have come to see a patient who must be located up here on the Oncology Unit. Her name is Cheryl Mammon."

The charge nurse looked up to the ceiling as if to scan her memory banks, and she replied, "No, no. She's not on this floor. Walk over here and lookie at the census on the EMR." Ms. Pagan grabbed Dr. Brewster by the pinky finger and dragged him over to face a computer terminal at the nurses' station.

Brewster stood and watched as she scrolled down the screen, and the name Cheryl Mammon was not to be found at all on the unit's fourth foor census list. She typed in the oncology group practice name and she found nada. She typed in a census query for all of the oncology patients who may have been misplaced on some other unit, and again she found zippo. Ms. Pagan shrugged her shoulders and called the operator to find out the exact location of Cheryl Mammon.

When the charge nurse hung up the phone, she looked at Dr. Brewster and explained that the patient was on the fifth floor and was admitted by Dr. Brown. Dr. Brewster thought that was a bit odd and asked, "The fifth floor is the hospice unit. Are all of your rooms here on the fourth floor filled up today?"

Ms. Pagan shook her head to answer no.

"Wait just a minute," J. D. Brewster continued, "there are two doctors on staff named Brown. One is a Caucasian who's a hospitalist, and the other is a black physician who's the director of palliative care. So, tell me, Ida Mae, which Dr. Brown is it? Is it the white Brown or the black Brown?"

The charge nurse intuitively knew something was awry and did not look back up to Brewster when she answered. "The black Brown, but technically he's not actually black. He seems to me to be more of a medium-brown Brown."

Brewster suddenly felt he was on a free-falling elevator. His old friend Cheryl, with whom he had lost touch with quite some time ago, appeared to be beyond the point of palliative chemotherapy treatment. That's why he and the nurse had trouble finding her on the EMR. She was on the hospice census, not the oncology census. Hospice patients had their own carve-out designation at Meyerland Memorial as they had one foot on a banana peel and another foot was already in a big hole in the ground. The job of hospice was to grease the chute and slide these terminal patients comfortably out of their current plane of existence. That is why these patients were not technically considered to be in the in-patient setting.

The charge nurse patted the doctor's shoulder, and she wished the best for his friend. As Ms. Pagan stepped away, Brewster opened the EMR from the computer terminal and saw that multiple cancer treatments had failed Cheryl. She was now in a bedridden state, with cancer involving her brain, lungs, liver, bones, chest wall, and spine. Cheryl had become a paraplegic when the cancer had spread to her spine, and she became paralyzed in her lower legs. Without success, the neurosurgeons had attempted to excise the tumor that was causing the pressure on her spinal cord. The lower back region was then treated with external beam radiation. However, all the treatment had failed, and the patient was left without any use of her lower limbs.

Brewster said aloud, to no one in particular, "A horrible situation, and nothing I could do about it."

In the medical terminology used by oncologists, Cheryl had a performance status level of ECOG 4. This meant essentially that Cheryl was on the launch pad to soon be transferred to a place that the hospice personnel euphemistically referred to as the "Eternal Care Unit", wherever that place may have actually been found. The Eternal Care Unit however, was likely outside of the realm of the space-time continuum that defines the universe. For Dr. Brewster, that colloquial terminology seemed a bit harsh but infinitely better than the other locker room expression bantered about by some of his colleagues. He knew a few older, cynical oncologists who used the slang phrase that when a patient had died, the body would carted away to take that big "dirt nap".

It appeared Cheryl had already agreed to DNR code status. *Do not resuscitate.* If her heart and lungs quit working, there would be no attempt at last-minute heroic medical efforts to revive her, and the natural death process would be allowed to occur. Dr. Brewster wondered how and when all of this could have happened.

Although he and Cheryl were no longer very close, he should have at least known she was battling this dreaded disease. Perhaps he could have done something, anything. The charge nurse attempted to assuage Dr. Brewer's angst and stated, "Lookie here. You get all of this sorted out and then you come back here, and I'll have you for lunch!"

How sweet of her to offer such a nice gesture at this difficult moment, although her grammatical structure was indeed a bit amusing. Dr. Brewster defaulted back to his usual modus operandi and tried to joke his way out of having to return to this nurses' station. With all that was going on, he could not really bring himself to eat anything at that particular time. Besides, if the truth be told, Brewster would have to acknowledge that for many years, he was never particularly comfortable in the company of people who originated from other racial or ethnic groups. When a life-changing event occurred on June 19, 1981, at precisely 11:48 p.m., Brewster was never the same.

As he had harvested these misgivings for years, he rarely missed an opportunity to poke a proverbial sharp verbal stick into somebody's eye. Brewster was accustomed to spewing intermittent shocking comments and insensitive jokes, essentially unaware that the era for such banter was long over. He enjoyed sparring with Ida Mae, and he just couldn't resist an opportunity to verbally joust with her in an aggressive manner. "I'd love to, Ida Mae, but I don't trust you Filipino gals. I know that you Filipinos have all come from a long line of cannibals."

The charge nurse howled in protest, put her hands on her hips, and then replied, "What do you mean? The Filipinos aren't cannibals."

Dr. Brewster wagged his finger at Ms. Pagan and replied, "Oh, yeah? What did the Filipinos do to Ferdinand Magellan in the year AD 1521? During his circumnavigation around the globe, he stopped in the Philippines just to cop a whiz and to pick up a few coconuts. Those godless savages from your home islands proceeded to club the poor bastard in the head, put him in a big pot, cooked him up, and then they ate him! I know for a fact that everybody from a certain village in the Philippines has the same last name of Pagan. That alone should tell you something!"

Brewster walked down the hallway toward the elevator, and Ida Mae called out to him with a toothy grin, "We didn't give ourselves that last name. It was bestowed upon us by the missionaries that came to the Philippines many centuries ago. You need to learn better our history, white boy. Besides, we didn't cook Magellan after we killed him. We just ate him raw! Portuguese sushi, yeah?"

Dr. Brewster laughed but did not look back to the charge nurse as he waved the back of his hand to her when he got onto the elevator to ride up to the fifth floor.

When Brewster got off the elevator, he walked directly to Cheryl Mammon's room, but he stopped dead in his tracks when he saw an African American woman with jet-white hair dressed in a sharp white pressed nurse's uniform standing right outside the door. He broke out into a cold sweat and dropped the NCCN cancer treatment guidelines that he had printed on Cheryl's behalf. He slowly approached the woman and got within three feet of her before he mustered the courage to speak.

"Oh my God. You're—you're Sister Buena!" How could this be? Brewster had known this woman all of his life, although it had been years since he had seen her last. This individual had even saved Brewster's life multiple times in the past, but as far as Dr. Brewster could tell, she had not aged a bit. "How is this possible?" Brewster asked. "Who are you? Better yet, what are you? Why are you here?"

The visage referred to as "Sister Buena" looked impassively at the doctor and replied, "Well, well, well, if it's not J. D. Brewster. Yes, I have indeed known you all of your life, and I'm somewhat surprised that you're asking me these questions. I thought you were brighter than that. I'm here for Cheryl. I introduced myself to her just recently. I told her I was a floating nurse from the temp pool. She's only known me for a short time, but she's already figured it all out by now. I guess she must be a whole lot smarter than you. I've been waiting for you to show up. Cheryl wants to reconcile with you but you have to hurry. I'm on a tight schedule, so you better go in and visit with her now. I suggest you make your peace with her. You need to do it now. The clock's ticking."

Brewster was not quite ready to come to grips with Cheryl's condition and what fate had in store for her. If Cheryl was actively dying, Brewster had grave concerns as to how she would be judged at the time of her passing. "I know that you think what I had done—no, what *we* had done—was wrong. I'm sorry you see it that way, Sister, but the action we took those many years ago was a righteous dispensation of much deserved clinical justice. Nothing more and nothing less. Surely you must agree with me by now."

"No, that was not your call," Sister Buena said as she shook her head.

"That man—that man we neutralized was evil," Brewster protested. "In fact, he was *pure* evil. Looking back on it now, I don't think that he was a redeemable human being. In light of all that he had done, I'm certain that he got what he deserved. He could have hurt or killed a lot more people."

Sister Buena pointed to the patient's room indicating that it was time for Brewster to make his obligatory visitation. Sister Buena raised her voice and spoke slowly for greater emphasis, "No, that was not your call."

J. D. went to the door. Before he entered, he turned and stated rather harshly, "I'll go in and see her now, but I'll be out in a few minutes. I need to talk to you. I'm serious. I have questions that need to be answered."

"No, that train pulled out of the station a long time ago," Sister Buena said, laughing. "Besides, I'm not the One you need to be talking to. Hurry up. You've got five minutes. I'm taking Cheryl home today. I'm on a tight schedule."

Brewster looked down, shook his head in disagreement, and said, "Cheryl is here on the Hospice Unit, and from what little I already know about her case thus far, I don't think she will be well enough to go home today. As she only has an ECOG 4 performance status and lower extremity paralysis, she's in a bed-ridden state and will not be able to participate in essentially any activities on her own accord."

Brewster looked up, but Sister Buena was gone. All through his life, Dr. Brewster had missed the big picture. Miracles had occurred in his career that he had never recognized. Several times in the past, he was on the threshold of medical and/or scientific breakthroughs, but he just could never connect the dots. Why should this time in his life be any different?

When J. D. entered Cheryl's room, he discovered a cachectic, acute, and chronically ill-appearing middle-aged woman who seemed to be twenty years older than her chronological life years. She had alopecia from the extensive previous chemotherapy administration that she had received. She had a Port-A-Cath venous access device embedded in her upper right anterior chest wall, and she was receiving a continuous infusion of intravenous morphine through this vascular access device.

Through her hospital gown, Dr. Brewster could recognize that she had already undergone bilateral mastectomy procedures. She had edema involving her left upper extremity, and her left hand appeared to be swollen to the point that she could not even flex her fingers. She had multiple ulcerated erythematous nodules popping through the skin of her left anterior chest wall that appeared to be small erupting volcanos. She was having involuntary episodic pauses in respiration, but then she would gasp and start breathing rapidly again before the pattern repeated itself.

When Brewster entered the room, Cheryl's daughter, Faith, was sitting in a chair at the right foot of the bed. She was wearing opaque wraparound sunglasses.

Cheryl opened her eyes and tried to focus her vision on the man standing beside her bed. At first she did not recognize J. D. Brewster, because the last time she had seen him, he still had brown hair and was forty pounds lighter. Cheryl weakly uttered, "It's you, J.D. I'm glad you made it. Well, tell me, Brewster, are you still out there trying to brew up trouble? That's what you always did best. You were a lightning rod for a whole mess of bad news." Cheryl smiled weakly and then gasped to take her next breath.

Brewster shrugged and replied, "Guilty as charged."

Cheryl then quickly dozed off back off to sleep. Faith jumped out of her chair and smiled broadly. She came to Brewster and shook his hand. When she had done so, the doctor made a conscious effort not to stiffen up. He actually allowed himself to pat Faith on the shoulder, as awkward as that was as an action for him to ever engage in. She put up her index finger against Brewster's lips to keep him from saying anything, and she pulled him out of the room.

She looked up at him and said, "Thanks for coming. I never really thanked you for helping out with my college tuition after my father died during my senior year at Trinity University. If you hadn't done that for me, I wouldn't have been able to finish school. I wish you had come to my graduation."

"At the time, I was glad to help you out," Brewster said. "It was the least that I could do, Faith."

"Well, I was surprised that you helped me out, because you were little more than a stranger to me. Mom was not surprised, though. She said that she knew you were the kind of man who would be able to step up to the plate and do the right thing," Faith said. "In fact, Mom said that even when you did a wrong thing in life, you always thought that you were still doing the right thing. I'm not sure what she meant by that. In any event, did you know that I'm now an insurance adjuster? I'm really happy how everything turned out for me in my life. Don't be mad, but Mother didn't want you to know anything about her cancer. She—well, she just thought when she came down with breast cancer you would've just yelled at her."

Brewster was stunned by such a comment, but he composed himself enough to say, "Faith, it is good to see you, sweetie." Brewster wanted to pay the young woman a compliment. However, as he didn't know quite what to say, what he stated was actually quite awkward. "I think you have really grown up to be a lovely young lady. Your teeth are perfect. You have the whitest and straightest teeth I think I have ever seen. I know your daddy would be proud of you now."

Dr. Brewster had to generate these superficial pleasantries before he got down to the brass tacks. Being cordial, polite, and complimentary are the lubricating oils that can reduce friction in social circumstances. Although he was not particularly adept at human-to-human interactions, Brewster at least understood that one societal fundamental norm.

At that time, there were three things Brewster needed to figure out. First, he had to find out if his encounter with Sister Buena was a real phenomenon or a figment of stress-induced auditory and visual hallucinations. "Faith, did Cheryl meet a floating nurse from the temp pool who was asked to come here by the chaplaincy service? Her name is, Sister Buena."

Faith nodded and replied, "Oh, yes, such a lovely person. She's come in several times to pray with Mom. She was the one who gave me your phone number."

Wow! Brewster wondered how Sister Buena had his unlisted phone number. Brewster pressed on and asked, "Faith, is your mom scheduled to be discharged to go into the home-hospice terminal care program?"

"Oh, no way," Faith responded. "Dr. Brown feels Mom would get better palliative terminal care if she stays here on the unit."

This relieved Brewster's concern about Sister Buena having said that Cheryl was going home that day.

What Faith said certainly answered the first question as to whether Dr. Brewster had taken leave of his senses. Sister Buena was real enough. Now, the next question in Brewster's mind had to be broached more delicately. If Cheryl had brain metastases, perhaps the frontal lobe filters in her cerebral cortex were adversely affected.

Maybe Cheryl slipped up and inadvertently told Faith already about the brutal, premeditated criminal act of homicide that Brewster had engineered thirty-five years ago.

If so, this situation could quickly snowball into a swift and painful introduction to the criminal justice system, which Brewster had skirted his entire life since graduating from medical school. He had to be absolutely certain that Cheryl did not spill the beans by some mistake. It was imperative what he, Feral Cheryl, the Wooly Mammoth, and a few other clandestine colleagues had been involved with would forever remain a secret. After all, there was no statute of limitations regarding what they had done.

The third thing that Brewster had to sort out was why Cheryl would have ever thought that he could ever possibly be mad at her, much less ever be inclined to raise his voice at her in anger. After all, he had known Cheryl since she was only eleven years, old and there was a time when she and Brewster were like family. Well, almost like family, although the doctor would readily admit that a vexing shadow of ethnic and racial nuances always sadly complicated his relationship with her.

Brewster was well aware that, at a societal level, these issues had always influenced the way Americans had looked upon and interacted with each other. This was true in the past, as it is now in the present time, and will likely remain so far into the distant future. The doctor long professed that human beings were basically tribal creatures. After all, it had not been all that long since our ancestors crawled out of the caves and climbed out of the trees.

Brewster gently probed for more detail and asked, "Faith, tell me how this came to pass. When was your mother diagnosed with cancer, and what has she gone through thus far?"

Faith shrugged her shoulders and proceeded to explain. "Mom was diagnosed with inflammatory breast cancer involving her left breast over two years ago. Her cancer doctor told her that with this type of cancer, patients are first treated with chemotherapy before they ever get a mastectomy. She was treated with several different types of chemotherapy drugs, including some stuff that I remember we called the 'Big Red'. That medicine made her heart weak after it was administered."

"The drug you're referring to is called doxorubicin, and it's well known to cause cardiac dysfunction from time to time," Brewster explained.

"A variety of other things were also tried, including some kind of drug that was extracted from the bark or needles from some type of nasty-ass, scrawny conifer tree," Faith added. "I remember that was the medicine made her hands and feet go numb."

"That must have been one of the taxane agents that you're talking about," Brewster explained. "There's no doubt in my mind that your mom was treated quite aggressively."

"Do you know why chemotherapy is so expensive?" Faith asked. "She received drugs that were made out of platinum. They gave her tons of anti-nausea medications that were only marginally effective. Sometimes she would vomit from the chemotherapy to the point that she was left with dry heaves that seemed to go on for hours."

"It sounds like she really had a tough time," Brewster sympathized.

"All of that would've been perfectly acceptable to my mother if only the drugs they tried on her had done her any good," Faith said with considerable frustration. "The cancer marched through everything that was tried. They even used radiation therapy to treat the tumor that had spread to her spine. They also used electrons to try and manage the painful open cancer sores that appeared on her chest wall."

Faith gave pause to her narrative, and Dr. Brewster pressed her for more information "Who was her cancer doctor who directed the treatment that she had received?"

Faith replied, "It was that young doctor with a peculiar last name, Dr. Brap. Did you know that his first name is almost as odd as his last name? His first name is Prap."

Dr. Brewster bit his lower lip to hide his disappointment. Poor Cheryl had been provided oncological care through the nefarious Dr.

Brap. He was a member of the "new breed". This was a derisive and demeaning term that the old-school oncologists like Dr. Brewster and his contemporaries used to describe the younger generation of physicians that looked upon the practice of medicine as only an eight-to-five gig. For this new breed, it was just a job like any other and not a true calling per se. These were the type of doctors that J. D. Brewster actively and openly despised. He considered them all to be a bunch of prima donnas that had "lifestyle" issues.

Members of the new breed of cancer specialists were generally vegans who considered burlap sack dresses and Birkenstock shoes as haute couture. They generally appeared on the borderline of being anorexic. Invariably, they had effete extremities that looked like pipe cleaners. Perhaps at one time they were stunt extras from a science fiction movie about the alleged gray aliens.

To make matters worse, Dr. Brewster believed that members of the new breed never seemed to be available at nights, weekends, or holidays, even when they were on call. If they were members of some kind of group practice, you could bet your bottom dollar that they would never willingly do one microgram of extra work if it was not specifically in their contract. As medical colleagues, Brewster felt that these individuals were quite useless.

Well, that was all water under the bridge. There was no sense at all in letting Faith know the contempt he had for Dr. Brap. At best, Brewster considered Dr. Brap to be little more than an ineffectual, dull tool.

"Oh, Prap Brap is a fine fellow and a good doctor. It sounds like Cheryl got the best attentive care that she could have received anywhere," Brewster said as he bit his lower lip. Faith seemed most relieved by Dr. Brewster's comment as she likely had doubts about the quality of care that her mother had actually received. Dr. Brewster still had to clear up a few more items. "Why do you think your mother thought I could ever be angry at her?" the doctor asked.

Faith had a ready and somewhat surprising response. "I think you know that my maternal grandmother had died from advanced breast cancer when my mom was only eight years old back in '65. Several years ago, you wrote my mom a letter making a very strong suggestion that she should get screened for the BRCA1 and BRCA2 oncogenes. She never followed your advice. If she had, perhaps she would've gotten the prophylactic mastectomies performed before she developed this lethal cancer. She was just stubborn and didn't want to have the tests done."

Brewster waved his left hand and said, "Realistically it's a possibility that she did indeed have a cancer gene that she could've passed on to you, but it is not going to change anything for your mother at this time. We've recognized several more oncogene markers in this day and age, above and beyond the first recognized BRCA1 and BRCA2 oncogenes. If you like, Faith, I could order you up a genetic panel if you are worried about any of this."

Faith rolled her eyes to the top of her head. "You don't understand! I got myself screened already with an advanced genomic panel," she explained. "I've inherited something even worse than the BRCA oncogene! I have the P-TEN mutation found in Cowden's syndrome. I don't know if black people are even supposed to have this genetic quirk. Maybe some white boy came along, jumped the fence, and contaminated our gene pool somewhere along the way. In any event, I now have a greater than eighty-five percent lifetime risk of contracting breast cancer, and maybe even dying from it!"

"Wow! I'm truly sorry to hear about this," Brewster said, somewhat surprised. It appeared that Faith had already figured out that she had an extraordinarily high lifetime risk of contracting and dying from not only breast cancer but also a variety of other malignant disorders.

"I'm also at an increased lifetime risk for thyroid cancer and endometrial cancer," Faith elaborated. "Mom must have the same genetic aberration. I'm getting a bilateral mastectomy and a total hysterectomy before I'm thirty. I'm twenty-seven years old now, and

I have to find some way to fall in love, get married, and have a baby before I pull the trigger and do what I have to do."

"Be brave, Faith," Brewster encouraged the young woman. After all, from a personal standpoint, Brewster was well aware that the primal instinct for reproduction was a powerful driving force in human beings. However, the biological fulfillment of having offspring was something that Brewster would sadly never experience.

"Maybe I'll just hire a sperm donor for a short-term and meaningless relationship. I don't want to end up like my mom or my grandmother," Faith lamented. "Wish me luck. I'm starting to vet sperm donors now. If I can't fall in love with somebody by the time I hit thirty, I'll consider a strictly straight-up test tube and Petrie dish kind of a romance."

With that comment, Brewster could only painfully laugh at the multilevel irony he had been confronted with. Above and beyond the whole issue of racial incongruity, there were indeed reproductive limits that he had to contend with ever since that painful and fateful night he had managed to survive on June 19, 1981. Obviously, Faith Mammon was totally oblivious of Dr. Brewster's own reproductive limitations. Following Faith's comment, Dr. Brewster recommended that they should go back into Cheryl's room to see if she could be awakened.

Faith agreed, and they entered the room together. Faith had folded her arms around Dr. Brewster as if he was an escort. She gently shook her mother's foot and said, "Mom? Mom? Mommy? Wake up, Mom–J. D. is here."

Cheryl blinked. Her pupils, which had been quite constricted, became slightly dilated as Brewster and her daughter came into focus. Cheryl's mouth was as dry as a tortilla chip, however once Faith moistened the inside of her mouth with a pink sponge swab, Cheryl began to speak. "J. D., I'm glad you're here. I didn't want you to be mad at me, but I wanted to see you before I die. I think I'm going to die today. It's okay. I'm ready. I'm ready, I tell you. Now, listen;

I'm DNR. Am I clear? *Do not resuscitate* me! I know you, and I don't want you to go all Captain Flag and whatnot on me. Just let me slide on out."

Tears started to well up in Dr. Brewster's eyes. He was starting to feel great pain and deep sadness, and it may have been the first time he had actually felt anything in many years. "I'm here for you, Feral Cheryl." Cheryl's eyes were bright yellow from a bilirubin level that was likely sky high as a consequence to her cancer-ridden liver. Her internal organs were in the process of shutting down from the advanced cancer that was consuming them.

"I love you, J. D. I've loved you ever since you took me to my senior prom after that other boy kicked me to the curb without any warning. That was good, because I wanted to go with you anyway. Lord, have mercy! I remember the way the other folks got all worked up into a frothy lather when little skinny ol' me shows up at the prom with a date. It was a white boy, to boot. I would have let you have your way with me, and twice on Sunday back then!"

Faith looked at her mother, and her eyes got wide as her jaw dropped open. "Momma, you're embarrassing me!" Faith looked at Dr. Brewster for some type of explanation, but none was forthcoming.

It was time to set aside the humorous banter, and Cheryl's face had suddenly shifted to a much more serious demeanor. "Yes, I was naughty, my child. More than you'll ever know. I've prayed to God that He'll forgive me for the great sin that I committed. Do you think He'll forgive me?"

"I hope that's the case, Cheryl," Brewster vaguely replied.

"Every night for these many years, I've long prayed for a day that would come when I would receive mercy," Cheryl confessed. "I kept our transgression a secret from everybody for all of this time. I never told another soul. As for me, I've been in search of redemption and perhaps even salvation. You see, J. D., it's not only for my sake or my very own soul that I'm now concerned about. I've petitioned our

Father in heaven to forgive the Wooly Mammoth, also. Lord, I do long to see him so."

"I don't know what great sin you're talking about, but I do know that that Daddy is waiting for you," Faith assured her mother. Faith furrowed her brow and looked at J. D. Brewster. Surely this man who had come to visit her mother must have known much more than he was saying.

"I've also prayed for you and Russian Bear. Willy and I both made peace with each other about the matter, but I know that you and Russian Bear—well, I just know you boys got damaged real bad and real deep over all of this. J. D., you need to get right with God. Can you bring me Arby?"

"Say what?" Brewster asked.

"Fuller!" Faith demanded. She was confused as a consequence to her encephalopathic terminal condition and sadly did not remember that Arby Fuller had committed suicide long ago.

"Not now, Cheryl," Brewster answered.

"Do it when you can," Cheryl said. "You have to get right with God, Brewster. I know He can forgive you, but I hope you can forgive yourself."

Faith had a strained look on her face as she continued to stare at J. D. Brewster for answers. The doctor made certain to avoid any eye contact with the young woman at that strained moment. Nonetheless, it was a great relief for J. D. to have learned that Cheryl had kept the great sin a secret.

A look of sudden relief and peace overcame Cheryl as she leaned back into her pillow. In her last moment of lucidity, Cheryl raised her left hand toward the ceiling and cried out, "Look! They're coming for me. They're coming for me now!" Those were her last words.

After several moments of inconsolable weeping, Faith turned to Dr. Brewster and said, "Did you see that? Oh my God, I think I saw miracle! Mom seemed to have had a slight glow about her entire body when she passed on. Tell me you saw that. Tell me that I'm not crazy, Dr. Brewster!"

Brewster shook his head to indicate that he had not seen any readily recognizable intersession of Divine providence. Brewster thought if there was such a slight glow that Faith had noted when her mother had died, it was just from the near-florescent jaundiced hue of Cheryl's skin, which was a result of her liver failure. The toxic elevation of her bilirubin level was a consequence of the cancer that had catabolized her. The cancer literally had eaten her, both inside and out. Nonetheless, Faith proclaimed that she had seen some type of miraculous vision that occurred when her mother, Cheryl, had expired.

Although saddened by the death of Cheryl Mammon, Brewster was optimistic that the great sin, at least for now, would remain a secret. Although Faith professed hope that the doctor would be able to stand and testify that a miraculous event had occurred, Brewster softly expressed his doubts about the entire phenomenon that the young woman witnessed. "Miracles do happen, but you never know who has been chosen to be the witness. I guess I just wasn't supposed to see this one."

Upon Cheryl's death, Faith intuitively knew something was rotten in the state of Denmark, and she was looking to Dr. Brewster for answers. She was truly clueless as to what possible nefarious activity her mother, and also apparently her father, had been involved with. Somehow, and very soon, Brewster needed to cut his way out of this new trap that had ensnared him around his ankles.

"Dr. Brewster," Faith asked, "what was this great sin that my mother was guilty of committing?"

3

LITTLE WHITE (AND BLACK) LIES

Faith Mammon forced a polite smile when a hospice nurse and a grief counselor arrived at Cheryl's room to offer words of comfort. Faith was asked if she wanted a session with the on-call chaplain, and the bereaved young woman had a specific request. "Could Sister Buena come by and hold a prayer service with me?" Faith was quite confused when she was told that no such person was an employee at the hospital or even registered with the chaplaincy service. Nor was such a person recognized to be a floating nurse from the temp pool.

The attending palliative care physician, Dr. Brown, arrived within the hour. As he greeted Dr. Brewster with a firm handshake, Dr. Brown shrugged. J. D. responded with a slow nod. Faith watched with curiosity as these two men, dedicated to the art of healing, had some mysterious way to convey their thoughts without utilizing a spoken word. As Dr. Brown made the official pronouncement of Cheryl's demise, the Neiman Mortuary service from Bellaire had arrived to take her body away to be prepped for the pending funeral service.

Dr. Brown asked the mortuary attendants to have somebody come by and drop off the death certificate at his office on Monday and he would finish the obligatory paperwork at that time. No postmortem examination would be requested, as Cheryl's passing was death by natural causes. As Cheryl's body was transferred to a transport gurney, she was covered with a fitted forest green velvet blanket. The plush green cloth would have looked as equally at home as if it were originally intended to be used as the cape draped over the shoulders of the Grand Royal Poo Bear during the proceedings of the local Ursa Minor Fellowship Lodge.

Dr. Brown spoke in a respectfully hushed voice to the mortuary attendants with a volume that was barely above a whisper. "Name of deceased: Cheryl F. Mammon. Cause of death: metastatic breast cancer. Official time of death pronouncement: Saturday, 2:15 p.m. Here's the hospital demographic sheet on her."

One of the mortuary attendants dutifully wrote down this information uttered by Dr. Brown to make certain the correct name of the dead person, the date of death, the time of death, and the cause of death could be neatly typed onto a standard blank death certificate form residing at the business office at the funeral home. The other attendant took the demographic sheet from Dr. Brown and inserted it into a binder.

The official death certificate document, once prepared, would soon be returned back to Dr. Brown after the weekend for his final signature. Following the return of the signed document to the Neiman Mortuary Service, the official death certificate would ultimately be delivered to the State of Texas Department of Vital Statistics. Then, and only then, would a gracious and righteous woman whom her friends had lovingly known as Feral Cheryl Mammon officially cease to exist.

After all of the minutia that surrounds a person's demise finally gets buttoned up, a dead person's earthly remains will finally be legally interred or cremated. Perhaps if one so wished in a last will and testament, a dead body could even theoretically be placed in a dumpster somewhere. Upon decomposition in a land-fill, the deceased would eventually be recycled back into Mother Gaia.

Needless to say, such a disposal process would need a signed approval from a local magistrate. The official would have to affirm that such a funerary request would be fully compliant with all the codes, rules, and regulations of the local municipality's Solid Waste Management Division. Maybe if one could be so lucky, one's former atomic and molecular subcomponents could become valuable fossil fuel in the distant future. It is all pretty rote, if you think about it. You're born, you live, and then you eventually die. Sadly, throughout the entire process, there's a lot of paperwork at the beginning, in the middle, and at the end of the whole ordeal. In addition, throughout the spectrum of life, there is also a shit-pot full of taxes one must pay along the way.

After Faith had composed herself, Brewster said, "Let's get some fresh air. Come with me to the hospital cafeteria. I'll buy you a cup of coffee and tell you everything you want to know." Brewster realized that many pointed questions were going to be coming his way, and he was trying to formulate plausible explanations for the incriminating comments Cheryl had made at the end of her life. When he soon would be asked the tough questions about the great sin that Cheryl had spoken of, it would be absolutely imperative that Brewster had conjured an audacious yet believable lie. He had to be able to throw Faith, who was a suspicious and bereaved young woman, off the trail of the actual truth. After all, Brewster's very own freedom, and perhaps his very own life, hinged on this matter.

When Brewster and Faith sat down in the hospital cafeteria for a cup of coffee, the interrogation began in earnest. "I need to know something," Faith said. "Did you ever have an affair with my mother?"

"What?!" Brewster asked. "You can't be serious."

"I'm dead serious. Did you ever come between my mother and my father as an interloper?" Faith asked with a scowl. "After all, she said she loved you."

So far, so good. Brewster could tackle this question with direct honesty. "No, Faith, it was nothing like that at all. Look, as you already know, your late maternal grandmother also died from breast cancer, and at a very young age. I never knew your maternal grandmother. Well, at least if I ever met her, I don't remember the event as I would've been around eight years old or even younger. However, I do remember your maternal grandfather. His name was Rex."

"That's right!"

"Well, after the Houston Astrodome was built in '65, Uncle John and Aunt Erna decided to buy a cigar store over on South Main. Apparently, business was only so-so, and Uncle John decided to try to market his tobacco store to the nearby black community. To make this cigar shop more palatable to black folks, John hired your grandfather Rex. John and Rex were friends from the time that they had worked for the postal service back in the late 1950s."

"I never knew about those details," Faith said. How did Mom get connected to your family?"

Brewster wanted to be absolutely certain that Faith was ready to hear about a very sordid and horrifically tragic event. "Faith, do you know what happened to your grandfather, Rex?"

"Well, I know that he was murdered," Faith answered. "That's how my mom, Cheryl, became an orphan. What I don't know is how she ended up staying with Uncle John until she grew up and went off to college. My mother really never wanted to talk about what happened to Rex."

"Let me fill you in," Brewster offered. "Oftentimes Aunt Erna and your grandfather Rex would work during the same shift at the cigar store. To make sure nobody got their feathers ruffled, Aunt Erna would attend to the white customers while Rex would offer services to the black folks. It seemed to be a good working relationship, and as best I know, the business had improved and everybody seemed to be happy. There was even a ten-by-ten-foot glass-walled smoking room, complete with sofa chairs. You're not going to believe this, but I remember seeing a white man and black man sitting together in sofa chairs in that smoking room. Dig this—they were actually talking to each other!"

"What?" Faith asked. "Are you throwin' a knuckle ball, Doc?"

"I saw it with my own eyes," Brewster replied. "They puffed on cigars and shared stories about the war! Now, mind you, this must have been around '67. As a boy, I found that actually hard to believe. Here it is now, a half century later, and I still think something like that happening would be as rare as hen's teeth today, much less than in the 1960s."

Dr. Brewster had hoped that Faith was ready to hear about the terror that occurred at the tobacco shop. "Then, something bad happened, Faith. Around the time that the Astroworld amusement park had opened in '68, the cigar store was robbed at gunpoint. Two urban thugs came into the store and killed Aunt Erna and your grandfather, Rex. Your mother, Cheryl, who was only eleven years old at the time, was also in the store on that fateful day. I guess she was in the back storage room doing her homework when it all went down. She was able to hide, but she witnessed the entire horrible ordeal."

Faith asked a question that to Brewster and his few living relatives was still a big mystery. "So, how in the world did my mother, who was an eleven-year-old black orphan girl at the time, end up living with your uncle, who was a white man, for more than seven years? Things like that just didn't happen back in 1968. Things like that don't even happen now."

Brewster shrugged his shoulders and tried to explain what little he knew. "Your mom had no other living relatives, and Uncle John just did what he thought was the right thing to do. Uncle John took your mother, Cheryl, under his wing until she graduated from high school and went off to college with a nice fat scholarship. It was beyond strange, though, and the situation was really weird if you think about it."

"I certainly agree."

"There was never any legal adoption or foster home arrangement as I recall," Brewster explained. "Uncle John just swept your mother up and took her home. That was all there was to it. Our family certainly didn't mind, and Uncle John tried to raise Cheryl as best he could since he had no children of his own. It's as clear as day that he tried to raise your mother in the same way that he would've raised an adopted white girl."

"I assume that's when you and Mom became friends," Faith correctly surmised.

"When we were young, Cheryl and I thought of ourselves as cousins," Brewster explained, "and as we were both the same age, we liked to hang out with each other. Does that seem odd to you? Well, a half a century later, it seems strange to me even now."

Faith shook her head in absolute astonishment. She asked, "What about the city of Houston Child Protective Services? Why didn't they ever get involved in this predicament? Look, I don't want to offend you, with you being a *white* person and all, but perhaps my mother would have been best served if she had been raised by a black family. Black people have a legitimate culture too, you know. It sounds like that she didn't get exposed to any of it during the latter years of her childhood."

"You're acting like that's a bad thing," Brewster said. "It would seem to me that your mother got a leg up on life."

"Of course you'd see at that way, Dr. Brewster!" Faith said. "After all, you're, well–*white.*"

"I can't argue with that logic. Perhaps you're absolutely right. Look, I don't want to sound out of line about this either, but I'll be straight with you. If Cheryl was a white girl and I was true blood kin to her, there is no way in hell that I would have been comfortable with her being raised by a black family if the tables were turned. It's clear that you and I probably feel the same way about this matter. Perhaps this isn't about race after all. Perhaps this is about culture. With your ethnic heritage," Brewster said, "you no doubt have a preference for black culture. I'm okay with that."

"With your ethnic heritage," Faith said, "you no doubt also have a preference for white culture. I'm okay with that, also. I asked you this before and you didn't give me an answer. What about the legality of the situation, or lack thereof, when Uncle John provided custodial care for my mom?"

Brewster took strong exception to what Faith had said. "Look here—it wasn't *custodial* care. Uncle John *raised* her, and he did it as best he could. In any event, the CPS didn't seem to know anything about it. Well, maybe that's not the right thing for me to say. Maybe the Child Protective Services organization was quite aware of the situation, but they just didn't give two shits about it."

"How could they not?"

"Think about it," J.D. answered. "Your mother was an eleven-year-old black orphan girl who was going to be raised by somebody who really wanted to take care of her. All's well that ends well. Maybe it was an open-and-shut case as far as they were concerned. After all, I'm certain there's a whole lot more paperwork involved in trying to adopt somebody compared to the paperwork that needs to be done when somebody dies. Life is hard. It's hard for everybody."

"Is this life really that much of a burden to you, Dr. Brewster?"

"Yes, Faith, life is indeed a burden," the doctor replied. "It is, at best, a mixed blessing. Paperwork sucks, and nobody wants to do it. Nobody wants to pay taxes either. Your grandfather, Rex, and Aunt Erna, weren't planning on being brutally murdered while working in a cigar shop. Bad things happen to good people all the time. In my humble opinion, we just need to grease the pipes, slide things along until we get to the finish line of life, and if necessary, slap on an occasional Band-Aid when we hit a rough spot or two along the way."

"I'm sorry you feel that way," Faith said, "but it offers me little insight into my mom's integration into your white family."

"What's wrong with that?" asked Brewster as he raised his voice. "Let's put down the race card for just one moment shall we? This will be just as hard for me as it likely will be for you. Are white people human beings?"

"Certainly," Faith answered. "On the other side of the coin, Aren't black people human beings?"

"Certainly. Now that we've agreed upon this basic tenant that white people and black people both belong under the Homo sapien taxonomic umbrella, let's both try to accept that fact. From our own personal perspectives, you and I might not be particularly pleased with that fact, but it's a fact nonetheless. This holds true despite the abysmal race relations that our country must contend with in this day and age."

"Fair enough, I guess," Faith conceded.

"In any event," Brewster continued, "no local or state agencies ever got involved with your mother's situation. Uncle John wanted to look after Cheryl after she was orphaned, and apparently that was all okay with your mother in light of the dreadful circumstances to which she was subjected. I guess when you look back at it, nothing else really mattered."

"Maybe so," Faith said, "but am I to believe that this story had a fairy-tail ending and everybody lived happily ever after?"

"The only fly in the ointment," Brewster said, "was that Uncle John eventually ran off the rails and he got a bit, well, how should I put this—sideways, I guess one could say. After Aunt Erna was murdered, he slowly evolved into a cantankerous old coot, to be honest with you. It had gotten to where none of the other family members really wanted to be around Uncle John. I was actually afraid of him, but your mother never seemed to mind Uncle John's quarrelsome demeanor. She always held John in high regard as long as I knew your mother."

Faith was intrigued and just had to know more. "What happened to the two goons who killed your Aunt Erna and my grandpa, Rex? Did they ever get caught?"

Brewster appeared pensive for a moment. He had to be very careful how he answered this particular question. If he told Faith the complete truth about what actually happened to the two men who murdered his aunt and Faith's grandfather, this great sin would jump right out of the bottle of moral decay and perform a tap dance right on top of the table in the hospital cafeteria for everybody to not only witness, but also for everybody to cast judgment.

Brewster had to be certain that he did not reveal too much confidential information about the matter. He came up with an appropriate, albeit vague answer to offer as a reply. "I have it on good authority that both of those nasty bastards are now, and for all of eternity, impaled on a slow-turning spit. They are getting cooked in the fires of hell as we speak. Pitchfork-toting demons are, in perpetuity, slathering spicy Texas barbecue sauce on their sorry asses."

Faith seemed most pleased with this answer, but she had more questions about other matters. "The way my mother said she loved you seemed to have a lot more passion than just the love that is usually shared between cousins. The way she was attracted to you at the time you took her to her high school prom seemed to be a bit, well—spicy! I truly believe that there were some deeper feelings between the two of you."

"You're reading too much into this, Faith," Brewster countered.

"After my father passed away, did you ever think about kindling a relationship with my mother?" Faith queried.

Without a doubt, it was now time to tell Faith a flat-out lie. No smokescreen, half-truth answers would likely fool Faith Mammon this time around. "No, it was not like that."

Faith didn't believe Brewster's response and asked, "Was it because you were white and she was black?"

Of course! That was it! Brewster was an old white man born in the South, an old white man born in Texas. There was absolutely no way in hell he could ever have a long-term relationship with a black woman. He had once taken Cheryl on a prom date, but that was the end of it.

This aversion to people of color was amplified now because of all the thick layers of prejudicial distrust that Brewster long harbored toward black people after what had happened to him on that fateful June night, back when he was in medical school in 1981.

Brewster had become a bona fide racist, and he knew it. He was ashamed of these feelings, but at least internally, he owned up to them. This emotional poison that permeated his soul was as tangible and as dense as the split-face concrete cinder blocks that were used to build the mausoleum in which he was entombed. He was never going to change at that point in his life. This was the precise reason that the friendship that Brewster once had with Cheryl and her husband, Willy Mammon, had eroded over time.

It was time for Brewster to put up some defensive shields in an effort to further his deception. "No, no, no, you've got that all wrong! Maybe there was a time in my life when I may have felt something like that, but you're talking to a modern man, now living in the twenty-first century who has now evolved way beyond all of that." What an industrial crock of squat Brewster had just spewed from his pie hole. Nonetheless, Faith seemed to be mollified by Brewster's exclamations.

She pressed on for more details. "Do you think my father had suspicions that Mom had any romantic notions about you?"

It was time for a rare truthful answer from Brewster this time. "Oh, heavens no, that was not the case. How could that ever be? I was the one who introduced Willy to Cheryl. Did you know that?"

Faith said she was unaware about that bit of history about her mother and father, and then she made a wistful comment. "I didn't know a lot of things about my father. He fought in Vietnam, and he got the Purple Heart for being wounded in the foot. Other than that, he never spoke about anything that happened during the war. I also asked him about his medical school training, and he would always wave me off, as if he never really wanted to talk about any of it."

Brewster understood perfectly, as he was certainly aware of some of what his long-departed, albeit estranged, friend had gone through. There was just no way that Willy Mammon could have ever really explained to Faith, or anyone else for that matter, what had really happened to him during the Vietnam War, much less what had actually occurred when he and J. D. Brewster had attended medical school together. Thirty-five years earlier, a mortal sin had been committed, and it was imperative that the crime remained a secret. No sir! That deed had to remain deeply buried.

Faith continued on with what little she had actually known about her father. "I think Dad really wanted to become a surgeon, but because he had that lifelong seizure disorder, he was not allowed to enter a surgical residency training program. That's why he settled on being a family practitioner."

Dr. Brewster thought for a moment. Was it a time for the truth, the half-truth, or perhaps a flat out, bald-ass lie? He chose option two and replied, "No, Faith, that's not quite right. Your father did *not* have lifelong seizure events. He sustained a closed head injury when he was in medical school." What Brewster had said to Faith up to that point in his retort was the stone-cold truth, but now it was time for him to fudge the facts just a bit.

Brewster continued, "As best as I can recall, he slipped on wet pavement when he was at an ATM at the bank. Automatic teller machines were a new technology back when your father and I were in medical school, and to be honest, I never learned to trust these devices. In any event, your father sustained a blow to his skull when he fell to the ground. He struck the back of his head on the pavement, and this caused a subdural hematoma. In layman's terms, this means that he had a bleed that occurred between his brain and a thick protective membrane around the brain that is known as the dura. In other words, he had a bleed that occurred between the brain and the skull bone. He underwent an operation to remove the blood clot that was forming inside his skull, but he was left with chronic and recurrent troublesome seizures, despite a variety of anti-epileptic medications that were prescribed for him over time. It was a real problem because Willy was not allowed to drive a car for a long time after that."

According to the rules established by the Texas DMV, any person who had a grand mal epileptic seizure would not be allowed to drive a car until it could be documented that he or she had been seizure-free for an entire year. Most states have similar rules and regulations to protect not only the patient who is afflicted with seizure activity but also the public at large. If somebody had a seizure while driving a car, something really bad could happen. Not only would the patient who suffered the seizure event be at risk for injury or death, but any unfortunate pedestrian or other commuter in the immediate vicinity would too. Unfortunately for Willy Mammon, he was afflicted with these periodic and seemingly random seizure events throughout the rest of his medical school training and well beyond. What happened to him had a markedly negative impact on the rest of his career. It also was directly responsible for eventually ending his life quite prematurely.

"Mother and I thought that he had finally gotten over his seizures when I was in high school," Faith interjected. "He had actually gotten his driver's license back from the state after all of those years, but unfortunately, Mom and I were wrong about him being seizure-free. You don't know how wrong we were about all of that. Even after he had been seizure-free for a full seven or eight years, another conniption fit finally struck him at the worst possible time."

"What happened, Faith?" Brewster asked. "Please don't tell me that your dad decided to quit taking his medication just because he didn't have any seizures for several years."

"No, that wasn't the case," Faith explained. "Despite the fact that he continued to take his anti-seizure prescription, he was destined to never get over his epilepsy. At the start of my senior year at Trinity University, my father was driving me up to San Antonio when he had another seizure. We were only a few miles away from campus when he started to shake and drool. Then something strange happened. It was as if some malicious force grabbed the steering wheel and pulled it hard to the right. The car ran straight off the I-10 Interstate Highway, and it crashed directly into a concrete abutment near the 410 Loop."

"Did you get injured?"

"I got banged up a quite a bit," Faith explained, "but I ended up with no major injuries or broken bones. I wish I could say the same from my father. The rapid deceleration and impact, however, ruptured by father's aorta, and he died at the scene, right there in front of me. It didn't matter one bit that we were both wearing seat belts. I just guess his number was up, that's all. I never really got over that."

Faith's mother had just died, and now she was remembering the pain of her father's premature demise. It was simply too much of an emotional burden for her to bear, and again she began to weep. Brewster was ashamed that he had not gone to Willy Mammon's funeral after he had died. He tried to think up some type of plausible excuse as to why he was absent from that bon voyage graveside service. As no explanation or apology could ever possibly be forth-coming, he looked away and remained mute.

Brewster accurately predicted, however, what interrogatory probes from Faith would likely be coming next. Brewster felt a bit unsettled, but he was nonetheless ready to break out the old smoke and mirror magic show and assuage Ms. Faith Mammon with sleight of hand and classic misdirection by non sequitur anecdotes. In other words, if he couldn't blind her with brilliance, he would try to baffle her with bullshit over the matter of the great sin that was on deck and ready to come to the plate.

Faith had been dancing around the six hundred pound Sasquatch that was in the room, but it was now time for her to try to tackle the disturbing comments her mother had made about the secret that J. D., her mother, and her father amongst others had apparently been deeply entangled. She began the inquisition. "Okay, Brewster, who was Russian Bear? What was the great sin from which my mother had sought redemption?"

Dr. Brewster took a big breath and tried to explain. Brewster first began with an unembellished true story when he said, "Russian Bear was a friend of mine and also a friend of your father, Willy, when we were all in medical school together. The exact fate of Russian Bear remains unknown, but it's long been presumed that he likely died a horrible death at the hands of the Calle Vampiro drug cartel in Mexico when he disappeared back in 1986. I don't know, but it's possible that he's still alive and being held as a slave."

"What are you saying?"

"A contact at the State Department one time in the past informed me of their fears that he could still be alive and is, for no other better description, a prisoner of war" Brewster said. "I'd hate to think that he's still alive and is now forced to do their bidding at gunpoint. As a doctor trained in emergency medical care, he would indeed be a valuable commodity that the drug cartel could coerce to patch up their wounded mules and coyotes."

"That doesn't make sense," Faith said.

"Well, after all, it would seem that even the workers for a Mexican drug cartel would require some kind of an employer-sponsored healthcare plan of some sort, don't you think?" Brewster asked sarcastically. "God forbid, but maybe my former colleague fit the bill. Russian Bear had a lovely wife named Larisa, but she was murdered when we were all in our senior year at medical school. From an emotional standpoint, Bear never fully recovered from this tragedy. In any event, he never remarried."

"How could he have ever gotten entangled into a Mexican drug cartel in the first place?" Faith asked.

Brewster resumed his story. "During his emergency room residency training, Russian Bear became deeply immersed in Christian missionary work and he helped run a charitable medical service through a group that was called the 'Doctors Across the Rio Bravo.' During what little spare time that he had, Bear elected to serve in a village of absolute rural squalor that was known as the town of Playa Caliente in Estado Tamaulipas. This was a place that I also knew well, as Russian Bear and I had both gone down there to participate in a volunteer clinic during a family practice rotation while we were in medical school many years ago. It was a dangerous place as I remember. On one occasion, we both got caught in a real pickle, and I truly thought Russian Bear and I would be murdered down there by two banditos. By the grace of God, a very fast Mustang, and a full take a gas, our lives were somehow saved."

Faith wanted details and asked, "Were you robbed down there, or exactly what really happened?"

Brewster resisted the temptation to get sidetracked on a tangential event and said, "That's not important now, Faith. What's important is that Russian Bear felt that he had a calling to return to Playa Caliente and resume charitable work at that Mexican fishing village. Your mother, your father, and I had all tried to offer Russian Bear very sage advice. We told him that it would be foolish for him to return to that place, as the State Department had issued a bona fide travel advisory for American tourists not to visit that part of Mexico."

"Why not?"

"We would later learn that the Calle Vampiro drug cartel had big plans to turn that village into a distribution hub for the business of exporting illicit recreational products to the United States. In return, the cartel would receive semi-automatic weaponry headed south."

Brewster momentarily paused but then added, "I have an acquaintance who is a crime detective on the Bellaire police department. I provided oncological care for his wife who sadly, has recently passed away. A while back, I told the detective the story about Russian Bear. He informed me that it was widely believed that *Calle Vampiro* had set up a full gunsmith shop in Mexico to convert common semi-automatic imports into fully automatic weapons. When the local townsfolks and a few honest but outgunned law enforcement officials at Playa Caliente became an obstacle to the drug cartel's business model, the entire township disappeared. Poof! Straight into thin air. When the town of Playa Caliente had vanished, so did Russian Bear."

Faith was stunned by this tale and asked, "How could such a thing happen in this day and age?"

Dr. Brewster became emphatic and started poking his index finger into the top of the coffee table. "If you don't believe me, take a look at a map of Mexico. Specifically, look at Estado Tamaulipas and follow Mexico Highway 101 south out of Matamoros. About eighty miles or so north of the Tropic of Cancer, the highway intersects with Mexico Highway 5. Follow this spur east toward the Gulf of Mexico as it heads through the Castillo Marshlands and crosses the Laguna Madre over to the barrier island where you can find El Mezquital, which is still there. Highway 5 is now just a dead-end road east of old El Mezquital, and I do mean dead. It stops in the middle of nowhere on the coast. There's nothing there now. I'm serious. In fact, I'm dead serious. Nada. Zippo. Nothing. There used to be the village of Playa Caliente due east of El Mezquital at the end of the spur. When the township disappeared, the cartographers at Rand McNally simply purged further references of that doomed village from any maps that they now publish about Mexico."

Faith shook her head in astonishment as Brewster continued. "It was as if the village had never existed. In all likelihood, the cartel is still down there in force and still causing trouble. The region is not more than a stone's throw from that part of the Gulf of Mexico to the big transportation hub in the South Valley city of Brownsville, Texas. As it turns out, the North American Free Trade Act seems to have been a big boon to the illicit drug industry. Big semi-trucks may now roll in an unregulated and unfettered fashion, and apparently, they're not often closely monitored. They transport produce out of Mexico and directly into the U.S. market. It's a two-way street as we ship manufactured goods back to Mexico, if you catch the meaning of my euphemistic expressions. It is all very sad, and all very disturbing."

The story about Russian Bear that Dr. Brewster had just told Faith was all quite true, but he told her the story simply to lay the groundwork for a big lie about what was really behind the great sin. Faith had found Dr. Brewster's story compelling but did not understand how this was connected in any way to some great sin. Faith asked, "Well, I can't see how you, my mom, or my dad could have had anything to do with the disappearance of Russian Bear. What am I missing in this picture?"

This is where Dr. Brewster went back into the wide-open throttle mode of lying to Faith. He had to step up his game now and sell the next fib to the young woman as best he could.

"You see, Faith, the great sin, as your mother called it, was simply the fact that the three of us did not do a good enough job in convincing Russian Bear not to go back to Mexico," Brewster professed. "Your mother, father, and I all knew that this missionary zeal that had possessed Russian Bear would someday get him killed. We were right. Your mother had always felt guilty about what happened to Russian Bear, and she blamed herself for his mysterious disappearance. It was nothing more than that."

"Why would Mom blame herself over this matter?" Faith wondered.

"As your mother was terminally ill with liver failure and brain metastases from her advanced breast cancer," Brewster falsely conjectured, "it was quite clear to me that her previous act of omission regarding what happened to Russian Bear was simply magnified in her mind as something much greater than it really was." Brewster paused to see if Faith was swallowing his layered diversionary tactic.

When it seemed that she was indeed absorbed by his sordid tale, he continued. "I'm certain that *if* your mother was of a sound mind when she died, she would have realized that whatever dangerous set of circumstances that Russian Bear had immersed himself into was something that he had done alone, under his own volition as a free man, with a free will, with a free mind, and above all, with a free soul."

"What about the person named Arby Fuller?" Faith asked. "Mom mentioned his name when she spoke about Russian Bear."

"I think you misunderstood what she said," Brewster again lied. "If I am not mistaken, I thought that your mother was asking for a fast food roast beef sandwich at the time. Perhaps if she ate one, it would have made her feel fuller."

"Well, if you say so."

Boom! Brewster sold it! It appeared that Faith bought the story. If that was the only truth about the great sin, even Dr. Brewster could have made peace with himself at that point. Sadly, there was much more to the story. An evil crime had been committed by Dr. Brewster and his long-dead friend Arby Fuller, in addition to Russian Bear, Cheryl Mammon, and her late husband, Willy. One day soon, Dr. Brewster was going to have to face this transgression from the past in a head-on fashion, once and for all.

Faith was visibly relieved and had a slight smile on her face as she looked across the coffee table at J. D. "Well, that was not such a great sin after all, I suppose. I don't think God in heaven would judge my mother very harshly over such an issue, do you? After all, we as human beings have been granted this gift of free will, and that means we must also find our own way. If we trip and fall on our faces, at least we were free to do so."

It was getting late, and storm clouds could be seen gathering through the hospital cafeteria window. "I'm glad now that my mom agreed to accept a DNR code status before she died," Faith said. "At first I had misgivings about this choice, but in retrospect, she clearly made the right decision for herself. There goes that free will gift, once again. When it comes my time to die, hopefully sometime in the far and distant future, I certainly hope I will show as much bravery as my mom showed today."

Brewster nodded in agreement. "Faith, I must tell you, I would hope as much for even myself."

Faith clearly remembered that her mother often said that everything in life happened for some greater, unseen purpose. Cheryl Mammon believed there were layers of harmonic vibrations, and everything in the universe seemed to be connected somehow. "You know, when Mom was orphaned and was taken into the unofficial foster care setting provided by your late uncle, she said it changed her life," Faith said. "She learned to appreciate classical music, she finished school, she went off to college, and finally she became a nurse. Her dream came true when she ended up marrying a doctor! You know, because of all that she had gone through in her life, she was always very comfortable being around white folks. That bothered me for a long time, but now I guess I should just accept that fact."

Brewster just couldn't help himself at that point. He retorted with a comment that perhaps any other black person may have taken umbrage. "Good for her. So, as it turned out, your mom was an Oreo cookie," Brewster said with a smirk as he tried to give Faith a tweak with an insensitive comment. "From my standpoint, that expression is meant to be a compliment to your mother. I think you know what I mean. As this old white man who is now sitting in front of you once said, 'She was black on the outside and white on the inside!' I think that about sums it up, don't you?"

Game on! Faith appeared not to be offended in the least. She laughed and wanted to take a poke of fun back at Dr. Brewster. Doing so, she also proceeded to stick a proverbial finger into the eye of idiosyncratic racial differences that were found within the very two people that were sitting across from each other at that coffee table on a lonely, dark Saturday afternoon.

"I like you, Dr. Brewster. I like you a lot, even if you're now this fat, slow-moving, old white guy. I'm truly sorry that you never had a fling with my mom before she died. I think it would've been good for the both of you. You know what I mean. As this young black woman who is now sitting in front of you has often said, 'Once you go black, you never go back!' I think that about sums it up, don't you?" They both had a good laugh over that banter.

With that, the young black woman, as she was so proudly self-identified, stood up and circled around to the other side of the coffee table where Dr. Brewster was still sitting. Without a further word, she gave him a kiss on the cheek. She then turned and silently disappeared out of the hospital cafeteria.

Brewster sat alone for several minutes with a now cold and untouched cup of coffee that was perched in front of him. He heard a loud clap of thunder that was immediately followed by the unmistakable sound of a heavy downpour from a late March rainstorm. He stared at the empty doorway exit to the hospital cafeteria, seeming to be lost in thought. No, that was not quite correct. Brewster was not seemingly lost in thought; he was just seemingly lost. He finally waved goodbye toward an empty doorway long after Faith had departed from his company.

As Dr. J. D. Brewster and Ms. Faith Mammon were incapable of diving future events, neither person was aware on that particular dreary day that they would never see each other ever again.

4

SEISMOGRAPH

The rain was still falling by the time J. D. Brewster returned to his home, and it was already late in the afternoon when the agitated physician felt that he was starting to become unglued. It seemed to Brewster that he was merely held together by the red stitching that could be found on the leather cover of a baseball. There was now a rupture developing at the suture lines of his very being, and Brewster was falling apart. He was about to witness his own wiring exceed the amperage load that his brain could safely manage. He was about to have a short circuit and blow a fuse.

He walked into to his home office and then closed the door, as if he needed privacy. His actions were a most odd thing to do, as he was a solitary man entombed in a mausoleum. It was time to have an account of where things stood regarding the five coconspirators and potential eyewitnesses to the great sin. Brewster was accustomed to thinking aloud as he never had anybody else to talk to. He began to run down the list.

"Here it goes. There were five people involved with this righteous act of justice. Where do they all stand now?" Brewster asked aloud. "Let me see. Cheryl Mammon, now dead: widely disseminated metastatic breast cancer. Willy Mammon, now dead: motor vehicle accident as a consequence to an acquired seizure disorder from a remote closed-head injury. Russian Bear, status unknown: missing now for thirty plus years. He is presumed to have been killed in action while he was an innocent bystander and witness to the drug wars going on in Mexico. Less likely scenario: prisoner of war status in the hands of the Calle Vampiro drug cartel. In any event, it's highly unlikely that he will ever be seen or heard from again. Arby Fuller Jr., now dead: he ate a bullet from his own gun as a consequence to chronic depression from post-traumatic stress disorder. How all very sad. That leaves only me, J. D. Brewster, MD. Wow, that's it! I'm the last man standing!"

Before he took a big sigh of relief, he realized he had forgotten to take account of Sister Buena. This would turn out to be the major underlying electrical current that added just enough additional amperage to blow out that already overloaded fuse box.

His self-directed monologue continued. "Just wait a minute there, buddy boy. You're not off the hook yet. There's that pesky Sister Buena. Well, she didn't exactly see what we did that night. When I ran into her outside of the stairwell that evening after what happened, it seemed as though she already knew something bad had gone down."

Brewster was a man who was generally slow on the uptake. Although he lacked basic intuition, he finally had an epiphany of sorts in his fevered mind. Although there was nobody for Brewster to talk to, he had to organize his thoughts and even attempted to answer his questions in a rational fashion.

"If Sister Buena is indeed a special messenger of sorts, as it would seem, I don't really have to worry about her at all. The only One I should really have any major concern about would be her employer. I'm certain, though, that when I cash in my chips, I'll have all of that covered. I'll likely get a pass for having good intentions."

Well, not so fast. After all, there's a rather famous old saying about the road to hell…

Undeterred, Brewster had grandiose delusions about the whole subject of a future day of reckoning. "Now that I am the last man standing, I'm *not* about to offer an apology, nor am I going to ask for forgiveness. I don't need forgiveness," he proclaimed in a defiant voice. "Someday, when I stand before the Creator of the universe at the proverbial Pearly Gates on my own day of judgment, I expect to receive a hearty pat on the back and a congratulatory, 'Job well done.' I expect St. Peter himself will offer me a fat premium cigar and a room with a nice view. I will ask for a veranda and a marble tub."

The tangential thought process exhibited by Dr. Brewster suggested that he was on the threshold of an emotional breakdown. "I want a rich, gold-colored, travertine tile floor. I like travertine. It's cool to the touch. On a hot day, I can lay upon it butt naked, and it will suck the grunge right out of my congested pores. Yes indeed, I will deserve all of that and a bag of jalapeño flavored potato chips to boot, to my humble way of thinking. I would anticipate that they have rock and roll in heaven, or at least country music. There's no way they'd put up with any of that angry, misogynistic hip-hop bullshit in heaven, I would venture."

The doctor paced in a circle about his home office. "What does God look like?" Brewster wondered aloud. "Man was made in God's image. Well, here I am. I'm a man. At least I used to be. As best I can tell, I'm certain God looks like me, whether or not I'm a man anymore. If He doesn't look like me, I'm totally screwed, blued, and tattooed. I shouldn't have to worry about any of that, though. If $A = B$, and $B = C$, then A, by infallible logic, must $= C$. Mr. Spock from *Star Trek* would be proud of me, that's for sure, that's for dang sure. Two wrongs don't make a right, but five co-conspirators certainly do."

Brewster stopped his seemingly incoherent rant and went outside to stand in the pouring rain. It was as if a house immolated in flames was suddenly being doused with a firehose. After becoming totally drenched, some semblance of stability returned to Dr. Brewster's mind, although any licensed and certified clinical psychologist would have had a most difficult time stating under oath that the doctor was truly in full control of his mental faculties at that moment. Once thoroughly soaked, Dr. Brewster returned to his study and began to slowly pace about the perimeter of the room.

Resuming his self-congratulatory line of reasoning, Brewster continued. "I'm certain now that this will all work out in the end. After all, my co-conspirators and I surgically excised what was essentially a malignant tumor from the transverse colon of society. Accolades for all of us are in order. Special kudos will no doubt be bestowed upon me by the Big Man Himself, as I was the one who engineered the entire successful enterprise. With my newfound gravitas, I will even be able to intercede on behalf of the lost soul that was previously assigned to the life of Arby Fuller Jr. I must definitely make a point of that. If Arby did not find redemption or salvation during this life, I certainly pray that he found it in the next."

Dr. Brewster was still standing just two feet due north of the delirium threshold, but he had the wherewithal to find a pen and paper as he continued his soliloquy. "Yes, I should write down everything that happened for posterity, if not at the very least to cover my own posterior. What we did together will likely be noted as one of the most magnanimous acts of collective altruism that will ever be found in the annals of recorded human history."

The physician began to write a chronological account as to what happened during his last two years of his medical school training. Was this going to be a confession? Oh, no. It absolutely would be no such testament. He simply felt an accurate record was long overdue about the matter. If he should wind up with a truthful written coherent account of what had occurred, the next question Dr. Brewster would need to ask would be to whom he could entrust such a potentially inflammatory record of events. He had to be careful, as what he and his colleagues had done might still be considered a capital offense. As he was the last man standing, it could be rightfully assumed that the criminal justice system would likely throw the book at him.

This would be the case even if he was fully exonerated by the *clinical* justice system. Even amongst his most jumbled thoughts, Brewster was still quite aware of that fact. He believed that such a potentially incriminating manuscript should remain hidden away until the last man standing became inert. J. D. Brewster had long known that he had become a deeply flawed individual, but he simply had no offspring to whom he could pass on such a testament. At least he took some comfort from the fact that on the future occasion when he would have to face his own personal demise, his particular chromosomal aberrancies and spiritual deficiencies would also die with him.

In a lucid moment, a thought occurred to Brewster. He had an adult niece and a nephew. His niece, Laura, had not settled into a structured lifestyle at that time, as she had gone to India to learn how to play the sitar while violating the laws of Newtonian physics. Laura was determined to levitate in the lotus position by gnostic negation of gravitational forces with her third eye focused on secret astral portals.

On the other hand, his nephew, Thomas, was one cool cucumber. He decided that he would send the manuscript to Thomas and give him specific instructions not to read the document until long after Brewster's ultimate death.

Thomas worked for a weapons contractor that was licensed with the Department of Defense, and he lived in Los Alamos, New Mexico. He had some type of job that required a top security clearance. As to what nis nephew actually did within the realm of his official job description as a special project procurator, Brewster was not certain. The lad could have been an engineer working on the next generation of stealth jet technology. Perhaps he was working on a handheld, quark-gluon, subatomic particle beam accelerator weapon. Brewster really had no clue as to what kind of projects that Thomas had been assigned. The only thing that was important, however, was the fact that his nephew was a trustworthy fellow. This was a man who could clearly keep a secret.

As J. D. Brewster penned his treatise, he thought about the late, great American author Ken Kesey, who had died from cancer a while back. Years ago, Kesey was once asked why he had only written two novels during the course of his lifetime, as he was a man who was roundly considered to be quite a gifted wordsmith. By no stretch of the imagination, however, would any literary critic ever accuse Mr. Kesey of being a particularly prolific author. He is as much remembered now for being a proto-hippy, hallucinogenic provocateur as he was for being a famous writer. Ken Kesey and his apostles who were once known as the Merry Pranksters, had a magic bus that was named Further.

Once Mr. Kesey and his crew got on that bus, they took a never-ending psychedelic ride into hippy history. It would seem that Ken Kesey had never returned from (warning: a double entendre is coming next) the trip. Kesey offered a profoundly deep answer to the question that was asked of him as to why he had quit writing after only two commercially successful publications. The author replied, "It is better to be a lightning rod than a seismograph."

J. D. broke briefly from his literary mission as he thought, *Oh yeah, Mr. Kesey? Why don't you just take another sip of that bullshit electric Kool-Aid horse piss that you and your happy, hippy loser friends used to swill down? What a fulminant load of existential crap! During the last two years of my medical school training, I became a lightning rod and much more. I was a psycho-magnet. I was a focal point of evil forces through no fault of my own. I was a portal into the Twilight Zone. I have my own demons from decades ago. They painfully remind me that what I had gone through was not anything like a bad hallucinogenic trip that one could get from popping a few funky mushrooms. No, you are wrong, Mr. Ken Kesey. I was a lightning rod once in my life, and I got struck by so many thunderbolts that my moral circuits got fried!*

Brewster suddenly became self-aware about a previously inexplicable decision he had made years ago. That's why he declared himself to have a DNR code status in an official notarized advanced directive.

"Do not resuscitate me. Do not intubate me. Do not touch me. Do not fuck with me," Brewster defiantly proclaimed.

He spent the last years under the radar in relative obscurity in a life of miserable solitude. Now that he was the last man standing, it was his turn to become a seismograph. Maybe this would help him find redemption and perhaps even the salvation that his friend Arby Fuller never found.

After several hours, Brewster finally took a break from writing his testament. He then did something that was, for him, utterly out of character. He went to his cigar room and pulled out a long fifty-two ring monster that was in his humidor. Never before had he allowed himself to smoke indoors. He clipped an opening into the cigar with his cutter, and then he lit the end of it with a burning cedar plank. He took a slow draw and artfully blew a perfect smoke ring that rose toward the ceiling. The hand-rolled cylinder of tobacco happened to be contraband from a nasty little communist island that was south of Florida. He held in his hand an authentic Cuban Churchill cigar, hand rolled by the Montecristo consortium. He thought that it was time for him to do his civic duty, and he destroyed that cigar by slowly burning it from one end to the other. That was the least that he could do for the country that he lived in but really didn't want to be a part of anymore.

As he was a man accustomed to order, symmetry, and sterility, he had never fired up a cigar within the confines of his own house before, even though he had built a glass-walled cigar room in his home. Years ago, he had known a doctor from Cuba named Sergio Balbona. Dr. Balbona had spent his entire career searching for the cause of Alzheimer's disease. Dr. Balbona had died before any discovery of substance was ever made, and Brewster knew that Dr. Balbona had thought that his own career in the neurological sciences turned out to be a failure. Brewster thought that nothing could be further from the truth. Even though Dr. Balbona never made it to the summit, his life was dedicated to a purpose. Even through failure, knowledge and wisdom can still be achieved. Brewster couldn't say the same thing in regards to his own life.

Dr. Balbona had once offered Brewster an opportunity to chat over a fine cigar and a Cuba Libre cocktail, but unfortunately, that celebratory occasion had never materialized. Brewster blew another smoke ring and said, "I pay homage to you, Dr. Balbona. You may have thought that your scientific endeavors were a failure, but in my eyes, your life and career were truly blessed. I, however, am indeed a failure."

Brewster returned to his office and found a partially written diary locked in a strong box from the time he started his medical school clerkship training. Although the diary was incomplete, it was nonetheless a valuable tool that jarred his memory on many of the surrealistic events he had witnessed.

When he sat back down at his desk, he turned on the radio to the 1960s rock-and-roll oldies station. He soon realized that he was again under cosmic scrutiny when he heard three songs in sequence. The first was the song "Nowhere Man" by the Beatles. This was followed by "Faking It" by Simon and Garfunkel. The third song in the triple play was "My Back Pages" by the Byrds, complete with Roger McGuinn magically performing the three-finger banjo roll on his signature twelve string "atomic" Rickenbacker. As if on cue, Brewster began to weep after he heard the last song, just as he had every other time that he had heard or sung that song throughout his entire life.

Even for a nearly deranged man who was generally devoid of intuition, Brewster had correctly realized that God in heaven was overtly affirming that the doctor was a flawed man who toiled at a life squandered in a morass of moral ambiguity while burdened by self-inflicted, unfulfilled potential. Years ago, J. D. Brewster had specifically been given a relatively straightforward pass-or-fail test in life. What was the outcome?

Brewster finally stopped trying to delude himself. As painful as it would be for him to actually admit, he clearly flunked the exam. Now it was time for Brewster to proceed with the task at hand, and he resumed the accounting of the events surrounding the great sin. Would this offer him any chance to extricate his very soul, long entrapped in his own personal bottle of moral decay? He could only hope that this would be the case. Although one could pray for Divine grace, it could never be a guaranteed commodity for any mortal being. That discretion was clearly in somebody else's wheelhouse. A supreme Final Arbiter would have to make such a decision regarding the ultimate fate of J. D. Brewster.

In the book of his life, however, that reckoning was scheduled to occur at some other time and at some other place. After all, he was only now about to enter the autumn of his life. As Brewster had rightly inferred, his heart may have long been dead. The rest of his internal organs, however, were still functioning at a peak level of performance. Even his brain would soon be rebooted. The only thing needed was to flip a few tripped circuit breakers in the fuse box of his cerebral cortex to divert away the current of negative energy that had consumed him for well over thirty-five years.

The needle on the celestial seismograph was always recording thoughts, commissions, and omissions as they occurred. It would seem at this time that the final chapters of the life of Brewster had not as of yet been written. The next course of events would indeed be duly noted however as his life continued to unfold. Perhaps for Dr. Brewster, the word *unravel* at the end of the last sentence would have been a more accurate clinical modifier.

Brewster composed himself and continued to put pen to paper. He was determined to try and finish writing his account of events before the weekend was over. Would his personal manifesto ultimately turn out to be a confession? Oh, yes. It absolutely would be such a testament.

5

HUMAN SUBJECTS

To help facilitate what would be an unpleasant trip down Memory Lane, J. D. Brewster dialed his recollections back to the very first week of July in the year, 1977. The young twenty-year-old Brewster at that time was considered to have been a "first-round draft choice" by the Gulf Coast College of Medicine at the Texas Medical Center in Houston. He was one of only a total of six individuals, derisively referred as the brainiacs to be accepted into the prestigious MD/PhD dual-training program. The other eighty-six student members of the 1977 medical school entry class were enrolled into the standard, straightforward MD educational program.

The usual length of training for a medical doctor was a total of four years, starting after one had already been awarded an undergraduate college degree. However, the students who were enrolled into the dual-training program were looking at six full years of postgraduate professional education instead of the usual four years necessary to get an MD degree. The dual program was designed to train future researchers in the field of medical science. The extra two years of training did not present too much of an issue to J. D., as he was the youngest member of his medical school entry class.

Through summer school work and CLEP testing, he had blasted through college in just two years when he graduated from Dick Dowling University in Orange, Texas, and he even left his almamater with two undergraduate degrees to mount on his wall. He had a BS degree in history and he also had a BA degree in the field of biology. He was only twenty years old when he first enrolled into the medical school.

The entry class of 1977 was only the seventh freshman class that this new university had ever seen. The Gulf Coast College of Medicine, like its neighbor, the Baylor College of Medicine, which was located just down the street, was a private medical school. The Gulf Coast College of Medicine campus was located on Cambridge Street just east of the Ben Taub Hospital complex and Lamar Fleming Street. It had a magnificent view of the famous Hermann Park and golf course located just across the street. It was a very crowded medical center at that time, and it still is to this very day.

There is not a whole lot of elbow room for three medical universities on one campus, no matter how big that campus may be. If one were to fly over the Texas Medical Center, one would find that it is actually geographically larger than downtown Phoenix, Arizona. In addition to Baylor and the Gulf Coast College of Medicine, there was also the University of Texas Medical School at Houston, which was another institute for medical training. This latter-mentioned school was obviously a state-funded medical college.

Unlike Baylor and its close rival, the UT Medical School, the Gulf Coast College of Medicine lacked prestige. It had no particular type of reputation, except for being a rock-hard institution where the children who were enrolled for the specific purpose of learning how to become doctors did not play in the sand box very well with each other.

Although his medical school lacked any other notoriety to speak of, this mattered little to J. D. Brewster. The only thing that had ever really been said by the other medical professionals in the Houston area about the Gulf Coast College of Medicine was that it had a peculiar militaristic approach to student education. In fact, it was known throughout the Southwest that the student dropout rate was higher at the Gulf Coast than any other medical school in the state of Texas.

As the Gulf Coast was thought by others to be a rough and tumble, crack-the-whip type of an institution, why would potential students think about applying to this medical school in the first place? The answer is that the Gulf Coast College of Medicine, unlike other medical schools in the state of Texas, offered solid tuition grants for financially challenged students. It also had an impressive financial scholarship program for students who were in the MD/ PhD program, as well as for any student who was in the top 10 percent of his or her class.

If Brewster could stay on his preplanned educational track, he would be on the launch pad to have both an MD and a PhD under his belt by the spring of 1983. With that, Brewster knew he could write his own ticket to any medical research firm or pharmaceutical company in the country. He actually looked forward to being locked into the basement of some laboratory somewhere. This would clearly minimize his social interactions with other living and breathing human beings. At that time in his life, he generally found other people to be annoying. Sadly, toward the end of his career, he would actually be starved for human companionship. As he would have been only twenty-six years old when he was tentatively scheduled to complete his six-year dual-training program, he would still have his whole life ahead of him. He had plenty of time in the future, he surmised, to foster a relationship with somebody if that was something he felt was ever truly needed.

Medical school had changed a lot over the last thirty-five years since Brewster was at the Texas Medical Center. In modern times, medical students are now introduced to patient care concepts and how to appropriately interact with individuals afflicted with a variety of different illnesses very early on in the course of their medical school training. However, this was not always the case.

When Brewster was in medical school many years ago, the first two years of his training were dedicated to straight classroom-based basic medical science studies. There was no type of introductory class to clinical care. As he was enrolled into a very new medical school, not all of the bugs had been correctly worked out of the curriculum. Even at UT Houston, which was also a relatively new medical school at the time, this state-funded institution had already found it useful to have an introduction to clinical care class incorporated into the second-year curriculum of the training program. The lack of direct patient contact during the first two years of the medical school curriculum would prove to be detrimental to many of Brewster's colleagues.

At that time, when students from the Gulf Coast College of Medicine had finished their second year of basic medical science training, they were essentially forced into the coliseum at the point of a lance to face angry lions, tigers, bears, and gladiators at the start of their clerkship rotations. This would happen even before the hapless and bewildered students had the experience of any living human patient contact. Respectively, these hostile adversaries in the coliseum of medical education that the students would encounter were in sequence as follows: the interns, residents, fellows, and attending physicians.

Brewster had often wondered why the upper echelon of his medical school failed so miserably in trying to foster a more rewarding clinical experience for students who were just entering their clerkship rotations. After all, wouldn't these students be colleagues at some time in the not-too-distant future? Sadly, at the Gulf Coast College of Medicine, that was not the case. This school had modeled its third-year and fourth-year clerkship training experience as a dehumanizing and degrading military boot camp program.

The unfortunate new students in their clerkship rotations were eagerly mauled, lacerated, or impaled by their adversaries, who would all attempt to make names for themselves by how much carnage could be left behind in their wake. The goal was to display their intellectual prowess in front of the senators and the emperor who were watching on with dispassionate indifference.

If a student was critically injured and lay mortally wounded in the arena, more times than not a senator watching in the coliseum would make the call. He or she would invariably take the extended thumb from the right hand and then would point it toward the base of the neck and then sweep the thumb across the anterior aspect of his or her own throat. By this action, an inambiguous instruction was given to the gladiator looming over the fatally injured student to administer a coup de gras.

Brewster had been semi-sheltered from these brutalities, at least initially. As he was in the dual-training program, he spent a year of clinical research after his first two years of classroom studies. Also, he had another leg up on some of his contemporaries. Although he spent a year doing clinical research working toward his PhD program, he had a chance to have a considerable amount of patient interaction during this time of extra training. He was actually awarded credit for two clinical rotations during his year of research. Over the course of the year of scheduled research, Brewster was able to obtain credit both for a hepatology and also an infectious disease elective rotation. His PhD research tract had overlapped both of these clinical subspecialties.

By 1980, J. D. Brewster was deeply immersed into a dual-pronged PhD research endeavor, and both were in the field of virology. Specifically, it was in the field of hepatitis research. He had been assigned two research professors. One was Dr. Yeshua Rabbi, and his field of interest was the active search for an effective hepatitis B virus vaccine. The research scientist had spent many years working on this project.

Dr. Rabbi was affectionately known simply as the Rabbi, and Brewster was his only research associate. Although an effective vaccine has now long been available in modern times, a bioprotective, attenuated inoculation that could have protected a human being from a full-blown hepatitis B viral infection did not commercially exist back in the year 1980. Rabbi and his young ward, Brewster, both believed they were on the threshold of perfecting the methodology to inactivate the hepatitis B virus. This was the first step necessary to move forward into developing a safe vaccine that would not inadvertently injure potential recipients with a viable infectious viral entity.

The other track of research that Brewster was involved with was the work he was doing with a multi-member team under the direction of Dr. Hank Holcombe. Uncle Hank, as he was known, was trying to isolate and identify the infectious entity that, at that time, was referred to only as the non-A, non-B hepatitis virus. This was a disease process that seemed to have the same transmission risks to human beings as the better-recognized and readily identifiable hepatitis B infectious agent. The problem was that the mysterious non-A, non-B entity did not seem to be easily conferred to laboratory animal models in any of the experimental research that had been done up to that point in time thus far. Brewster and his assistant research biologist, who was named Rip Ford, were already erroneously contemplating that the virus was Homo sapiens specific. All of the laboratory subjects to date appeared innately immune to inoculation attempts.

In any event, J. D. Brewster had completed his first mandatory year of his PhD training, and it was now time for a day of reckoning. He was scheduled to meet with both of his mentors, Dr. Rabbi and Dr. Holcombe, that very afternoon with the other members of the Human Subject Committee in conjunction with Dr. Harrison Reed, who was the head of the PhD program, amongst others who were also involved with the dual-track plan.

Brewster would have to give two presentations concerning the status of both of his viral research projects, and the school's Human Subject Committee had to make certain that these fields of research were appropriate from the perspective of medical ethics.

Harrison Reed would be there to make certain any research program undertaken could have a potential financial benefit to the medical school. All of these factors would eventually have bearing as to whether Brewster would be allowed to continue working toward a PhD degree in the university's dual-training program.

"You need to relax, Mr. Brewster," the Rabbi said with encouragement. "I've been through many of these dog and pony shows, and it's all just an annoying formality."

Brewster had serious reservations that the ordeal would be a benign experience. After all, he didn't get along very well with Harrison Reed. He knew that the PhD program director was a dyspeptic snake ready to regurgitate a ball of non-digestible fur and bone scraps, likely to be the earthly remains of the last medical student that Reed had voraciously consumed.

"I don't know about all of that, Dr. Rabbi," Brewster said. "To make matters worse, Dr. Beathard is scheduled to make a guest appearance this afternoon."

The vice chairman of the PhD program was a duplicitous man with a fragile ego named Dr. Bruce Beathard. Brewster wondered why the vice chairman could be such a disagreeable person. Perhaps it was because Dr. Beathard lacked tenure. Perhaps it was because Dr. Beathard had anger management issues as a consequence to the unsubstantiated rumors of chronic alcohol abuse. Perhaps it was because there was some validity to the rumor that he had been twice overlooked for a promotion. In any event, Brewster never felt comfortable in the presence of either Dr. Beathard or Harrison Reed for that matter.

Dr. Beathard had openly complained in the past to anybody who would listen that his direct political rival at the medical school, and the overt target of his ire, Dr. Denny Sassman, had graduated from an *osteopathic* school of medicine and not from a more prestigious *allopathic* college. As Dr. Beathard wore his heart on his sleeve, it was no secret at the Gulf Coast College of Medicine that the professor was furious that Dr. Sassman was drawing a better salary. Whatever the matter, Beathard's behavior was quite unpredictable. At times he was supportive and collegial, but his demeanor could change on a dime.

On more than one occasion, J. D. was shocked to find Dr. Beathard to be unspeakably cruel in his derisive critique of the student's scientific research.

In light of these adversarial relationships with the directors of the PhD program, Brewster held the conviction that if he had ever crossed Dr. Reed or Professor Beathard in the wrong way, a heavy hammer would be brought down upon his head, which would effectively end the student's enrollment in the dual-training program. There was a lot of work to be done before the meeting that afternoon. Brewster had to sit down and compose an outline for the presentations he was expected to deliver to Dr. Reed and the other physicians who would be in attendance that afternoon.

Above and beyond that looming congregational soiree that was scheduled to take place in the upstairs conference room, Brewster had a fair amount of clinical work left to do on Dr. Holcombe's non-A, non-B studies that were ongoing up until the last minute. There were two patients who were in the hospital that day who were infected with the mysterious viral entity. He had a duty to harvest the free-flowing ascites fluid that was swishing about in their abdomens, and then he had to schedule a time when he could expose the potentially dangerous infectious fluid to additional different laboratory animals. It had to be ascertained, once and for all, if the mysterious infectious agent could actually be transmissible to nonhuman organisms. That would be imperative in isolating and identifying this troublesome infectious entity.

Brewster had secretly fantasized that he would be the one to isolate the evil, non-A, non-B virus. If that happened, the genomic and species designation of the mysterious virus in question, once identified, would be named after Brewster! International fame and recognition would be his for all time. Fat, sweaty television talk show hosts would throw themselves at him in an attempt to get exclusive interviews.

He would be invited to spend the night in the Lincoln Bedroom at the White House, and at a remarkably reduced cost compared to what the other usual influence peddlers would generally have to pay. As he was no longer an athlete, it could not have been expected that he would ever have had his picture found on a box of Wheaties. However, he was certain that the snot-nosed little bastard they called Mikey would have had to pack up his grit and make room for a picture of Brewster to appear on the cover of a box of Life cereal. That stuff tasted a lot better than those crappy wheat flakes anyhow. Brewster could anticipate that one day he would open a new, financially lucrative line of sushi-flavored cigars that ex-presidents and other dignitaries would be honored to have displayed in their own personal humidors.

Yes indeed, it could be a win-win scenario! No accolade could be greater in the annals of medical science than to have a virus or microbe named after the individual who discovered it. One caveat to that consideration is that it probably would have been somewhat unwise to have considered any type of an intimate physical relationship with any woman who allegedly had a sexually transmitted disease previously named in her honor.

Brewster wandered down into the dark bowels of the research sector where he was assigned a work station adjacent to the animal laboratory. The biologist who was a member of Dr. Holcombe's research team, Rip Ford, manned a nearby desk. Like Brewster, Rip Ford was a Houstonian. He graduated with a master's degree in biology from Texas A&M in '74 and was the better part of a decade older than J. D.

The couple who had adopted Rip had no children of their own, and Rip, to his knowledge, had no identifiable bloodline kinship to any known persons. With scattered freckles, red hair, and chronic solar damage to his nose and cheeks, Rip Ford was likely of Irish descent if anyone were to venture a guess at his ethnic origins. The medical research scientist had contemplated going to medical school years ago, but he didn't fare well on his two attempts at taking the

MCAT entrance exam test. Rip Ford was insightful enough to realize that his career choice had probably worked out for the best, as he actually didn't enjoy being around other human beings any more than Brewster did. Well, at least not enough to actually serve in the capacity as a medical physician.

Brewster spent an inordinate amount of time poking Ford in the eye with a sharp stick. It was not so much that he disliked his research associate, per se. It was just that, by and large, his working relationship with the research scientist had somehow turned into a big pissing contest of bluster and bravado.

Brewster didn't have any time that late morning in June to engage in any locker-room banter, so he gave a direct heads-up announcement to his associate. "All right, Rip, right about now I'm up to my elbows with assholes and alligators, and I don't have any time to flush the pot or drain the swamp. Don't mess with me right now, okay?"

"Brewster, you are such a major league cry baby", Ford replied without looking up from his workstation. "I won't talk to your sorry ass today, if you promise not to talk to me either. Do we have a deal?" Without saying a further word, the two men shook hands, and a fragile detente had been established, which allowed Brewster the liberty to write up the outline for the pending grand inquisition.

The Rabbi had been trying to successfully engineer a chemical method to inactivate the hepatitis B virus but still somehow maintain the critical viral features that could allow an antigenic presentation to the host's immune system. This would hopefully engender future long-term host immunity. The goal was to try and protect the host, if at a future time the host had ever actually encountered a viable infectious viral load. His efforts, which previously included chemical baths of ethanol and formaldehyde, alone and also in sequence, had all failed in the past.

With Brewster's expertise in using an electron microscope, a new idea was germinated to try to inactivate the hepatitis B virus by not only utilizing a combination of various chemical baths but by also adding the experimental technique of trying to freeze dry the damned thing. The idea came about when Brewster was recruited to work with Dr. Rabbi on the vaccine project. When using an electron microscope, a specimen can only be viewed by a beam of electrons bombarding the subject matter while it is virtually isolated in a vacuum chamber. The whole process of subjecting organic material into a vacuum chamber desiccates that material. This essentially is the freeze-drying process. Perhaps subjecting the hepatitis B virus to both a combination of chemicals and also freeze drying it in a vacuum chamber could successfully inactivate the entity and eventually allow for the creation of a commercially viable vaccine.

During World War II, thirty-five years before Brewster had begun his research studies, the boys across the street at Baylor University were the first to utilize the freeze-drying technique to store whole plasma. This of course was done to provide the copious blood products that were needed to save the lives of wounded Allied soldiers on the frontline battlefields. The technique was successful, but it was soon proven that this freeze-drying technique, when used alone, was totally useless in preventing the transmission of viral hepatitis infections. After the end of World War II, the freeze-dried plasma industry had essentially disappeared.

Brewster and his Rabbi had devised a two-stage process to try to denature the virus, and that included exposing the infectious agent to both a formaldehyde and ethanol detergent bath, and then freeze drying the material. Afterward, the hepatitis B virus would be rehydrated and then the whole arduous process would be repeated. Thus far, in their experimental animal models, the process was proven to be quite safe. No subject animal ever showed any active hepatitis B infection. Their technique was therefore totally successful in neutralizing the infectious virus.

Soon they also anticipated being ready for a pilot trial on human subjects (i.e., financially destitute medical students who needed to jam a few extra shekels down into their pockets). Rabbi and Brewster would definitely need approval from the Human Subject Committee to take their research to that next level. All this amazing amount of work was accomplished by only two dedicated individuals, Dr. Rabbi and his young but talented assistant and PhD candidate, J. D. Brewster.

There was only one problem about their technique. It seemed to work in a way that was considered to be too good of a fashion. The procedure they had stumbled upon must have totally disintegrated the virus completely without leaving any type of immune-stimulatory trace. None of the test subjects that were exposed to the denatured virus injections showed any evidence of immunological seroconversion. If they had, that would have been perhaps tantamount to biological immunity to a future host challenge with the real living virus. It was as if the animal models had been injected with nothing more immuno-stimulating than sterile water!

What the Rabbi and Brewster had been doing was pure and simple overkill, essentially knocking out a fly with a sledgehammer. They had broken down the viral corpse beyond the point that it could be recognized by the host as a potential threat. That's why no immunity was conferred to the test animals. Brewster and his Rabbi had to take their foot off the accelerator and then try again with different, less drastic techniques.

The problem was not likely insurmountable, however. Nonetheless Brewster had to be able to gloss over this setback to the Human Subject Committee and the PhD Committee, especially to Dr. Harrison Reed. In other words, if he couldn't blind them with his brilliance, he would have to baffle them with his bullshit. Brewster could pull it off. It was in his basic nature. After all, he was a Texan, and bullshit is what Texans do best.

There was another issue to consider, and that was the proverbial ace card that Brewster held up his sleeve. It was something that Dr. Rabbi didn't even know about, and Brewster planned to surprise everybody about the matter during the conference that was scheduled that afternoon. After all, a bit of showmanship never hurt in such a situation. The West German pharmaceutical firm, Leben Kur, AG, sent a letter to Brewster, erroneously thinking that he was the director of the hepatitis B virus research that was being conducted at the Gulf Coast College of Medicine. It was a brief letter of introduction that expressed corporate interest in the acquisition, by a preferred stock offer, of the research data that had been accumulated about the hepatitis B inactivation technology.

In abstract form, Dr. Rabbi and Brewster had presented some of the preliminary data of the work that he and Brewster had done at the most recent International Hepatitis Symposium that was held that past March in San Antonio, Texas. It looked like Dr. Rabbi and Mr. Brewster had actually raised a few eyebrows on different corners of the planet with what they had accomplished thus far.

The other tract of research that Brewster was doing was with the team that had been assembled by Hank Holcombe. The crew was trying to isolate the non-A, non-B hepatitis virus, and that line of investigation was certainly much less productive, to say the least. From a historical overview, it would not be until a full decade later from the time that Holcombe and his team had started to investigate the mysterious virus when the nasty little pathogen would finally be isolated by some other research team in the year 1989. Only then would the name of the infectious virus be officially changed from the designated label of the non-A, non-B hepatitis to its now confirmed and new conventional name: the hepatitis C virus.

As it would eventually be confirmed in the late 1980s, this virus was so difficult to isolate because it only infected humans and chimps. Obviously, Dr. Hank Holcombe's research team was not privy to that important bit of information in the year, 1980. It's curious to now realize that no other primates can be infected with this virus, including any of the other great apes. Other than the misfortunate chimpanzee, even the gorillas and the orangutans, which are also some of our closest relatives on the planet earth, are naturally immune to this infectious agent.

Sadly, it would turn out that the reluctance that J. D. Brewster and Rip Ford had about utilizing higher primates in the experimental process would ultimately doom Dr. Holcombe's research project to abysmal failure at the Gulf Coast College of Medicine in the very end.

Years later after Brewster would complete his fellowship training, he was finally able to draw a direct contrast between the hepatitis C virus and the better understood hepatitis B virus, which was first isolated way back in the year 1966: The B virus agent could fortunately be grown in a variety of different animals, including transgenic mice, woodchucks, and several birds, including the common duck. That fact made this infectious virus a fairly easy entity to evaluate in a laboratory setting. Unfortunately, this did not hold true at all for what would eventually be called the hepatitis C virus.

The difficulty in getting this entity to actually infect other living organisms was directly reflected in the fact that J. D. Brewster and Rip Ford ended up sacrificing a total of sixty trans-genic mice, twenty-four Fischer and thirty-four standard white laboratory rats, twenty-four ducks, twelve woodchucks, twelve white rabbits, and six rhesus monkeys. It was all done in seemingly cruel futility. At the end of his career, Brewster still had considerable misgivings about what he had done in the name of medical research.

Despite repeated attempts of conveying to these unfortunate creatures the non-A, non-B viral infection, there was no sign of any hepatitis or even any hepatic dysfunction at all in any of these animals at the time that post-sacrifice, necropsy evaluations were undertaken. To be frank, both Brewster and Ford were literally quite sick of killing such a large number of laboratory animals without having anything to show for their efforts.

Earlier in the year, injecting whole blood obtained from infected human patients into the animal subjects was proven to be completely unsuccessful. The next phase of the experimental study was based on injecting processed plasma obtained from infected human beings into the animal test subjects. Again, this failed to induce any evidence of infectious hepatitis that may have been transmitted to the lower life-forms.

With a new novel idea that perhaps the unidentified virus was more likely to be shed into the abdominal ascites fluid of infected human beings, but without having any true confirmatory empirical evidence, the presumed infectious ascites fluid would be drawn out of the abdomen from the human subjects to be utilized for the third trial at transmitting the mysterious non-A, non-B hepatitis virus into an animal model.

The potentially dangerous fluid was painfully, and repeatedly, administered into the animal subjects by the injection of the infected liquid directly into their livers. The transgenic mice were injected with a tiny thirty-gauge needle. This type of small needle was also utilized to try to infect the baby ducks. Unfortunately, all of the other larger critters were hit with a fairly large-bore, nineteen-gauge needle.

It should be noted that the woodchucks would put up quite a fight. They often showed their overt displeasure about the abuse that they were receiving by trying to viciously bite Brewster and Ford at every available opportunity. One could surmise that the animals found the overall experience to be somewhat of an unpleasant ordeal.

Some of the tests subjects died immediately from the trauma to the liver and intra-abdominal hemorrhaging. However, the majority of the animals survived the inoculations until they were ultimately sacrificed. Once they were dead, their livers and other organs were scrutinized for any signs of infection caused by the mysterious non-A, non-B virus. Of course, it was all done without any anesthesia. They were, after all, just animals. Unfortunately, not one of these tests subjects, irrespective of whatever mammalian or avian species they may have been taxonomically assigned, ever showed any sign of contracting the non-A, non-B hepatitis virus.

This meant one thing only: lower mammalian and avian lifeforms appeared to be completely impervious to this mysterious virus. If so, it was then time to start subjecting the great primates to these types of dreadful inoculation procedures. Would it work? No one knew for certain during this historical time frame of scientific research. Viral transmission certainly did not work in the rhesus monkeys. After all, did not human beings, the great apes, and the humble rhesus monkey all share a similar genetic blueprint?

Research biologist Rip Ford was clearly reluctant to take the project to that next level. Brewster also had serious doubts that he actually had the personal intestinal fortitude to wander down that dark pathway. They both felt it would be morally objectionable to do the same types of experiments to the non-human primates, even though the success of Holcombe's team would have been a great benefit for humankind. Such are the vagaries of the human heart and the complexities of the human soul.

Because of a congenital anomaly that required the previous surgical extraction of his left testicle many years before, J. D. Brewster was only walking around on the planet with one testicle at that time in his life. If he was going to be pressured to proceed with infectious inoculation attempts on the great primates, he would be determined to put up a stiff fight about the matter. If he got steamrolled in the process, then it would be highly likely that his only remaining testicle would end up on a skewer and given to that dyspeptic snake and acting director of the PhD program, Dr. Harrison Reed.

A testicular presentation on a silver platter to the director of the PhD tract of the dual-training program would have seemed, perhaps, to have been a bit melodramatic, but Brewster's only gonad was a large one, indeed. If his only existing industrial gamete factory unit was about to be lost through a public administrative orchiectomy, then so be it. He would insist, however, that the lone resident that was still occupying space within the confines of his blue-tinted scrotal sack should receive at least as much reverent deference as what King Herod had bestowed upon the head of the Baptist when it was delivered to Salome.

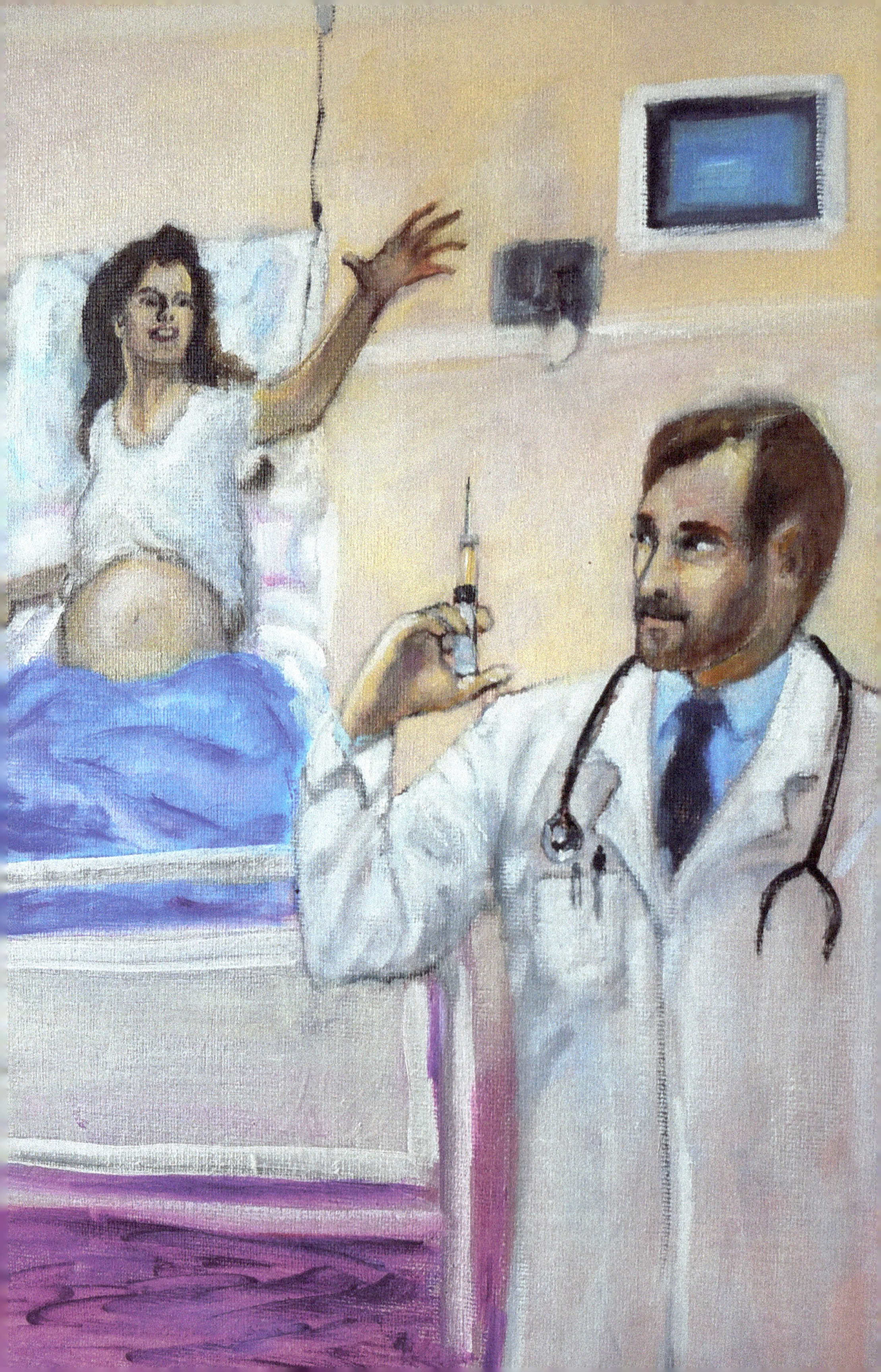

6

PARACENTESIS

Brewster had buttoned up the outline he had written out for his afternoon presentation, and then he put the papers in a manila folder for safekeeping. He turned his head to Rip Ford to offer a word of appreciation about the ceasefire they had previously agreed upon, which allowed Brewster to finish the task at hand.

Rip responded, "Good luck today. I know your PhD post is on the line, but my ass is in a perpetual sling over this situation too. This better go down well for the both of us. Look, we haven't hammered this out officially, but you and I have tortured and sacrificed nearly one gross of laboratory specimens, and we have nothing to show for it."

"Our research project is going nowhere in a hurry," Brewster conceded.

"You and I both know deep down inside that Uncle Hank, Harrison Reed, and maybe the whole damned universe wants us tee-up the great apes," Ford surmised. "My counterpart, Zip Talbot, says those big boys are all tucked in over at the lockdown kennel. Dr. Denny Sassman said he's ready to pull the trigger whenever we are. Both of those guys want to talk to us about the project."

"Is Uncle Hank really ready for us to take it to the next level?" Brewster asked.

Ford shrugged his shoulders and answered, "I don't know what's officially on the agenda from his standpoint. He talks to me, and I have no idea what he's saying half the time. His accent, dialect, language, or whatsoever the hell you want to call it is a foreign tongue to me."

"I thought I was the only one at this university who has trouble discerning what he says," Brewster opined.

"As far as I can tell," Ford said, "the entire sophomore class is enveloped in a fog whenever he gives a lecture. It's as if that television preacher Rectal Roberts smacked Dr. Holcombe across the forehead, and old Uncle Hank's very essence has been taken hold of by a country bumpkin edition of the Holy Spirit."

"Now, we just a minute," Brewster pleaded. "You're going to get hit by a bolt of lightning, and you need to be standing on the other side of the room."

"With all of those indecipherable, West Texas, Trans-Pecos, mumbo-jumbo idioms," Ford complained, "I need to have a translator present to cut through all of the Gomer Pyle horse shit that Uncle Hank spews. I can tell you this, though. I'm not about to shoot up one more mouse, rat, duck, woodchuck, or rabbit. I'm sure as hell not going touch another one those little bastard organ-grinders that just shit everywhere either."

Brewster had to laugh at Ford's accurate, albeit scatological, reference to the Rhesus monkeys, and he then added, "You know, there are a lot more mammalian and avian species to consider in the subphylum of vertebrata, all under the greater cordate phylum, that are still left out there for us to consider."

"Very funny, brainiac! I'm serious. I'm William Barrett Travis at the Alamo. I'm drawing a line in the sand. I absolutely will not tackle a dog, cat, baby pachyderm, pigmy rhino, armadillo, wombat, emu, platypus, koala, squirrel, Sasquatch, bat, or bald eagle. Not gonna happen, buddy boy. No how, no way! That's a road that leads straight to hell." Ford continued, as if he had just pulled up a bad command card during a popular board game. "Go to hell. Go straight to hell. Do not pass go. Do not collect two hundred dollars!"

Brewster said, "If we're going to start playing Monopoly, I want my play piece to be the little dog."

"No, not the little dog," Rip countered. "Your Monopoly piece should be a pile of dog poop. This isn't a game, Brewster. I swear, if Uncle Hank wants me to waste any more of my life chasing windmills, I'm going to politely tell him that he can put his head up his own ass and take a flying leap."

"You can't do that," Brewster cautioned. "You're too young to draw Social Security retirement benefits, and you're just too plain stupid to get another job anywhere else."

"Nice," Ford sarcastically responded. "I wonder, what would be the rough translation of that basic East Texas insult that I had just levied into say, the bullshit vernacular, Gomer Pyle, West Texas, Trans-Pecos horse shit that Uncle Hank would more likely comprehend? I might add right about now that the personal slight I previously conveyed about our country-fried boss was delivered in a conventional and perfectly spoken form of the English tongue."

"That's a hell of a lot more than I can say about the peculiar language that Uncle Hank seems to speak." J. D. commented, realizing that his research colleague could be a bit loquacious from time to time.

"Hey, Brew—what do you know about this new disease that has just popped up called GRID?" Ford asked. "It stands for gay-related immunodeficiency syndrome. From what I have read in the newspapers, it seems to be an illness that's only attacking people in the homosexual community."

Brewster confessed that he knew nothing about it and asked Ford to tell him more.

Ford replied, "It seems to be an illness that predisposes people to atypical pneumonias, and scary Kaposi's sarcoma, which causes nasty purple plaques to form on the skin. The patients afflicted with GRID are also at risk for mycobacterial and fungal infections. If this is an infectious disease caused by a virus that is currently only in the gay community, it will eventually break out and affect heterosexual people also. Maybe you and I can get on the ground floor and start looking into this peculiar phenomenon."

Years later, Brewster would remember this conversation that he had with Rip Ford. His research colleague was of course referring to the disease that is now known as AIDS. In the year 1980, it was widely referred to as GRID, and very little was known about this problem at the time.

"I think we have too much on our plate right now," Brewster replied, "although you are welcome to ask Dr. Holcombe his thoughts about the matter."

"You know," Ford said, "I think I'll do just that."

"I am a bit worried about Uncle Hank," Brewster commented. "He has that troublesome psoriatic plaque that developed on his left forearm, and it seems to cause him a fair amount of grief. It's interesting. Apparently it's not painful, but he said the itching sensation was intense. He seems to scratch and pick at it all the time. It's been excoriated to the point that I now occasionally see the site actively bleeding."

"It doesn't matter. Whatever is chewing on Hank's skin, you already know darn well that our boss is on the hot seat, just as we are," Rip added. "I know for a fact that this slime-ball, Dr. Reed, has been breathing down Hank Holcombe's neck.

"Uncle Hank is now feeling the branch starting to creek, and I'll venture he doesn't like it one bit," Brewster noted. "I'll know a lot more how things are going to shake out after this afternoon's meeting."

As Brewster walked toward the door, Rip Ford had one more salient comment. "In the bigger picture, I really think we're pissing on the wrong fire hydrant. I really don't think that this entity we're looking for can cause an infection in any other living organism besides human beings. At this point, I hypothesize that if this thing is a virus, it's strictly species specific."

That was a hypothetical assumption that Brewster had already conceded. "You know, I don't usually agree with anything you say, but I think you're hitting the nail on the head. Where does that leave us? Should we all just pack up our bags and go home then?"

Rip Ford raised his index finger to make a point and lowered his voice to make certain that Brewster knew he was on the level. "Look—I won't like subjecting these noble creatures, who may very well be our very closest relatives extant on this planet, to inoculation experiments any more than you would. Now, we might be the only facility within the Texas Medical Center that has the capability to do primate-based research, but make no mistake about it—we're certainly not the only laboratory on this planet that is trying to isolate this damned virus."

"Well, what are you saying?" Brewster asked. "Are you on board with this or not?"

"I don't know just yet," Ford answered indecisively. "No matter what happens, whatever data we gather about any experiments that we'll eventually perform upon the great apes will be critical. If these inoculation experiments are successful and we can eventually prove that this hepatitis virus can infect any of these great apes, a scientific breakthrough of such magnitude will eventually lead to the ultimate identification of the damned virus."

"You have to be brave enough to speak the name of the enemy that is trying to kill you in order for you to mount an assault against it," Brewster said philosophically.

"Precisely!" Rip said. "Once the virus is identified someday, maybe somebody can start working on a vaccine or a treatment for it. This will then be a great benefit for all of mankind."

Brewster wasn't sold on the idea. If the research project ran into a brick wall with the great apes, then surely his aspirations to be granted a PhD degree would be left unfulfilled. "That's all fine and dandy, but what if we fail? Maybe we should quit while we're behind and go on to something else altogether like this new GRID mystery."

Ford shook his head and replied, "You don't seem to get the big picture, do you? Deep in my heart, I actually do believe that any experiments we will perform on the great apes will also be doomed to failure. If we learned that this virus is indeed species specific and we can't transmit the hepatitis infection to these big primates, this would be just as important for all of us to know. That would be data that our team could publish in a peer-reviewed journal, and you could still get your coveted PhD degree. God knows what you would do with your miserable life if you actually graduated from this place with a dual degree. I would not be in the least bit surprised if one day I ran into you while you're driving around Bellaire in an ice cream truck peddling frozen lime sherbet bombs to elementary school children."

"Kiss my ass. If I nail down a PhD, it would indeed be important, but it's not paramount to me," Brewster admitted. "Look, I know you don't like to talk to me about religious or spiritual matters, but I believe that there is indeed an absolute truth that is the common denominator in this experimental equation. It would be a sin to inoculate and then sacrifice the big primates. I just wouldn't be able to pull the trigger."

"Knowing you, I don't think that you'd be able to ever pull the trigger. Think about this for minute, Brew," Ford counseled. "Suppose we strike out at the plate and we prove that the non-A, non-B entity is indeed Homo sapiens specific. In the grand scheme of God's universe, look at all of the good that we would have accomplished. It would likely deter *any* other research team in the world from using the great ape as an animal model for further experimental purposes. Can't you see?"

"I'm not following your line of reasoning," Brewster countered.

"Even if we had to throw a hand grenade into the locked-down kennel and kill every one of the big boys that are now incarcerated down there," Ford explained emphatically, "we might be able to save their kin that are still free and swinging through the trees from a similar grizzly fate. It's primate altruism, get it?"

Brewster finally understood what Rip Ford believed all too well, and then he replied, "No greater love hath one monkey than one who would lay down his life for others. Yeah, sadly, I *do* get it."

Rip Ford overtly wished that Dr. Holcombe and his team would abandon the search for an appropriate animal model host for this mysterious virus. He suggested to Brewster, in only a half-joking manner, that they should proceed with the direct vivisection of prisoners that were already infected with the unidentified infectious entity. After all, they were a captive audience within the penal system, especially those who were on death row.

Ford believed that such miscreants would be superb subjects for these experimental studies. He ventured a dark thought that if he could utilize real human subjects in such a fashion, Brewster could readily find viral buddings on the hepatocytes of these doomed prisoners with the help of an electron microscope. It could all be done while the prisoners were still breathing! Of course, these human subjects would need to declare themselves to have a DNR code status before the vivisection could proceed.

That would be a most excellent way for such wretched human refuse to repay their debt to society for whatever evil deeds they had perpetrated. Unfortunately, to Ford's way of thinking, it was highly unlikely that the Human Subject Committee would be particularly enthusiastic about a specific suggestion concerning prisoners to be utilized in open vivisection procedures. First, getting a consent form procedure permit signed without overt coercion might prove to be a bit of a daunting task. The second issue was that the court of world opinion had apparently frowned upon such "gray area" research activities since, oh, around 1945, when the Nazis were found guilty of actively engaging in brutal and lethal medical experiments on concentration camp victims.

"Hey, brainiac," Ford asked, "you're going to tap that prisoner, E. Rockholder, are you not? Why don't you just bring his whole liver down here instead? Would it be considered perhaps a bit gauche to do experiments upon living human subjects, especially those consigned to death row? I've met Rockholder, and he is, without a doubt, the most dangerous and vile human being I have never encountered in my entire life."

J. D. responded as he walked out of the lab, "Rockholder is *not* on death row to my knowledge, although that has nothing to do with the price of tea in China. You scare me, Ford. Someday your evil and creepy thoughts might start to rub off on me." Sadly, Brewster's concern about external negative influences would one day come to pass.

As if on cue, Dr. Holcombe entered the lab and bumped into Brewster as he was on his way out the door. Uncle Hank offered, as best could be told, a word of encouragement for the pending tribunal that was scheduled for later that afternoon.

"I'm cornered up to be your cut man!" Dr. Holcmbe exclaimed. Don't you worry none, boy. Suck the beefy boys up to 'round yer tonsils 'n hunker down fer a twister. Whowee!"

Brewster looked over to his colleague for help in understanding what Dr. Holcombe had said. Perhaps Rip had the ability to translate Uncle Hank's Trans Pecos diction into the English language, but unfortunately, Brewster's research associate was left dumfounded.

Ford could only shrug his shoulders in apparent ignorance.

As with the translation difficulties that had plagued Rip Ford, Brewster usually had no real idea as to what Dr. Holcombe was ever trying to say. Be damned if it didn't sound good, however. Brewster responded to the boss of his research assignment with a vague, yet enthusiastic response. "Whowee!"

———◦◦◦⊰◉⊱◦◦◦———

Brewster had to go to the medical unit and collect abdominal ascites fluid out of two hospitalized patients prior to the scheduled 12:30 p.m. meeting. Although he had spent one full year doing clinical research, the hepatology and infectious disease specialty services had greeted him with open arms. Brewster had a wonderful learning experience with these two services, and he became proficient at performing physical evaluations, especially with the help of DeGowin's treatise on performing bedside physical exams. He at least had become adept at recognizing when he encountered an abnormal physical finding. He also had gained procedural skills that would've been the envy of the other students.

He became confident in the use of rigid anoscopes and proctoscopes, and most importantly, he became quite skilled at performing the bedside paracentesis procedure. This, of course, was the surgical procedure utilized to remove abdominal ascites fluid from the unfortunate patients who were afflicted with advanced cirrhosis as a consequence to the underlying non-A, non-B hepatitis virus infections. Initially, he was carefully instructed and supervised to make certain he had these procedures down cold. As no mishaps had occurred at the midpoint juncture of his training, the residents and fellows would let him fly solo in doing these procedures. For a medical student to be allowed to engage in that level of clinical activity was relatively unheard of.

At the end of Brewster's career many years later, he was actually quite surprised as to the variety procedures he was allowed to perform in 1980. In regard to the modern standard of care, the paracentesis procedure is now usually performed in an interventional radiology suite in the hospital in order to utilize ultrasound imaging to isolate the pocket of abdominal fluid that is required to be safely drained. This extra effort is now done to reduce the small but very real risk of bowel perforation that may occur when a long needle is inserted into a patient's belly. During Brewster's training, however, students and residents would be taught the art of finding the location of abdominal fluid by percussing the abdomen and then listening and feeling for changes in resonance that could indicate the likeliest safe place to introduce the needle into the abdomen.

The first patient he was going to visit was a person he had known well over the past year—a thirty-four-year-old nurse named Kelli Krause who previously flew on the hospital-based Angel Flight helicopter ambulance service. The Angel Flight ambulance service was the brainchild of Dr. John "Wayne" Gray. Dr. Gray was a former army trauma surgeon and now a staff physician at the Gulf Coast College of Medicine. He served as a trauma surgeon, and he was also coiled tightly onto the organ transplant harvest team. He was able to incorporate emergency care technology utilizing helicopters for the nascent trauma program, just as it had been done on the battlefields of the Vietnam War.

About two years prior to her current admission, Kelli was on a helicopter ambulance flight that had been directed toward an accident that had occurred at the 610 Loop crossover at Texas Highway 59. Some poor soul was trying to change a flat tire in the emergency lane when he got clipped by a passing car. Unfortunately, this individual was crushed in the accident. The fellow who had run him over was apparently stoned out of his mind, and he ended up crashing the guard rail barrier. The inebriated driver responsible for the fatality was also injured in the accident.

After the helicopter ambulance arrived at the accident site, IV fluids were initiated in the field in an attempt to resuscitate and stabilize the inebriated and injured survivor of the mishap. That's when things went horribly wrong. Kelli got a finger stick from a needle at the crash site, and she unfortunately had contracted a fulminant case of non-A, non-B hepatitis. This infectious disease that she had contracted was about to lead to her premature demise. How could it possibly be that this virus could be so easily transmitted from one human being to another but not to any other identifiable species? It truly was a conundrum that deserved intense scientific investigation.

Most often, Kelli would come to the outpatient hepatology clinic on Thursdays and get a paracentesis procedure done as necessary to remove the excess fluid that was building up in her abdomen. This was usually done in the clinic when she had designated outpatient status and she was not actually actively enrolled into the hospital. However, on this day she had become so ill that an admission to the hospital was warranted.

When Brewster arrived to the floor, the charge nurse, Ms. Irene Segulla, directed the student to the patient's room for the first paracentesis procedure. Many of the other nurses on the med-surg unit looked upon Brewster as a troublesome neophyte. However, Irene had become quite fond of J. D. Brewster. The charge nurse would often go out of her way to make sure that the medical student avoided the political pitfalls that might have otherwise torpedoed his clinical training. Irene was a Texan from the ocean side village of Bacliff, and she held the strong conviction that Texans should look out for each other.

"Kelli has signed her procedure permit consent form. The GI service fellow, Blomeo Colima, is already in the room. He's setting up the paracentesis trays and lining up multiple five hundred milliliter Vacutainer bottles to help decompress the patient's abdomen," Irene explained. "I am really proud of you. Dr. Colima has given you the green light to fly solo on this paracentesis procedure. Don't forget, you'll also have one more to do after this one is finished."

"Thanks, Ms. Segulla," Brewster replied. "I'll drop off the first load of ascites fluid at the nursing station before I tackle the second job."

The senior gastroenterology fellow, Dr. Colima, appeared to be visibly upset when Brewster entered the room. "Brewster! Come here, come here! I need to show you something, my young brainiac friend."

Blomeo Colima was completing his postgraduate training within just a few weeks. Dr. Colima had lived his entire life in the middle-class suburb of Meyerland, and he was eager to leave the city of Houston once and for all. Conservative by nature, he was most unhappy with the massive increase in the population of his once-beloved city, and he no longer had the patience to put up with the buckled concrete, potholes, and nerve-jarring traffic that now perpetually plagued the major trans-urban arteries of the Bayou City.

Complicating matters, Blomeo was a man who invariably wore his heart on his sleeve. He had a short fuse by nature, and his well-publicized confrontations with administration over the fact that he had been on call every other night for the last year only solidified his irascible reputation.

He took Brewster by the arm, guided him out into the hallway, and then said, "This is a golden teaching moment, and you're going to learn a clinical pearl that you're not apt to ever forget."

"What gives?" Brewster asked.

"Listen, I can't believe this," Dr. Colima said, "but Kelli Krause is on her last legs. This will likely be the last time that you'll need to drain her belly."

Dr. Colima was a strikingly handsome individual. Standing at six feet, three inches tall, his dimpled chin and sharply trimmed sideburns made him a heartthrob among the nurses working on the med-surg unit. Sadly, Colima was too busy to even be aware when women would overtly flirt with him.

The alarming comment that Dr. Colima made about Kelli was quite distressing to the medical student. "I don't know what you're talking about. Are you telling me that this is going to be a terminal admission?"

Dr. Colima pursed his lips and nodded. "I want you to drain as much fluid as you possibly can out of her and get her comfortable. Do it now. I truly believe this may be the last time that we have an opportunity to be with her. She's dying."

Brewster was stunned. He had just seen Kelli on an outpatient basis a month before, and she certainly did not seem to be critically ill at that time. Brewster asked, "How is it that you claim to know that she's on her last legs, as you say?"

Dr. Colima opened up the patient's chart and went to the lab section. He answered, "Look, you'll never see this in any type of textbook, but she has what I call the Dr. Blow Sign. If you've got it, box city, baby! Adios, muchacha! It is a one-way ticket to the eternal care unit. Sayonara, senorita! It's the big sleep. It's all over now, baby blue."

J. D. pressed for clarification and asked, "Okay, show me. What's the Dr. Blow Sign?"

Colima pulled a pen out of his pocket and started to point out some of the alarming laboratory parameters to Brewster. "Don't ever forget what I'm going to teach you. It's all right here in black and white. The patient's direct bilirubin is now greater than her hematocrit. Her serum creatinine is greater than her hemoglobin. Her albumin is less than or equal to 1.0. Mark my words: This patient is about to go into the death spiral of the dreaded hepato-renal syndrome."

Brewster had never encountered a case of a patient afflicted with the hepato-renal syndrome. "Spell it out for me. What's going to happen?"

"It's simple," the gastroenterologist fellow explained. "When the liver gets this sick, it makes the kidneys go bad. When the kidneys go bad, it makes the liver even worse. I don't think we will be able to pull her chestnuts out of the fire this time. As Dandy Don Meredith used to say, 'Turn out the lights, the party's over'. I think that it's highly unlikely that she'll live long enough to see the end of the week."

Brewster had found that the clichés that Dr. Colima had so flippantly tossed about were truly disgusting. However, Colima was indeed correct. After his days as a medical student, Brewster had never really learned of what had ever become of Blomeo Colima.

Nonetheless, the Dr. Blow Sign was an expression that eventually found its way into the permanent lexicon of the house staff and students at the Gulf Coast College of Medicine. It turned out to be a clinical pearl that Brewster could bank on for the rest of his career.

Brewster shook his head in sadness and asked, "Dr. Colima, does she know this? I don't know what say to her."

Colima put his hand on Brewster's shoulder to reassure him and replied, "Stay frosty, brainiac. She's down-stream to it. I already made her a DNR code status. She knows that her life has drawn to a conclusion, and I truly believe that she has made peace with God and her fate. Oh, one last thing. Do you believe in karma?"

"No. It's just a bunch of mumbo-jumbo bullshit," Brewster answered.

"Perhaps that's not quite the question that should be asked. Do you believe that God sometimes has a cosmic sense of irony?" Dr. Colima asked.

"Obviously," Brewster said. "I have encountered so many weird things that seem to be intertwined; it can't be coincidental. I hope I don't sound as if I'm delusional, but on more than one occasion, I feel as if I'm being scrutinized by the universe. To paraphrase the Bard, life is but a play, and the whole world is but a stage."

"Well, Brew, you're spot on," Colima agreed. "It's strange, but there seems to be some type of mysterious, harmonic, unifying wavelength that vibrates throughout the whole of creation. Sometimes it seems that everything in the universe is connected somehow. Maybe sometimes God just needs to rub our collective noses in the diddly-squat to remind us miserable human beings just how truly screwed-up we really are down here."

Brewster furrowed his brow and asked Dr. Colima, "What is this—a new theological edict recently found amongst the Dead Sea Scrolls?"

"You're a heathen," Colima said.

"No," Brewster said. "I'm on the level. Maybe biblical scholars should codify your pontifications as the Acts of the GI Fellow, authored by the newly ordained apostle, Blomeo Colima!"

"All right now, you sacrilegious bastard," Colima said. "I don't want to be standing this close to you when you become a lightning rod and get struck by a thunderbolt. You have a well-deserved representation of brewing up trouble. Right about now, I think you should be standing way the hell over there." Colima pointed to the far end of the ward. "I mean it!" Colima was apparently not joking.

Brewster tried to smooth Blomeo's ruffled feathers. "I'm sorry, but I'm just not following your line of reasoning."

Colima continued to point down the hallway and wagged his finger. "After you get Kelli squared away, the next belly that you're going to tap belongs to that dirtbag prisoner known as Rockholder. He was brought in today by the department of corrections to specifically get his belly tapped, but he was running a high fever when he got here. He might have spontaneous peritonitis. That's why I put aerobic and anaerobic culture bottles and an EDTA tube out there for you on top of the Mayo table."

The medical student watched with curiosity as the GI fellow pulled out a small ceramic statuette of a dog out of his pocket, rub it three times with his right thumb, and then secure the small figurine back into the pocket of his laboratory coat.

Although what Dr. Colima had done was inexplicable, Brewster thought that he was already on the bus with what was going on. With hubris and unfounded bravado, Brewster said, "Culture up, cell count, diff, and Gram stain. Check. Should I send for cyto-spin and chemistries also?"

"No, dumbass," Colima replied. "We don't need cytology or chemistries as that would just be a waste of money and resources, and it would not tell us anything, as we're pretty sure as to what's going on. E. Rockholder was admitted to the hospital from the outpatient hepatology clinic for empiric antibiotic treatment and to get his belly tapped. That's it. You do remember this shit-box sociopath, right?"

J. D. shrugged his shoulders, as he had known this prisoner/patient throughout the course of the past year. "Well, I don't recognize any cosmic harmonic convergence of the planets that might be going on here, but yeah, I know this guy. What's the big deal? I've tapped his belly two times before in the past. Give me the lowdown and tell me what I'm missing."

Colima had pulled within just a few inches away from Brewster face. "I didn't know anything about this maggot throughout all of the time that he was coming in here to get his belly drained. Today, my curiosity just got the best of me. I just had to ask the correction officer who always brings him in here from the prison a most basic and obvious question: why was this Rockholder character locked up in the big house in the first place?"

"Who was the correction officer you spoke with?"

"The fat guy, Arby Fuller," Blomeo said. "Have you met him before?"

"I know Arby well. He strikes me as being a really smart person, although he's certainly jaded about life in general," Brewster answered.

"You nailed down his persona, all right."

"I'll be the first to admit that Rockholder has been nothing but verbally rude and abusive to me in the past," Brewster said, "but what else can you tell me about this guy?"

"Check this out," Dr. Colima continued. "I found out that Rockholder has had multiple convictions for the crime of vehicular homicide. He just can't seem to help himself when he gets high. He has a compulsion to get behind the wheel of an automobile and flat out kill people. I don't know why the guy hasn't been sentenced to life in prison without any possibility of parole."

Brewster recalled the opinion Rip Ford had rendered about E. Rockholder. "The research scientist working with me on Holcombe's hepatitis study is convinced that Rockholder is the most wretched, vile, and evil entity currently residing on the planet earth. I don't know about that, but I'll certainly feel safer walking about on the streets of Houston if this guy is going back to prison as soon as we're done with him."

Blomeo disagreed. "I can't speak on your behalf, but I personally won't feel any safer unless justice is done to this dirt bag. I mean real justice. This is Texas. Better yet, as far as I'm concerned, he should get the big needle so he can permanently go nighty-night. Yeah, that's the ticket! Bedtime for Bonzo, baby blue. Some asshole judge and an idiotic parole board let the sumbitch back out onto the streets a while back so he could go about his business to kill more people. This just goes to show you what a messed up criminal justice system that we have in this country. I truly believe this is the reason why God is rubbing our noses in it."

Dr.Colima looked from side to side to make certain that no hospital staff members were lurking about in the hall and listening in on his conversation with the medical student. Certain that nobody was paying attention to what he was saying, he continued. "Well, let me tell you about the big cosmic connection here. I can hardly believe this myself, but E. Rockholder is the bastard from whom the nurse Kelli Krause contracted her lethal infectious hepatitis. I shit you not! When she went out on the helicopter ambulance flight to pick him up after a motor vehicle accident that had occurred a few years ago, she got a nasty needle stick from this loser. That's right. I can't make this up. She tried to save his sorry ass, and she's going to end up dying for it."

Yet again, Brewster observed Dr. Colima pull the small ceramic figurine of a dog from his lab coat pocket. On this occasion, the GI fellow rubbed the ceramic token no less than six times after clutching it tightly.

Dr. Colima had a point of cynicism to convey about the whole tragic event. "Okay, here is the second clinical pearl for the day. This is another lesson that you should also never forget. Are you're ready? Here it is: No good deed goes unpunished. That's it. Remember it. I'm going to give you a pop quiz about it later today. Now, you found out today what Rockholder has done to Kelli Krause. That's not the whole story. I want you to make a point of talking to this dear, sweet, mellow yellow fellow. He has four tattoos of teardrops on his face under his right eye, and two more teardrop tattoos under his left eye.

I want you to specifically ask him what those teardrop tattoos are actually all about."

"To what end?" Brewster asked. "Will it be akin to an enjoyable, personal, transcendental astral holiday with a Hindu guru?"

"It will be better than that!" Colima exclaimed. "You really need to know what Rockholder is all about. It will definitely brighten your day. I'll tell you that once you learn what this guy has done in the past, you will be ashamed that he's a white man. Just to make absolutely certain that you realize that I am not joking about any of this, I'm going to give you a final exam about Rockholder later today, also! No cheating. Rest assured, I'll shake you down to make certain that you're not sneaking in any crib notes before you take the final exam," Colima proclaimed sarcastically.

On the third occasion that the GI fellow retrieved the glazed ceramic statuette from his pocket, curiosity finally got the better of the medical student. "What in hell is that thing you keep dicking around with? Brewster asked. "A good-luck charm, maybe?"

"It is more than that," Blomeo said. "It is an amulet to ward off evil spirits. Technically, what I hold in my hand is an effigy of the 'Colima' dog, just like my surname."

"Colima dog?" Brewster asked. "Never heard of such a thing." Brewster asked.

"In pre-Colombia times, the Mesoamerican people would place dogs around cenote pits and deep-shaft burial sites. If a corpse had returned from the dead as a vampiro or a ghoul, the Colima dog would supposedly bark like crazy to warn the villagers that danger was nigh."

"So," Brewster asked, "is Rockholder a ghoul?"

After a moment of thoughtful contemplation, Blomeo Colima finally gave a cryptic reply. "After you find out what he's done in the past, I'll let you be the judge of that."

"Be that as it may, the Rabbi told me that we shouldn't ask patients who have come into the hospital from the prison system as to what crimes they may have committed," Brewster protested. "I was told that to ask any patient who was a prisoner who had a conviction as to why they were incarcerated would be considered to be somewhat rude and impolite."

Colima chuckled malevolently and replied, "Come on, brainiac, are you kidding me? So, the Rabbi said it would be 'rude and impolite'. Are you shitting me? You need to grow a pair! The Rabbi is a liberal. What he said is bullshit liberal thinking right there. I know for a fact that the Rabbi actually voted for that spineless Jimmy Carter back in '76. He was actually bragging about it!"

"What's wrong with that?" Brewster asked.

Although he was Hispanic, Colima was a staunch conservative firebrand. For personal reasons, he had strong misgivings about one particular political decision that the Carter administration and the State Department had made. "God, almighty, that toad of a president of ours actually gave away the Panama Canal! I'll have you know that my great-grandfather died while working on that project. He was a tender on a railroad, flat-car mounted steam shovel. He was hired to go down there because he was a Mexican, and he could speak Spanish to the Panamanians."

"You must be very proud that your great-grandfather was involved with this great feat of engineering," Brewster said in a rare insightful moment.

"I don't know if he had yellow fever, malaria, or the plague. I don't know why he died down there, but it doesn't matter. He helped build that canal, and you're correct about one thing, Brew," Colima said. "I am indeed proud of that. In my opinion, working on the canal was the most important thing anybody in my family has ever done. When he died, he got buried along the banks of the canal. To this day, nobody knows even where. That peanut farmer from Georgia just gave the canal away. Just like that. To my knowledge, our country didn't even get shit out of the deal. I'll never forgive him for that."

"I was not aware of that fact," replied Brewster.

"You need to turn on the television and wash down the evening news once in a while, junior." Colima pulled the medical student close by the lapels of his white jacket and added, "Can you imagine Carter coming out of a place like Georgia? I thought that the state of Texas and the state of Georgia fought together on the same side during the Great War against Yankee Aggression."

Brewster concurred. "They did indeed."

"I'll bet someday in the future the Panamanians will end up selling the damn thing to the communists," Colima projected. "That would serve the United States right, because the average American is a politically ignorant dumbass. I swear to God, Brewster, if I ever find out that you plan on voting for Carter during the upcoming presidential election in a few months, I promise you that I'll come back to Houston and kick your balls into orbit! Do you understand me?"

Brewster put up his hands in defense. "I won't do that. Cross my heart and hope to spit."

Blomeo Colima concluded, "Just do as I say. You go ask Rockholder what the teardrop tattoos on his face are really all about. You'll hear a really cheerful and heartwarming story. If you're left with any liberal ideations after you talk to Rockholder, I'll personally go out and buy you a pair of your favorite liberal, loser, unisex Earth Shoes myself. I'll even throw in a disco album of the Village People. You come back and find me after you get through tapping the fluid from those swollen bellies."

Little did Brewster know, the Texas Medical Center was about to be clobbered by a fearful tempest on that day in June. A violent storm was rolling down on the vicinity. Unfortunately, it was not a storm that would be regularly recognized in any conventional atmospheric or meteorological subcategory. It was a storm in the form of two human predators.

Since the late 1960s, two particularly evil and dangerous individuals were involved in a long-term crime spree. The target rich environment where their malevolent activity occurred was scattered over a very wide territory that spread all the way from the North 610 Loop and down to the Astrodome. They specifically targeted the Greater Heights, the Montrose area, the region now referred to as the Museum District, the Texas Medical Center area, and the district south that went all the way to the other side of the Loop between S. Main and Fannin Street.

The two hoodlums used to hit convenience stores, liquor outlets, and tobacco shops. With the advent of security cameras and also in-store silent panic buttons that could be triggered by shop employees, that particular line of work was becoming far too dangerous. They had distilled their skills down to carjacking expensive, high-end, and collectible vehicles. White people were a much easier target. As the majority of violent crime that is committed upon the black population is actually perpetrated by other black people, the black citizens of the city of Houston tended to be quite wary of these two individuals whenever they were on the prowl.

Unfortunately, the majority of white people who were generally going about their business on a daily basis tended to let their guard down if they were ever approached by these two characters. The two career criminals always wore disguises whenever they did a job, sometimes dressing up as common laborers and even hipsters wearing mock turtlenecks and sports jackets.

They only did a job once every two or three weeks, and they also never hit the same neighborhood twice in a row. The caution they had taken in executing their criminal enterprise ensured they had never been caught during their twelve-year crime spree. As they were self-proclaimed black supremacists, they would generally spare the victims who were of African American descent from excessive physical violence. However, if the opportunity arose, they would often attempt to beat a white victim to death, and they enjoyed doing it.

Their names were Darryl Hewrett and Cleophus McDonald. Kicked out of the local chapter of the Black Panthers in 1967 because of their overt propensity to commit acts of excessive violence, they considered themselves to be rogue warriors in the struggle against white oppression. This argument simply gave them justification for their long-term criminal enterprise.

Cleophus McDonald had believed that his name sounded too "plantation white," so he ended up legally changing it to Mumbo Jamar Apoo. This was simply a name that McDonald had made up out of whole cloth. As it would turn out, it was a moniker that had nothing to do with the Islamic faith. If the truth be told, McDonald knew absolutely nothing about the Muslim religion anyhow, except that monotheism was a cornerstone of its belief system.

To reduce the likelihood of ever being caught and convicted, the two hoodlums would only refer to themselves by their foul, self-ordained nicknames. As insulting as it would seem to other people, both black or white, the two men took great relish in respectively referring to themselves with abhorrent derogatory labels: "Smeg Nog" and the "Big Nig." They would refer to each other in such a disturbing manner openly among themselves. These inflammatory nicknames were *meant* to be highly offensive, as the two men held each other, and even themselves, in considerable disregard.

Mumbo Jamar Apoo called the shots, and he did not tolerate any dissent from the slightly smaller man called Smeg Nog. The two criminals were not friends. In fact, they did not like each other one bit. At best, they only tolerated each other. Secretly, the Big Nig had serious concerns that his accomplice was foolish and careless. On the obverse side of the coin, Smeg Nog believed that the Big Nig was an overbearing brute. Nonetheless, they had a successful criminal enterprise, and their chop shop near the outskirts of downtown had flourished.

A major, well-deserved criticism about the city Houston at the time was that it was a boom town that had grown so fast that the sprawling metropolitan area had outstripped the resources of the local government to provide adequate police protection, safe roads, or even sane zoning laws. These chaotic "growth pains" were the exact reasons why this criminal enterprise engineered by Smeg Nog and the Big Nig remained under the radar of the Houston Police Department for over a decade. With the crime they were about to attempt, however, they would no longer be incognito. In fact, they were about to have a very large target painted on their chests. The two violent criminals reached Hermann Park and then proceeded to stroll over to the employee parking lot at the Gulf Coast College of Medicine. The would-be carjackers appeared to casually stroll about, but they were actually waiting to ambush some poor soul. They would find their hapless victim soon enough.

7

HOMICIDAL IDEATIONS

Brewster went back into the room of Kelli Krause to proceed with the planned paracentesis. The student was devastated to see the declining condition of the young woman. Sadly, her ascites was so massive that she looked as if she was twelve months pregnant. Her skin was bright yellow, as were her eyes. Her cheeks were hollow, and she appeared to have little if any residual muscular reserve. The swelling in her lower extremities was of such a magnitude, that her feet looked like loaves of butter-crust sandwich bread. She had a gummy residue on her skin as her very serum was leaking through her pores. The young woman looked frantic and was pleading for help.

"J. D., hurry, hurry! Get me tapped right now. Please, I just can't stand it."

J. D. smiled at Kelli and tried to calm her anxiety by speaking to her with a soothing and reassuring voice. "I'm here, Kelli. Let's get your belly drained." The only problem was that the medical student was incapable of calming his own personal anxiety about the fact that Blomeo Colima had professed that Kelli Krause was actively dying. Brewster raised the head of her bed to a forty-five-degree angle, which would allow her gas-filled bowel to float to the top of the abdomen. The ascites fluid would then pool below the distended umbilicus.

Brewster prepped the infra-umbilical site with swabs of Betadine and then he used a small amount of local lidocaine anesthesia to make certain the procedure was not too painful. Using a "Z-track" technique to reduce the possibility of a persistent post-procedure abdominal fluid leak, J. D. Brewster quickly struck oil. He connected the hub end of the needle to a firm plastic tube that was soon affixed into one of the Vacutainer bottles. A yellowish and transparent fluid, which looked very much like urine, was rapidly sucked out of the abdomen of the unfortunate patient. As bottle after bottle began to fill up, a look of relief finally appeared on the young woman's face.

"Kelli, are you feeling better?" Brewster asked.

The patient gave out a big sigh of relief and replied, "Oh, I'm feeling much better indeed. Thank you."

"It was my pleasure. I mean that," Brewster said, as he was just as relieved to see Kelli's discomfort abate as she was.

"J. D., is your team any closer to being able to identify this hepatitis that I am infected with? If I am going to die from this, I'd find comfort in that my body fluid contributed to your scientific endeavors somehow."

Brewster shook his head. "No, Kelli, I don't think so. We're not even close to getting this damned thing nailed down yet."

"You know, J. D., I have been a nurse now for twelve years, and it has been an honor and a blessing for me to have had this profession. I don't know about this premonition that I've had for a while, but for some reason I think that I am getting closer to the finish line of my life."

"Stop right there, Kelli." Brewster proceeded to fabricate a monumental lie. "I have it on good authority that you should be tiptop in no time."

"You can't kid a kidder, Brewster. Blomeo told me the score," Kelli sadly replied. "The clock is winding down. I can feel it! If that's so, my only regret is that I missed a chance to be loved. If it had happened, even for a fleeting moment, I think I would truly feel that my life was complete. I guess it just wasn't meant to happen for me. I hope that doesn't happen to you too. It is the awareness of our own mortality that gives our very lives any meaning at all. What do any of us have? If a person is lucky, maybe he or she will have about a number of four score or so spins around the sun. That's it. That's all we get."

"I don't know about that, Kelli," Brewster interjected. "Eighty years of life may be too many for some people but not enough for others."

"I can't help but be philosophical about all of this," Kelli implored. I believe that we are all called to find some tangible mission that is righteous and good. Once we recognize that this calling may be our destiny, it's then our duty to try and accomplish this calling to the best of our God-given abilities. This divine commission to such a purpose gives our lives a deeper meaning."

"I used to think life had a deeper meaning," Brewster confessed. "After seeing the cards you were dealt, I have serious doubts about your perception that life is a Divine commission."

"Listen to me! I have never seen the purpose of my own life clearer to me than I do at this very moment. This is my conviction. Should we not also surely strive to pursue love and happiness along the way of this mystical journey, no matter how fleeting? I suggest you consider the same." What Kelli Krause had professed would turn out to be a recurrent dogmatic theme that would perpetually revisit J. D. Brewster for the rest of his life.

Brewster would soon discover that Blomeo Colima was quite right on the trinity of truth that he had predicted earlier that morning: (1) The Dr. Blow Sign, as a clinical pearl, had turned out to be a powerful, negative-outcome prognostic indicator. (2) No good deed goes unpunished. (3) Kelli Krause had made peace with God and her fate. She would die the next day.

J. D. had loaded a half-dozen bottles of ascites fluid onto a roll cart and pushed it out to the nurse's station, as it would eventually have to be transported down to the laboratory for future animal inoculation experimental studies. The GI fellow had previously instructed Brewster that he needed to wrap up the bottles of infected fluid into heavy duty, red vinyl biohazard bags, but the student was now behind schedule. He made a mental note to himself that this task would have to be completed as soon as the second paracentesis procedure was accomplished. As he had a mandatory meeting with the research committee later that afternoon, it was imperative for him to proceed with the paracentesis procedure on the very next patient, who just happened to be the evil and dangerous imprisoned convict, E. Rockholder.

As he entered the room, he found that Rockholder, as usual, was closely guarded by the transportation correction officer, Arby Fuller. At five feet, eight inches tall, Arby was considered a man of only medium height, although his protuberant girth, massive biceps, and body weight of 224 pounds ensured that he was nonetheless a formidable figure.

Although he was only in his late twenties, Arby Fuller was already experiencing a considerable amount of alopecia. The correction officer was afflicted with a classic distribution of hair loss that is typically referred to as common male-pattern baldness.

In the rough and tumble world of the Department of Corrections, Arby Fuller was a man who nonetheless could readily hold his own against the vilest or occasionally puerile incarcerated individuals. The general population of prisoners was well aware that Officer Fuller was quite proficient with the swift dispensation of prison yard justice through his black baton. He would happily wield the disciplinary device at any time against any troublesome adversary, oftentimes requiring only the slightest of provocations.

Officer Fuller had lived most of his life in the Texas Hill Country town of Fredericksburg, but his family moved to Houston during Arby's last year in high school. His father owned a modest automotive repair shop not far from the Texas Medical Center, and he hoped his son would someday take over this business enterprise. Unfortunately,

Arby never grew accustomed to getting skinned knuckles or grease imbedded underneath his fingernails when he worked at trying to repair disabled vehicles.

"Arby, it's good to see you again," Brewster said. After he shook hands with the correction officer, he turned his attention to the prisoner who was dressed in an orange jumpsuit. His left wrist was shackled to the bed railing with handcuffs. After learning that Rockholder was a man who apparently had a lot more bite than bark, Brewster looked at the prisoner warily.

E. Rockholder was originally from New Jersey, and he moved to Houston in the early '70s with plans of jumping on board the rapidly expanding oil industry along the Texas Gulf Coast. Incapable of holding a steady job as a roughneck, Rockholder was fired time and again for on-the-job drug use and fighting with fellow oilers working on various offshore drilling platforms. The non-A, non-B infectious hepatitis that Rockholder had battled for the better part of a decade had left the man with a yellowish jaundiced hue. Although his gross general appearance easily afforded him the ability to pass for a middle-aged individual, the prisoner, nonetheless, was certainly not a man to be trifled with.

He had wavy salt-and-pepper hair that he wore in the style of a Mohawk, and his arms and torso were festooned with a variety of obnoxious pornographic tattoos. His abdomen was distended as a consequence to infectious ascites, but his face appeared to be particularly menacing. Rockholder possessed icteric sclerae, and his irises, which were nearly black, made his eyes appear demonic.

Although Rockholder had been through more than one paracentesis procedure in the past, Brewster was compelled to explain the circumstances to him yet again. "Hello, sir. I've heard that the fluid has re-accumulated in your belly and that you're now running a fever. I understand that you've already signed the procedure permit consent form, so I believe that we're ready to proceed with draining this fluid out of you. I'm going to send some of the fluid down to the laboratory to make certain that you don't have some kind of active superimposed bacterial infection in your abdomen above and beyond the mysterious hepatitis that you're afflicted with."

"What in hell are you waiting for? Just do it," Rockholder said.

"I will," Brewster said, "as soon as I'm finished explaining everything to you. In addition, we'll be taking some of the fluid down to the research department where I work. As you may recall, we're performing experimental studies to try and determine the underlying nature of the hepatitis that appears to be troubling you. The team that I'm working with is not certain, but we believe the trouble is caused by a yet to be identified virus of some type. We've done this paracentesis procedure on your abdomen several times over during the past few months, so you should know the routine by now."

Rockholder didn't even bother to look up at J. D. Brewster when he replied, "Shut up with your bullshit and just get it done, you nasty little whore. I don't have all day."

"Well, I bid the top of the morning to you too!" Brewster said sarcastically. As with the previous patient, Brewster prepared the target site for the paracentesis procedure, and then he proceeded to drain the fluid out Rockholder's abdomen. As explicitly instructed by Blomeo Colima, Brewster was compelled to ask the prisoner about the extensive teardrop tattoos that regaled his pitted and scarred face. "Mr. Rockholder, you certainly have some interesting tattoos, especially the ones on your face. While I'm in the process of sucking this fluid out of your belly, why don't you tell me the story about what these tattoos are all about?"

"Careful, Brew; you're about to wander down a dark path," Arby Fuller cautioned. "You'll end up getting caught deep in the briar patch. It happened to me when I first met this man. When I previously learned what he had done, I was forever changed. I was no longer able to see the light. You're going to get lost in the forest, and when you do, you won't be able to find your way back home. For

God's sake, buddy," Arby said softly but emphatically, "you don't want to go there. Trust me on this."

"You're absolutely right," Brewster said. "I don't want to go down this path, but I've been given strict orders by Dr. Colima. I simply can't walk away empty-handed."

The prisoner didn't answer the medical student's question and appeared to be lost in thought. Brewster was persistent and repeated the query. "I'll bet it is all water under the bridge now. You can tell me. Well, that is, of course, if you're not *afraid* to tell me what happened." Brewster was about to learn a fundamental lesson in the biological science of herpetology. If a person is looking at an alligator basking in the sun on the edge of a swamp, perhaps it would be unwise to take a sharp stick and poke the deadly reptile in its eyes.

The prisoner motioned with his index finger for Brewster to come closer, and he said, "It's a secret. I'll tell you, but I'll have to whisper it to you." Brewster leaned forward toward the prisoner, but that turned out to be a big mistake.

Without a warning, E. Rockholder lunged with his unshackled free right hand at J. D. Brewster and grabbed the back of his collar. As he pulled the startled student to within an inch of his face, the prisoner said, "Listen to me, you snot-nosed little cock-sucker; I killed a bunch! It was a bunch, okay! Happy now?"

Brewster jammed the heel of his right hand under the nose of the assailant. As J. D. fell back, the corrections officer pulled out a nightstick and snapped it sharply across the left patella of the violent convicted criminal. As Rockholder recoiled in pain, Arby Fuller calmly grabbed the prisoner's free right hand and proceeded to handcuff it down at the lower edge of the bed frame. The forced hyperextension of Rockholder's right arm at the elbow turned out to be a most uncomfortable position for the convict.

The exaggerated spread-eagle position reminded Brewster of what it must have looked like for an infidel to have been subjected to the rack during the dark ages. Strangely, that pleased Brewster immensely as he looked down upon the shackled human refuse with utter contempt.

Arby Fuller then spoke as if he was addressing a child. "Now, Rockholder, be a nice fellow."

Brewster could not help himself, and he displayed an uncharacteristic malevolent streak of his own when he added, "Yes, Dr. Colima told me that you were a mellow yellow fellow. I'll admit that the GI doc was quite correct when he explained that you were a jaundiced man. Ergo, he got the 'yellow' and the 'fellow' descriptions quite right. However, I'm not so sure about the 'mellow' part. I think Blomeo tried to oversell that specific alleged attribute just a bit. Nah, I'm just not feelin' it."

With a broad grin, Arby Fuller deftly twirled his baton only inches away from the prisoner's face. Once the pain from the sharp strike on his kneecap had started to subside, E. Rockholder thought it would be the better part of valor to cooperate, and he began his story.

"In '74, I was doing some major league speed. I was messed up, and I was driving fast down into a dead-end cul-de-sac. Some momma bitch was pulling into her driveway, just coming back from the shopping at the grocery store. She probably bought milk and cookies and that kind of bullshit. She got out of her car to open her garage door. I guess that cunt was too stupid or too poor to own an automatic garage door clicker. She left her two rug rats in the back seat."

"Don't tell me you hurt those kids," Brewster pleaded.

"Oh, yeah, buddy boy; I hurt 'em. I hurt 'em big-time. Later at my trial proceedings, I found out those kids were three-year-old twins. That's why momma bitch had the little bastards tied down into those child seat gizmos. I tell you, it was like shooting fish in a barrel! It was all just way too easy. She was standing in front of the car trying to open up the garage door, and that's when it happened."

"What did you do?" Brewster asked, although he was actually afraid to hear the answer.

"Like I said, I was all messed up, didn't know I was on a deadend street, and I slammed into the back of her car at about thirty miles an hour. Her car exploded! Man, what a rush! Her rug rats got trapped inside the car, and I got to watch them get incinerated. I pinned the lady up against the house so she couldn't move an inch to escape. Sweet! Bitch got to watch her kids go up in flames. You could see them squirming back there, screaming like howler monkeys. What a trip!"

Brewster had never encountered an evil and deranged sociopath before. "Holy shit! 'What a trip!' Is that what you said, you sick son of a bitch?!" The medical student cocked his head sharply toward the correction officer and asked, "Why is this bastard still allowed to breathe?"

"Your obvious hostility toward our esteemed guest suggests that you're a likely proponent of the death penalty," Arby surmised.

"Up one street and down another," Brewster replied. "Revenge is sweet. And you?"

"Not for the reasons that you'd think," the correction officer clarified. "Many convicts have told me that life in prison without any chance of parole is a fate far worse than the death penalty. After all, if you're on death row, you'll only get the needle once. If a man is facing life in prison, he'll die a thousand times."

"Well," Brewster asked, "what is it then?"

"My enthusiasm for the death penalty is for practical reasons. First, we have a fiscal responsibility for the taxpayers of the great state of Texas. The juice in a needle doesn't cost very much. The same can't be said for the cost of sticking a dirt bag like this in a warehouse for years on end."

"Makes sense," Brewster agreed.

"There's more to it, though," Arby added. "Tell me; what is the name of the place where I work?"

Brewster didn't see where Fuller's line of reasoning was headed, but he answered the question nonetheless. "The Sharpstown Correction Facility. Why?"

"What a joke. We don't correct *anything*," Arby said. "The main reason why I believe in the death penalty is that the needle will reduce the potential danger of turning loose repeat offenders. Think about it. Although I wasn't a whiz at high school math, by my calculations, the death penalty will reduce the potential risk of repetitive violent crimes committed by previously convicted felons by one hundred percent." Arby Fuller smiled as he leaned back against the wall and repeated the figure with even greater emphasis. "One hundred percent!"

Brewster leaned over and whispered into the prisoner's ear. "Well, how about that, Rockholder? Would you like the needle? I'm going to petition the state to allow me to be the one who gets to push the plunger. I don't know if you'd like it, but I certainly would." Rockholder seemed to be generally surprised at Brewster's threat.

"You should have been there, and you would have felt the same rush I did. It was like an extra hit of speed. The bitch starts waving her arms around and started to bellow like a sow popping a litter of piglets before she was also overtaken by the flames."

"That's enough. Shut up, asshole!" Brewster commanded.

Realizing that he had a golden opportunity to further torment the medical student, Rockholder began to quickly dart his tongue in and out of his mouth as if he were a poisonous viper.

"It reminded me of the old television show, *Lost in Space*. Do you remember the robot that belonged to the character they called Mr. Smith? Whenever that little red-headed bastard on the television show got into trouble, the robot would flap his arms around like a bird. He would shout out in his mechanical voice, 'Danger, Will Robinson, danger!' That always cracked me up."

Brewster became nauseous. "I can't hear any more of this."

"I'm not done yet," Rockholder said. "I'm rolling up on the best part of the story. Somehow, I didn't get a scratch in the accident, so I got out of my car, sat on the lawn, and watched it all go down. I was cracking up, like I was watching an old television rerun. I was digging the scene, so I just leaned back and lit up a blunt. That is when things really got groovy."

Officer Fuller turned to J. D. and said, "Do you see the type of bullshit I have to choke on when I'm assigned to babysit this slime wad? I warned you, Brewster. I specifically told you not to talk to this bastard about the crimes he committed. If you end up with a life time of nightmares, that'll be on your head, pal. Did you listen to me?"

"No," Brewster answered sheepishly.

"No, of course J. D. Brewster didn't listen," Fuller ranted from a third-person point of view. "Why would some dumb ass named J. D. Brewster listen to any pearls of wisdom bestowed upon him by a man named Arby Fuller? After all, Arby Fuller is only the world's greatest corrections officer. Yes, indeed. He's a man endowed with vast practical experiences in the universe of the criminal justice system."

Fuller stared at Rockholder momentarily and asked, "Tell something me, shit bird; is there any obvious correlation between pearl and swine?"

"Look, screw, that's above my pay grade," the prisoner replied. He turned toward Brewster and blew him a kiss. "Why don't you ask bottom boy over here? I'm sure this little pussy knows the answer to that question."

"Shut up, Rockholder," Brewster demanded.

"Listen up, cupcake. This'll put a smile on your face. This is when things turned into a major league laugh riot." The prisoner was absolutely determined to torture the medical student at that point. "Check this out—the husband of that bitch and her two kids was at home, and he came outside when he heard the commotion. His wife was still writhing about, although she was already on fire. Her two young boys were very much like a skewered bratwurst that would sizzle and pop over an open fire at a Boy Scout overnight camping trip."

"Shut up, Rockholder!" Brewster's order was again ignored.

"They weren't moving at all by then," Rockholder explained. "Dude tried to get the garden hose turned on to spray down his wife and kids, but it was all too late. They had gone up in flames! What happened next was really far out. Dude goes back inside the house, and he gets a forty-five-caliber pistol. I thought for sure he was going to pop me, but he put the gun in his own mouth and blew his brains out all over me."

"Shut up, Rockholder! You're tied down, asshole. I can bust you up, and there's not a damned thing that you could do about it." Brewster threatened.

Brewster's warning went unheeded. "There was like red shit and gobs of greasy snot that I got showered with. Man, was that a hoot, or what?" Rockholder asked. "I was looking right into the guy's eyes, and I was smiling at him when he pulled the trigger."

The prisoner proceeded to open his mouth as if he was wrapping his lips around the barrel of a gun. "I can tell you right now that he was already dead before he swallowed the lead. Know what I mean? So, I'll take credit for killing the bitch, the two bastard children, and her husband also. That's why I have four tear-drop tattoos underneath my right eye. That was strong work on my part, if I may say so myself. I'll admit that I admire this dude who ate a bullet from his own gun. A man has to be brave to commit suicide."

As if demonically possessed, Rockholder leaned forward and looked at Brewster directly in his eyes. "Even if you ever wanted to kill yourself, and I'm sure you will someday, I'll bet a little whore like you wouldn't have the balls to ever pull the trigger. When the time comes for you to put a gun in your own mouth, the only thing you'd do is suck on it like you want to suck on my cock right about now!" Rockholder looked at the medical student with contempt and added, "You're a pussy."

The transformation of J. D. Brewster had already begun. He started to slide down a long and slippery slope into a very dark and cold place. He started to tremble a bit, but he had a plan already formulated, and he shared it with the correction officer. The medical student even spoke about it openly. He laid out his deepest thoughts right in front of the demon prisoner that Brewster was convinced was evil incarnate. "Arby, if a prisoner tries to escape, how much force are you authorized to use?"

"Depends on the situation," Fuller explained. "Some poor slob convicted of cheating on a tax return is one thing. A killer, well ..."

J. D. jerked his thumb at Rockholder. "What about him?"

"This scum sucking dirt bag?" Fuller asked. As the correction officer slowly worked his jaw in a horizontal motion for but a brief moment, a malicious grin edged into the corner of his mouth. "Lethal!"

"Nice!" Brewster replied.

"I always wondered if you were aware of the clandestine clinical justice system at this institution," Fuller said. "Maybe it's time for you to get a formal introduction. Do you think we'll be able to pull this off?"

Up until now, J. D. Brewster had been oblivious to the culture of institutionalized retribution that had percolated under the surface at his very own medical school. Little did Brewster comprehend, he was soon destined to become the judge, jury, and executioner amongst his peers in the illicit dispensation of what Arby Fuller referred to as clinical justice.

Brewster proceeded to expound on his new, frightening homicidal ideations. "There will no doubt be a postmortem inquest. You have to be able to bring him down with one blow."

"The reason being?" Arby asked.

"Multiple strikes to the back of the head would look quite suspicious to a forensic pathologist. Remember—we would have to make it look you were simply trying to subdue him when he became an acute physical threat to my well-being."

"What would be the outcome if he survived a single blow to the head?" Arby asked.

"Good question. He'd likely end up critically injured. After all, this prisoner has liver failure, and the coagulation proteins that are naturally produced in his liver are already decreased from the usual amount that might be found in a healthy patient's circulation."

"So, no matter what, things will likely get wet and sticky," Fuller said.

"If he has a major blowout," Brewster elaborated, "we're looking at a crimson tide."

"I'm downstream to you," Fuller said. "I've always liked the color red. Go 'Bama!"

"Roll tide!" Brewster chimed in. "The visual cortex is where the interpretation of optical images takes place in the posterior aspect of the brain," Brewster explained. "I strongly recommend that this area should be your specific target zone for the blow that he would receive from your baton."

"I can do that," Arby confirmed. "I won't miss."

"Good! If death or blindness from such a blow was not an immediate result, it is nonetheless highly likely that the prisoner would end up in a prolonged vegetative, comatose state. Over time, he would end up getting foul, putrid, pre-sacral bedsores, and his flesh would eventually rot down to the bone," the medical student professed.

"I'm sporting a stiffy just thinking about it!" Arby confessed.

"Well," Brewster said, "keep it zipped. I don't want to *ever* see your plumbing! Am I clear? In any event, if he ever gets gangrene, we could actually bring in therapeutic maggots and allow them to eat away at his necrotic flesh. I would pay good money to see that. I don't think we'll need to have him sign a DNR designation form before we proceed."

"Well, if the blow did not kill him outright," Fuller commented, "those potential alternative clinical results would also certainly work for me. How about you?"

Brewster pursed his lips and nodded in affirmation as the left side of his mouth slowly curled into a malevolent grin. "Let's quit jerking off and get this done."

E. Rockholder turned to Officer Fuller and asked, "Say, what in hell you boys talkin' 'bout?"

Arby just smiled and replied, "My friend and I were just commenting as to how much we were enjoying your story, so please tell us more. We really want to hear what else happened to you. You still have two other teardrops under your left eye to tell Mr. Brewster about."

"Well, the next part of the story is not too happy," the prisoner reported. "I got arrested, and the judge threw the book at me. He sentenced me for seven damned years in prison at the Sharpstown Correction Facility. Can you believe that shit? Seven whole freakin' years!"

"Wow. Seven years?!" Brewster's intonations were saturated with sarcasm. "Frankly, I'm astonished. I would have guessed that the judge who had originally sentenced you, if he actually had his head out of his ass, would have sent you up the river for, oh, I don't know, maybe seven thousand years. Yeah, that's more like it."

The prisoner was totally oblivious to the hostile statement that the medical student had made. The vicious sociopath replied, "No, it was only seven years, not seven thousand years. Seven thousand years would have been a really long time. The scariest part about being in prison is that I had to keep on the QT about the two kids that I had incinerated. The general prison population doesn't treat other convicts very kindly if they know the death or abuse of children was caused by another inmate."

The correction officer scratched his chin and said with a smile, "I can see why you'd want to keep the matter a secret. Yes indeed, Rockholder; it would be a real shame if the general population of prisoners ever found out what you had done to those twins."

"I know," Rockholder said, "I've been lucky so far."

"To be honest with you, I'm really quite surprised none of the other convicts are aware of this already," Fuller said with a grin. "Just to think that an accidental slip of the tongue from a correction officer to the other inmates could have bought you a visit from some bent-nose like Nick the Shiv or Joey the Bull! After all, if the word ever gets out about what kind of man that you really are, they'd cut you to ribbons."

"I hope not. Those two guys scare the hell out of me. Other than that, I really enjoyed being the big house my first time around," the prisoner explained. "I would have been happy to have stayed there, because the drugs that you can get in prison are much better than what you can get out in the street. Although the drugs cost a lot more in prison, I can usually get a good deal because I'm a lover, not a fighter."

"You were convicted of vehicular homicide on more than one occasion," Brewster observed. "How in the world did you get out of prison the first time after only serving a few years behind bars?"

"Simple! The parole board asked me what would happen if I was released from prison. I told them I would get a job and go to church every Sunday," Rockholder said with a chuckle. "Well, it appeared they believed me, but I thought I was just being funny at the time. After all, I never thought that the parole board would be stupid enough to believe anything that I ever said."

"Well, seeing some of the incredibly stupid things that the parole board has done in the past," Fuller said, "I for one, am not particularly surprised."

"In any event, my comments were good enough for the parole board to make a decision about me, and I was released from prison early. It's what I deserved!" Rockholder crowed. "I love our criminal justice system, don't you? So, tell me; I didn't understand what you boys were talking about earlier. What are you planning on doing with me?"

Brewster ignored the prisoner's question as he taped a white hand towel over the door window to block the view of anybody who may have been passing by in the hallway.

To create a distraction, Officer Fuller asked the incarcerated demon to continue. "Don't worry your pretty little head about a thing.

The student was just explaining to me that he wanted to perform a specific neurological procedure to take a better look at what's in your mind. You've told us a really nice story so far, Rockholder. Now walk it home."

Rockholder wrapped up the tale of the multiple teardrop tattoos. "As soon as I got out of prison, I got stoned and went out driving on the loop. I just wanted to fire up a big blunt while I listened to some tunes on the airwaves. Suddenly I clipped some asshole that was changing a flat tire on the 610 loop. I squashed him like a grape. He got snagged by the undercarriage of my car. I could hear him like scream and shit, but I didn't stop. Finally, he busted loose, and my rear tire went over his head. Dude went all freakazoid when I was done messin' with him. When I crushed the dude's skull, it went flat and it got all big around. About as thick as an eighteen-inch deep-dish pizza, I'd say. So that's where the fifth teardrop tattoo came from," Rockholder recalled with great personal satisfaction.

Although both of his arms were now shackled, he tried it to wipe the sweat from his face against the front of his orange jumpsuit when he added, "I got this final sixth tear drop tattoo a bit too soon, however."

"Well, did you kill another person or not?" Brewster asked. "You can't score a trophy like a teardrop tattoo for simply being a good boy and eating all of the spoiled meat loaf that they throw down on your lunch tray."

"It's to celebrate some bitch that I heard got hepatitis from me. The nurse that flew out on the helicopter to pick me up when I got into that wreck on the loop accidentally got a needle stick from me. Sucks for her. I now hear she gonna die from my hepatitis. Just goes to show you, no good deed goes unpunished. Stupid bitch deserved every bit of it. She should've stayed out of my way," Rockholder smugly concluded.

⸺ooo▪◉▪ooo⸺

Brewster immediately realized he had just experienced another jarring event of déjà vu. For a brief moment, Brewster's mind was transfixed on an event from when he was a junior-high school student. He recalled the bizarre practice at his parochial school where the administration would consign the frailest, oldest, and most visually impaired nuns to monitor the recess period. This was the very fate that poor Sister Santa Sangre had faced.

Although she was a strikingly tall woman, Brewster recalled that Sister Santa Sangre was infirm, with a senile tremor. In addition to poor vision, the octogenarian was also sadly afflicted with drastically diminished auditory acuity. Despite these physical limitations, the good nun was nonetheless assigned the daunting task of trying to patrol the playgrounds during the recess period. She struggled valiantly in her noble efforts to maintain some degree of order and civility amongst the evil Catholic school children who were little more than vertically challenged demons spawned within the bowels of hell.

Sadly, Sister Santa Sangre would be totally oblivious to the violence that was in orbit about her. With her advanced age of eightytwo years, she could not readily discern when some kid was getting a vicious beat down or if some other fragile and spindly child was being shaken down by bullies for his or her lunch money.

As recorded in the Gospel of Matthew, the itinerant preacher from Nazareth at one time had rendered the beatitude which proclaimed that "the meek shall inherit the earth." Well, that might very well be true, but the demon children spawned within the bowels of hell will most assuredly inherit the playground.

One particular bully that Brewster remembered was a brute named Nick Bustamante who tended to run amok on the playground. Brewster recalled an extraordinarily grim day when Sister Santa Sangre was praying on her rosary beads when she had passed by Bustamante. As she walked past the heathen in reverential solace, Bustamante picked up a baseball and threw it directly at the back of her head. Once the projectile was launched, he shouted out, "Sister, help! I need you!"

As the nun pivoted to see what was awry, the baseball that had been hurled at her smacked her right in the forehead. The tall, elderly nun fell like a redwood tree that had been cut down in the forest by stout lumberjacks.

Bustamante, feigning concern, ran up to the semiconscious nun and said, "Oh, Sister, Sister! Some very bad boy threw a baseball at your head. I'm here to help you!"

The elderly nun, perpetually filled with grace, uttered, "Bless you my child, bless you."

After an ambulance arrived, Sister Santa Sangre was scraped off the playground and carted away. Brewster confronted his classmate and asked him why he would do such an evil deed.

Bustamante smugly replied, "Stupid bitch deserved it. She should have stayed out of my way." As the traumatic childhood memory receded as quickly as it had appeared, Brewster became a man suddenly focused on a mission of retribution.

Something deep inside the medical student was now irrevocably fractured. He was indeed ready to kill E. Rockholder. Arby Fuller had specifically warned J. D. Brewster not to talk to the evil criminal, but the medical student failed to heed the correction officer's dire warning. After Rockholder cheerfully recalled the vehicular homicide he had committed, Brewster truly felt that his very soul was now somehow critically injured from the wicked tale that the criminal had rendered.

Brewster was compelled then and there to end the life of the prisoner. In his heart and mind, he would never be able to fully ascertain the nature of the primal forces driving this compulsion to kill another human being. Would the murder of this prisoner, as vile and evil as Rockholder was, be an act of rage, an act of vengeance, an act of righteous indignation, or an act of clinical justice? Brewster was not able to conger up any type of rational explanation at the time, nor would he likely ever.

"Okay—I've heard quite enough of this," Brewster said. "Let's get to work, Fuller. We've got very little time to pull this off. Let's get him out of those handcuffs, and then we'll prop him up in front of the door."

"I'm ready to rock and roll. Lay it out for me," Arby petitioned.

"When I set him up correctly, you'll know what to do," Brewster instructed. "The cover story we'll use is pretty straightforward: You had to remove his handcuffs to reposition him after the paracentesis procedure was completed, and that's when he charged me. He was simply a wild and rabid animal that had to be put down."

Fuller noted that a favorable and coordinated strongly written cover story concerning what was about to occur would no doubt be in order.

As the brain of E. Rockholder was addled by hepatic encephalopathy as a consequence to his advanced liver failure, he did not actually grasp the fact that the two other men in his hospital room were actually planning his murder. It was being openly planned right in front of him, and there was nothing he could do about it.

Brewster told the prisoner, "Okay, Mr. Rockholder, I need you to get out of bed and stand with me in front of the door. I'm going to do a neurological assay on you. I want you to follow my fingers with your eyes while you're standing in front of me, but you have to keep your head absolutely still. Do you understand what I'm saying to you?"

"Droopy dog," Rockholder replied, "I'll do anything to get out of these handcuffs, even for just a little while."

The prisoner was removed from his handcuffs, and Brewster positioned him to stand in front of the door, while he held the shoulders of the soon-to-be dead man to steady him.

"Okay, Mr. Rockholder," Brewster said, "I'm just about ready to find out what your brains look like by this pending invasive neurological exam that I am about to perform on you. Mr. Fuller is going to assist me."

Arby Fuller was filled with great resolve as he lifted the nightstick and prepared to deliver a mighty and fatal blow to end the life of the evil psychopath.

Just before Arby Fuller pulverized the skull of the prisoner, an elderly black woman with white hair entered through the doorway and asked if anybody who was present in the room was in need of spiritual guidance or prayer.

"Madam, we're really busy right now. I'm going to have to ask you to leave." The visage looked familiar to Brewster, but he could not remember her name. Had he met her before? Brewster believed that may have indeed been the case, but he was not absolutely certain. Oddly, she had no name badge.

The woman was not about to take no for an answer. "I'm a float nurse from the temp pool, but in my spare time I'll make rounds for the chaplaincy service if they get into a pinch. Pardon me for being so bold, but it would seem to me that *everybody* in this room is in need of redemption. I need to intercede now, as I'm on a tight schedule."

"Thank you, lady, but I assure you, there's nobody in this room looking for redemption or perhaps even salvation. Now, if you don't mind, I'm about to perform a complex neurological examination on this patient. As you may gather from the fact that he's wearing an orange jumpsuit, this fellow is not only a prisoner, but he's also a cold-blooded killer to boot! I'm going to have to ask you to leave this instant. Let me see you out."

No sooner had Brewster somewhat rudely dispatched with the uninvited guest in a bum's rush out the door, there was another unexpected interruption. It was as if the hand of providence was purposefully disrupting the best laid plans of mice, men, and co-conspirators in the act of murder.

Blomeo Colima burst through the door of the patient's room and seemed irate. "Brewster, what in hell are you doing? Get this guy back in bed and tie him down. I'm not happy with you right about now, Mr. Brainiac."

Brewster and Fuller both thought they had been busted. Because of the stressful circumstances, Brewster briefly lost the vision in his left eye, and the peculiar phenomenon lasted for several seconds. Was it the onset of a migraine attack, a transient ischemic event, or perhaps a self-limited episode of psychogenic blindness? Brewster was not certain. However, his temporary medical malady was indeed most frightening. Fortunately, his symptoms quickly receded. Both Brewster and Fuller took a sigh of relief as soon as they realized Dr. Colima was completely oblivious about the pending murder that had been inadvertently thwarted.

"You screwed up big-time, buster!" Colima loudly exclaimed. "You left the paracentesis fluid on a roll cart right beside the nurse's station. You didn't have them doubled-bagged in the mandatory red bio-hazard bags. What were you thinking?"

"Hang on, Blow! I'll go out there and take care of the situation right now."

"Too late for that," Colima said in frustration. "The damage has been done already. The ascites material is theoretically highly contagious. If a bottle fell off the cart and had broken on the ground, it may have contaminated another patient or staff member. They could have gotten infected with hepatitis, you idiot."

"I've got this under control, Doc," Brewster said. "I'll go out there and fix it right now."

"Stand fast! Hear me out," Colima commanded. "If a bottle had broken out there, your career would have been over before it had ever started. Cash in your chips, bucko. Grab the big pink slip. Get on the bus. Take a one-way trip back to Lodi. Not to mention potential lawsuits that would have you legally embroiled until hell had frozen over."

"A headache maybe, but no harm, no foul," Brewster said defensively. "It's all good! I'm going to take those specimen bottles down to the laboratory right now."

"There is indeed a big harm, and also a big foul, you asshole," Dr. Colima countered. "Kristina Coffee and her boss from the Department of Occupational Safety and Infection Control found the cart, and they went grape ape. Oh, hell, it was worse than that; they went purple monkey shit all over me! I just got written up. I'm going to get spanked by the administration over this. You did this, but I'm responsible for your actions. Get out of my sight before I decide to kick you out of the band."

There was nothing further that Brewster could say. Dr. Colima was now in hot water, and Brewster felt completely dejected because his own careless behavior was responsible for the GI fellow's circumstances. Somehow, the medical student had to find a way to make things right.

While Arby Fuller directed Rockholder back into bed and secured him with the handcuffs, Colima turned his seathing rage toward the prisoner. He pointed a finger at Rockholder and began an unexpected tirade. "Rockholder, I have never seen a slime ball like you before in my entire life. While I was filing away your procedure permit consent form on the chart, I saw under the section where it said 'patient compensation' that you added twenty dollars and a pack of smokes every single time we perform a paracentesis on you. On top of that, you forged my signature on the document!"

"If you want my belly fluid," Rockholder said, "you pay me."

"Is that so?" Colima asked.

"Pay, pay, pay, pay, pay!" Rockholder chanted incessantly.

Blomeo Colima didn't respond any further to the prisoner's request for financial compensation. The doctor continued, "You have the balls of a brass monkey. I'm through with you!"

Dr. Colima looked at J. D. and whispered a valid point. "This is exactly why convicted criminals should be excluded from the pool of potential blood and fluid donors for Uncle Hank's hepatitis study. It was a mistake from the get-go. I should have fought a lot harder for that specific patient-pool exclusion criterion."

Turning back toward the prisoner, Colima said, "I don't care if the Gulf Coast has a contract to provide medical care for prisoners incarcerated at the Sharpstown Correctional Facility. Once you get over your fever, I'm going to do everything that I can to make certain that your ugly ass never shadows the doorway of this institution ever again."

In a dignified and polite manner, Rockholder managed to query, "So, does that mean you won't suck any more water out of my belly?"

Dr. Colima failed to answer the question, but nevertheless a hostile gaze was returned.

The prisoner lunged forward as if possessed and cried out, "Well, if that's the case, you can just suck the sweat off by balls, you pig!"

Blomeo wryly grinned and seemed to have a twinkle in his eye when he contemplated his next course of action. He addressed Officer Fuller with a specific surprising request. "Arby, let me borrow your nightstick right now. I want to beat this bastard's brains out."

Fuller replied, "Well, funny you should say … That exact subject matter actually seems to have been the main topic of conversation for almost the entire morning!"

Colima calmed down, and as he left the room, he turned to Brewster and said, "Sorry I lost my temper with you. I need to talk to you in little while. Come find me out on the floor."

After Dr. Colima left, Fuller looked at Brewster and stated the obvious. "I guess we dodged a bullet on that deal."

Brewster, always the Southern gentleman, graciously said, "I want to reward you for the hard work that you do by offering you a fresh cup of hot java." Brewster paused for a moment before he asked, "Tell me—how do you take it?"

Fuller responded, "Well, how do I take it? That's an excellent question. I'd like to believe that, by and large, I'm trying to do something good for society. I'm protecting John and Jane Doe from the horrors that we have locked up behind bars. If what you've asked me is not a rhetorical question, some days I'm not exactly sure exactly how I'm able to take it. Sometimes it feels like I'm taking it up the ass sideways with an eighteen inch, split-face concrete cinder block."

Brewster interjected, "No, dumbass, I mean your coffee. How do you take it—sugar and cream?" They both had a laugh over that.

Brewster returned to Rockholder's room to find that the prisoner had fallen asleep. J. D. had brought Fuller a cup of coffee with two packages of powdered creamer and one package of artificial sweetener. In addition, Brewster had managed to rifle the refrigerator in the nurse's lounge, where he found a piece of pecan pie. "It looked like this piece of pie I found was about to go bad. I suspect that it may have been in the refrigerator in the nurse's lounge since at least early this very morning. You better eat it now, but I didn't find a clean fork."

Fuller mustered a curious expression on his face and asked, "How could a piece of pie go bad if it has only been in the refrigerator for a few hours?"

"The piece of pie had belonged to a nurse named Missy Brownwood. If she finds out that I absconded with it, I assure you something will really go bad for me. Finish up your pie and let's bust out of here. Dr. Holcombe is granting a fifteen-minute interview down in the auditorium at noon today for the Your Witness News program. Check this out; my friend Medhi from the cafeteria is setting up a table with snacks and soft drinks. I know for a fact that he'll bring a couple of pecan pies and sandwiches for folks to snack on. I want to saddle up to those goodies and book out before the festivities begin. After all, at twelve thirty, I have a feeling that I'm going to get raked over the coals at the Human Subject Committee meeting."

"Good luck with all of that, but I have to stay here and keep an eye on the dirt bag," Arby explained as he pointed his index finger at the prisoner. "Score me a sandwich if you can." Fuller suddenly had a burning question to ask Brewster. "Since you mentioned this upcoming Your Witness News television interview, is it true that your cousin Antonia Alabaster is one of the consumer protection ambush reporters who works for Martin Zinfandel on channel four's Your Witness News program?"

Brewster replied, "That's indeed true. She got her degree in journalism at UT, and she joined Your Witness News after Zinfandel hit the big time. As you may recall, he broke open the story about the house of ill repute that was discovered in that warehouse in Casa Gato Grande, just west of Houston. In 1978, they came out with the hit Broadway musical about the whole sordid event and it was called, *The Best Little Warehouse in Dixie.*"

Fuller noted, "Your cousin has such a cool gig. I like the Thursday-night segment called 'Roachaurant Nightmares' when the reporters raid nasty diners and find roaches, rat shit, and rabid raccoons residing in restaurants. What I don't know is this; how does Martin, his crew, and the health department get to these places so quickly once patrons find something nasty when they're out dining somewhere?"

"There's a simple answer for an easy question," Brewster said. "Martin Zinfandel used to be a constable with Harris County. From what I've been told, he's still very tight with the cops. Martin has several different teams out on patrol at any given time. If a restaurant patron finds something nasty, the only thing that particular person has to do is to call 1-800-EAT-SHIT. Martin or his crew members are guaranteed to be there at the restaurant within twenty or thirty minutes after receiving the call. My cousin has been assigned to the Texas Medical Center/North University Place sector."

"Wait, Brew, this is Houston," Fuller said. "I'm not certain if you've been paying attention to current events, but the traffic out there sucks. It sucks all the time. You can't even get across the street in only twenty or thirty minutes in this damned town."

"Dig this," Brewster explained. "If a call comes in, the police will escort the TV crew and the Health Department inspectors to get to the offending restaurant lightning fast. The TV station also pays good money, depending on what kind of putrid or disgusting filth is found inside the establishment."

"Like, how much scratch are you talking about?"

"They'll pay a boatload, I tell you. For example, a live roach found in somebody's salad is worth two hundred bucks," Brewster explained. "If a patron finds rat grunt in their soup, it's worth three hundred dollars. There's a sliding pay scale for the whistle blower depending on just how nasty something might be. God knows how many bills you could cheerfully stuff into your own pocket if you were to ever accidently stumble upon a dead 'possum on a platter or maybe find road kill-o armadillo on a meat hook in the back of some Cajun restaurant somewhere. I know for a fact that the television station will also flip a Jackson to the officers providing the police escort. Except for the restaurant involved, it's a win-win situation for everybody. Whowee!"

"Is your cousin married?" Fuller asked.

"Don't go there, dipshit. She is indeed married, and no, I will *not* introduce you to her."

Sporting a huge grin, the most grateful correction officer started to consume his tasty treat. "You did something nice for me today, and now I'm going to do something nice for you. Speaking of finding a roach in your salad and rat grunt in your soup, I want to give you my silicone cockroach that I got at a novelty store on Fannin. It means the world to me, but I want you to have it."

Arby reached into the pocket of his trousers and proceeded to extract an artificial insect that was two inches long and complete with a pair of antennae that would wiggle about with the slightest breeze or vibration.

"What in hell do you do with this damned thing?"

"Now listen—this is the most realistic-looking fake bug that I have ever seen. I've often used it to torment the prisoners. I'll drop it onto their lunch tray or slip it inside a sandwich that they're about to eat just to piss them off. Keep it with you. Someday you'll need this artificial insect when you decide that it's time to flip over the tables of the temple mount money-changers."

Brewster chuckled as he examined the silicone roach and said, "You're right; I must admit this is likely the most realistic-looking synthetic, coprophagic creepy-crawler ever made! I'm honored that you gave it to me. Not only will I cherish this invaluable commodity," Brewster added sarcastically, "but I'll keep it toasty warm in the top pocket of my consultation jacket. You're absolutely the best, Arby. Someday I might need to play a nasty prank on somebody in the future. Whenever I pull it off, I'll be sure to let you know how well it all turned out. By the way, I'm sure you've dropped this silicone bug on Rockholder's lunch tray in prison in the past. Well, how did the fucker respond?"

"I've never had the chance," Arby answered.

"Why not?" Brewster asked. "If anybody in prison needs to be shit upon, it's certainly this joker."

"He's a chain smoker and he uses copious amounts of illicit recreational drugs, but I've never seen him take in food or fluids. Not once. Not ever. Nobody else has, either!"

"What?!"

"I have my own ideas about what that-that thing is that's chained down to the bed rail in front of us might actually be, but I'd rather keep my personal theories to myself."

As Rockholder suddenly lunged forward and darted his tongue rapidly in and out of his mouth, Brewster fell back out of harm's way and asked a most pertinent question. "Is he, well-what is he?"

"Stop right there, junior," Arby answered. "I've said too much as it is. You're a bright boy. You need to figure it out on your own accord."

After Arby Fuller had finished his slice of pie, the medical student made a motion with his index finger to indicate that the hospital room of E. Rockholder should be vacated for a private discussion. Brewster felt that the boundary between what was right and what was wrong had been breached, and he needed clarity from his new-found friend. The two men walked out into the hallway and stood in silence together for several moments before Brewster sheepishly addressed a most pressing question. "What in hell happened in there?" Brewster asked in a low monotone.

Brewster received a nonchalant response, as if an acquaintance was making a casual commentary about something as trivial as the weather. "Nothing. I assure you. Not a damned thing happened in there today."

100
Confidential: For Corporate Eyes Only

8

PAYOLA

J. D. Brewster was not certain what dark force had overtaken him, but he realized that he had never previously met an evil entity that was more of a living and breathing demon than it was a human being. Once the feelings of rage toward Rockholder had subsided, Brewster prayed that such a vicious and malevolent energy would never have the opportunity to swallow him whole like that ever again. Sadly, for the medical student that would simply not be the case.

Brewster returned to the nurse's station with the additional bottles of infectious ascites fluid that had been collected from Rockholder. The charge nurse, Irene Segulla, was waiting for him. She pointed to the wheeled cart that had been loaded up with several bottles of the previously collected contaminated ascites fluid, and then she rebuked Brewster for his careless behavior.

"You better get this cart down to the laboratory right now, young man. Put those bottles into a red bio-hazard bag before you take it down the elevator. In the future, you need to stop and think about what in hell you're doing."

"I'm truly sorry, Mrs. Segulla," Brewster said. "I promise that it will *never* happen again."

"I'm worried about you, Brewster," the nurse said. "I don't want to see you getting into more trouble about this mistake. Maybe I'm just revealing my unfulfilled maternal instincts that are starting to spill out. I just want you to know that I have you and Blomeo Colima covered."

"How is that, Ms. Segulla?" Brewster asked.

"The infection control team entrusted the official complaint about you and Blomeo with me. They instructed me to file the report with administration, and I have it right here in my hot little hands." Irene Segulla proceeded to wave the two-page document in front of Brewster's face. She continued to demonstrate her ultimate benevolent intentions with a most mischievous grin on her face. "I want you to watch me file this complaint about your misdeeds with administration. I'm going to do it right now!"

Irene walked over to the locked wooden chest that held scrap confidential medical record documents that needed to be shredded. She stuffed the report into a slot that was on the front panel of the box to make absolutely certain that the formal complaint would be destroyed. Apparently, the document would never leave the medical ward!

"Thanks!" Brewster said with the smile. "If I was the kind of guy who would give out hugs, I would clearly give one to you, Ms. Segulla."

"Please, call me Irene."

"No," Brewster said, "I'm going to officially call you my surrogate mother!"

"I'm honored, J. D."

"You should be," Brewster said. "After all, I plan to be the best surrogate son that you ever had!"

"Well, since I've never had a son, surrogate or otherwise," Irene said with a laugh, "you'd fit the bill for being the *worst* surrogate son that I ever had, also!" Brewster made a conscious effort to not stiffen his body when Irene gave him a hug.

Brewster added the bottles of fluid that had been collected from Rockholder onto the bottom shelf of the roll cart after that infectious material had also been safely put in a red bio-hazard bag. He took the material down to the laboratory to drop it off with Rip Ford. By then, it was almost the noon hour, and Brewster only had about thirty minutes before the grand inquisition was scheduled to take place with the PhD program director and the Human Research Committee.

J. D. Brewster stopped by the auditorium before noon, where Dr. Holcombe was being prepped for a brief interview by a reporter from the Your Witness News television station. The interview was going to be broadcast over the airways as a "human interest story" about the perils of infectious hepatitis. Brewster was about to meet a man he had previously befriended. His name was Medhi, and he was an attendant at the hospital cafeteria. Medhi was setting up a small buffet table inside the auditorium with an array of snacks, including an urn of coffee, doughnuts, slices of pecan pie, and finger sandwiches. It was absolutely imperative for Brewster to obtain a slice of pecan pie to replace the one he had stolen from the nurse, Missy Brownwood. He had to make good on this, or else there would be hell to pay. He'd been caught in the past stealing food from the nurses' refrigerator, and the experience could only be described as something that a honey badger would have likely encountered if it had raided a hive.

When Brewster went out of his way to first meet Medhi in June of '79, the medical student's initial intentions were actually rather dishonest and nefarious at best. Brewster's original design was to only feign a friendship with the young man to only manipulate the cafeteria attendant into providing Brewster with free meals from time to time. Brewster actually had no desire to have Mehdi as a friend, much less anybody else for that matter.

As it turned out, Medhi was actually a much more interesting individual than Brewster could have ever imagined. Mehdi was previously a medical student in Tehran, and Brewster learned that Mehdi and his family were driven out of their homeland in February of '79 because of his family's support for the Shah of Iran. Mehdi and his family became refugees once a political coup forced the shah and his followers out of the country at the point of a gun.

Political convulsions in Iran established an iron-fisted theocracy that would subsequently rule the country. Medhi's father was a petroleum engineer, and he readily found work at a refinery in Houston. Although they were granted asylum, life for his son became a much greater struggle. Unable to get readmitted into a state-side medical school, Mehdi accepted an unfulfilling job as a hospital cafeteria attendant until he could figure out what he was supposed to do with his life.

Even though Brewster had never planned to be anything more than an acquaintance to the cafeteria attendant as an avenue for an occasional free meal, the inevitable happened, and Brewster had actually found himself concerned about the young man's future welfare.

If Mehdi was ever going to become a doctor, he would have to start over from scratch. That meant Medhi would eventually have to take the arduous MCAT examination. Brewster stepped into the role of being a tutor to the refugee in an effort to help the young man do well on the standardized medical school entrance exam. In return for his tutorial services, Mehdi took Brewster bow-fishing for gar on the Trinity on several occasions.

Although he was from Iran, Medhi considered himself to be a Persian, and he referred to himself in such a fashion. It made sense. As the Iranian government was holding American embassy personnel as hostages at the time, the American people were extraordinarily hostile to the Iranians then, as now. There was just as much anger toward the useless and ineffectual Carter administration at that time, as it seemed to be completely incapable of resolving the hostage situation.

Once Brewster entered the auditorium, Mehdi said, "Hello, my friend! I have a treat for you. I put it in a brown bag for your lunch later on. It's a meat loaf sandwich!"

Brewster appreciated the gesture, but he waved off the bag and said, "Mehdi, I just can't eat any meat loaf. Not now, not ever. Please take it away or I just might barf on you."

The cafeteria attendant expressed a look of dismay and asked, "Are you the type of Christian who is not allowed to eat meat on certain days? My meat loaf is really very good, and I want you to have some."

Brewster replied, "No, it is not that. I think it is okay for Catholics to eat meat on Fridays now after the Vatican II resolutions, but I have a story about meat loaf that I rarely tell anybody. I want to tell it to you just to make certain that you know that I'm not being rude to you."

Brewster took a deep breath, and he hesitated for a moment before he revealed to his friend a horror story about the medical student's childhood. "I was only three years old when my father passed away, and my mother had to go back to work as a nurse. She got a job at the VA Hospital. Before my brother and I were old enough to go off to school, she would leave us at a children's day care facility that used to be over on South Main Street. It was called the Town and City Children's Center. It was a dreadful place that I can still vividly remember to this very day. The proprietor of the establishment was known as Mrs. Arlington. Although I was only three or maybe four years old at the time, I remember that she looked like a Grinch."

Mehdi looked concerned. He was not sure what Brewster was talking about. "What's a Grinch?"

Brewster responded, "The way I see it, that's the saddest thing about you being a godless infidel."

"What did you call me?" Medhi asked. "It looks like I now have the sad misfortune of confronting a fossilized Templar knight."

"Unless you need a Q-tip to clean the wax out of your ears, I believe you heard me the first time," Brewster laughed.

"Must you be a pig every day of your life?" Medhi inquired. "No matter how nice I am to you, you come around here and yank my scrotum. I don't know why I give a shit about you."

"Spare my life!" Brewster said with feigned indignity. "Just last Tuesday you called me an uncivilized barbarian."

"If the shoe fits …"

"Look," Brewster said. "I just can't believe that you don't know anything about the Grinch. You can't be that ignorant!"

"Go ahead and insult me," Mehdi scoffed with a grin. "Whenever you try to do it, you just make me laugh. I can't tell at times whether you're a funny comedian or just a funny bigot. I don't care. I'll continue to feed you no matter who or what you are, because deep down inside, I believe you're a good man."

"Thanks!"

"Actually, come to think of it," Medhi said, "I don't believe that at all! Don't think for a minute that I haven't figured out the cornerstone of our so-called friendship."

"Oh, yeah?" Brewster asked. "Well, I'm all ears, and you have my absolute undivided attention. Spell it out for me."

"It's quite straightforward when you think about it; we're using each other," Mehdi said confidently.

"That's bit of an oversimplification, don't you think?"

"No," Medhi replied, "not at all. You're giving me tutorial assistance on passing the MCAT exam so I can have a chance to get readmitted to medical school, and I'm sneaking you free food. Don't get me a wrong, as I'm okay with this arrangement. Perhaps it's an example of primitive capitalism."

"How so?"

"We're engaged in a mutually agreeable exchange of goods and services," Mehdi opined. "Despite this fundamental economic co-dependence, I like you, Brewster, and frankly I hope you like me. Nonetheless, you are truly one of the most peculiar human beings I have ever encountered!"

Brewster grinned and said, "I'm a man of many talents, but sometimes I'll admit that the shirt I'm wearing doesn't always match my trousers. So, I'm odd; what of it? I was born here in Texas, and maybe that explains everything.

"Everything indeed," Medhi agreed.

"In any event, my Persian friend, it seems to me that you don't know anything about Christian traditions," J. D. said. "One of the great things about being a Christian is that you get to watch excellent cartoons on television around the holiday season. I am talking about *Charlie Brown's Christmas* and *The Grinch that Stole Christmas* featuring the late Boris Karloff who provided the voiceover for the cartoon creature in the title role."

"If the foundations of your religious beliefs can be found on a celluloid reel of animated film," Mehdi said, frowning, "I hereby fully retract all of the nice things that I just said about you!"

"Now, see here," Brewster countered. "I'm telling you right now that this is all seriously good, spiritually fulfilling entertainment. Check this out: the Grinch was a mythical, large, and hairy bi-pedal creature that lived in a cave. He terrorized the citizens of a place that was called Whoville. The town was comprised of crappy, one-room, neo-lithic communal dwellings, jam-packed with extended family members. These relatives were likely to be inbred, micro-cephalic cretins."

Brewster was compelled to incessantly joust with the cafeteria attendant. "I would surmise Whoville was very much like the urban squalor to which you and your people, Mehdi, are most likely accustomed."

"I'll have you know that I lived in Tehran," Mehdi said. "At the time I was there, it was a fairly cosmopolitan city. Incidentally, if you offend my former homeland one more time, I'll bury you up to your head in a hill of fire ants, and then I'll stone you to death!"

"Okay, okay; don't be so sensitive!" Brewster said. "Anyhow, after the Grinch gets infected with an acute case of mosquito-borne viral endocarditis, complicated by a chronic overindulgence in methamphetamines, the creature developed cardiomegaly."

"What a load. I've lived in Texas long enough to recognize bullshit when I hear it," Mehdi said.

"Be mellow. I'm about to reveal to you an important clinical vignette. You want to get back into medical school someday, don't you? Well, I can guaran-damn-tee you what I'm about to tell you will appear on the next MCAT entrance exam. You see, the poor bastard's heart got too big," Brewster explained. "High-resolution CAT scan imaging studies confirmed that the heart of the Grinch had hypertrophied to over ten times it's normal size, but the cardiac ejection fraction was quite low and it was probably well below twenty percent."

"So, this Grinch had a weak heart?"

"You could say that," J. D. confirmed. "With a projected life expectancy that was thought to be only on the order of a few months, the Grinch converted to Christianity. He became a Benedictine Monk who vowed a life of chastity and poverty. He continued to work in a cave with a dog named Max, and together they translated the Bible into an Indo-Iranian branch of human speech that is widely known today as the Farsi language. In the end, after all the infidels in Whoville had been successfully proselytized, everybody lived happily ever after."

After Brewster's eloquent line of bull, Mehdi was obviously more confused than ever. "So, this Grinch is a Sasquatch, no? I spotted a documentary about these mythical creatures on TV awhile back. It was truly fascinating stuff. What does this Grinch have to do with the meat loaf sandwich that I had made for you?"

"Look," Brewster replied, "at the childcare center, Mrs. Arlington, a.k.a. the Grinch, once served me meat loaf for lunch when I was a child. The meal was disgusting. It was spoiled, I tell you, and I just couldn't eat it. Since I refused to ingest the putrefied lunch, Mrs. Arlington took the plate of meat loaf and set it out on the kitchen counter at the daycare center. The same routine would happen every day until I would finally break down and consume it. As best I could tell, this daily routine would have continued until I finished that piece of meat loaf, no matter how long it may have taken. She just left it out there on the kitchen counter without any foil or plastic covering over it, or anything like that. She didn't even put it into the refrigerator at the end of the day."

Mehdi was skeptical. "Are you telling me the truth?"

"Scout's honor!" Brewster confirmed. "Soon, the meat loaf was growing fuzzy mold on it. This whole ordeal went on for at least a week or more. One day she brought it to me, and there was even a large cockroach sitting on the top of that wretched plate of spoiled food. I remember the bug had big antennae that were moving all around, as if it was sizing me up for a meal. Secretly, I had hoped that the cockroach would eat the spoiled meat loaf before I would have to. Finally, things were starting to get out of control. Mrs. Arlington started to beat me because I wouldn't eat her goddamned meat loaf."

Mehdi commented, "If somebody did that in my country, the shah would send over the secret police to pay this Grinch lady a visit, and she would never have been seen from or heard of again. Where was your mother during this dreadful time?"

Brewster replied, "That's a good question. My mom was afflicted with pathological grief after my father had passed away. She was totally oblivious of anything that was going on in life. She never recognized that I would come home at the end of the day with bruises or other injuries. I actually thought at the time that my mother hated my brother and me, as she had always blamed us for the death of our father. In retrospect, she may very well have been complicit in the abuse I was receiving at the hands of Mrs. Arlington."

"I don't know of any mother who would allow her child to be treated in such a fashion," Mehdi said.

"One would think," acknowledged the medical student. "Anyhow, the daily beatings started out slowly. First, I just got slapped around a bit. After a week or more had passed, she finally broke the fifth finger of my left hand. That's why I have a dog-leg in that finger to this very day. I remember she grabbed my arm at the wrist, held my pinky finger in front of my face, and said, 'This is what happens to bad little boys who don't eat their meat loaf.' Then, bam, she just snapped it like it was a pencil."

To emphasize what he had just said, Brewster pulled a ballpoint pen out of the top pocket of his white consultation jacket and broke it in front of Mehdi's face. "I remember being momentarily startled, and then I started to scream out in pain. Mrs. Arlington then started to stroke my hair and brush my cheek as if she was trying to soothe me. I remember her saying, 'There, there now, my sweet child, try not to cry.' No sooner had she said that, she slammed my face back down into the desktop, and my nose started to bleed."

"Was there nobody around to help you?" Mehdi asked.

"My older brother, Bill, was there, and he watched the whole thing in terror. The poor little guy was only five years old, and he was powerless to help. Take a look at what the fifth finger of my left hand looks like today." Brewster held up his left hand to show Mehdi that he had a very crooked pinky.

"Things got a bit rough for me after that," Brewster said. "Mrs. Arlington touched the blood on my face and began to roll it between her thumb and index finger."

"Was she a vampire?" Mehdi asked. "She sounds like she was an evil Mexican vampiro."

Brewster shook his head, "No, no, you're not listening! She was a Grinch, not a vampire or an evil Mexican vampiro, whatever in hell that is. I decided to finally eat the meat loaf, and to try and put an end to the beatings I had been receiving. I took a bite of the vile and spoiled food, but I immediately vomited. Well, no offense, Mehdi, but that was the straw that broke the camel's back. I was absolutely certain that Mrs. Arlington was going to murder me."

"What happened?"

"Now, I was quite small as I was only about three or four years old," Brewster recalled, "but I remember that she grabbed me by the left arm, and she began swinging me around as if I was a chained hammer to be thrown in an Olympic field event. I remember I got slammed up hard against the wall, and I was really injured quite badly. I sustained a fracture to my left humerus, and it tore the axillary nerve in my arm. That's the reason why I have a completely atrophied deltoid muscle in my left arm today. It never developed any further, and I cannot abduct that arm more than thirty degrees away from my body even now as an adult."

Mehdi asked, "How did you live through such an ordeal?"

"I think even Mrs. Arlington knew that she had gone beyond the point of no return," Brewster replied. "She went off to call my mother to explain to her that I had apparently been critically hurt. I remember her lying to my mother on the telephone that I had sustained the injuries while I was playing with some of the other children on the playground in her outside backyard. She had a jungle gym and a swing set, so what she had reported was completely feasible."

"Don't tell me this lady got away with her crimes?"

"I don't know for certain, but in the end, everything worked out okay," Brewster answered. "After she had spoken to my mother, she called the ambulance service to report that a child under her care had been seriously injured while playing in the backyard of the child care center. She asked for the ambulance to come right away. I think now, looking back on it all, she could have gotten away with it."

"Maybe what you experienced as a child is a contributing factor to your occasional hostile and caustic comments," Mehdi added. "At least it seems so to me. Well, in any event, you survived somehow."

"Did I really? To this very day, I'm just not too sure about that," Brewster mused. "I remember an elderly black woman with white hair had suddenly showed up. She was dressed up like a nurse, all in white. She must have been a person that Mrs. Arlington had just hired, as I had not seen her before. To this very day, I remember that she said her name was Sister Buena, but I'm not sure that I remember what she exactly looked like. In any event, she scooped up the rotten meat loaf and put it into a paper towel, and then she made it disappear."

"Sounds to me somebody was looking out for you."

"I don't know—maybe so. This lady whispered into my ear that it was okay to lie to the Grinch upon her return from speaking on the telephone. Before Mrs. Arlington had returned to presumably finish me off, the black woman with white hair simply vanished after she said that she was on a tight schedule and that she couldn't stay. In any event, I think she may have saved my life. I told the Grinch lady that I somehow had managed to choke down all of the putrid meat loaf after all. A detente had been achieved, and I soon ended up at the hospital to get my broken arm, fractured finger, and bloody nose attended to."

Mehdi asked, "Whatever happened to this Grinch lady?"

Brewster replied, "I don't rightly know. I fantasize that she was convicted by a WWII war crimes tribunal to have been a fascist collaborator and that she was sent off to spend the rest of her miserable days at the Spandau prison with the convicted Nazi named Rudolf Hess. All that I know is that the Grinch lady and the black woman named Sister Buena were gone after I had recovered from my injuries. The daycare center was suddenly under new management, and I never got hurt there again after that."

Mehdi then asked, "So what you're saying is that you'll not be eating the meat loaf sandwich that I made for you, is that right?" It would appear that Brewster and his friend Mehdi were cut from the same cloth when it came to seeing the big picture.

Brewster concluded, "Mehdi, what I really need is a slice of pecan pie wrapped up in some foil. I can promise you that if I don't come up with a slice of pecan pie within the next few minutes to deliver to a very feisty nurse named Missy Brownwood, there's a very good possibility that I will end up disappearing just like that Grinch lady I just told you about!"

Mehdi laughed but was able to oblige the student's request and soon Brewster was on his way.

While Brewster was working his way back upstairs, he passed Bruce Beathard, who was going in the opposite direction. The vice chairman of the PhD program was headed downstairs to the outside employee parking lot. A thick brown envelope was clutched tightly in his right hand. Dr. Beathard's mind was reeling with anxiety about the white-collar crime that he was about to commit. When the two men had passed each other, Dr. Beathard stopped Brewster and said, "J. D., I'm going to be at the conference that's scheduled at 12:30 p.m. today, but I might be a bit late. When I get up there, I should have some new and important information that will have direct bearing on the hepatitis B vaccine study that you're working on with the Rabbi."

Brewster suddenly felt as if a yellow flag was hoisted to the top of a pole. "Dr. Beathard," the medical student asked, "is it going to be good news or bad news for us?"

"What do you think? I'll be there you soon. Keep your powder dry until then." With that cryptic statement, Dr. Beathard smiled maliciously as he turned and disappeared down the stairwell. If pressed, Beathard would have readily admitted that he strongly disliked J. D. Brewster. He always thought that the medical student was little more than a poseur. As such, Dr. Beathard was a man secretly driven by ulterior motives when it came to matters concerning the brainiac who was enrolled in the dual-training program. Brewster would soon learn that a man driven by ulterior motives was indeed a potentially dangerous individual.

Complicating matters, Beathard had long been a critic of Brewster's research adviser, Dr. Yeshua Rabbi. Beathard was obviously irritated by the snail-like pace that the Rabbi adopted in his pursuit for the discovery an effective neutralization bath for the hepatitis B virus. Although Beathard would have been enthralled to see both

J. D. Brewster and Yeshua Rabbi unceremoniously dismissed from the Gulf Coast College of Medicine, the vice chairman of research realized that he had to keep his personal feelings in check. He had to maintain allegiance to whatever course of action was ultimately best for the medical school.

Unbeknownst to anybody except Dr. Harrison Reed, Dr. Beathard was on a clandestine mission. It occurred to Dr. Beathard as he left the hospital that perhaps he had inadvertently said too much to the medical student when they had passed each other on the stairwell. By then, it was too late. The meeting on the parking lot was already set, and the clock was ticking. The brown envelope Beathard tightly held was a pure and simple monetary bribe. Beathard was on his way to buy confidential information concerning the research data that another group of hepatitis investigators had accumulated. The information was regarding a different, yet parallel hepatitis B vaccine program sponsored by an industrial behemoth.

Funded by the highly efficient pharmaceutical giant Merck Sharp and Dohme, it appeared that this other viable hepatitis B vaccine program was much closer to reality than Brewster or Dr. Rabbi would ever realize. Dr. Beathard had suspected that this competing research was far ahead of the work that Brewster and the Rabbi had accomplished to date. The vice chairman anticipated that if this was true, it would be the death knell for the work that Brewster and the Rabbi had accomplished over the past year.

As Beathard had entered the parking lot, he passed within mere yards of two black men who were dressed in black sport jackets and wore white mock turtlenecks. They had goatee-style mustaches. Dr. Beathard thought it was a bit curious that these two men were dressed in this fashion on such a warm, early summer day.

The medical school professor was totally unaware that the two thugs had erroneously believed that the doctor was going to be an easy mark. When Dr. Beathard glanced over his shoulder and realized that the two men were closely following him, the two men who were in pursuit suddenly veered off in a different direction.

"Hello! How are you boys doing today?" Beathard called out to make certain the two men were aware that they had been spotted. When they failed to reply, Dr. Beathard had the uncanny suspicion that the two men were watching him to see what car he was getting into. After all, Beathard looked like a wealthy white doctor—just the likely person who might get assaulted and beaten to death with a lead pipe.

Instead of entering an expensive private vehicle, Dr. Beathard made certain that the two men had seen him enter a rather inexpensive airport rental sedan that also held another occupant sitting in the driver's seat.

"Oh, shit! We've been made, big man! Let's bail," the lesser of the two men said with alarm.

"Cool your tool, Smeg Nog," the bigger man replied. "You need to be patient, I tell you."

The two thugs elected to bypass the particular mark that they had previously sized up for a vicious backside assault. They started to look for an easier target that owned a nicer set of wheels. The two would-be carjackers meandered off in another direction while Dr. Beathard and the industrial spy he was scheduled to meet sat down together to conduct their clandestine, and most assuredly, illegal business trans-action.

When Brewster made it back to the medical floor, he again ran into Irene Segulla. He asked the charge nurse if Missy Brownwood had taken her lunch break yet. When Ms. Segulla replied that Missy was still seeing patients, Brewster replied that he had a piece of pecan pie that he needed to leave in the refrigerator for her.

Irene Segulla asked, "Well, why would she need an extra piece of pecan pie? I know she brought one from home that she's planning on having for lunch today."

Brewster replied sheepishly, "I know for a fact that the piece of pecan pie that she brought from home went bad. Being the nice guy that I am, I felt it was my duty to replace it with a slice of pie that would be safe for her to eat."

"You're always brewing up trouble, aren't you?" Irene responded. "Go find Blomeo. He's down the hall, and he wants to talk to you about something. When you're done, however, I need to ask you a favor. I need to go out and run some errands during lunch. I had trouble starting my car this morning. Missy Brownwood says that you know a lot about cars and that you have a fancy, fast one. I was wondering if you might be able to go down to the parking lot and to take a quick look at it. I know that you have a meeting upstairs in about twenty-five minutes, but I don't think this will take too long."

Brewster smiled and replied, "I owe you big-time, Irene. I'll be happy to take a look at it. I must say, though, Missy Brownwood talks too much. I'll be back in a minute."

Brewster found Blomeo Colima in the physician dictation room and was happy to report that Ms. Irene Segulla had saved their bacon. She had shit-canned the complaint written up about the two of them that was submitted to her by the Infection Control monitor. Colima was relieved to hear that, but he wanted to talk to Brewster about a different matter altogether. Specifically, it was about a pending extracurricular event.

"Well, as you know, my fellowship training will be completed in just a few weeks, and I'll be leaving Houston. With my departure, I guess that will be the end of our band, DNR. I wanted to let you know that I really enjoyed the times we performed together. We have one last gig to do, and it's on the Fourth of July."

Brewster was happy to hear that and asked, "Did we get invited back to Guano Dick?"

Colima replied, "Yes, but the other guys don't want to drive all the way to San Antonio to do just one show on the River Walk. I think you'll like our venue, though. It's the sister club of Guano Dick located down on Bellaire Boulevard just before the railroad tracks. It also happens to be a 1960s retro-styled club, and it's called Guaiac Dick."

"What will the crowd be like?"

"As best I know," Colima explained, "most of the girls that will be at the club will likely be in their mid-thirties. I know that you dig fat, old, hippy chicks, so this should make you very happy. It'll be a blast. Sadly, it'll be the last time that I'll ever see you guys. Band practice will be a few nights from now at the clubhouse in my apartment. I've reserved time for us to run through our two sets."

"I will definitely make it a point of being there, Blow."

"You better," Colima said, "because it's time we mix things up a bit. The apartment manager doesn't mind as long as we don't crank up the volume too loud. I have a surprise for you boys. I have a new guitar that I'm going to break out, and I want to add a new song to our last set. I want to close with it."

"Fill me in." Brewster expressed curiosity as to what the new song might be. "What's the tune that you want to do? Maybe I don't know the lyrics."

Colima was coy and said, "All in good time, young grasshopper. Just consider it to be a going-away present to myself. In regard to knowing the lyrics, you are a very strange man indeed. You have an encyclopedic memory regarding every top one hundred hit that was ever released between the years 1960 and 1970. I've never seen anything like it before."

"I'm not so certain that you're paying me a compliment right about now."

"I'll be honest with you, Brewster," explained Dr. Colima, "you're *way* beyond strange. You're a freak. You're a likable freak, but a freak nonetheless. I have no doubt in my mind that you already know the lyrics, so I am not going to bother to tell you what the song is until we practice it in my apartment clubhouse."

"Thanks for the vote of confidence," Brewster replied. "I hope you're right about all of that."

"I actually wish that I had bothered to buy a guitar like this new one that I now have," Dr. Colima wistfully lamented. "Way back when we first formed up as a band, I actually wanted to buy it over a year ago, but I just didn't have the money for it at that time. I won't lie to you; it cost me a shit load, Brew. If I had this guitar when we first teamed up, I'm certain that we'd now be the opening act for the Rolling Stones the next time those old geezers plan to go on tour." Both men laughed at Colima's penchant for hyperbole.

"Where exactly are you going to be setting up your private practice once you leave the Gulf Coast?" Brewster asked.

"It will be here in the state of Texas," Colima responded, "but otherwise, I'd rather not say. Once I split, I don't want anybody to try and hunt me down. This place has been like a bad dream to me, and I want to forget that I'd ever been here. There, I said it. I'm sorry I feel that way, but it is the truth."

"Really?"

"Some things happened here that I'll never get over," Colima said. "There are many evil things that I've witnessed here that I wouldn't even be able to tell a parish priest if I ever went back to receive the sacrament of confession. Nobody would believe me. In fact, I wouldn't even believe it myself unless I was an eye witness."

The medical student glanced over the GI fellow with an admixture of apprehension and curiosity. "Like what?"

"Bad things," Colima answered. "*Real* bad!"

It was obvious to J. D. Brewster that Dr. Colima was not about to elaborate at that point.

"I don't have any business skills," Blomeo confessed as he tried to change the subject, "so all I'll say is that I am going to join an established practice where I don't have to worry about billing, employees, payroll, withholding taxes, and all of that other happy horse shit, bullshit that makes the world go around."

Brewster asked, "Do you have any other pearls of wisdom for me before you permanently lay down tracks to bail out of here?"

"You'll personally know that I've made it to the top-shelf in life when you see that I get my book published someday," Colima replied.

Brewster laughed and said, "Well, I didn't know that you were writing a book. What's it all about?"

"The operative title at this time is *Dr. Blow's Honey Bun Diet,*" Dr. Colima answered. "The subtitle is *There's Always Somebody Fatter than You.* Now, I know you dig fat chicks, so don't drop trow and sport a woody on me. The book will be filled with pictures of fat women in bikinis. How cool is that? I've already worked out several chapters. The first one will be entitled 'No Good Deed Goes Unpunished.' Like it?"

Brewster chuckled and rhetorically asked, "Why am I not surprised?"

The second chapter will be called, 'The Benefits of Cholesterol.' In this section of the book, I'll take the counter-intuitive stance that the consumption of cholesterol in high doses is actually quite good for the human circulatory system. Cholesterol can and will make your coronary arteries as hard as a rock, and I think that would be a good thing. I will also make the argument that fat and grease are also healthy dietary items, as they will make the inside lining of your coronary arteries slippery. Therefore, fat, grease, and cholesterol will help prevent blood clots from occurring according to my largely unsubstantiated scientific theories."

"You're a freaking genius!"

"I'd like to think so. I'm actually surprised that it took you so long to come to that conclusion," Blomeo said, laughing.

"Now, wait just a minute," Brewster protested. "The people who read this book might believe your bullshit. You might be held liable someday if you actually put those crazy ideas of yours on paper."

"If you're not going to enjoy reading my second chapter, Brew, you're going to blow a fuse when I tell you what's next. The third chapter will be entitled, 'The Perils of Exercise.' In this section, I will provide the scientific evidence that when a human being is born, he or she has already been given a genetically predetermined number of heartbeats."

"What are you talking about?"

"You see, a person shouldn't squander his or her lifetime limit of heartbeats by jogging, playing sports, or running up and down a stairwell. To hell with that crap. After all, if I'm going to develop tachycardia over something," Colima boasted, "it better be while I'm sitting on a beach and getting a rubdown with coconut oil by a herd of nubile, semi-clad, Polynesian females!"

"That's the ticket!" Brewster exclaimed. "I smell a Pulitzer prize! I want to garnish a slice of the pie when it comes to movie rights." They shook hands, and for the time being until the band's scheduled practice session at Colima's clubhouse, the two men parted company.

While Brewster and Dr. Colima were enjoying a lighthearted social visit, Bruce Beathard was engaged in a much more serious conversation going on in a white rental sedan down on the employee parking lot. Beathard had never met a person who claimed to be a pharmaceutical spy before, and he was aware that he had to quickly vet this stranger. The research department's vice-chairman had to make certain that the information that the spy possessed was on the level about an alleged parallel hepatitis vaccine research program. If verified, this alternate scientific research would be in direct competition with the experimental studies conducted at the medical school.

After all, he was not about a hand over an envelope filled with $5,000 cash for a bogus line of bullshit. Beathard had broken the ice and asked the elderly stranger, "So, do I get to know your name, or should I just call you Dr. Mole? Or maybe it's Mr. Mole. How would you like to be addressed?"

This stranger replied, "Of course I won't tell you my name. However if you must call me something, just Mole would be fine, sans prefix, suffix, or a specific title of any sort."

"How do I know if the information that you brought is legitimate?" Beathard pressed for disclosure.

"Reed set this up. That should be enough for you to know that my information is on the square."

"How long have you known Harrison Reed?" Beathard asked.

"Are you trying to make small talk, or are you vetting me?"

"Come on. Give me something here. After all, if we get pinched, both of us are going down."

"Just keep your mouth shut and you and I will both be able to walk away happy from all of this," the Mole replied. "Reed and I were both associated with the CAD boys after the end of the Korean War. We got a grant from Galveston, and it was our team that did the first breakdown on the chemical composition of atheromatous plaques. We also had a functional dog lab. We studied why our canine friends were relatively impervious to the ravages of coronary artery disease. Dogs can eat cholesterol-laden food, including meat, fat, grease, and even their own turds. Although they can get some seriously bad butt-breath, they generally don't get the same clogged coronaries like human beings do. We were determined to get to the bottom of that interesting anomaly."

Beathard needed clarification and asked, "Who were the CAD boys?"

The Mole was clearly annoyed and responded, "So, you call yourself a research scientist and you proclaim that you don't know about the CAD boys? Frankly, that's pathetic. The CAD boys were the members of the Coronary Artery Disease Study Group, initiated by UTMB. I'm surprised you didn't recognize that acronym."

Beathard had taken offense to the Mole's overtly hostile mannerisms and retorted, "I'm only thirty-eight years old. I wasn't around three hundred years ago when you and Antonie van Leeuwenhoek had invented the microscope, old man."

"A little respect is in order here, boy!" The Mole countered. "After all, you need me more than I need you. I'm here as a favor to Harrison Reed. If you don't see it that way, you're more than welcome to take your five grand and shove it up your ass. Don't let me stop you."

This meeting was starting to go south in a hurry, and Beathard had to salvage the situation before the pharmaceutical spy got cold feet and disappeared. Dr. Beathard responded, "Okay, keep your shirt on. Let's both try and be civil about this matter and get this deal done. How are you associated with this hepatitis B vaccine technology?"

"It's all right here in this binder," the Mole replied "I was an assistant to the principal investigator who successfully figured out the chemical bath that was necessary to neutralize the virus. I attended the San Antonio symposium this past March, where Dr. Rabbi and his associate, Mr. Brewster, presented the abstract data that they had accumulated regarding their own efforts to paralyze the virus, but to keep it intact from an antigenic standpoint. I realized that Brewster and the Rabbi were on the right track, but they were easily several years behind my team."

"What's in this for you?" Beathard wondered.

"Five grand."

"Bullshit," Beathard said. "Be straight with me. Tell me right now why you're risking what's left of your career by betraying your principal investigator."

"Let's just say that I have an axe to grind. I did a lot of work on this project, and I deserve some credit. I wrote a research paper to get our data published, but the PI buried the treatise because of his alleged concerns regarding the release of our proprietary scientific methodology. In any event, I wanted to crank out just one more publication before I crawled into my backyard hammock and called it quits. I guess it's not going to happen," the Mole lamented.

"I would surmise that you co-authored a lot of publications in the course of your career." Beathard asked, "What possible difference could one more published scientific paper make at this point in your life?"

"It's my legacy. In the future, when I'm long dead and gone, how else will anybody know that I ever even existed? In any event, the big pharmaceutical company, Merck, is taking our initial research to the next level, and they brought in the heavy artillery. They're far along in having a commercially viable vaccine available based on the work we did. I suspect that an effective hepatitis B vaccine will likely hit the market within the next two years."

"What?! That soon?" Beathard asked with considerable alarm.

"Yeah, junior," the Mole confirmed, "it's coming out that soon, and I promise you that it's going to be a home run. Out of my personal respect for Harrison Reed, I don't want to see the Gulf Coast College of Medicine throw valuable resources down into a bottomless pit. The Gulf Coast is in a race that you boys just simply cannot win."

"Let me see what you have."

"Pay me now, and then I'll let you have this binder," the mole said as he pulled the scientific document away from the reach of Dr. Beathard. "No money, no lookie. No matter what, you're going to pay me the five thousand dollars first to finalize this transaction. You better hand me that envelope and let me examine its contents before we go any further. If you're not down with all of this, we'll go our separate ways. If you walk away from this deal, however, I'm going to tell Harrison Reed that you're a major league asshole. Rumor has it that you have a burr up your paltry pecker because you've been passed over for a promotion a time or two."

"Frankly," Beathard said, "that's none of your goddamned business."

"Well, it most certainly is," the Mole replied. "If you queer this deal, I'll make sure that Reed pummels your sorry ass. You'll be slinging hash and washing dishes with the camel fuckers down in the hospital cafeteria before it's all said and done if I have any say-so in the matter!"

Dr. Beathard passed over the thick envelope of money to the stranger. Once the Mole examined the envelope's contents, he handed Dr. Beathard the large binder of scientific secrets. Dr. Beathard quickly scrutinized the confidential information destined to soon torpedo all of the arduous work that had been done by Dr. Rabbi and his research PhD candidate, J. D. Brewster, over the past year. "In five minutes, I have to go upstairs and meet the members of the Human Subject Committee. It's going to take me much longer than five minutes to digest all of this. In a few words, can you give me a corporate summary?"

"Oh, yeah," the Mole said with a laugh. "In fact I can. Go pay a visit to your stock broker. Do it today. Buy Merck, and buy it bigtime! You can thank me later…"

9

TERMINAL CORROSION

Back on the medical ward, J. D. Brewster found Irene Segulla. The student said, "Let's go down and take a look at that Cutlass of yours. I can take a peek, but now we only have twenty minutes or so to get this done. My mandatory conference is on deck." The charge nurse was happily agreeable to Brewster's offer.

Irene was a funny and loquacious middle-aged lady of Italian ancestry. With her corrective lenses, as thick as a double-decker corned beef sandwich, her eyes appeared to be the size of golf balls. When Brewster and the charge nurse reached her car which was located on the employee parking lot, he had her pop the hood so he could take a look as to what may have been the problem.

He noted a thick white flaky residue on both battery cables where they were affixed to the battery posts. Brewster instructed, "Look here; this is your problem. You have terminal corrosion, and this nasty crud is swallowing up your battery posts and cables. If you clean that crap off, you just might be able to get enough charge to get your car started. I'll bet gophers to gonads, however, that you will eventually need a new battery."

"How do I clean it off?" she asked.

Brewster replied, "It is easy as pie. Pecan pie, specifically. Take one of the urinal collection buckets and a disposable toothbrush out of the clean utility room. There's a box of baking soda in the back of the refrigerator in the nurses' lounge. You can find it right behind a large carton of cottage cheese and beside a package of unopened Cotto salami. I hope somebody eats that salami pretty soon, or otherwise it might go bad. If that salami reaches the threshold of its expiration date, I'll have to personally intervene before the situation gets dangerous."

"That package of salami happens to be mine, young man," the charge nurse warned.

"On the other side of the box of baking soda is a Ziploc plastic bag that has two pieces of fried chicken. One is a drumstick, and the other is a wing. By the texture of the fried chicken, I believe it's highly likely that the chicken may be the Colonel's extra-crispy variety. I'll have you know that's my favorite! I would mainline fried chicken intravenously if I could," Brewster proclaimed.

"How in the world does this have anything to do with my dead car battery?" Irene asked. "Stay focused on the task at hand, Mr. Brewster, or else I will relinquish your status as my designated surrogate son."

"I'm sorry," Brewster said. "I got off track. Where was I? Oh yeah—you'll need to fill the clean urinal bucket with water and bring it back down to your car, along with the box of baking soda and the disposable toothbrush. Pour the baking soda over the white deposit on the battery posts, and then carefully add water. Scrub vigorously with the toothbrush, and that should help take care of the problem, at least temporarily. I tell you what—I actually have a few minutes, so let's see if I can help you take care of this problem right now."

"Not now, J. D.," Ms. Segulla protested. "Blomeo said you had an important meeting this afternoon, so you better not tackle my dead battery until your conference is over. I don't want you to get grease or anything nasty on your hands or clothes before your meeting."

Brewster noticed two fairly muscular-appearing black males strolling about in the parking lot. The men had caught the attention of J. D. Brewster when the individuals stopped and peered over the roof of an automobile that was located about ten parking spaces away. Although it initially seemed to Brewster that Irene Segulla's 1972 bronze Oldsmobile Cutlass was being carefully scrutinized by the two strangers, the medical student was able to convince himself that he was only imagining things. After all, prejudicial thoughts of that nature could quickly qualify him as being a racist. At that point, Brewster believed that the best course of action would be to mind his own business as he proceeded to attend to Ms. Segulla's disabled vehicle.

In the meantime, it had dawned on Irene Segulla that the medical student seemed to know too much information about the contents of the refrigerator in the nurse's lounge. She looked at Brewster with curiosity, and then she took the index and the middle finger of her right hand and made a V. She repeatedly poked it into the lenses of her own eyeglasses. After repeating this motion three times, she finally took her index finger and jabbed the tip of Brewster's nose to confirm that she was watching him closely. It was a rather amusing action for Brewster to behold, especially since Ms. Segulla had eyes that appeared to be orbital planetary bodies as a consequence to the magnification from the thick lenses of her eyeglasses.

"J. D., how could you possibly know the contents of the refrigerator located in the nurses' lounge? There is a sign on the refrigerator that warns medical students and house staff to stay the hell out of there."

Oops. Busted! It would not be the first time that Brewster was caught with his hand in the proverbial cookie jar, and it certainly would not be the last.

In vain, Brewster tried to defend himself. "Ms. Segulla, I love the nurses that work on your floor. I worry about them all the time. I have grave concerns that you and your staff might be exposed to dangerous and toxic food-borne pathogens. You might all be ingesting food that could very well spoil at some point."

"Oh really, now?"

"From firsthand personal experience," Brewster proclaimed, "I am considered to be a recognized regional expert in the particular subject matter of what could be the tragic consequences if a human being unwittingly ingests spoiled food, especially meat loaf. I try to check out your refrigerator quite frequently as a public service courtesy to all of you, just to make absolutely certain that none of your staff members are about to eat any food that is on the threshold of going bad within the next few days or weeks."

Irene didn't believe a word that she was hearing. "Do tell…"

"I'm serious!" Brewster said. "If something is about to go bad in your refrigerator, I will sacrifice myself and eat it just to keep you all out of harm's way. I love you guys, and I would happily throw myself on that hand grenade in order to save the nurses on the med-surg unit. I gladly perform this noble service if and when the circumstances are dictated by these largely unrecognized perilous conditions."

"You're a regular prince."

"I am indeed," Brewster concurred "For example, just earlier today I found a slice of pecan pie that had belonged to Missy Brownwood. I'm absolutely certain it was about to go bad. To spare Missy from her planned near-future ingestion of a potentially dangerous dessert item, I gave that piece of pie to the correction officer, Arby Fuller. You will be relieved to know that after he ate that slice of lucious pecan pie, he noted no untoward ill-effects."

"You're so full of bull I'm surprised that your eyes aren't brown," Irene said.

"Can't you see? The pecan pie was sitting in the refrigerator, probably for two or three hours at a bare minimum. I found that piece of pie, and I just had to give it to the Arby. As a correction officer, he surely had the skill set to discern if that slice of pecan pie was dangerous or not. Frankly, it's hard for me to fathom that you're unable to appreciate what I'm trying to do here. We're talking about self-sacrifice here. We're talking about altruism here."

Ms. Segulla was not particularly amused and replied, "No, we're talking about BS here. If I ever catch you stealing food from the lounge refrigerator, I will hand you over to the nurses. You'll be flogged and then impaled. I'll personally see to it that you'll get hung out to dry. Ouch! Let me know how that'll work out for you. Something tells me that you won't be seeing a resurrection from the dead at the end of this story." As it would turn out one day in the future, Ms. Segulla would not be quite right about her last prognostication.

Brewster put up his hands in self-defense and said, "You're absolutely correct. I'm full of just a ton of bull. Trash-talking is part of my birthright. I'm a Texan, after all."

Ms. Segulla was appeased by his confession. "J. D., you seem to be a very lonely young man. Do you have a girlfriend?"

Brewster thought that it was sweet that she had asked. Irene was trying to connect to Brewster at some deeper level, but nevertheless, the medical student tried to keep his guard up. He was certainly reticent to allow himself to feel too much. That would be dangerous. "Now, Ms. Segulla, I'm happy without girlfriends."

Ms. Segulla seemed embarrassed and added, "Oh, I'm sorry, dear. I didn't know that you were one of those homo-satchels. Were you born that way, or do think it's an acquired sexual orientation disorder?"

"Wait!" Brewster responded. Clearly, there was a breakdown in communication. "I'm not gay!"

"Yes, I know that you are not a happy person," Irene said. "If you're one of those homo-satchels, I promise I won't judge you. I just want you to enjoy your life."

"Wait!" Brewster pleaded. "I don't think you understand what I am trying to say. I'm not a happy person, but I'm *not* a homosexual by any stretch of the imagination. I'm just not at a point in my life where I would want to be involved in a relationship. Look—I have to scram in a couple of minutes. I need to finish up so I can get out of here." Brewster lowered the hood of Irene's automobile, as it was now time for him to go upstairs for the mandatory 12:30 p.m. Human Subject Committee conference.

Mrs. Irene Segulla had an additional sincere thought to convey to the young medical student. "Before you leave, I want to tell you something that happened to me. Back in 1950, I was thirty years old, and I was finishing my master's degree in nursing. I fell in love with a young man who was maybe five years younger than me at the time. His name was Flavius Gordon, and he was from Wink, Texas."

"Wow. The rock 'n' roll star Roy Orbison came from Wink, Texas," Brewster said.

"How in the world did you possibly know that?" Irene asked.

"I am, without doubt, a font of useless information," Brewster proudly said.

"Well, I am indeed impressed," Irene said. "Flavius went by a shortened version of his name, and everybody but his mother usually called him Flav. When he was in grade school, somebody gave him a special nickname. J. D., I'll bet that you can't guess the nickname that my fiancé had."

Brewster thought for a moment and then answered, "I'll guess that his nickname was Flash Gordon. After all, any kid that came of age during the late 1930s was probably a big fan of the Olympic athlete and serial movie actor Buster Crabbe as he battled Ming the Merciless in outer space."

Irene looked pleasantly surprised and said, "Wow, I really can't pull anything over on you, Mr. Brewster! When Flav was still a teen, he proudly fought with the Marines at the Battle of Okinawa in World War II. After the war, he was able to go to college on the GI Bill. He was called back up during the Korean War and served as a lieutenant. He was sooo handsome! He proposed marriage to me before he went off to fight in the Korean conflict. Before he was shipped out, he gave me a single yellow rose."

"That's beautiful," the student said.

"It's my most precious memory," Irene said. "He told me I was his Yellow Rose of Texas, which I guess was quite true as I was born in what is now the little fishing village of Bacliff. He promised to give me a whole dozen roses when he returned! Can you imagine such a thing? To this very day, nobody has ever given me a dozen roses. Gracious me, that would be something to behold. I still secretly hope I'll come home from my shift someday and I'll find a dozen roses waiting for me. That's silly of me to think that way, isn't it?"

Brewster found that he was incapable of answering what was essentially a rhetorical query. Even if he tried to say something at that time, the medical student's larynx had welded shut. For some reason, he was unable to speak at that precise moment.

Ms. Segulla pulled a tissue paper from her purse, but her voice remained steady, and she was emotionally firm in her resolve to continue. "Anyhow, I thought that it would be best if we waited to get married until he came back from the war. Flash went missing in action and was a presumed prisoner of war. To this date, I don't know if it was the evil communist Chinese or those godless North Korean animals that took him away, but he never came home."

Brewster composed himself enough to ask a question. "Does Uncle Sam still consider him to be a prisoner of war?"

"I can't bring myself to even consider the possibility that he might still be living three decades after he disappeared." Ms. Segulla removed her eyeglasses and dabbed away at a single tear from her left eye. "God forgive me, but I pray that he died quickly. I know exactly what happened to our American servicemen who were captured and interrogated by the enemy during the war. You know, a lot of those boys never came home."

Brewster was a historian, and he knew the facts. "Sadly, thousands of American servicemen simply disappeared."

Irene fired off a volley of difficult questions for which there were no obvious answers. "Do you really think that any of our boys are still being held by those bastards after all of these years? If so, are they still being tortured? For what purpose could our boys still be held as captives? Well, what else can I say?"

"Don't let your mind go there, Irene."

"I can't help it," the nurse explained. "I missed my chance to grab the gold ring. The days had turned into weeks, and the weeks had turned into months. The months had turned into years and the years then turned into decades. Suddenly, my whole life had passed by."

Brewster shook his head in sadness and was finally able to comment in a faltering voice, "I'm grieved to hear about all of this."

"I kept thinking to myself that I would find somebody else to love," Irene said. "In the end, love never came by my way again. Perhaps I was being punished because I was in love once, and I let it slip through my fingers. Maybe that's it. This's what I have to face because it was the wrong decision not to get married when my fiancé went off to the Korean War. You see, I have this huge house filled with all kinds of nice things that mean absolutely nothing to me, as I'm all alone."

"You have friends, Irene."

"Friends? Yes, I do. A life partner? No, I don't," she replied. "Even if I was destined to have become a widow after only a few months or a few years of marriage, perhaps I would have had a baby before my husband was lost. If I had a baby, part of my husband would have lived on in the child that we would have shared. I guess that's about it. I never got reconnected to anybody else after that."

A strange fleeting pallor had overtaken Irene's face, despite the midday summer sunshine. It was as if she had been transiently enveloped by a shadow. "I don't know about this premonition that I've had for a while, but for some reason, I think that I am getting closer to the finish line of my life. If that is so, my only regret is that I missed a chance to be loved. If it had happened, even for a fleeting moment, I think I would truly feel that my life was complete. I guess it just wasn't meant to happen for me. I hope that doesn't happen to you too."

For Brewster, his very soul was shaken by an unmistakable, peculiar déjà vu event in what Irene Segulla had said. He previously heard the exact same proclamation from the nurse Kelli Krause the day before she died from hepatitis.

"It's the awareness of our own mortality that gives our very lives any meaning at all. What do any of us have? If a person is lucky, maybe he or she will have about a number of four score or so spins around the sun. That's it. That's all we get."

"Hang on there, Irene. I need to ask you something. I know you were good friends with the nurse Kelli Krause before she died. In fact, she used to be one of your coworkers. Tell me; did you ever have this very same verbatim conversation with her that you're having with me now?"

"No, J. D.," Irene answered. "Why would I?"

"Oh, it's nothing I guess. Perhaps I'm just imagining things."

"I can't help but be philosophical about all of this," Irene explained. "I believe that we are all called to find some tangible mission that is righteous and good. Once we recognize that this divine calling may be our destiny, it is then our duty to try and accomplish this calling to the best of our God-given abilities."

"I don't know if I've been consigned some kind of tangible mission. If so, I sure as hell don't know what it is. I wish somebody would walk right up and spell it out for me in black and white," Brewster said.

"It doesn't work that way. You have to find your own purpose in life deep inside yourself. This commission to such a purpose gives our lives a deeper meaning. This is my conviction. Should we not also surely strive to pursue love and happiness along the way of this mystical journey, no matter how fleeting? I suggest you consider the same."

Brewster was washed over by a tidal wave of surrealism. What could this disturbing episode of déjà vu possibly mean? For a brief moment, the student was fearful that this event was actually a harbinger of early schizophrenia, but fortunately the frightful notion quickly subsided. Maybe it was God. Maybe it was the universe. Maybe Brewster should have been paying better attention.

The medical student felt as if Irene was on a mission now to bring emotional redemption and perhaps even salvation to a heathen lost in the wilderness. Brewster's soul was boxed up tightly in bubble wrap and stuffed into a closet down in the basement lab where scores of experimental animal subjects had been sacrificed in vain.

"Listen to me; it seems that you're lost in your work. I'm afraid that you've forgotten how to live like a human being," the nurse said. "Open your heart, son. Feel something, anything, before the chance to actually do so is forever gone."

It must have been a terribly bright day. Brewster had a hard time keeping his vision focused on Ms. Segulla, and he had to put on a pair of sunglasses that he had taken out of his top shirt pocket. Perhaps the air pollution in the city of Houston was at a high concentration level that day. Perhaps the bright sunlight was just affecting his vision. Perhaps he was just now starting to pay attention.

"You know, J. D., there is a person I want you to meet. I have a very nice niece named Stella Link. She works as a secretary for that psychiatrist, Dr. Corka Sorass. She is several years older than you, but she's a full-figured girl. Dr. Blomeo Colima said that you're attracted to girls that are, well–*huge* for no better word. Well, I don't know about that, but Stella does have very big bones, and her teeth are very straight. She has a beautiful face! Her head is perfectly round like a basketball!"

"Ms. Segulla," Brewster feigned, "you're scaring me!"

"I don't know about you, but I don't trust skinny girls," Irene opined. "I don't think that thin women are attractive at all, do you? A woman should have the figure of an apple. She should have an enormous bosom that could suffocate a man. Choke the life right out of him unless he sprouted a set of gills to breathe. You know what I'm talkin' about?"

Brewster interjected, "You're starting to embarrass me, Ms. Segulla! Perhaps I should not go out on a date with her until I devolve non-mammalian, extra-pulmonary oxygen absorption organs above and beyond the physiologic air-exchange plumbing that I was originally born with."

The charge nurse did not take her foot off the proverbial accelerator one bit. "No, J. D., life is way too short for you to you to change through some kind of reverse evolutionary transformation. I suggest that you get a snorkel or perhaps you should learn how to hold your breath a lot longer! You just need to start doing some breathing exercises before you take her out on a date. I forgot to mention that she's a hippy."

"Well, I won't mind a bit if she was a hippy chick."

"My description of her is in the present tense, not past tense," Irene explained. "She wears flowers in her hair, but I must admit that they're plastic. She went to San Francisco in '67, and she's had flowers in her hair ever since. I wish the poor child would learn how to wear a brassiere, but I guess it is hard to find something that would nicely fit when your chest size is fifty-six triple E. She came up to have lunch with me a few weeks back, and she saw you on the ward. She told me she thought you were *sooo* handsome."

Brewster thought that perhaps there were a lot worse ways to die than suffocation. Ms. Segulla climbed out of the driver's seat of her disabled automobile and got up on her tip-toes to give Brewster a kiss on the cheek.

"I know you are a shy person," Irene observed. "That's why I told Stella that she should ask you out for a date instead of her waiting to hear from you. They say that women are liberated now. Don't worry, son. I'll make her promise to me that she won't permanently injure you. At the very least, I'll make sure that she doesn't disarticulate any of your major joints, avulse any of your appendages, fracture your spine, or otherwise hurt you very badly on your first date together. Don't fret; I'll have a word with her. I'll specifically request that she refrains from wearing fish net stockings or tying you down with leather straps until you at least take her to a nice Italian restaurant. I hope by now that the poor child has at least learned not to rush into things. Oh, I forgot to mention; she likes to eat. In fact, she likes to eat a lot."

As Brewster turned away to hustle off to the 12:30 scheduled mandatory meeting, he turned to call back toward Ms. Segulla. "That's very considerate of you, Irene, as I'm afraid that my bones are readily fractured and I suffer from easy bruisability. Don't worry about trying to get those battery posts cleaned up. Harper from maintenance is down by the foyer trying to get the sliding-glass entry door operational. I'll tell him what is going on with your car. He's a gear head, and he'll know what to do." With that, Brewster disappeared back into the medical school complex.

J. D. had kept his word. The maintenance man, Harper, was wrapping up his work at the entryway, and Brewster told him about the predicament that Ms. Segulla was in.

Harper responded with enthusiasm about having the opportunity to take a look at the engine displacement under the hood of Ms. Segulla's Oldsmobile. "I bet she has a three fifty tucked under the blanket. Yeah, I'll be right out and take a look at it. Unless her car has been designated to have a DNR code status, I should be able to provide mouth-to-carburetor resuscitation and bring the beast back to life in short order. Tell her to sit tight, Brew."

With that, J. D. Brewster disappeared into the elevator.

Ms. Segulla thought, in all likelihood, she would end up having to take her car to an automotive service shop to get a new battery. She had taken the ignition key off the rest of her key chain and poked the key back into the ignition slot. She turned the key one more time in frustration, and the only sound that she could be hear was the rapid and annoying click of the starter solenoid. It was not receiving enough juice to engage the starter's teeth to mesh with the transmission's flex plate. Sadly, the engine just refused to turn over.

As the noonday sun beat down upon the parking lot, Irene left the driver's side car door open to catch the small amount of breeze that was wafting across the asphalt. She kept the key inserted into the ignition slot while she waited for Harper to complete the maintenance work on the hospital's entry door. Once the repairman had finished this task, Irene was hopeful that he would give her a hand in arousing her now-dormant vehicle. If Ms. Segulla had any idea of what was about to happen to her, she would have fled on foot in terror as Smeg Nog and the Big Nig approached the nurse while she was still sitting in the driver's seat of her car.

Smeg Nog and Big Nig were both from Houston, and sadly, none of them had ever ventured outside of the state of Texas. Cleophus McDonald (a.k.a. Mumbo Jamar Apoo, a.k.a. the "Big Nig") completed his eighth grade, but he never went on to high school. He was forced to drop out of school when he was thirteen years old to help support his mother and sister. He claimed that he never knew his father, but that was not the case.

Prone to violence, Cleo's father long terrorized his family. Once divorced, Cleo's father would begrudgingly pay child support, at least on rare occasions. He would do so by personally dropping off a check at his former home from time to time. That was all well and good, except for the repulsive demand that he was rightfully obliged to receive sexual gratification from not only his ex-wife but also from his teenage daughter. After all, the wretched beast believed that it should have been considered a *privilege* for his ex-wife and daughter to be the financial beneficiaries of the modest monetary obligations Mr. McDonald was burdened to pay as a consequence to the legal declarations outlined in the marital dissolution decree.

On every single occasion, the mother would refuse to allow her ex-husband to have his way with his own daughter in this sexual capacity, and sadly, this would result in the woman and her daughter receiving a vicious beat down. Whenever Cleophus tried to defend his mother and sister during these horrific events, his father would rear back and throw a haymaker that would slam the boy down to the floor with a black eye, a bloody nose, or much worse.

By the time Cleophus was sixteen years old, he had become quite a physical specimen, and it was finally time for retribution. One afternoon when the adolescent returned from his job as a dishwasher at a nearby restaurant, his father was again found in the act of violently raping his sister. A sharp blow to the back of his father's skull, administered by a claw hammer, quickly quelled the elder McDonald's insatiable wanton sexual perversions. After the father was knocked unconscious, Cleophus gladly handed the hammer over to his sister as she had demanded. She then proceeded to pulverize the man's skull until she was exhausted.

Once done, it was then the mother's turn to engage in an identical macabre, ritualistic catharsis. Cleophus waited until the middle of the night to dispose of his father's corpse upon the nearby railroad tracks. Cleophus made certain that the dead man's skull was propped up directly upon one of the rails and an empty bottle of vodka was strategically placed underneath his late father's torso. Once the partially decomposed and mutilated corpse was eventually discovered, the authorities assumed that the man was in a drunken stupor when he was flattened by a passing freight train in a terrible locomotive/pedestrian accident.

Perhaps it would have been the better part of valor for the McDonald's to simply go to the police and tell them what had happened. After all, the adolescent boy was only trying to protect his mother and sister from being savagely raped. This, however, would not be the course of action that Cleo and his family elected to engage. The members of Cleo's clan decided to keep the whole grizzly event a secret.

As long as he lived, Cleophus McDonald would never tell another soul that his father had repeatedly raped his mother and sister.

As long as he lived, Cleophus McDonald would never tell another soul that he had murdered his father.

As long as he lived, Cleophus McDonald would never tell another soul that his father was a despicable white man …

———◦∞◦❰❂❱◦∞◦———

Darryl Hewrett (a.k.a. "Smeg Nog") grew up less than a mile from where Cleophus McDonald lived as a boy. Oddly, the two individuals never met each other until they began their life of crime in '68. Darryl did manage to graduate from high school, although the only class he had excelled in was automotive body shop. Despite this fact, Darryl had never been gainfully employed.

The two men originally met each other when they were both members of the local chapter of the Black Panther Party. Because of excessive violence demonstrated against other members of the paramilitary/political organization, in addition to the overindulgence in illicit recreational drugs, both men were expelled from the party in 1967.

Darryl had an enormous scar on the dorsum of his right arm, and he proudly displayed the nasty injury to anybody who asked about it. When Darryl was in junior high school, he made the egregious mistake of entering a soda fountain shop emblazoned with a sign over the front door that said "Whites Only." When told to his face that a "person of color" would not be served in that particular establishment, he quietly left the restaurant without causing an incident. Unfortunately, the same could not be said for one of the patrons who followed the young boy out on the street and assaulted him with the glass from a broken soda bottle. Darryl Hewitt was able to flee to safety, but not before nine square inches of bloody skin and muscle from his right forearm had been violently extricated from his body.

195

Could acts of violence actually result in an individual degenerating into a full-blown, violent, sociopathic racist? That question is certainly food for thought ...

———∘∘⊙∘∘———

To avoid suspicion, the hoodlums had loitered about at the far end of the parking lot and were totally unaware that the Oldsmobile Cutlass was paralyzed with a bad battery. Smeg Nog and Big Nig jogged up to the open car door, and one of the brutes asked, "Ma'am, 'scuse me. My man here and I needs to ax you a question. Where 'da white wimins at?"

Confused by the seemingly unintelligible question, Ms. Segulla looked up at the two men who were standing beside her car. As their backs were toward the nearly overhead sun, she had to squint to look at them. Unfortunately, she did not get a good look at their facial features. Ms. Segulla tried to shield the bright sun with her left hand and asked for clarification as to the nature of the question that was asked of her. "Come again?"

Smeg Nog had chuckled and turned to his slightly taller accomplice. "Cum again? Okay, bitch. We is a gunna cum again and again until you needs to up and wipe that shit off o' yo' face and swallow down what I be blastin' in yo' mouf."

The Big Nig started to sing a nasty little ditty that was sung to the old tune, "She'll Be Coming around the Mountain." As the end of a three-quarter-inch threaded lead pipe was jammed through the thick left lens of the eyeglasses that Ms. Segulla had been wearing, her assailant began to sing. "I'll be riding six white wimins when I cum, when I cum." His compatriot in the crime joined in the chorus without missing a beat.

Irene Segulla's left eyeball exploded. Crushed like a kumquat, the gelatinous intraocular contents blasted onto the dashboard as if it were a tablespoon of citrus marmalade. The second blow from the lead pipe pulverized her zygomatic arch. Her face was crushed. The gentle, middle-aged nurse offered no resistance. She could not even muster up a scream. She was forcefully yanked out of the driver's seat and the two urban thugs cast her aside, much the same way that an unwed teenage mother would fling out a dirty diaper onto the parking lot at the local Walmart shopping center while sipping from a piss-warm can of beer that had lost its carbonation.

The two vicious assailants jumped into the Oldsmobile and attempted to make their escape. If only the engine had turned over at that point, perhaps Ms. Segulla would have been spared further injury from her tormentors. Unfortunately, that was not to be the case. When the car would not start, the two men got out of the car and casually strolled back toward their victim, who was lying on her back with her left arm reaching up to the heavens.

The taller of the two men spoke first in a calm and almost serene voice. "Now lady, dat weren't right you tryin' to sell us a used car dat jes' willn't fire up. You is a dishonest merchant, and I is gonna have to report yo' lily white ass to da Betta' Bidniss Bureau."

The man known as Smeg Nog started to twirl the lead pipe in his hand as he confided to the semiconscious woman that a heinous transgression of such egregious magnitude could not go without a stern reprimand. "Lady, I be from da Betta' Bidniss Bureau, and I hear dat there has been a formal complaint filed against you."

Ms. Segulla put her hands together as if she were in prayer. She humbly pleaded, "I did nothing to your people. Don't do this to me. My parents are Italian and they immigrated to this country long after slavery was over."

It could not have been choreographed better. The two thugs raised their gloved fists in triumph, purposefully mocking the two Olympic athletes, Tommie C. Smith and John Carlos, much as if the two assailants had just respectively won the gold and bronze medals for the two-hundred-meter-dash competition at the 1968 summer Olympic games that had been held in Mexico City.

They exuberantly shouted together, "Let the beatings begin!"

Fortunately for Ms. Segulla, the bloodthirsty and boisterous war chant shouted out by the evil perpetrators had not gone unnoticed. About six rows away in the employee parking lot, Dr. Beathard and his accomplice in corporate espionage both got out of the sedan that they had been sitting in to see what was causing such a commotion. Beathard had exclaimed to the Mole across the roof of the car, "Oh my God! That's Irene Segulla. I know her! She's the head nurse on the med-surg floor. It looks like those two bastards are trying to beat her to death!"

The Big Nig grabbed Irene Segulla by the hair and pulled her over to the curb at the sidewalk. He propped her head against the curb and asked sarcastically, "Is you comfy?" The two men proceeded to kick Ms. Segulla in her face until she had completely lost consciousness. They were very careful not to strike her skull. To do so would kill her. That was not their objective on this particular day. Their mission was to simply destroy the life of a helpless and harmless middle-aged white lady. A botched carjacking had devolved into a straight-up, black-on-white race hate crime. Nothing more and nothing less.

The Mole had responded to the exclamations made by Dr. Beathard and said, "We've got to do something!" Although the Mole was well into his latter sixties, he began to instinctively charge the two assailants with utter disregard for his own well-being. Beathard wisely stopped the older man and said, "No, wait! Those men are armed with a pipe. We just can't run up there empty-handed; we'll get our brains bashed in! Open the trunk of this car. Do it now, goddamnit!"

The Mole had opened the trunk of the rental car and pulled out a tire iron, handing it to Dr. Beathard. The Mole then grabbed the jack stand riser bar and held it above his head as if it were a battle axe. Both men had looked at each other, and without a further word, ran toward the melee. They shouted out a rebel yell the likes of which had not been heard since Pickett's Charge.

Coming through the front door at the same time was the maintenance worker, Harper.

Behind him were two other good Samaritans who happened to be cousins. They were leaving the hospital after paying a visit to an elderly relative who was suffering from a kidney stone. Although the cousins readily recognized that Ms. Segulla was a white woman, there was no way these two good Samaritans were about to allow some innocent hospital employee to get beat to death right in front of their eyes just because she belonged to a different race. Although the Samaritans were unarmed, Harper was wielding a very large wrench.

The two assailants quickly realized that they were outmanned. It looked as if John Q. Public was about to dispatch with the two thugs in what would have been a most violent act of well-deserved street justice. It was time to sound the retreat. Smeg Nog turned to his taller business associate and said, "It's time to bail out, Big Nig! I mean it! John Wayne n' da' cavalry is a comin'!"

With that, the two men were forced to prematurely discontinue the most pleasurable recreational activity that either of them had enjoyed in quite some time. They turned to sprint across Cambridge Street and immediately disappeared into Hermann Park while the vigilante posse was in hot pursuit. Unfortunately, this would not be the last time that these two vicious and evil men would cast their dark shadows upon the Texas Medical Center.

Gulf Coast College of Medicine

10

CODE GRAY

When Brewster arrived at the upstairs conference room for his 12:30 p.m. mandatory meeting with both the Human Subjects Committee and members of the PhD training program, he was pleasantly surprised to see a tray of po'boy sandwiches sitting in the middle of the conference table. As he previously rejected the meat loaf sandwich that was offered to him by Medhi, the medical student was actually quite hungry by the time the conference was scheduled to begin.

Anybody who had lived in Houston during that era would remember a certain delicatessen shop that was located on South Main under the shadow of the Astrodome. It served up fabulous po'boy sandwiches out of what used to be an old, red railroad caboose that had been turned into a restaurant. Unfortunately, that old railroad car has now faded into history. To his last days, Brewster would long remember the tasty treats, piled high with ham, provolone, hard salami, a layer of dill, and topped off with Cajun sweet red pepper and cabbage chow-chow.

The six members of the Human Subject Committee were already present, as well as Harrison Reed, who was the director of the PhD training program. There were two other members of the PhD program who had already arrived. Those individuals were Dr. Regina Clemmons and Dr. Sergio Balbona. Brewster did not really know any of the members of the Human Subject Committee, but it was not really pertinent for him to have made their acquaintance. The Human Subject Committee was basically the moral conscience for scientific research being conducted at the Gulf Coast. It was the arbiter, if you will, for ethical behavior in the setting of medical experiments. The only thing that Brewster, the Rabbi, and Uncle Hank actually needed from this committee was a simple thumbs-up to allow the continuation of their research projects. Once Rabbi and Brewster overcame the problem of complete viral destruction and then successfully induce biological immunity in an animal model without causing an active hepatitis infection, the Rabbi and Brewster would then be ready to proceed with a human pilot study. They could not go forward unless they had that blessing from the Human Subject Committee.

Dr. Clemmons was the only African American on the PhD committee. A nephrologist by training, her field of interest was studying the changes in renal integrity when the kidneys were exposed to nephrotoxic agents. Dr. Clemmons spoke with a high, squeaky, and weak voice. Brewster could readily discern that it was really quite a strain for her to speak at all. For anyone versed in the art of medicine, the root of her problem was plain to see. A keloid scar that ran across the anterior aspect of her neck confirmed that at some point in time, her thyroid gland had become rather quarrelsome. A surgical resection, followed by radioactive iodine treatment, made the rebellious malignant gland go away, but she would be committed to a lifetime of replacement oral thyroid hormone therapy.

Brewster, for some reason, recalled a passage from the Matthew 5:29: "And if thy right eye offends thee, pluck it out and cast it from thee …" Perhaps Matthew was addressing the appropriate surgical intervention necessary to extricate an ocular malignant tumor.

Although mildly proptotic, Dr. Clemmons was nevertheless a very handsome woman in her early forties. "The Rabbi tells me that you're skilled with an electron microscope," she said. "I'm currently planning on doing an experiment where I subject the kangaroo rat and the Fisher three forty-fours to the new chemotherapy drug called Cisplatin. We know that this drug can cause damage to the kidney, but we're not certain as to how. I was wondering if you could be so kind to take some electron micrographs of renal specimens to try and give us a better idea about how this drug can cause renal injury." Brewster replied that he would be honored to assist with her endeavors.

Another physician who was a member of the research committee present that day was Dr. Sergio Balbona. A neurologist by training, Dr. Balbona was a Cuban refugee who had spent his entire career of research trying to find the key to unlock the actual etiology of Alzheimer's disease. He tried to explain to J. D. Brewster a postulated theory that the neuro-fibrillary plaques found in the brains of patients with Alzheimer's disease were a deposition of pathological metallo-proteins.

When Brewster finally started to wind down his career decades later, the medical community was actually no closer to finding a truly effective treatment for the dreaded mentally incapacitating disease than they were back in the year 1980 when Brewster was in medical school.

Brewster conveyed his best wishes to Dr. Balbona and hoped that he was successful in his neurological investigations. "It's the human mind that puts us at the very top of the food chain. Without a healthy noodle, nothing else really matters, does it, Dr. Balbona?"

The neurologist agreed. "¡Sí, sí, sí!"

Brewster followed up with another question. "Señor, ¿eres Cubano, no?"

"¡Exactamente!" Dr. Balbona beamed. "I was able to escape Cuba in 1964 when I was only eighteen years old. My father knew of a fisherman who owned a six-meter skiff, but it had no motor. In fact, I don't think it was ever designed to accommodate an engine. Anyhow, my father was a clever truck mechanic and he knew the location of a wrecked lorry that—"

Dr. Balbona was rudely interrupted by Dr. Reed, who could not bear to hear anything derogatory about his beloved perception of socialism or communism. "I can't believe you ever wanted to leave a worker's paradise like Cuba. Perhaps you should regale Mr. Brewster with your tales of fiction on your own time."

Balbona glared at Reed and said, "To me, it would be a very sad day indeed if it would ever take a foreign Latino from Cuba like me to have to come all the way over to this country and explain what actually made America great in the first place. Freedom and capitalism go *mano con mano*."

With that, Sergio sneered at Dr. Reed. Dr. Balbona then pointed to himself and then at J. D. Brewster. The doctor put his hands together and rapidly moved his fingers up and down over his thumbs. Brewster was delighted and agreed. "Necesitamos hablar mas."

Dr. Balbona nodded and added, "Otra ocasion, ¿sí? Perhaps we can do it over a Cuba Libre and a nice fat cigar from my homeland."

As Brewster grabbed a sandwich, Dr. Yeshua Rabbi and Hank Holcombe entered the conference room together, each taking a chair on either side of Brewster in an obvious attempt to guard his flanks during the pending inquisition. The only person from the PhD committee who was obviously absent was Dr. Beathard, but he was expected shortly.

"Dr. Holcombe," Brewster asked, "how did your television interview go today?"

"Finer than frog's hair!" Uncle Hank replied. "With a tiddlywink and a dash of cayenne, that reporter didn't know if it was time to reel in a catfish or bite down yonder and spit out her plug on a knotty pine. Whowee!"

Baffled, the only thing Brewster could respond was, "Whowee!"

Suddenly, an alarm was broadcast over the PA system from the flush-mounted speakers that were located in the ceiling tiles in theconference room. An automated voice repeated, "*Code gray*!

Employee parking lot. *Code gray*! Employee parking lot."

Dr. Balbona shook his head in sad disappointment "There's been another breech in security. I remember about five or six months ago, somebody got carjacked in that same parking lot. They never did catch those two assailants, and the victim was seriously injured. We have security that patrols out there now, but they only come around about every half hour or so. I am telling you, we need to get security cameras out there ASAP."

Oddly, everyone in the conference room at that moment seemed rather complacent about the emergency announcement. There was a major change in attitude however, when the automated voice over the PA system began to broadcast a different dire message: "*Code blue*! Employee parking lot. *Code blue*! Employee parking lot." With that announcement, the dozen people that were in the conference room rushed to the plate glass window to look down on the employee parking lot, which was directly below them.

Dr. Holcombe pointed. "Look over there! There's our old boy Beathard with a bunch of other folks chasing two fellows over into Hermann Park."

With fascination, the conference attendees watched until the figures disappeared into the tall pines. Three of the five men carried some type of makeshift weapon brandished above their heads. They looked like Vikings who were hoisting broadswords and double-bit medieval axes. Soon they were obscured by the trees and a cloud of dust.

A pair of Houston police cars came rolling down Cambridge Street with their lights and sirens blaring. One of the squad cars had turned right and entered the employee parking lot. The other police cruiser made a hard left turn, crashing over the curb, and then actually drove off into Hermann Park, skirting through the trees at breakneck speed. It was quite an amazing sight to behold. Below them, there was an unidentified female figure lying on the asphalt. Her was head propped up against the curb of the sidewalk that led toward the medical school entrance. There was blood pooling all around her, and her identifying features were obscured by what appeared to have been a large, gelatinous, crimson cephalopod that had taken up residence upon her shattered face.

Dr. Clemmons commented, "Oh, good! Dr. Bryan and the ER team just arrived. I hope that poor soul is going to be okay." The injured individual was suddenly overtaken by a swarm of industrious army ants that came pouring out from the emergency room. They loaded the injured woman onto a wheeled gurney and then quickly whisked her away to the repair shop to get a major overhaul.

The committee members returned to their chairs in stunned silence, and the Rabbi made a request. "I believe we should take a moment and offer a silent prayer for whoever that victim is."

Reed scoffed at the suggestion. "No, we are not going to do that. It's already twelve thirty-five and we're behind schedule. It is time to get to work."

The medical student took umbrage at what Dr. Reed had said. Always one to brew up trouble whenever he could, Brewster chimed in with Dr. Rabbi. "Oh, I disagree, Dr. Reed. We certainly have the time to do just that. I for one, am going to bow my head and say a silent prayer."

"It's against the law to pray in public," Reed said.

"Although secular," the Rabbi said, "this happens to be a private institution. Besides, you obviously don't know anything about the Constitution."

"I don't know," Brewster chimed in, "but perhaps there are one or more godless heathens or angry atheists in this conference room. If that's indeed the case, I'm quite certain that the rest of the committee members at this meeting don't really care. As Americans, we're granted the right for freedom *of* religion, not freedom *from* religion. We should be able to exercise our first-amendment rights as guaranteed by the Constitution."

That statement was truly a stroke of genius on the part of J. D.

As the old saying goes, there's strength in numbers. J. D. Brewster concluded, "After all, we live in a free country, Dr. Reed. You're entitled to your own religious beliefs, or lack thereof, as the case may be."

Except for Dr. Reed, the other members in attendance respectfully bowed their heads to pray. Brewster, however, refrained from bowing his head, and neither did he close his eyes or even say a prayer. Instead, he found secret delight in taking the opportunity to watch the face of Dr. Reed turn a dull claret hue.

—∞◦}◦◦{◦∞—

Although trained as a cardiologist, Harrison Reed had spent the majority of his career as a glorified paper-pusher, either at high-profile major medical centers in various locations throughout the country, or toiling as a mid-rank medical school administrator here or there. Reed was not a Texan by birth. He was originally from Oakland, California. A hypocritical leftist, Reed was secretly delighted that he bailed out of Oakland before the time, in his own words, that it was over taken by "angry Negroes."

Although he lived in the Lone Star State for many years, he always felt out of place. Harrison Reed never looked upon Texas as his home; it was just some dreadful place where he lived and worked.

Dr. Reed was recruited to round up the PhD training program at the Gulf Coast College of Medicine from the institution's very inception. Prior to accepting his current faculty position, Reed parted company from the St. Francis College of Medicine under rather mysterious circumstances. Never married, his personal life remained a big secret. An unsubstantiated rumor had circulated throughout the Gulf Coast College of Medicine for many years that Harrison Reed got the boot from his prior post after graphic photos of sadistic sexual bondage scenes and torture were found amongst the pages of a manuscript that he had presented to the St. Francis College of Medicine's Audio/Visual Department to be transferred into overhead slides for a lecture

207

that Harrison Reed was slated to present to a sophomore class of medical students. Allegedly, the pornographic pictures in question were inadvertently transferred onto overhead slides and then subsequently loaded into Dr. Reed's projector cassette. Needless to say, if that particular rumor was indeed true, one could only imagine the chaos that had ensued in that particular lecture hall when Dr. Reed started to click through the slides on the overhead projector!

Like many young men from what is now known as the Greatest Generation, Reed served in the military during World War II. Manning a position as a loader on a 40 mm antiaircraft pom-pom gun, Reed saw considerable action in the early course of the war during the Battle of Coral Sea in the Pacific Theater.

After the war, Harrison Reed moved to Texas, where he enrolled in the less-than-reputable Mule Shoe State Teacher's College with the help of the GI bill. Surprisingly, he performed quite well at this small liberal arts institution that incidentally had no obvious reputation of any sort regarding state rank, much less any notoriety at a national level. Nonetheless, his undergraduate academic success afforded him the opportunity to get accepted into medical school.

Upon completion of medical college and postgraduate education in internal medicine, Dr. Reed also received fellowship training in cardiology. Harrison Reed had joined the CAD research team at the UTMB in Galveston. If the truth be told, this was Dr. Reed's only claim to frame. He was able to ride this self-promoted reputation as a top-shelf research scientist throughout his entire professional career, although he truly had not done any serious or substantial medical research of any value since the mid-'50s.

As it turned out, Harrison Reed was an academic fraud, and he knew it. Nevertheless, he somehow was able to bluff his way through life and climb the ladder of academia to his current prestigious post at the Gulf Coast College of Medicine.

—◦◦❯❮❖❯❮◦◦—

The moment of silence was fractured by another police siren. As the conference attendees looked back out the window, a blue pickup truck that had police markings pulled up on Cambridge Street at Hermann Park. An officer ran out of the park and approached the truck. In his hand, he had what appeared to be a black suit jacket. Two large shepherd dogs that had been restrained in separate crates in the back of the pickup truck were released at the edge of the park. The officer let the animals take a good sniff of the jacket. The two canines looked at each other and then at the officer. Under their own volition, the two wolf-like creatures bolted off into the woods like Fourth of July bottle rockets that had been lit with a punk. Clearly, they were dogs on a mission.

As the Big Nig sprinted through the park, he had already stripped off his jacket, mock turtleneck, beret, and goatee and cast them aside. Underneath his outer disguise was a black T-shirt and jogging shorts. He looked over his left shoulder and was pleased to see that he was easily outpacing the posse that had pursued him into the forest. He then looked over his right shoulder to ascertain the whereabouts of his accomplice. Although the smaller man was keeping pace, the Big Nig was stunned to see that Smeg Nog was still clad in his primary disguise.

"What in hell are you doing, Smeg?" The big man panted. "Drop your duds!"

Smeg promptly obeyed the big man's orders, and it was none too soon. "Dogs! I hear dogs!"

With only seconds to spare, the two men jumped into the getaway car that was parked adjacent to the Hermann Park Zoo just as the two pursuit canines threw themselves at the now closed and locked driver's side door. The shepherds snarled and barked at the closed car window, but to no avail.

As the car pulled out of the zoo's parking lot, the dogs realized that their quarry was escaping. The frustrated canines nonetheless pursued the two criminals into the traffic on Cambridge Street, immediately East of the Texas Medical Center. Smeg was behind the wheel of the car, and on more than one occasion, he was petrified with fear from the persistent police shepherds.

During the pursuit, the dogs were able to pull up to a parallel position with the escaping vehicle on the frequent occasions when stop-and-go traffic would intermittently ensnare the two assailants who were attempting to flee the vicinity. At the time that the dogs were able to approach in close proximity to their prey, they would bark ferociously.

Suddenly, there was an open break in the traffic line. Smeg crushed the accelerator pedal, and the two vicious criminals sped away to the relative safety of their chop shop near downtown. The eyes of the big man sitting in the passenger's seat were peeled wide open, and he was incapable of even blinking until the proverbial coast was clear. All the while, he incessantly commanded his partner in crime to obey a very specific, yet truncated order: "Drive! Drive! Drive! Drive! Drive!"

Dr. Clemmons noted, "If they had to break out the dogs, it means the perpetrators have gotten away. Look, I see Bruce now!" Leading what appeared to be an exhausted band of men, Dr. Beathard and the others slowly crossed the street back over to the employee parking lot. He bent over and put his hands on his knees, along with another fellow who appeared to be a man about in his mid to late sixties. It was, of course, the man that Beathard had referred to as the Mole. They looked like book ends. Both of the men were bent over and standing abreast as two police officers were taking statements from them, and also from the other individuals who had valiantly given chase to the perpetrators deep into to the park before the violent thugs had finally made their escape.

Yet again, the attendees resumed their seats. J. D. Brewster looked over to Dr. Holcombe, who was wearing a button-down oxford shirt with a bolo tie. Although Dr. Holcombe clearly had a gauze dressing covering a troublesome rash on his left forearm, blood had oozed through the dressing, and it had caused a maroon, sero-sanguineous stain on his white shirt sleeve. On several occasions, Brewster saw Uncle Hank scratch away at the skin plaque, despite the gauze dressing.

Dr. Clemmons spoke up. "Hank, did you try any steroid cream on that psoriatic rash that you have on your arm?"

Dr. Holcombe replied, "It's a wild boar up in the carrot patch. I was washing down my curlies, and I stumbled upon a goober high up in the man funk. I'm lining up the dermatodes to take a cookie cutter and bite this damnation. Hopefully, they'll be able to give me the skinny once and for all. Time to saddle-up a surgeon. Old John Wayne Gray needs to pluck the goober. If he doesn't, I'll just have to do it myself. I'll have the crab pickers give me a low down, and hopefully, I won't be in need of their services. Straight-up, the boom is out at ninety and I got the sheets in my teeth pulled hard like an old pole cat dancing with a blue tick. Whowee!"

Now, J. D. Brewster was from Texas. He was fluent in just about every form of the Texas language that was identified by linguistic scholars. He could fluently speak Coastal Plains, East Texas, Hill Country, Northern Prairie, Panhandle, and Valley Tex-Mex. He was even fluent in straight-up Mexican, which was almost as good as having the ability to speak refined Spanish. However, Brewster had never mastered Trans-Pecos Texan. More times than not, Trans-Pecos idioms and colloquial expressions would leave Brewster bewildered.

Back in the late 1960s, the old *Star Trek* television series had an episode where Spock had to invent a device that was called a "universal translator." It looked like an electric toothbrush, but the machine had the ability to translate the thoughts of some horny, amorphous, female, plasma entity into the English language. The members of the crew were in peril from the plasma being, but once Spock and Captain Kirk had figured out that the electrified blob of raspberry-flavored gelatin just wanted to hook up in a three-way, tag-team match nookie sandwich, everything else worked out okay. After all, if the crew members of *the Starship Enterprise* figured out how to make a handy universal translator, why didn't Brewster have one to communicate with Hank Holcombe?

J. D. frowned with concern about Dr. Holcombe's worsening chronic rash and suspicious axillary lymphadenopathy. Could it be a malignant disease process? Oh, yes, that certainly might have been the case. Hank tried to put everyone at ease when he said, "Y'all are swamp-stridin' on the down low like you strapped on a gator. Remember—this is Uncle Hank over here. Whowee!"

The technique that Brewster had used to try and respond to the Trans-Pecos research coordinator was to generally head bob in a slow, counterclockwise circle. By doing that, he would cover both an answer of yes and no, if by chance he was being asked a question from Dr. Holcombe. However, even that was never a certainty. The other technique Brewster had employed was to regurgitate a short verbal editorial of the idiom that Dr. Holcombe had just uttered, either in the form of a question or exclamation. Then Brewster would add Uncle Hank's favorite expletive at the end of the reply. A perfect example of this defensive response is when Brewster replied, "Strapped on a gator? Whowee!" The other attendees at the meeting apparently had no trouble in understanding the Trans-Pecos Texas language at all, as the others had nodded their heads in agreement and affirmation to Dr. Holcombe's peculiar reassurances about his own questionable health status.

Brewster had hoped throughout his entire life that one day the Republic of Texas would again have the wherewithal to secede from the Union, as he had long felt that the United States of America was on the wrong track. If that had ever happened, he felt that with his background in history he would be an excellent candidate to be on the Independence Committee. He thought it would be reasonable to offer the Trans-Pecos region of Texas in a straight-up trade for the entire state of Oklahoma.

After all, every damned football player on the roster at the University of Oklahoma and Oklahoma State came from Texas anyway. Now was just the right time to bring those prodigal sons back home. Most assuredly, natives from the Lone Star state were finding it quite tiresome when the Okies would brazenly raid across the Red River, kidnap Texas women and children, and then beat the crap out of the Texans in a game of football.

To paraphrase LBJ, it would be much better to have those Okies inside the tent and pissing out, as opposed to having them outside the tent and pissing in. Okies were somewhat like Texans anyhow. They just weren't quite as accustomed to the undeniable pleasures of using indoor plumbing or having toilet paper any more sophisticated than an old Sears and Roebuck catalog. Do bears shit in the woods? Why, most certainly. However, so do Okies. If the truth be told, Brewster had actually held the toothless ridge-runners from Arkansas in even lower regard than Okies.

"Looks to me that Bruce Beathard is going to be down there for a while," Dr. Reed stated. "Although we have a quorum, we can't pull the trigger until he gets here. J. D., I'd like to ask you some questions. Do you mind if I call you J. D.?"

"Yes, you can call me J. D. because that's indeed my name. It's actually on my birth certificate. To be honest with you, I don't think that the letter J or the letter D actually stand for anything in particular. May I call you Harry?"

Dr. Harrison Reed, who already had his feathers ruffled, harshly replied, "No, you may not. I only allow my friends to call me Harry."

J. D. Brewster bit his lower lip to keep from laughing. The medical student had speculated that Dr. Reed had never heard the nickname Harry in the past because it was highly unlikely that he had any friends to speak of.

Reed was getting over a recent black eye. He said that he had fallen off an exercise treadmill, but there were unsubstantiated rumors floating about that he tried to grab the reproductive unit of a stranger who was standing beside him at a public urinal in the Astrodome who happened to be a member of the Mexican Marauder motorcycle gang. Reed's sexual overtures apparently resulted in a severe beat down. Brewster had thought to himself that if the rumor was really true, he would have asked for a ringside seat to have witnessed such a scandalous event. Brewster had some marginal compassion for Dr. Reed, as penis envy was reportedly a terrible burden to bear.

Brewster felt that people like Dr. Reed should not be allowed into the Republic of Texas in the first place. At the very least this type of evil being should be restricted to the confines of the Austin city limits. A person like Dr. Reed should be forced to wear a shock collar. Any attempt at sneaking across the Edward's Plateau in an effort to infiltrate and corrupt the established realm of conservative ideology would result in an immediate and painful death by electrocution.

Harrison Reed continued. "I assume that you know the six members on the Human Subject Committee that are joining us today.

Brewster responded, "I have not met any of these people prior to today. If you would be so kind to introduce—"

"Do you mean to tell me that you have been doing bench research for an entire year and you don't know any standing members of the Human Subject Committee?" Dr. Reed rudely interrupted. "I find that, quite frankly, rather shocking. Shocking, I tell you, shocking!"

Brewster was just about to tell Harrison Reed to pucker up and plant one. Fortunately, reason stayed his tongue, but not for long.

Once composed, Brewster replied with sweet sarcasm. "No, I guess that I've just been working way too hard on the projects that Dr. Rabbi and Holcombe have been involved with. I just don't get out and socialize very much like you are able to do, Dr. Reed." Brewster turned to the members of the human subject committee and genuinely spoke from the heart. "Ladies and gentlemen, I will definitely make a point of meeting each one of you individually after today's conference."

The Rabbi, who had been quiet up until that point, dug the heel of his shoe sharply into the top of Brewster's foot underneath the conference table. Dr. Rabbi attempted to reel in the rebellious student in an effort to quell the skirmish that was being waged between his protégé and Dr. Reed. If it did not get under control now, this skirmish could break out into open warfare. Ever the politically correct mediator, the Rabbi asked, "Dr. Reed, are there other queries that you have for Mr. Brewster? He will be happy to answer any questions that you may have."

Dr. Reed ignored the Rabbi's question and said, "I certainly hope that we can get this meeting on track pretty soon. I know Dr. Beathard is going to have specific information to tell us about hepatitis B vaccine research."

Brewster realized that Dr. Rabbi was somewhat alarmed when he asked, "What is it, Harrison? I need to know what's going on."

Dr. Reed replied, "I'll be on the square with you, Dr. Rabbi. I honestly have no idea. We'll just have to wait until Bruce makes it back upstairs to fill in the details. In the meantime, I need to find out a little bit more about the brainiac that's working with you. J. D., I'm looking at your dossier. How's your health?"

Brewster found that to be somewhat of an odd question as it was only a few weeks before his twenty-third birthday. He replied, "Why, I'm fine, sir. Thanks for asking."

Reed pressed on. "Looking at your medical file, it appears that you had a bad injury to your left arm when you were only a child. Has that left you with any residual problems?"

Brewster shrugged his shoulders and replied, "I don't have a functional left deltoid muscle. It doesn't bother me too much, but it limits the abduction of my left arm. Nonetheless, I get by."

Reed continued with this peculiar line of questioning. "Does cancer tend to run in your family? What kind of testicular cancer did you have in the past? Was it a seminoma? Choriocarcinoma? Yolk sac? What exactly was it?"

It would absolutely be totally inappropriate to ask that kind of question in the twenty-first century. Courtesy of the HIPAA rules and regulations, that kind of information concerning intimate details about a person's health would, by law, remain private. The year 1980, however, was a very different time.

Initially, Brewster felt that he had nothing to hide. "I didn't have testicular cancer. The only person who ever had cancer in my family was my uncle, Cotton. He came down with gastric cancer a while back. He underwent a lap, but the doctors found that he had extensive metastatic disease involving the mesenteric lymph nodes and his omentum. He was declared to have a DNR code status and died soon after. That's the only blood relative that I know of who ever had a diagnosis of cancer. What makes you think that I ever had some type of malignant disorder?"

"I have your medical record from the mandatory physical examination that the Family Practice Department performed on you when you were admitted into the Gulf Coast College of Medicine," Dr. Reed replied. "The exam is dated July 14, 1977. Under past medical history, subheading, 'Surgical Procedures,' it's noted that you're now status post a left orchiectomy. You apparently have only one remaining gonad."

If Dr. Reed was trying to goad Brewster's gonad to anger, it was not working. J. D. Brewster certainly was not embarrassed by his predicament; however, he saw absolutely no bearing on how his personal medical circumstances could be of any consequence to the research projects that he had been involved with.

"Oh, that," Brewster replied. "I got the orchiectomy because I had a nonviable, undescended left testicle. The procedure was done when I was only a kid. I didn't have cancer, but my clinical condition was certainly considered to be a precancerous state at the time."

"Okay," Dr. Reed said, "I get the picture. That *is* quite enough."

"I couldn't agree more," Brewster said. "To be honest with you, now that I think about it, I shouldn't have answered *any* of these questions. My physical maladies are none of your business. It's not that I'm ashamed in any way of what I've been through in life, but to be frank, it's got nothing to do with my two research projects. I don't want to play this game anymore. If you keep up this line of questioning, I think I'll take my ball and go home!"

At that point, Dr. Balbona, began to laugh out loud. The research scientist clearly enjoyed seeing Dr. Reed's cage get rattled.

Once again, Dr. Rabbi had taken the heel of his shoe and jammed it down hard against the top of Brewster's foot to try and distract the young man from committing educational suicide.

Dr. Reed was clearly annoyed and stated, "Well, I'm glad Sergio has had a little laugh over all of this. Are you through now, Dr. Balbona? Perhaps it's time we find out what kind of man that J.D. Brewster really might be."

11

MD/PHD/(AND A LOT OF) BS

r. Reed got out of his chair and walked over to the window. With his back turned to the conference attendees, he continued the interrogation of J. D. Brewster to either embarrass the student, discredit him, or both. "So, J. D., I see that you and your high school team were winners of the Parochial School Science Challenge for the western regional United States back in the year 1975. You got published when you were a senior in high school. Tell me all about that."

Brewster wondered if he was being set up like a bowling pin. He replied, "First off, the credit goes to my high school buddies that were on the project. I just directed traffic. We started a two-year study using the rat as an animal model. We had a total of forty rats divided equally into an observational control group and the other that we referred to as the stressed group."

Brewster took a sip of water, cleared his throat, and continued. "The control group was pampered and treated as pets. The stressed group, to be frank, was tortured both physically and psychologically. In regard to the matter of physical stress, we would run an intermittent low-voltage current through the cages of the stressed rats at totally random times. Arbitrarily, we chose to do it four times a day. The electrical shock sessions would go on for three-second duration cycles. The electricity was generated and modulated by a standard commercial electric cattle fence transformer."

Dr. Clemmons voiced concern regarding the abuse that the test animals had been subjected to in this amateur experimental project. "What was the amperage in the voltage that you utilized on your test subjects?"

"Just enough to startle and annoy the animals," Brewster explained. "I must say, our technique worked quite well. Additional psychological stress was provided by a hungry neighborhood ally cat that would be allowed to paw at the subjects through the cages in which they were housed. The objective of the experimental study was to see if we could induce cardiac disease in the rats that had been recruited to participate in the stressed group."

"You were just high school students," Dr. Clemmons asked. "How did you pull this off?"

"One of the members in my research group had a father who was a staff member on the pathology service at the M. D. Anderson Tumor Institute," Brewster explained. "None of the animals were purposefully sacrificed. We simply followed their lives until the point of natural death. They were then subjected to postmortem evaluations courtesy of the pathologist who worked at M. D. Anderson. No microscopic studies were undertaken, but the thoraco-abdominal viscera and the brains of the test animals were evaluated by gross examination."

Dr. Holcombe was curious about the results and asked, "What did you boys stumble upon?"

Brewster replied, "The results were striking. The median survival of the pampered, controlled group was sixty-seven days longer than the experimental arm of the stressed group. As predicted, the experimental arm had significant cardiac and adrenal gland hypertrophy. What we did not predict, however, was the overwhelming evidence of increased neoplasia that was clearly found in the stressed group.

"You found cancer?" Reed asked.

"Now, this idea that stress may actually be a trigger for malignant disease is not a new concept. Galan had made that claim in his dissertation 'De Tumoribus' well over two thousand years ago. The evidence however, even now, is still a bit soft. What we found was certainly thought provoking. Maybe physical and psychological stress can actually contribute to the cause of cancer in human subjects. It's anecdotal, but where there's smoke, there may be fire."

It had appeared that Dr. Holcombe was intellectually stimulated, and he said, "Hot diggity, son! You just got timbered-up my tally-whacker like a tall tallow tree. Yes, indeed. You stuck your mitt into the big dipper to grab a craw-daddy, and you pulled yourself out a snipe! I'll bet it crawled up your long johns and blew soot up your chimney! That's for sure, that's for dang sure. Whowee!"

What was strange to J. D. Brewster was that the other members at the conference all nodded their heads in solemn agreement. How could it have possibly been that they knew what Uncle Hank was talking about? It sounded to Brewster, as best he could determine, that he needed to perform a mandatory, STAT evaluation of his own undergarments and specifically search for some type of unsavory critter that may have nestled into his under shorts. If some uninvited occupant had taken up residence amongst his curly cues, he hopefully would be able to rapidly dispatch with it by shaking it down a pant leg.

Years later, Brewster would wonder if that was the alleged thrill that the television political hack, Chris Matthews, had once noted when he infamously alleged that something had vigorously traversed up one of his lower extremities when Obama ran for president in 2008. By Matthews account, this sensation must have been quite pleasurable...

The probe by Dr. Reed continued. "You went to Dick Dowling University in Orange?"

Brewster replied, "Yes. I had a full ride."

Dr. Reed shook his head as if he were confused. "You could have gone elsewhere, and you decided to choose this small, obscure liberal arts college located in the triangle. I don't imagine that there are more than twenty-five hundred students enrolled there at any given time. Why on earth would you choose an institution of such marginal repute?"

Brewster assumed Dr. Reed had not heard him the first time. "Asked and answered. I had a full ride."

Dr. Reed studied his navel momentarily after he had returned to his chair and then proceeded to delve deeper into Brewster's background. "Did you continue your research at Dick Dowling?"

Brewster was actually appalled that Dr. Reed was trying to vet him. He had been at the Gulf Coast College of Medicine now for three years, and nobody had ever subjected him to such a line of questioning about his past. He could not shake the distinct feeling that he was going to be boxed into a corner and Dr. Reed would eventually crack a lead pipe across the back of his head.

Brewster replied, "Yes, but nothing panned out any further. Dr. Beverly Bartholomew was my research adviser. She had a great idea that the pathological effects that had been noted in the murine subjects from my high school experiment had to be a consequence to one of the acute stress hormones. The work that we did at the university level was obviously much more sophisticated. We subjected the test rats to the acute-phase, fight-or-flight hormones of epinephrine and norepinephrine. The theory postulated was that it was likely one or both of these two hormones that were responsible for any potential increased risk of cancer. What did we find? Nada. Zippo. Nothing."

"To be frank," Dr. Reed opined, "there's something blatantly discordant here, even to a casual observer. It would seem that you never generated a second published paper on your research. This is a fundamental problem with modern research. Investigators are fearful about publishing a negative report. I assure you right now that the study you did in high school was certainly thought provoking. If I was involved in cancer research, I would agree with the ideas of your research adviser from Dick Dowling. Dr. Bartholomew had conjured the next logical course of investigation."

"Well, I agree but it was a negative study. A negative report doesn't move the ball forward," Brewster said.

"That's not correct, J. D." Dr. Balbona said. "As a negative report was never submitted for peer review, there's nothing else out there in the medical or scientific literature that would currently prevent future researchers who are evaluating the etiology of cancer from repeating the same dead-end experiments over and over again. To me, it would seem that this would be just as important as the first paper published on this matter."

"I'm wondering, why you didn't further pursue this question about the possible relationship between stress and the onset of malignant disease once you were accepted into the dual program at our college of medicine?" Dr. Reed.

"I'm not sure. I guess I wanted to throw my hat into the ring on some other project."

"Why did you decide to tackle completely unrelated fields of research? Hepatitis B and also non-A, non-B hepatitis were totally unrelated to your primary realm of investigational experience?" Dr. Clemmons asked. "You had no previous practical 'hands-on' at all in this separate discipline of virology. I can't speak for the other members of this committee, but when you were admitted to the MD/PhD dual-training program I was under the impression that you would continue your basic science research into the etiology of malignant diseases. I think you might be missing the big picture by directing your attention away from the field of oncology. I can't tell you what to do, but my advice is for you to consider changing horses and getting back into cancer research. I truly believe that you were actually very close to one or more major scientific discoveries."

There was a question now on the table for which Brewster had absolutely no legitimate answer. "I guess I walked away from the cancer study at Dick Dowling while it was still in progress. Well In any event, I thought I would try my hand at some new endeavor once I had been accepted into the PhD program here at the Gulf Coast."

As it turned out, Dr. Clemmons was completely correct. Brewster failed to recognize a major opportunity that could have led to some important breakthroughs in the understanding of the role between psychological or physiological stress and the onset of malignant diseases.

Years later when scientists eventually discovered a dose-dependent relationship between the adrenal gland acute stress hormone, epinephrine, and the ABCB1 oncogene's affiliation to a P-glycoprotein cancer protective moiety, it finally dawned on J.D. Brewster that he made a mistake. He should have listened to the advice that Dr. Clemmons once offered. He should have kept his nose to the grindstone and continued his basic science research into the etiology of cancer.

While engaged in his undergraduate work, Brewster was on the threshold of an important scientific discovery that he was actually quite close to stumbling upon. If he had continued additional cancer research during the dual-training program at the Gulf Coast, he would have likely made the connection. Sadly, he didn't see the big picture.

A mercurial oddity, Brewster lacked the discipline to stay focused on only one task at a time. This was a deeply embedded character flaw that Brewster would never overcome. His lack of intuition would haunt him throughout his whole career and also his personal life.

Dr. Reed shifted gears. "It looks like you graduated from Dick Dowling University in just two years. Not only that, you had dual majors. Somehow, you managed to get a BA in biology and a BS in history. Even I must admit that was an impressive accomplishment, although it was achieved at a second-rate or maybe even a third-rate university. How did you manage to pull that off?"

"This query is coming from the man who got his undergraduate degree from the Mule Shoe State Techer's College in Sheep Fart, Texas?"

"We're talking about you now, not me," Reed answered.

Brewster was bemused by the backhanded compliment. "I went to a parochial high school that had a project for the senior students called the Momentum Program. It allowed students who were in the top ten percent of the senior class to take a full load of college-level courses. By the time I had graduated, I had twenty-eight hours of college credits already. When I enrolled at Dick Dowling University, I also skipped out more than an entire year of college by taking the CLEP tests."

Dr. Balbona was not sure what J. D. was referring to and asked, "What is CLEP?"

"Whowee, it's nasty, Sergio!" Professed Dr. Holcombe.

Dr. Clemmons knew better and replied, "CLEP stands for the College Level Examination Program. I swear, Hank, you are a naughty boy!" She flared her nostrils at Dr. Holcombe, and he returned the sentiment of mutual arousal.

Brewster felt a bit awkward at the overt display of sexual tension and interjected, "I don't recall the cost of the tests, but as Dick Dowling wanted me on board, I was given a grant that picked up the entire tab. I remember taking enough exams to get thirty-six hours of college credit. In conjunction with the 28 hours I already received from the Momentum Program, I had sixty-four hours of college credits before I even set foot upon the Dowling campus. The only downside from taking these CLEP exams is that I only got a score of pass or fail. As that was the case, that meant I couldn't screw up on any of my formal courses."

Dr. Rabbi added, "We need to kill more time while we wait for Dr. Beathard to come up from the parking lot. Explain to Dr. Reed and the other members of the committee what else you needed to do to get through college in such a short amount of time with degrees in two separate disciplines."

Brewster replied, "The rest was easy. I took summer college courses also. I obtained sixteen credits of summer college credit at the University of Houston immediately after I graduated from high school. I put away another sixteen hours of college credits between my first and second year at Dick Dowling University. Those thirty-two hours of extra credit that I salted away allowed me to graduate from college in just two years. Don't ask me the total number of credits I had under my belt when I left Dick Dowling University, but it was in the one hundred forty range I would guess."

Without looking up, Dr. Harrison Reed asked, "What's the rush? What are you running to? Or perhaps, the better question would be, what are you running away from?"

Brewster squirmed a bit, as Dr. Reed had hit a raw nerve.

"It would seem that you are on a dead sprint to get through life as quickly as possible," Dr. Reed observed. "I have generally found that the people that are rushing through life like this are the kind of people that are actually afraid of the very life they have been given. Would you be the type of person that I could pigeonhole into this category? Maybe to you, life is not a blessing but a burden."

Of course, that was precisely the case. Although Brewster was a deeply flawed man, he could not let on that Dr. Reed was correct about that assessment, or right about anything else for that matter. The medical student was able to maintain a poker face and nobody overtly recognized that he was a man living out his life in an emotional vacuum. "No, sir," Brewster said. "I'm simply goal directed."

"Fair enough." Dr. Reed continued to make small talk. "Did you participate in any sports while you were in high school or college?"

Brewster replied, "I ran track in high school, and I also ran a few months of track during my first year in college. My less-than stellar athletic career ended when I sustained a stress fracture on the metatarsal head of my left great toe. Although my foot allegedly healed up, it still bothers me to this very day. I don't know why I never really got over that injury. In any event, I was a quarter-miler, and I also ran on the 1,600 meter relay team. My best split ever was 48.7 seconds, and to be honest, that was only fair for a white boy. I couldn't compete against the blacks. No offense, Dr. Clemmons, but that's a fact. The black guys were beating me by two or more full seconds in the quarter."

"What are you saying, Brewster?" Are you implying that blacks are naturally faster than whites?" Dr. Clemmons asked.

Brewster was afraid to answer the question, so he focused his reply in the most narrow of parameters that he could possibly address. "I don't know. I'm only speaking from personal experience."

Years later, Brewster would be saddened by the fact that human beings were no longer able to talk about or even express admiration for any of the subtle differences that existed between ethnic groups, various races, or even the pleasurable and objectively measurable differences found between those humans who were born with an XX chromosomal arrangement versus those who were walking around with a set of the XY genetic complement. Perhaps the mythical pair of long johns that Hank Holcombe had spoken about just had too much starch in them.

It was now well past one o'clock in the afternoon. There was no sign of Bruce Beathard as of yet. The meeting was at a standstill until he arrived to convey the new information he had that would have a likely an impact on the hepatitis B vaccine research project. An awkward silence had overtaken the conference room, and the only sound Brewster heard was Dr. Reed clicking his ballpoint pen at a steady pace of one-second intervals.

After several more minutes, Dr. Clemmons felt compelled to break in the icy silence. "What do you do in your spare time, J. D.? Any hobbies?"

"As for now, I am the lead vocalist in a rock-and-roll band that performs 1960s music. Nothing serious, but we have played at a few bars and parties. We are usually paid with just enough money to buy gas. Sometimes we're compensated by adult beverages, and that's okay with me. We only had one gig ever outside of the Houston city limits at a blast from the past called Guano Dick. It's a dance bar on the River Walk in San Antonio, adjacent to the Kangaroo Court restaurant. Go-go dancers came out of the ceiling in wrought-iron cages, festooned in white boots and miniskirts. A lot of aging hipsters hang out there, so it was like stepping into a time-warp."

"How amusing," Reed said with disdain.

"Our next and very final performance will be down on Bellaire Boulevard on the Fourth of July at a place called Guaiac Dick," Brewster explained. As you might guess, it's a club owned by the same fellows that manage Guano Dick in San Antonio. Our lead guitarist is Blomeo Colima, and he's finishing his fellowship training in July. The band will no doubt dissolve upon his departure."

Dr. Holcombe was scratching away at the plaque on his left arm but was nonetheless intrigued about Brewster's band. "What's yer handle?"

Brewster replied, "We call ourselves DNR. Last year we tried a different name and called ourselves the Sucking Chest Wound. For some reason, that name was not particularly palatable to the members of our audience. If anybody likes 1960s rock-and-roll music, you are all invited to come down and watch us perform. We always open our first set with a song from 1966 called 'I Fought the Law' by the Bobby Fuller Four."

Dr. Holcombe surprised Brewster when he said, "Whowee! I saw those boys in El Paso back in the mid-sixties before they hit the big time. They laid down the tracks to that song at the now-defunct Mustang record label. Bobby Fuller died soon after those boys recorded that song, but he could pipe it like a fricasseed chickadee in a gnarly skeet. Whowee!" Now, that was surely something everybody could agree upon.

"In a gnarly skeet?" Brewster asked as if surprised. "Whowee!"

Dr. Reed had been disengaged from the previous conversations as he was reviewing Brewster's college transcripts from Dick Dowling University. "Mr. Brewster, if this works out for you, you will end up with an MD, PhD, and BS degree, but I note that you have your BS degree in history. You have the lesser BA degree in biology. If you were originally planning on going to medical school, how did that come to pass?"

Brewster replied, "It was purely by accident. My main interest in history is focused on the American Civil War and also on World War II. I took electives to investigate both of those historical periods. I had written a total of three term papers that were deemed to be good enough to have been published in the specialty warfare magazine *Slings and Arrows* in 1978. Getting published was considered master's-level work, and that credit propelled me to get a BS degree in history. You know, most universities only offer a BA in history. Dick Dowling is a rare exception."

"You didn't include that information on your resume when you applied to medical school," Dr. Reed noted. "What were these articles about?"

"Each article was constructed around the theme that a singular, simple oversight at a focal point in time changed the entire outcome in the course of human conflict," Brewster replied. "The first article I wrote was about the War Between the States. Civil War historians have argued it was Robert E. Lee's impetuous decisions on July 3, 1863, that lost the war for the Southern cause. I hold a different perspective. During the Battle of Gettysburg, Robert E. Lee ordered J.E.B. Stuart and his Comanche to outflank Seminary Ridge and attack the Union troops under George Meade from the rear. Stuart encountered just a few mounted Wolverines that he should have easily swept aside, but he was afraid that he had encountered a much larger defensive force. Instead of pressing on with his attack, he sounded retreat. Because of Stuart's failure to see the big picture, Pickett's Charge was not successful. The South never again mounted another major expeditionary force to attack the Union head on."

Dr. Balbona wanted to know more and asked Brewster about the other two articles that had been published in the *Slings and Arrows* magazine.

"Regarding the attack on Pearl Harbor," Brewster continued, "other historians have made the argument that Admiral Yamamoto failed because his aerial armada was unable to find and sink any of the U.S. aircraft carriers that had left Honolulu and were out on maneuvers. I hold a different perspective. I made the argument in my article that Yamamoto's big mistake was his failure to expend any ordnance on the oil reserves of the Pacific fleet. If he had done so, the U.S. Navy in the Pacific Theater would have been crippled for six to twelve months, and Japan would have won the war before it had even started. Because of Yamamoto's failure to see the big picture, the attack on Pearl Harbor was ultimately a failure. When Imperial Japan was unable to knock the United States out of the war with the attack on Pearl Harbor, the fate of the Japanese Empire was sealed."

"That's fascinating. I'm actually learning a lot from you today,"

Dr. Balbona said with interest. "What about the third article that you penned for *Slings and Arrows*?"

"My last publication on a historical subject was one I wrote about the Nazi atomic bomb project. Other historians have made the argument that the German bomb project was put on the back burner in December of 1941 when Albert Speer elected to pour Nazi resources into the V-1 and V-2 jet and rocket programs instead of atomic weapon research. While superficially true, historians should ask an important question: was that decision made only because of limited wartime resources and time constraints? I think not. I hold a different perspective. German physicist Walter Bothe was assigned the task of calculating the best material to utilize as a modulator in a uranium fission reactor. While Fermi and the allies had chosen graphite, Bothe made a mathematical miscalculation and erroneously concluded that graphite was unsuitable material for a nuclear reactor. Instead, the Germans had chosen to use heavy water, which was a much more difficult material to work with."

"Why was this decision an issue?"

"Although heavy water could theoretically have been used as a neutron modulator," Brewster noted, "it turned out to be a problematic course of action. Heavy water, in addition to be more difficult to work with, was a limited resource. As a case in point, the Nazi nuclear reactor, known as Kiln Four at Leipzig, went critical when there was an accidental heavy water leak, causing the device to blow up in the summer of 1943."

"What happened?" Dr. Clemmons asked.

"This was an enormous setback for the project," Brewster explained, "especially after the research into atomic weapon development had already been scaled back. In addition, the only source for heavy water was the Norsk Hydro-electric plant, and the allies proceeded to bomb that dam into nonoperational status. Enormous quantities of heavy water that had been collected for the project were also destroyed by saboteurs."

"We had better scientists," Dr. Reed noted.

"Quite true. As it turned out, the titular head of the German atomic bomb program, Werner von Heisenberg, was lazy. He never even bothered to check Walter Bothe's faulty math. Because of Heisenberg's failure to see the big picture, the plan to create a functional Nazi nuclear reactor wasn't successful. Unable to perform neutron multiplication experiments or to have the ability to ever breed plutonium," Brewster concluded, "the German atomic bomb program never reached the finish line."

"If Bruce doesn't get here by one thirty, we'll need to cancel this meeting and reschedule for another time. Is everybody okay with that?"

"No, absolutely not," Dr. Rabbi said. "I'm sorry, but I need an answer today about our hepatitis B project. To be honest, I'm quite alarmed about this alleged new information Dr. Beathard may have concerning hepatitis B vaccine research."

"What about you, Hank?" Dr. Reed asked.

"I'm paddling the same canoe upstream as the Rabbi."

"Okay, here we are," Dr. Reed reluctantly acquiesced. "We'll try and stick this out as long as we can. Just so everybody is aware of our time constraints, we're going to get the boot in about an hour. The Dietary Service Department is lined up to use this conference room next."

Dr. Clemmons changed the subject and said, "It doesn't hurt to chit-chat. What can you tell us about your family, J. D.?"

"I guess my inspiration to pursue a career in medicine came from my mother," Brewster replied. "She was an RN, and she achieved a bit of notoriety as she was the first scrub nurse under DeBakey when the first open heart surgeries were done in Houston after the war. She's now long retired, but I do try to see her on occasions. She lives in Bellaire and has for many years. My father was a lieutenant in the navy and served in the Pacific Theater. He graduated from the University of Houston before the war broke out, which enabled him to enter the service with the rank of an officer. In 1949, he used the GI bill to get his law degree from UT. For several years, he worked with the FBI on their organized crime task force before he joined the DA's office. Unfortunately, he had premature coronary artery disease, and he died when I was only a small boy. I have an older brother named Bill who works for the Tenneco oil company."

With the conclusion of Brewster's mini-dissertation about his own life, Dr. Reed looked up with an obvious scowl on his face. "Mr. Brewster, you had an impressive GPA of three point seven when you graduated from college. However, I am looking at some of the courses that you took at Dick Dowling. I'm astounded at the lengths that you had gone through to try and buff up your GPA. I find that, quite frankly, rather shocking. Shocking, I tell you, shocking."

This was the attack Brewster had been expecting, despite all of the superficial pleasantries that had been previously expressed. Reed came down hard. "You got three hours of college credit for taking a course called Film Appreciation? Are you kidding me? Tell me, Mr. Brewster, did you just watch movies in that college class?" Brewster replied, "Yes, but I had to write up a one-page critique over each of the films that I watched. I must have written up a dozen or more reports for that particular class!"

Reed openly laughed at the medical student. "That doesn't seem to be much of a challenge. Here is another college course that I must also ask you about. You got three hours of college credit for taking a course called Extraterrestrial Life. Are you kidding me? Tell me, Mr. Brewster—were there any field trips associated with that college class?"

This was about to get very ugly. "Oh, yes," Brewster answered. "We went to the planetarium at the north end of Hermann Park." Brewster stood up and jammed his chair hard against a conference table. "What's this all about? I was approved by this medical school's Admissions Council to enroll at this institution. I've been here now for three years. I believe that it's quite inappropriate for you to put the only gonad that I still possess into the meat grinder like this. If you don't like who I am or what I am, deal with it. Your tactics of intimidation are not going to force me to resign my position, if that's what you're thinking!"

Dr. Reed waved Brewster off and continued. "There were over a thousand applications for a hundred entry positions. Just how thorough could we possibly be with this admissions process? It's quite clear some reprobates such as yourself may have slipped through the cracks. Here is another course that looks quite suspicious to me. You took a course called Art Appreciation. Tell me Mr. Brewster, what in hell could you get out of a course like that?"

Brewster felt that his ears and the back of his neck were starting to feel hot. "I can tell the difference between Cubism and a Cuban, by God!" He responded to Dr. Reed.

Dr. Balbona was obviously pleased and shouted out, "Arriba!"

Dr. Reed quickly admonished the Cuban physician with a glance and continued the inquisition. "Oh, joy! Here's another course I have to ask you about. Did you actually take a course in college called 1960s Discotheque Dancing? You only earned a B in that course. Please tell me this is a joke."

It was now time for Mr. Brewster to go on the offensive. "It was absolutely no joke. I learned how to do the Twist, the Boogaloo, the Monkey, the Bird, the Batman, the Loco-motion, the Shimmy, the Swim, the Jerk, the Fly, the Temptation, the Limbo, the Gator, and also the Skate. Did you know that there were two variations of the Skate? Well, you should. One was the Egyptian, and the other was the Hitchhiker. I learned them all. The only dance I was not able to master was the Mashed Potato. I found that particular dance to be quite difficult. To do it correctly, the dancer must exert a considerable amount of internal rotation of the lower extremities. As I told you, I had a stress fracture on the metatarsal head of the great toe of my left foot from running track. I found that the Mashed Potato caused me a great deal of grief when I tried to pivot on the ball of that foot. I hope I have given you a correct forensic and anatomical overview as to why I only made a B in that course."

Dr. Reed was furious at that point and asked, "How could a course like that be of any benefit to you?"

Brewster did not skip a beat and retorted, "Asked and answered. I previously informed you that my rock-and-roll group, DNR, performed at the Guano Dick dance club in San Antonio. Fat older women dancing in birdcages wearing white go-go boots really dig me. Do I have to spell it out for you?"

Dr. Hank Holcombe grabbed Brewster's elbow and exclaimed, "That sounds like you're havin' more fun than a crippled three-toed mountain ape on a wombat run. Whowee!"

Brewster was quite pleased that Uncle Hank could see the big picture. "A wombat run? Whowee!"

Dr. Reed was not about to let Brewster have the last word on this matter, and the intentions of the PhD program director were now unmistakable. He was going to try to drive Brewster out of the dual-training program. "Mr. Brewster, when you were in college, you tried to buff your GPA by taking powder puff fluff. Well, boy, your transcript is filled with fluff! You, sir, are a fraud." Reed stood and slammed the top of the conference table with the open palm of his right hand and then added, "When you try to buff with fluff, it indicates what kind of man you truly are."

Earlier that day, Brewster had felt homicidal thoughts toward the prisoner named E. Rockholder. Those hostile impulses were returning now, and Brewster struggled to keep his emotions in check. "How dare you call me a fraud? I know for a fact that my MCAT entrance examination scores placed me in the top fifteenth percentile for the 1977 freshman class at the Gulf Coast."

"Sure, sure, sure," Dr. Reed said. "When you buff with fluff, a man like you would certainly have more time to prepare for that MCAT entrance examination. Is that right?"

Brewster continued his offensive tactics. "Don't be naïve, Dr. Reed! Every single one of my medical school colleagues who has any gray matter between their ears is certainly smart enough to buff with fluff. Yes, it's what I did! In fact, dollars to doughnuts, it's what we *all* did! I'm not ashamed of it. Go ask any of my medical school colleagues; they're not ashamed of it either. There are specific criteria that need to be met to get enrolled in medical school. I met those criteria. In fact, I met all the requirements in spades. That's why I'm here. *Everybody* in my entrance class met those criteria. When you get accepted into a medical school, you get a fat envelope in the mail. Well, I got the fat envelope. Who in hell cares how I got it?"

Dr. Reed was about to throw the book at J. D. for gross insubordination when Bruce Beathard finally entered the conference room and made a casual understatement. "It looks like I'm about forty-five minutes late. I'm sorry, but my lunch hour was somewhat unpleasant."

Dr. Clemmons clapped her hands and said, "Welcome back, superhero. What happened out there?"

Dr. Beathard was covered with sweat, and it looked as if he had taken a shower with his clothes on. He had grease on his right hand, and it had smeared onto his jacket and shirt. He replied, "I was down in the parking lot conducting some business when it appeared that one of our nurses was being beaten to death by two hoodlums. I don't know if she put up a fight, but it appeared that they wanted to steal her purse, or car, or perhaps both. Maybe I'm wrong and they just thought it was the right time of day to go out and beat the hell out of some poor soul. All that I do know is that they got away with nothing, as we managed to chase them away into Hermann Park. The police were still looking for them by the time that I made it back up here to the conference room."

"Who was the victim?" Dr. Reed asked. "Is it anybody that we know?"

"Of course," Beathard replied. "All of you know her. The victim is the day-shift charge nurse from the med-surg floor, Ms. Irene Segulla. She's now blind in her left eye, and she sustained extensive facial trauma. She had a blowout fracture, and her nose, mandible, and maxilla were all pulverized. She's going to be in surgery for a long time. I'll be frank with all of you; she may have sustained lethal injuries."

Dr. Reed rightfully determined that it was time for a fifteen-minute break, and he encouraged everybody to get up and move about. He told Dr. Beathard to go to the staff washroom and get freshened up before the meeting resumed. "Take a break, everybody. We've been stalling all of this time with meaningless chit-chat because Dr. Beathard was occupied with more important matters. Now that this situation has been rectified, let's reconvene at one thirty. By then, we'll be one hour behind schedule, but we still have two items on the agenda that need to be tackled today. Come hell or high water, according to Dr. Rabbi and Dr. Holcombe, we'll have to get this done today. I still think we can wrap this up before the Dietary Service comes in here and boots us out. Brewster is going to fill us in on the progress of the hepatitis B vaccine study that he's been working on with Dr. Rabbi. After that, we need to hear from him where things stand in trying to isolate the non-A, non-B hepatitis entity that he's been working on with Hank Holcombe. I'll see all of you momentarily."

Brewster sat in stunned silence after learning what happened to Ms. Segulla. He felt guilty about the whole matter. After all, if he had simply stayed in the parking lot a bit longer and helped out with her dead car battery, perhaps none of this would have happened. While the student was wallowing in self-recrimination, everybody else left the conference room—except for the Rabbi.

Yeshua Rabbi was a brute with a barrel chest and large hands, although he was in his mid-sixties. He looked like a larger and more powerful edition of the former secretary of state during the Nixon administration, Henry Kissinger. The Rabbi was a man of few words. When he did speak, however, he had a distinct, thick Eastern European accent.

Once everybody else had departed the conference room to take a short break, Dr. Rabbi stood up and grabbed the combative medical student by his left arm and pulled him out of his chair. Brewster got pushed up hard against the wall, and Dr. Rabbi got only an inch away from his face.

Fearful that he was about to be physically injured, Brewster closed his eyes. His mentor quietly said. "J. D., what in the hell is wrong with you? You better start showing some restraint here. If Dr. Reed pulls out his puny pecker and proceeds to piss on your pants, you better persevere! He's getting the better of you. Take it like a man. Next time, before he zips up his fly, you'll offer to dab the dew from his lily with your necktie. Am I clear?"

After Brewster had sheepishly confirmed that Dr. Rabbi's orders were crystal clear, Yeshua Rabbi stormed out of the room once he had released the student's lapels. The stunned but ever-rebellious medical student's legs were shaking when he collapsed at the conference table as if he was but a crumpled and discarded paper coffee cup.

12

PIMP AND PONE

By 1:35 p.m., J. D. Brewster had already composed himself as the rest of the conference attendees were returning to their seats. The student was quite preoccupied about what had happened to Ms. Segulla and was also quite ashamed that he did not have enough initiative to act upon his suspicions about the two carjackers who were walking about in the parking lot before the assault had occurred. If he had done so, perhaps he would have scared away the two individuals.

That was, however, just wishful thinking on his part. If the truth be told, Brewster would have received a pipe upside his head if he had approached the two thugs. While Brewster was obviously concerned about the fractured face of Ms. Segulla, he was also concerned about his fractured relationship with the Rabbi. Would the recent altercation with the Rabbi lead to the student's dismissal from the dual-training program?

The student was surprised when Dr. Rabbi sat right beside Brewster as if nothing at all had happened between them. He patted Brewster on his knee and said, "J. D., my son, knock 'em dead with the update about our research program! I would like to make a motion that the Human Subject Committee give us a straight up-or-down vote at the end of today's session as to whether we will be able to proceed with a pilot study utilizing human subjects in the next phase of our hepatitis B vaccine project."

The motion received a second affirmation but the formal roll-call vote was immediately tabled until the medical student could present his formal report. Nonetheless, Brewster felt relieved that the altercation with the Rabbi was already water under the bridge.

Dr. Reed kicked off the session. "Well, now that we have Bruce Beathard here, we can finally begin this meeting in earnest. There's no more time for small talk. No more Mulligan strokes from the tee box. Mr. Brewster, you are now officially up to bat. You are obliged to give us a state of the union address on your projects with Dr. Rabbi and Hank Holcombe."

Brewster began. "Let me first start off by giving everybody an update on my hepatitis B vaccination project with Dr. Yeshua Rabbi, as we have certainly made considerable headway. I have handouts for everyone to specifically see how we devised a technique to neutralize the hepatitis B virus. As you'll note, our technique includes utilizing both a multistep chemical bath process, in addition to a freeze-drying desiccation technique. Dr. Rabbi and I are absolutely one hundred percent certain our technique neutralizes the virus completely. The next step is to get formal approval from the Human Subjects Committee to allow us to start an in-house pilot study on human subjects."

A member of the Human Subjects Committee asked, "Do you actually have a protocol at this time for us to review? Typically, a feasibility pilot study will usually incorporate somewhere around one or two dozen human subjects with the objective to make certain that the product is safe in human beings."

"Mr. Brewster is working on that as we speak," Dr. Rabbi replied.

"Well, on behalf of the other members on this review board, we thought that a protocol would be available as for us to review at this time," the committee member pointedly said.

"I need to ride you hard over this matter, Yeshua," Dr. Beathard complained, "as this seems to be a recurrent theme of procrastination on your part. I can't blame Mr. Brewster over this issue, as you're the chief cook overlooking this pot of chili. It's not only about this hepatitis B vaccine project, but it seems to be an issue with every endeavor you've undertaken at this institution."

"Stop right there, Bruce," Dr. Rabbi said defensively. "I'm offended you're unable to recognize the great work that we have accomplished over the course of just one year. What's the matter with you? You're not even looking at this report that Mr. Brewster has passed out. Open your eyes and see what I'm talking about. This meeting is already behind schedule. We're running out of time."

"You're sadly mistaken. As far as I am concerned," Dr. Beathard sneered, "you've *already* run out of time." Although not particularly adept at grasping the nuances of human-to-human interactions, Brewster readily perceived that the vice-chairman was now exhibiting open hostility toward his mentor.

"If and when the time comes, a stipend should be offered to individuals who are willing to sign up for a pilot study," another committee member said. "You might find it troubling, but the university will not pay a stipend directly to any person who wants to participate in a pilot study. It is up to you, Mr. Brewster, to hammer out some way with Dr. Rabbi to allocate a small honorarium of financial compensation from the general grant money that the university has already set aside for your project."

Dr. Reed bypassed Brewster altogether and addressed the director of the project. "Dr. Rabbi, how many of the experimental animal subjects have sero-converted to a state of confirmed immunity?"

Dr. Rabbi knew this hard question was coming. He replied, "None, but we were not officially looking for the development of immunity at this point. Before we can look for the development of immunity in the animal models, we had to first confirm that the material we inoculated them with was indeed safe and it would not result in an overt infection from an activated hepatitis B virus."

In an attempt to deflect the uncomfortable questions in Dr. Reed's interrogation, Dr. Rabbi added, "Mr. Brewster, is there anything else you would like to add to your optimistic report?"

J. D. Brewster was filled with pride, and he thought that he was going to deliver some surprising news that would be well received by his mentor, the Rabbi. Brewster began, "Recently, Dr. Rabbi and I presented in abstract form this new information about our virus neutralization technique. We provided the pertinent information on a poster board at the conference in San Antonio this past March. It appeared to generate some interest. I have in my hand an introductory letter that I received from the West German bio-pharmaceutical company, Leben Kur, AG. They want to buy out the hepatitis B research work that we have done to date!"

There was a round of applause from the attendees, and even from Dr. Reed. He was obviously pleased that there was potential economic benefit to the college of medicine that appeared to be close at hand. Everybody looked relieved except for the Rabbi, who had cradled his forehead in the palms of both of his hands and remained silent.

When Brewster's mentor raised his head, his face was filled with anguish. "Listen to me everybody; we can never do business with these people! Not now, not ever." The collective members of the Human Subject and PhD Committee looked about with confusion concerning Dr. Rabbi's statement.

Dr. Rabbi stood and slowly removed his jacket and draped it over the back of his chair. As he rolled up the left sleeve of his dress shirt, he exposed a series of numbers that had been tattooed onto the ventral aspect of his forearm. Underneath the row of numbers was a triangle. Perhaps it was a tattoo of the Greek letter delta. In any event, the numbers and the symbol appeared indistinct, as the ravages of time had made them look as if they had been smeared. The tattoo was indeed many decades old. Those who were present quickly and painfully realized that the Rabbi had received the tattoo when he was incarcerated as a young man. Sadly, the meaning of it all was dreadfully clear.

Dr. Balbona broke the awkward silence and asked, "Auschwitz? Dachau? I'm sorry, Yeshua. I never knew. Did everybody who was sent to the extermination camps get a tattoo?"

"I was at sub-camp three at Monowitz," Dr. Rabbi replied. "The victims who were sent off to get immediately gassed and then turned into ash did not get tattoos. There was no need for that. Only the working slaves got the tattoos."

"What does this have to do with the Leben Kur pharmaceutical company?" Dr. Balbona asked.

"It has everything to do with it," Dr. Rabbi explained. "Once the SS figured out that I had medical training, I was pulled out of the chemical factory and sent over to assist the Nazi physicians with their experiments that they were conducting on the *untermenschen*, or sub-humans, as we were so fondly referred to. As it turned out, Leben Kur and the SS had a hand-in-glove arrangement."

J. D. was stunned and realized the misery that his mentor must have endured. He added, "Dr. Rabbi, I thought that I knew a lot about the subject of World War II. To be honest, I believe I learned enough to actually teach the subject matter at a university level. I just don't understand the implied connection you're making between the war and a minor, rather obscure German bio-pharmaceutical firm. What—well, what happened to you?"

When the Rabbi turned his face toward Brewster, it appeared that the professor had aged another twenty years. Dr. Rabbi answered, "I doubt that any of you would have known about the grizzly details. It was a big secret. Yes, I know that many of you are quite aware that medical experiments were carried out on human subjects at the concentration camps. However, it is unlikely that you are aware that these brutal and barbaric experiments were funded by many of the German pharmaceutical companies that had existed at the time. One of these companies was Leben Kur, AG. As you can plainly see, this company is still very much in business to this very day."

"To what degree was this company involved in human experiments?" Brewster asked.

"You'd have to ask them," the Rabbi answered, "but I do know that funding for these medical experiments was paid by Leben Kur, AG, directly to the SS."

Dr. Clemmons noted, "I was aware that some types of medical experiments were performed on concentration camp victims, but I certainly did not know that human experimentation was funded by German pharmaceutical companies. What types of experiments were performed on these poor souls?"

Rabbi took a deep breath and continued. "The Nazis would put human subjects in ice water and see how long it would take for them to die from hypothermia. They would skin human beings alive to see how long it would take for a person to die if they didn't have any intact integument. No anesthesia was utilized during these procedures; however, I must compliment the Nazi doctors for at least having the decency to utilize properly sterilized medical equipment when a prisoner was subjected to vivisection."

"Please, Yeshua," Dr. Clemmons said with an obvious look of horror on her face, "no more."

"After all, when it came to surgical procedures the Nazis were quite hygienic. Perhaps my terminology is not quite correct. Maybe the word I was looking for was *eugenic*. Anyhow, I also remember that they would sequentially burn victims alive to see what percentage of body surface area could be destroyed by third-degree burns, and how long subjects could survive such an ordeal."

"What could possibly be gained by these pseudo-scientific experiments?" Dr. Balbona wondered.

"Think about it for a moment. If a soldier suffered a burn injury and he was facing a fifty percent or greater chance of up-front mortality from the ordeal, the limited medical resources that were available to the Nazis during the time of war would likely warrant that medical care would be withheld from such an individual. It all makes practical sense, I suppose."

"I guess it makes practical sense," Brewster added, "if one were a Nazi."

Dr. Rabbi had a dark and disturbing story to tell. As he became glassy-eyed, he drifted back into time to relive the horrors of his incarceration. He was compelled to give testimony to what he had witnessed. "The Nazi physicians would take a person and burn ten percent of the body, then twenty percent of the body, and so on, until the subject finally died in agony. From what I witnessed, they used a blowtorch to burn off a victim's skin."

"Stop, Yeshua," pleaded Dr. Clemmons. "I believe that's enough."

"I'll always remember the high-pitched screams when the subjects were chained down and were slowly incinerated," elaborated Dr. Rabbi, oblivious to Dr. Clemmons's protests. "I'm not certain as to why, but the screaming usually stopped abruptly after about the time that sixty percent of a victim's skin had been burned away. At that point, the victims would look on almost placidly while they were being immolated with a blowtorch."

"Stop, Dr. Rabbi," Regina Clemmons again asked. "I don't want to hear any more of this."

Emotionally, Dr. Yeshua Rabbi was a boulder rolling downhill, and he was gathering undeniable momentum. "I always wondered about that oddity. Do you think it might have been from a release of internal endorphins as somebody was being cooked alive? The victims were very much like a skewered bratwurst that would sizzle and pop over an open fire at a Boy Scout overnight camping trip."

For Brewster it was yet again another peculiar episode of déjà vu. After all, did not the evil prisoner, E. Rockholder, say the exact words to the student, almost verbatim? What did it mean? Was it part of some type of cosmic puzzle that he wasn't smart enough to put together? For a brief moment, the experience caused Brewster to develop a transient decrease in the visual acuity of his left eye. He rubbed his face vigorously. Fortunately, his vision completely cleared after only a few seconds.

"It was the Nazis who confirmed the ten percent burn/ten percent mortality rule; there is a ten percent risk for mortality expected for every ten percent of third-degree body burn that was inflicted upon a human subject. For example, if somebody had received ninety percent third-degree burns over his or her entire body, you could be assured that the victim was looking at a ninety-percent probability of up-front mortality. You could take that to the bank," Dr. Rabbi summarized.

As an afterthought, Dr. Rabbi added, "Oh, I almost forgot. There were also inoculation experiments where infectious agents were directly injected into—"

"Please, stop," proclaimed Dr. Clemmons in a voice that was brimming with panic. "For the love of God, I have heard more than enough!"

With continued pleadings from Dr. Clemmons, the Rabbi finally snapped right back into the year 1980. He realized that he had gone too far and apologized to everybody in the room.

After a moment of stunned silence, the sarcastic and incredibly cruel Dr. Reed stated, "Thank you, Yeshua, for that lovely trip down Memory Lane."

"Well," Dr. Beathard asked, "where do we stand with all of this? Personally, I really don't care if Leben Kur collaborated with the damned Hun in the past. That's ancient history, as far as I'm concerned. Trust me on this—if this drug company wants to do a straight-up deal right now, we should strike while the iron is hot."

"This clandestine Nazi collaboration that Leben Kur allegedly had with the Nazis may prove to be problematic to our medical college down the road," Harrison Reed surmised. "To be honest, I suspect Dr. Rabbi is telling the unembellished truth about this matter. In the future, if this ever sees the light of day, it would give our institution a black eye if we ended up doing business with this particular pharmaceutical firm. Therefore, we just can't risk having any financial arrangement with these people."

"Wait," Dr. Beathard petitioned, "we should only conclude this matter with a formal vote. I'm warning you, Dr. Reed; you'll be making a big mistake if you decide to give Leben Kur a cold shoulder after the offer that they tendered."

"No, Bruce, I don't think so." Dr. Reed ordered, "Don't start an argument with me about this situation! This matter is certainly not open for further debate, much less a formal vote. It's time to move on."

Brewster had erroneously assumed that the PhD training program director had moral qualms about dealing with a company that overtly supported the Nazi regime. However, was that indeed the case? For Dr. Reed, perhaps what was even more important than any potential lost revenue or ethical considerations was the institution's fledging reputation, or lack thereof, if the truth be told.

Reed concluded, "I demand that we now table any thoughts about selling the data Dr. Rabbi and Mr. Brewster have acquired regarding the neutralization of the hepatitis B virus to a third party, especially one that may have funded Nazi experiments."

"Thank you, Reed," the Rabbi said with considerable gratitude.

"We'll see if you'll be thanking me later," Dr. Reed replied. "I think it's time to turn the floor over to Bruce Beathard to hear about what new information he has obtained that will have bearing on Rabbi and Brewster's research project. Bruce, please fill us in on what you've learned about competing efforts to develop a new hepatitis B vaccine for commercial purposes."

"Gladly," Beathard replied in a raised and angry voice while he darted his eyes about the room, as if something sinister was afoot. The medical student had just witnessed the research scientist being publicly spanked by Dr. Harrison Reed, and Brewster looked over to Dr. Rabbi nervously with raised eyebrows.

After Dr. Beathard was rebuked by his boss, the vice chairman of the PhD program was now intent on crashing the hepatitis B vaccine project into a brick wall. If Dr. Reed elected not to consider selling the hepatitis B vaccine research project to a foreign entity, so be it. If the medical school lost its entire investment on this dead-end research project, so be it. Beathard was now livid, and he wanted to actually bring fiscal harm to the Gulf Coast College of Medicine after his suggestion of selling out the hepatitis B vaccination data to the German pharmaceutical company was rejected. His hostile demeanor clearly implied to the other committee members that something bad was barreling down the turnpike, and it was headed straight toward J. D. Brewster and Dr. Yeshua Rabbi at breakneck speed.

"It looks like it's my duty to get this meeting back on track," Bruce Beathard said. "Now, Mr. Brewster, it seems that you have had only one a year of bench work in the laboratory. I understand that you haven't had any patient contact or done any clinical rotations as of yet. Is that correct?"

Brewster replied, "No, sir. At the end of June I will officially have two clinical rotations under my belt, so I have indeed had a fair amount of patient contact at this time."

Dr. Beathard seemed superficially pleased and asked, "So, is it safe to assume that you know how to play the game pimp and pone? It's an important teaching tool that we use here at the Gulf Coast."

Brewster answered, "I certainly understand when a student gets a pimp job from a resident or a fellow, but I don't exactly understand the part about giving back pone. To be honest, I'm not even sure what the word *pone* exactly means. Is the game pimp and pone something like going out for trick or treat on Halloween?"

Dr. Holcombe tried to be helpful and offered an explanation. "Pone is like getting all swolted up."

What in hell did that mean? Everybody else in the conference room nodded their heads as if something profound had been said, but Brewster had furrowed his eyebrows in abject confusion.

"Is that a good thing or bad thing?" Brewster searched for clarity. "Can you use the word *pone* in context? Can I buy a vowel?"

Dr. Holcombe proceeded to expound his definition. "For your edja-makay-shin, I will put the word *pone* in a sentence you kin sabe. Listen up now and I'll give you a crystal-clear example: 'When I saw them there necked tarts, I commenced to get all poned-up like a stomped on horny toad.' Whowee! Do you see what I mean?"

"My synapses are starting to run out of neurotransmitters," Brewster replied. "I better start talking to somebody who speaks the King's English as a primary language. If not, I'm going home right now."

Bruce Beathard tried to assuage Brewster's angst and said, "Don't be fooled when Uncle Hank employs prolific country-bumpkin verbiage. As you well know from your work with him, he's a first-rate scientist. Allow me to expound on the rules of the game that we call pimp and pone."

Brewster suddenly realized that he was about to end up on the gummy side of some malicious act of psychological torture that was about to be done in the name of medical education.

Dr. Beathard continued, "A person can only get a pimp out by somebody higher up in the food chain. For example, it's legal for an attending physician to pimp anybody downstream. He or she can and will pimp a fellow, a resident, an intern, or student. A fellow can only pimp a resident, intern, or student. A resident can only pimp an intern or student. By the rules, an intern can only pimp the student. You're not allowed to pimp uphill; you can only pimp downhill. Get it?"

Brewster needed a bit of clarification. "Who can the student pimp?"

Beathard scowled and raised his palms at the ceiling and said, "Nobody! There's no life-form that is lower than a medical student." Dr. Beathard turned to Harrison Reed and asked a rhetorical question, "How did this guy ever get into the dual-training program?"

Without waiting for an answer, Dr. Beathard turned his attention back to J. D. and said, "Well, there you have it. It's standard to get pimped with three questions. The pimp will start the game by calling out 'batter up' to somebody lower in the food chain, and then the fun starts. The person who is getting pimped is called the batter. If the pimp stumps the batter two out of three times, then the pimp has won the game. If the pimp stumps the batter three times in a row, then the pimp has not only won the game, but he's pitched a shutout. It's proper etiquette for the pimp to point a finger at the batter after a shutout and proclaim, 'No hitter!' Get it?"

Beathard continued, "Conversely, every time a batter answers a question correctly, then the pimp gets poned. If the batter is able to pone the pimp two out of three times in that round, then the batter won that game. If a batter is smart enough to answer three questions in a row correctly, then he not only won that game, but he was good enough to have hit a grand slam. It is proper etiquette for the batter to point a finger at the pimp after a grand slam and shout out, 'You got poned!' Okay, Mr. Brewster, let's play a round of pimp and pone. Batter up!"

Brewster jumped out of his chair and stood at attention when Bruce Beathard asked the first question. "First pitch: Is the hepatitis B virus a RNA or a DNA type of a virus?"

For Brewster, the answer to the first pitch was easy. "It is a DNA virus."

"Very good," Dr. Beathard confirmed. "Second pitch: What organism causes Chagas disease?"

Brewster knew the answer to that question also and thought it would be fun to interject some humor. "The bug is called trypanosoma cruise control or some such critter."

Dr. Beathard replied, "You are not as dumb as I thought. It's 'cruzi', not 'cruise control.' Don't be a jerk-weed. You're not a stand-up comic. If you know the right answer, just spit it out. I'll give you credit this time."

Now it was time for Dr. Beathard to subject Brewster to the last question in the round of pimp and pone. "Third pitch: When was the last recorded case of smallpox?"

Fortunately for Brewster, this third question was also in his wheelhouse. "Through the hard work of the World Health Organization, the smallpox virus has been essentially eradicated from the planet earth at large. The virus is now only viable in certain licensed research laboratories. I suspect, however, that certain countries are able to batch produce a weaponized version of this bug to be used as a tool of mass destruction in case there is ever an outbreak of biological warfare."

"Look, Brewster, don't give me lecture on the history of infectious diseases that afflict human kind," Beathard complained. "Just answer the question!"

"Okay by me if you don't want me to explain things in detail," Brewster said. "It was just two years ago in 1978 when the last recorded case of smallpox had unfortunately occurred. It happened when a mishap transpired at the Birmingham School of Medicine."

"You got it right, junior. You can pipe down now," Beathard ordered.

"I'm just getting to the good part," Brewster said, oblivious to the fact he was starting to annoy Dr. Beathard. "It was a laboratory accident that resulted in two cases and one death. As I recall, the research scientist who was responsible for the mistake that caused the outbreak became so distraught that he committed suicide. I'm not certain about all of the details, but I believe he ate a bullet from his own gun. If you put the barrel of a gun in your own mouth, you have to be brave to pull the trigger. In any event, it was all a very sad affair. Correct me if I am wrong, but I believe I just hit a grand slam. Dr. Beathard, you just got poned!"

The attendees politely clapped, and Dr. Beathard stated, "You see? That's just how easy the game is played. You just poned me! That felt really good, did it not?"

Brewster readily agreed with that sentiment.

Brewster realized that Dr. Reed and the members of the Human Subject Committee were becoming impatient, as one attendee was tapping his finger against his wristwatch while another began to shuffle papers about rather loudly. It was clearly time for Bruce Beathard to now reveal the secret information that he had harbored about hepatitis B vaccine research.

Dr. Reed pressed Beathard to get to the point and said, "Bruce, this meeting will be ending in twenty minutes. As we have some serious time constraints here, I strongly suggest that if you have any new information that will have bearing on the hepatitis B vaccine investigation, that you reveal it now. We haven't even had a chance for Brewster tell us about his other research project as of yet."

Dr. Beathard was not deterred and stated, "It's important for me to make sure Brewster understood how to play the game pimp and pone, as I have a big revelation coming right now." Dr. Beathard turned to the Rabbi and declared, "Batter up."

Dr. Rabbi vehemently protested and said, "Bruce, you can't pimp me. I'm a full, tenured professor at this institution. I don't want to rub your nose in it, but you don't even have tenure. At this rate, if you ever try a little stunt like that again, you'll never be offered a permanent post at this institution. Don't insult me. You're only pegged at an assistant professorship level. Remember it's against the rules to pimp up the food chain!"

The Rabbi was correct. Dr. Beathard had just committed an egregious pimp and pone protocol violation. "There are apparently institutional rules about this game called of pimp and pone," Brewster interjected. "You just taught me these rules, and now you're violating them. If you're going to break the rules right off the bat, I'm not going to play this stupid game, either."

Although stung by another rebuke, Beathard still held all the cards. The vice chairman nodded and nervously pulled at his neck tie, while he plotted his spiteful revenge against the Rabbi, who just pulled out a piping hot dish of crow from the oven and jammed it into

Beathard's face. Thoroughly embarrassed, Beathard pointed back at J. D. Brewster instead and said, "Batter up. First pitch: Does the name Dr. Maurice Hilleman from Philadelphia mean anything to you?"

Brewster shook his head to indicate that this was a name not familiar to him.

However, the name was quite well known to the Rabbi. Yeshua actually appeared to be suddenly terrified. He reached up and stretched out his arm across the abdomen of J. D. Brewster, who was still standing. The defensive action was as if the research scientist was trying to protect his student collaborator from some great calamity.

Bruce Beathard was just warming up. "I forgot to tell you, J. D., you're able to ask for a pinch hitter in the game of pimp and pone. If you do get stumped, you're permitted to ask for assistance from a colleague. So, Rabbi, do you want to help out your protégé or not?" Dr. Rabbi sat in stunned silence as he had already figured out that an unwelcomed heavy hitter was apparently looming on the sidelines. If called up from sitting on the bench, the deployment of this particular heavy hitter would indeed be a game changer, and the Rabbi knew it.

"So, Yeshua," Dr. Beathard continued, "does the cat have your tongue? Well, Brewster, it seems your mentor knows who Dr. Maurice Helleman is, but you don't. Well, let me fill you in. During World War II, Helleman developed a vaccine to protect American serviceman from the Japanese Encephalitis B infection. In the early 1960s, he developed the MMR vaccine. Frankly, he is considered to be the world's greatest virologist and vaccinologist. He's apparently one demanding taskmaster to work for with a reputation for being a perfectionist, but nonetheless, he is a steely-eyed stud of the first order. He is now officially under contract with Merck."

Brewster was starting to sense that his research project with Dr. Rabbi was about to be derailed.

Bruce Beathard continued, "Second pitch: Would you like to take a wild guess as to what the good Dr. Helleman has been working on for the last few years?"

Brewster and his mentor both remained silent, but by then, the Rabbi had also arisen out of his chair. It was as if both the student and the professor were standing before a judge and were awaiting a penitentiary sentence after the conviction of a crime that the two men had committed together.

Beathard asked, "Is the suspense starting to make you boys twitch just a bit? He happens to be working on a vaccine for the hepatitis B virus, and I must tell you that he's far ahead of where you guys are at this time."

In a flat and barely audible monotone, Yeshua Rabbi asked, "You know this how?"

Beathard disregarded the question and continued with his painful revelation. "Can you guess how Helleman figured out a way to inactivate the virus without completely destroying it? It seems what you boys have done here at the Gulf Coast was to develop a technique that completely destroys the virus without leaving any trace."

"You don't know that for certain, Bruce," countered the Rabbi.

"I'm afraid I do, Yeshua," Beathard replied with confidence. "You boys created a product that doesn't engender any immune response from the animal test subjects. Well, it appears that Helleman and his crew made the breakthrough that took the Merck pharmaceutical company to the next level."

Bruce Beathard turned to address the other members of the committee who were present at the conference table. "While Helleman and the Rabbi appeared to be on a similar path, Dr. Helleman's team found that they could actually denature the virus with a combination of formaldehyde, urea, and pepsin. This chemical bath worked without going through the extra effort of adding a freeze-dry step to the process that Brewster had developed."

"You know this how?" Dr. Rabbi asked.

"I must admit, you guys got very close," Beathard confessed without specifically answering Dr. Rabbi's question. "You picked formaldehyde and ethanol for your chemical bath, but it didn't occur to you to drop the ethanol from the equation and add pepsin and urea instead. Yes, you boys indeed got close. Very close, as a matter of fact, but no Cuban cigar."

Dr. Beathard reached into his briefcase and pulled out a thick binder and motioned with his hand that the document should be shared among the committee members. "I have only one confidential handout that I've acquired, and I will pass it around for the other members at this meeting to review. This material can't leave this room with anybody except for me. I'll need to destroy all of these documents as soon as this meeting has drawn to a conclusion."

Again, the Rabbi asked, "You know this how?"

Beathard ignored the Rabbi, as if he was nothing more than a misfortunate armadillo that had been pancaked by a pickup on an open highway. Beathard appeared to enjoy inflicting these fatal wounds on the Rabbi's research project. He turned toward Dr. Rabbi and Brewster and said, "Please sit down, gentleman. I'm almost finished here."

For Brewster, the game of pimp and pone was not yet over. "Get ready," Beathard warned. "Here comes the third pitch: Do you have any idea how close Merck is on getting this vaccine to the market?"

"I would anticipate by your unbridled enthusiasm for our very own research project that is apparently going down in flames," Brewster said with sharp sarcasm, "that Merck's vaccine is right around the corner."

"It's even closer than you think," Beathard clarified. "The vaccine they developed is now well into Phase III trials. If all goes well, the FDA will likely approve that this vaccine gets launched next year, or maybe in '82 at the latest. To convince all of you of the veracity of this information, I'll show you in this other folder that I have reports that will show you the short list of the trade names that the Merck marketing department is now considering to label their new vaccine. Ladies and gentlemen, Dr. Rabbi and Mr. Brewster are probably three to five years behind what Helleman and his crew have done for Merck thus far."

Beathard smirked at J. D. Brewster and said, "I've just pitched a shutout."

Although there was no applause, Bruce Beathard took a bow, and then he poked his index finger on the sternum of J. D. Brewster while he triumphantly proclaimed, "Better than that, I just pitched a no-hitter! Boy, you just got pimped."

Brewster had transiently lost the vision of his left eye. He bent over and cupped his left hand over his eye socket, but fortunately this symptom would rapidly subside. This frightening phenomenon was appearing with greater frequency, but fortunately the medical student was, as of yet, not left with any apparent residual neurological deficits when the symptoms spontaneously receded.

As for the Rabbi, he bowed his head and softly whimpered. "You know this how?"

An angry Dr. Balbona pointed his finger at Bruce Beathard and harshly accused him of pharmacological espionage. "I'll tell you how, Rabbi. Beathard had a spy inside Merck. He had a spy, I tell you! By God, we could all go to jail over having this information. After Ms. Segulla was assaulted, I saw a man down in the parking lot who was wearing a gray suit. He was standing right beside you when the police arrived. I think that fellow must have been the one who revealed to you this confidential information. After all, Harrison told us that you had an important meeting down in the parking lot before today's conference. Was this man your stockbroker, or was he your spy?"

Dr. Beathard refused to answer. He simply smiled while he shrugged his shoulders.

"You hung us out to dry, Bruce. What were you thinking? Tell me something; how much did it cost us to get this information?" Dr. Clemmons wanted to know.

Beathard raised his voice and slammed his fist on top of the conference table. "What a bunch of ingrates that I'm surrounded with!

It's better to have learned about this information now than after we ended up dumping another quarter million dollars down this shithole, dead-end project. Grow up, boys and girls, grow up!"

"Did you green-light this scheme, Harrison?" the Rabbi asked.

"I find that inference rather shocking. Shocking, I tell you!" Dr. Reed replied.

"That doesn't matter now," Dr. Beathard said. "What do you think I was talking about when I suggested that we unload Rabbi's research project to Leben Kur? You people should have listened to me. Too late now, I guess. In deference to Dr. Rabbi's sensibilities, Dr. Reed said, 'No dice.' Dr. Reed is the arbiter here, as he claims to have the final word on this matter. The Great Oz has spoken, or so it would seem."

Harrison Reed was clearly irritated. "I don't appreciate that. Do I have to put you in the same doghouse as Brewster?"

"Look, we're not going to get to the finish line on this, no matter how you slice it," Beathard elaborated. "If we can't dump this turkey upon some other group of morons, we'll have no choice but to kill it and bury it deep. We'll just have to act like it never even happened to save us from a shit-storm of embarrassment."

"I object to your criticism," Brewster said in protest. "We did good work here. We did important work here."

"Really? Maybe so, Brewster, but you guys didn't win the gold ring. Why should this be any different than any other research project that has been done here at the Gulf Coast? After all, if there's one thing that we seem to excel at around here, it's unmitigated failure. It's what we do, and damnation if we don't do it extraordinarily well. Perhaps we should just be proud of that fact," Dr. Beathard said in disgust. "So tell me, is everybody ready to walk away from this?"

Just like that, the last eight years of the life of Dr. Rabbi had accounted for nothing at all. He was now in his late sixties, and realistically, this was the last chance for him to try and grab what Beathard called the gold ring. He painfully realized that he was approaching the end of his career. When he would eventually climb out of the saddle and wander out into the desert someday, he would leave no legacy. He would have made no major scientific breakthrough for which he so desperately yearned.

Brewster would have believed that this setback would have made Dr. Reed ecstatic. That was, however, far from the case. Although there was personal animosity between Dr. Reed and Brewster, it really was quite imperative for Brewster and the Rabbi to be successful in their experimental endeavors. The university, after all, had a lot of money riding on this project.

Before anyone had completely closed the casket on the hepatitis B project, Dr. Clemmons asked Brewster, "Can you or Dr. Rabbi see any other potential commercial or scientific value in continuing with your current path of investigation?"

Looking back on what happened years later, Brewster wished that he could have hit a magic freeze button. All of the members of the PhD committee had IQs well north of 140. Somebody in that conference room should have seen it. J. D. should have seen it. Sadly, the research funding at the Gulf Coast College of Medicine was so heavily invested toward the successful development of a hepatitis B vaccine that everybody missed the big picture. Of course, there was scientific and commercial value in continuing with what Brewster and the Rabbi had discovered! It had nothing to do with developing a vaccine, however. The two scientists had inadvertently discovered the methodology that may have rendered blood bank systems around the world much safer.

Their technique would have completely destroyed viral pathogens that would have otherwise been transmitted through the transfusion of human blood products. At that time, patients who received blood transfusions were very much at risk for contracting dangerous viral infections. Several years in the future, blood products would be made much safer through detergent and lyophilization techniques.

Brewster would later be tormented by his myopic view of the horizon. Why did Leben Kur, AG, want to buy this technology that he and Dr. Rabbi had developed on behalf of the Gulf Coast College of Medicine? This particular minor league pharmaceutical company, after all, had never manufactured *any* vaccines in the past. Their focus was on blood product support. Before he would graduate from medical school, Brewster one day would be filled with self-loathing once he finally figured out what had transpired.

Brewster extended his index finger into the air in an attempt to postpone the rendering of an answer to the question asked by Dr. Clemmons. He wracked his brain to try and understand why a German pharmaceutical company had expressed such great interest in their research project, but he was incapable of putting the pieces of the puzzle together. The answer should have been an emphatic yes to the question Dr. Clemmons asked. If only Brewster and Rabbi had stayed on track, the gold ring would have been there for the taking.

Sadly, Brewster and the Rabbi had blinders on, as they were totally focused on trying to find a vaccine for the hepatitis B virus.

In the end, they were oblivious to any other potentially beneficial applications for their scientific discoveries.

Dr. Rabbi, seemingly lost in despair, told Dr. Clemmons and the other attendees that the project had come to a dead end. At that instant, Brewster could have written and published another "Missing the Big Picture" installment article for the Slings and Arrows magazine.

In an instant, Brewster had become J.E.B. Stuart. Because he missed the big picture, the Stars and Bars and the Lone Star flags would not flutter together in the breeze over the state of Texas. As it turned out, J.E.B. Stuart was a failure.

In an instant, Brewster had become Admiral Yamamoto. Because he missed the big picture, the flag of the Rising Sun would not flutter in the breeze over the Pacific Rim. As it turned out, Admiral Yamamoto was a failure.

In an instant, Brewster had become Nobel Laureate Werner von Heisenberg. Because he missed the big picture, the ugly red flag with the Aryan swastika rune would not flutter in the breeze over Europe. As it turned out, Professor Heisenberg was a failure.

In an instant, J. D. Brewster had become the man he was always destined to be. Because he missed the big picture, a great laboratory breakthrough just waiting to be found would never flutter in the annals of the history of medical scientific discoveries. At that moment, despite the minor victories he had previously enjoyed in life, Brewster believed he was a failure.

His fate and that of the hepatitis B research project was sealed when Brewster turned to Dr. Clemmons and finally answered her question. "No, I guess I cannot think of any scientific or commercial benefit that can be rendered by going any further down this path of investigation."

With that, Dr. Rabbi picked up his jacket, which had been draped over the back of his chair, and silently slipped out of the room, more as an ethereal cloud of ash to be scattered to the four winds than a previously well-respected research medical scientist.

⸺∘∘❀∘∘⸺

Although he was emotionally spent, the torment that Brewster had to endure was not yet over. Dr. Reed had pointedly said, "Brewster, you need to pull it together right this minute. It's now time for you to tell us about the second research project you're working on with Dr. Holcombe. Are you making any headway into finding out the etiology of the non-A, non-B hepatitis infection?"

Brewster tried to stifle a sigh of despair, but then he began. "The non-A, non-B hepatitis infection is clearly a horizontally transmitted infectious disease process. However, the team assembled by Dr. Holcombe is having difficulty finding any animal models we can successfully inoculate. Our attempts to transmit the infection to rats, rabbits, ducks, woodchucks, and lesser monkeys have all been a failure to date. I'm going to pass around copies of a summary to all of you here today to show you just how our project has gone over the past year."

Dr. Reed intoned a harsh critique. "Quit screwing around. You and Dr. Holcombe are a whole year into this research project, and it's going nowhere. It's time for you to break out the great apes. We have a total of six of those big boys currently residing in the lockdown kennel. This institution spent a great deal of money to have these creatures sent to us from Africa and Indonesia."

"Hang on, Dr. Reed," Brewster said defensively. "Our team is paddling the boat in that direction as we speak."

"No," Reed said. "That's simply not the case. I know for a fact that those beasts have been down there for many weeks now, and they're just gathering dust. I also know for a fact that Dr. Holcombe *wants* to take this project to the next level, but for some reason, he's getting pushback from you and also from the research biologist, Mr. Rip Ford. It's time for you to put these big primates to work for us!"

Brewster was about to feel the big squeeze that he had anticipated. He always felt that he wanted to help the world but not actually be a part of it. Nonetheless, he was clearly resistant to inoculating the great apes with blood or serum that had been harvested from patients afflicted with the mysterious non-A, non-B infectious entity.

Brewster objected, saying, "It may come to that, but I have thought of some other animal models that may work just as well."

He was immediately cut off by Dr. Reed, who said, "We have two pan troglodytes, two beringei, and two pongo pygmaeus specimens available right now to take this project to the finish line."

So it was finally coming down to this. Brewster quickly realized that Dr. Reed had employed an age-old technique to remove any emotional conflict any of the committee members may have had about using higher primates for the purpose of medical experiments. By the conscious effort of referring to chimps, gorillas, and orangutans by their specific scientific names, laboratory researchers had made it much easier to subject our closest living relatives to experimental studies, and eventually, if necessary, sacrifice them in the name of medical science.

Brewster knew it was far easier to kill something if it had an abstract label. After all, it was likely to be much simpler for an abortionist to vacuum out the "products of conception" or to terminate a "fetus," as opposed to accepting that abortion is the killing of an unborn human offspring.

It surely was easier for the Nazis to exterminate six million undesirable *untermenschen* than to admit that they were actually committing mass genocide on six million fellow human beings.

It surely was easier for research scientists to sacrifice a pan troglodyte than to actually admit that they were killing a chimpanzee. "I clearly see where this is all headed," the medical student protested in vain. "Words have meanings, and the words we use obscure the truth of what we do."

Reed was at a loss for what was seemingly a non sequitur response. "What are you talking about? You've already wrapped your lips around the barrel of this gun. Be a man. If you're too weak to pull the trigger, you shouldn't be in the dual-training program."

Brewster ignored the comment and simply shook his head. Further elaboration about his concerns regarding this particular ethical dilemma would have been an act of futility. Yes, specific words do have meaning. The student sadly realized that to change the sterile words that Dr. Reed had used, it would first require a spiritual enlightenment in the scientific culture that was commonly shared. After all, abortionists use euphemisms, Nazis used eugenics, slimy, self-serving politicians within the beltway use spin, and primate experimentalists use taxonomic genus and species. Oh, what a web we weave when we practice to only deceive ourselves …

Despite what Brewster had previously believed, Dr. Holcombe was definitely not going to be in Brewster's corner after all. "Look here, J. D. You got to up and bip through the six-hole stiff, like a diamond back rattler snake. Bip! Bip, bip, bip! The clock is tickin', boy. Tick! Tick, tick, tick! It's time to chomp down yonder quick, like a June bug on a banana stick! Whowee!"

Dr. Clemmons admonished Holcombe, saying, "What you said about a June bug on a banana stick makes absolutely no sense at all."

Brewster thought that finally there was another rational and sane human being inside that meeting besides himself. Sadly, he was wrong about that conception too.

Dr. Clemmons asked, "Didn't you mean to specifically say that it was time to chomp down yonder quick, like a cicada on a mulberry branch?"

Holcombe looked embarrassed and turned to J. D. to offer clarification. While he again scratched ferociously at the pruritic plaque on his left arm, Dr. Holcombe apologized. "I'm sorry, son, I was trying to utilize a folksy double-extended metaphor as a teaching tool, but my chromiums got all jacked as they went into a high-scan mode. My mouth was moving before my gray matter got into gear. It's no wonder why you looked like you were confused."

Then Holcombe looked to Dr. Clemmons and said sweetly, "I didn't know you were particularly fluent in Trans-Pecos."

Dr. Clemmons winked at Hank and added, "I'm sure there are a lot of things I can teach you."

Annoyed, Dr. Beathard said, "Okay, you two, let's focus on the task at hand."

Just then, Brewster remembered an old TV show from the late 1960s called The Prisoner starring the late, great British actor named

Patrick McGoohan. It was a bizarre story about a retired secret agent whose name was Number Six. He was held as a prisoner against his own will at a Victorian-styled, surrealistic inferno that was called "The Village." Appropriate for the era, the show was infused with psychedelic overtones. It was avant-garde and very heady stuff for its time.

The problem for secret agent Number Six was that he could never tell what was real and what was illusory. The major thematic dilemma that washed over the audience that had watched this short-lived series was that even the viewers could not tell whether the protagonist in the show was crazy and all the other characters were sane, or vice versa. J. D. had come to the realization that he was the prisoner, secret agent Number Six. He was clearly starting to have trouble discerning where reality ended and where madness began.

It was time for Dr. Reed to conclude the meeting. "There's still an open motion on the floor previously submitted by Dr. Rabbi that must be addressed, although it's quite obvious that he's already departed from our company. There was a request for the Human Subject Committee to vote on whether a pilot study utilizing human subjects will be approved for the current hepatitis B vaccine experiment."

"This is just an unnecessary formality, Harrison," Dr. Balbona said. "Must we do an actual head count?"

"Despite the devastating news presented by Dr. Beathard that the research project is going to be a dead-end experiment for the Gulf Coast College of Medicine, we're still obligated to vote on the matter if we want to formally end this hepatitis B vaccine study once and for all," Dr. Reed replied. "I must now ask for a definitive answer from the six members of the Human Subject Committee who are present today to either give a thumbs-up or a thumbs-down decision regarding the motion on the floor."

All six members of the committee put the thumbs of their right hands to their own necks. In unison, the members made a swift sweeping motion across the anterior aspect of their throats.

Dr. Reed concluded, "With that, we'll take Dr. Rabbi's and Mr. Brewster's hepatitis B vaccine study off life support, and we'll sadly declare that the project at this time has been declared to have a DNR code status."

13

PUMP JACK EPIPHANY

Days later, déjà vu occurred when Brewster again encountered Dr. Beathard in the stairwell. With every episode of déjà vu, Brewster began to believe he was under some type of cosmic microscope and all of his thoughts, deeds, and misdeeds were now being scrutinized. The inescapable feeling was becoming quite unsettling. As before, Brewster was walking up and Beathard was walking down the steps. Brewster bristled with resentment when Beathard stopped him to have a word with him. Anticipating another round of criticism about the failed hepatitis B vaccine research project, Brewster was actually surprised when Dr. Beathard asked, "How's Ms. Segulla coming along?"

"It seems that she's making progress," Brewster replied. "They're weaning her off the ventilator, although she's having considerable difficulty tolerating the liquid feedings through her gastrostomy tube. Her jaw is still wired up and likely will be for some time. I have not had a chance to see her today, but I'll definitely make a point of doing so."

Beathard nodded and asked Brewster for a favor. "Please be so kind to give her my best when you see her today. Call me at my office and give me an update when you get a chance. I'm truly very fond of Irene, but for some reason, I'm just not feeling brave enough to actually go into the ICU and see her myself."

Brewster promised to keep Beathard up to date when he had the chance. After a stop for breakfast in the cafeteria with his friend Medhi, he planned to go back down to the lab. Apparently there was new work to be done, as Ford told J. D. that they had been assigned an expanded project by their team leader, Dr. Holcombe.

When Brewster finally made it down to his workstation, Ford was waiting for him. "You're quite a popular fellow today."

"Why, thank you," Brewster replied.

"Actually, I'm being sarcastic," Ford said. "You're so dense, you probably wouldn't recognize sarcasm if it jumped up and bit you square in the ass."

"What now?"

"To be honest, you're persona non grata right about now. More than one person wants to open up a can of whup-ass on you. I just happen to be one of them," Ford said.

Brewster scowled at his colleague and asked, "Who put a roach in your corn flakes this morning?"

"You sandbagged me. You told me the other day that you would *not* agree to proceed with bringing the big primates online into the next round of inoculation experiments. Well, Uncle Hank is now off getting his skin and lymph node biopsies done today to find out what's causing that nasty rash on his left arm. Before he split, he left me this memo that says you agreed on moving forward to try and induce non-A, non-B hepatitis infections in the big boys in the lockdown kennel."

"I did no such thing!"

"I don't believe you," Ford said. "I swear—you're a deluxe, industrial-strength asshole."

Brewster put both hands in the air as if he was a foiled carjacker who was surrounded by the police. "Stop right there. I had nothing to do with any of this. I assure you that I did *not* agree to move forward with the great apes. Dr. Holcombe snookered you. He's trying to box us into doing something we'd rather not." Brewster had successfully defused the situation, and the head of steam that was swirling between Ford's ears had started to decompress.

Ford revealed the new instructions that had been given to him by Uncle Hank. "Well, here's the set up: Dr. Holcombe wants us to write up a timeline as to when we will subject the big primates to contaminated blood, serum, and ascites body fluid."

"A formal protocol?"

"You got it," Ford confirmed. "We have to get this done now. Hank is taking a three-day sick leave over his rash and this enlarged lymph node business. When we get it finished, both Zip Talbot and Dr. Sassman have to sign off on the protocol."

"How in hell does Talbot have any authority over our project?" Brewster asked. "After all, you and Talbot have the same rank. That would be like me giving you permission to blow your own nose."

"You just don't get, do you?" Ford asked. "If Uncle Hank says jump, we're supposed to jump. In any event, I really don't know why Hank needs that much time off for those simple biopsy procedures. If he is sick of anything, I'll venture it's from looking at you and me."

"He's a good man, but he certainly wasn't in my corner at the Human Subjects Committee meeting the other day," Brewster complained.

"Can you make an educated guess as to what's causing the rash on Uncle Hank's arm?"

"I'm not sure," Brewster replied, "but I'm afraid that whatever it is, it may be something nasty. The other day at the committee meeting, he told us that the rash was spreading to other parts of his body. Well, I guess we'll know soon enough."

"I almost forgot," Ford added. "Talbot wanted me to remind you that your band, DNR, is going to have practice at the clubhouse located at Blow's apartment complex."

"Thanks. I'd forgotten about that. You mentioned that somebody else wanted to beat my ass. Just who might that be?" Brewster asked. "Yeshua, I presume?"

"No, the good Rabbi is in a foul mood, and he must be off sulking somewhere," Ford surmised. "I never had a chance to tell you that I was quite sorry that they pulled the plug on your hepatitis B vaccine study. At least, Brew, you have one viable research project that's still in the hopper. Perhaps you and I will have more success in trying to nail down this non-A, non-B hepatitis virus."

"If we don't, I'll have to forego my big dream of getting an MD/PhD degree. If that happened, I'd have to get a real job someday and I'd be forced to interact with other Homo sapiens on a daily basis. Perish the thought!"

"That would suck for you. Your inability to do any real work certainly hasn't escaped my attention. Nonetheless, I would bargain with the Devil himself if we could get out of having to use the big primates in our future experimental studies," Ford lamented.

"Well," Brewster said, "as you probably know, if you want to bargain with the Devil, I've been told that you can generally find him loitering about down at the crossroads. That being said, who else wants to put a voodoo hex on me besides you?"

"You'll love this," Ford answered. "The other individual who's got a burr up his ass about you is also upset with me. That person is Dr. Denny Sassman. With the trouble that Uncle Hank has been having in and out of the lab, Sassman has been elevated to the secondary investigator position on the non-A, non-B hepatitis study."

"Good for him. He deserves it. Tell me, though—what's he upset about?"

"I didn't tell you that Sassman had a mandatory meeting set up for us to see him the other day, and I just blew it off."

"What in hell is the matter with you?"

"Did you know his nickname was Dr. Sasquatch? Well, it fits the bill. After all, he's a large and hairy beast of a man."

"Why did you blow off the meeting?" Brewster asked. "You should've told me about it, and I would have gone over to his office and talked to him. I like Denny, and I think he likes me. At least he used to ..."

"I know he wanted to give us a pep talk about using the big primates in the hepatitis study, but I just could not bring myself to meet him face-to-face," Rip said. "He called back this morning before you came down to the lab. He still wants to meet with us. Right now, in fact. He said, and I quote, 'no ifs, ands, or buts, buttheads'!"

It was now Brewster's turn to be angry. "Damnation, Ford! Now he's pissed off at us. You should have at least told me about that previous meeting. If you didn't want to have a face-to-face with Denny, that was your business. You can't go around making decisions on my behalf. You're making me look bad here!"

"Relax, grasshopper," Ford responded. "We'll get all of this smoothed over. Besides, you're making yourself look bad all on your own accord. You don't need any help from me in that regard."

"First things first," Brewster said. "I have to see Ms. Segulla this morning, and I'll be back in just a few minutes. When I return, you and I will *both* go and find Dr. Sassman to have that little chitchat. Perhaps it will be a civilized congregation and we can have this meeting over a spot of tea." With that, Brewster headed up to the ICU.

The practice of medicine had changed dramatically since Brewster was in medical school back in 1980. The old concept of a single intensive care unit has evolved into subdivided, multiple subspecialty units at most modern hospitals. Instead of one ICU, one may now find a cardiac care unit, medical intensive care unit, and a surgical intensive care unit, with different specialists hovering about like busy bees in each of these care units.

A cornerstone of the standard of care when Brewster was in medical school involved the deployment of internal medicine specialists to manage the ill who were hospitalized, but things have also evolved over time concerning this matter. In the modern era, there are now two newly recognized specialists who handle this task. One is called the hospitalist, which manages patients who are on the regular patient care wards, and the other is the intensivist, and these physicians manages patients who are in the intensive care units.

Years later when J. D. Brewster was approaching the end of his career, he wondered about the pros and cons of such a system. The presence of hospitalists and intensivists would likely improve patient care. However, the skill sets that an internist would acquire during the course of his or her early training would no doubt eventually erode over time.

When Brewster reached the ICU, something was awry. Stall number four where Mrs. Segulla had been hospitalized was now empty. The linens had been stripped from the bed and cast into a corner of the room, and the unit custodian was wiping down the thick, vinyl-covered hospital bed mattress with a bleach solution. Brewster thought to himself that this was good news, as it must mean that Ms. Segulla was well enough to have been transferred to the floor. However, optimism turned to panic when the hospital operator told Brewster over the phone that no patient with the name of Segulla was still registered at the facility.

Brewster felt lightheaded. He went out into the hallway to the nearest nurse he could find, and he asked if she knew what happened to the patient who was previously in stall number four. The nurse turned and saw that Brewster was wearing a name badge that designated him as a student. She was not about to degrade herself by answering a question from some inferior life-form, so she sneered at him and walked away. This didn't seem possible. Ms. Segulla was the day-shift charge nurse on the medical floor. How could it be that the hospital operator didn't seem to know anything? To make matters worse, some disengaged unit nurse, who was an alleged colleague of Ms. Segulla, just didn't seem to give a shit about the situation!

The medical student saw a young woman wheeling a nebulizer machine past him, and Brewster thought perhaps she could be of help. "Pardon me, but do you know what might have happened to the patient that was in stall number four? The patient was one of our own. It was Nurse Segulla from the med/surg floor. She got hospitalized several days ago, and now she's disappeared. I just talked to the telephone operator, and I was told that she's not registered here anymore."

The young woman replied, "I'm from the RT Department, sweet cheeks. Does it look like it's my turn to be in the barrel? I don't think so. Go ask the ward clerk." When the therapist departed, she assumed the persona of Sergeant Schultz from the old television show *Hogan's Heroes.* With an exaggerated German accent, she said, "I know nothing, nothing, nothing!" Brewster's panic had turned into outright terror. Perhaps Ms. Segulla had suffered a lethal myocardial infarction or perhaps a catastrophic pulmonary embolic event. She might have died!

Brewster rushed off to find the unit clerk. He found that she was on the telephone, and he was quite certain that she was not conducting business as she was giggling and sweet-talking somebody. Brewster attempted to interrupt her, but he was quickly rebuked.

"What's the matter with you? Can't you see that I'm talking on the telephone? I'm busy here."

Brewster took two steps back and remained quiet.

The unit clerk was not mollified one bit. "Quit lurking about. You're making me nervous. Go stand over in the corner, you little pervert, and don't look at me like that."

This was not the first time Brewster had had a run-in with this particular intensive care unit ward clerk. The overt hostility displayed toward *all* medical students who were passing through the intensive care unit while on various clerkship rotations was indeed quite inexplicable, although there were unsubstantiated rumors that the clerk at been previously jilted by a senior student a while back.

For whatever reason, she would viciously project her ire upon any medical student who had the audacity to actually speak to her. Brewster backed up and leaned against the wall. As he folded his arms together, he became an eyewitness to the bizarre event that had happened next.

Brewster wondered if Blomeo Colima was right; perhaps there was such a thing as instant karma. John Lennon, one of the Beatles, certainly sang about it. Depending on one's theological persuasion, it may or may not exist. In any event, when karma, or a reasonable facsimile of it occurs, it can be a wondrous thing to behold.

As Dr. Marek Cannon, one of the internal medicine physicians on staff, was walking down the hallway, he had a serious purpose to his step. When the unit clerk noticed that he was walking her way, she quickly hung up the telephone because she knew she was about to get scolded.

Dr. Cannon appeared to be angry, yet he spoke in a calm voice. "Yesterday, I received a consult request from Dr. Reynolds to do an evaluation on the patient in stall number eleven. I did the consult and dictated the report on the transcription machine, but it's nowhere to be found. It is your job as unit clerk to make sure that consults are put on the chart in a timely fashion. This is a patient care issue. Now Dr. Reynolds thinks that I blew off his consult request. There is now a new order submitted by Dr. Reynolds for a second consult request to be done by *different* internal medicine physician. This makes me look bad."

The ward clerk furrowed her brow and simply looked back at Dr. Cannon.

"I spoke with Mrs. Blight who is in the transcription department, and she said that my transcription was finished and she actually had brought it up and handed it directly to you earlier this morning. What happened to it? Did you lose it?" Dr. Cannon demanded.

When the ward clerk again failed to reply, Dr. Cannon suddenly felt a pounding sensation in his right temple. "Before I leave the unit, I want you to put a call down to Mrs. Blight in the transcription department and have her generate another copy of my consult. Once done, I need you to get that report on the patient's chart ASAP. Do it now before you cause me to have a stroke!"

The unit clerk rolled her eyes and then stared back at the attending with implacable disdain.

Her insubordination did not go unnoticed for long. Dr. Cannon blew a gasket and poked his index finger toward her face and raised his voice. "Do it. Do it now!"

The unit clerk then picked up the telephone and seemed to call down to the transcription department. As soon as Dr. Cannon had turned and gone back down the hall to see another patient, the ward clerk ended her ruse and hung up the telephone back onto its receiver. Brewster erroneously thought it would be a good time to approach the unit clerk and ask about what happened to Ms. Segulla.

Brewster knew there were generally four ways to get somebody to answer a question. The primary method was to use honey. This would usually work in about 99 percent of the time in human-to-human interactions. If that method proved to be unsuccessful, then it might be time to try vinegar. If the second method failed, then option three would warrant the employment of bile. As a last resort, the final option boiled down to the threat of physical violence, be it a shank, a shiv, a beat down, or a brick bat if ever necessary.

Although he was not particularly skilled at interpersonal relationships, Brewster wisely considered it would perhaps be best to try an approach with honey, at least initially. He again addressed the unit clerk and asked most politely, "Madam, now that you are off the telephone, I would like to see if you might know what happened to Ms. Segulla. She was the patient that was in stall number four. I certainly hope that I'm not intruding upon your busy schedule."

The unit clerk was in no mood to cooperate with a pesky medical student who was at the bottom of the totem pole as far as the issue of political influence at the hospital was concerned. "Who are you? It seems that you keep coming around here and cluttering up my hallway. I don't know what happened to the patient, so will you please just go away? Don't bother me again."

It was clear to Brewster that honey was useless. His attempt at civility was met with futility.

It was time to go to option number two and try vinegar. Brewster said, "Now, I'm not here on my own accord. I was asked to come here by Professor Beathard. He will not be particularly happy if I have to go back and tell him that you did not want to cooperate with me. All you have to do is to tell where Ms. Segulla may have been transferred. In light of the most unpleasant conversation you've already had with Dr. Cannon, I would suspect that your long-term employment at this institution may very well be in jeopardy if you decline my invitation to cooperate with me at this time."

To the unit clerk, Brewster was an annoying moth hovering about a lightbulb. At that point, Brewster didn't even warrant a swat from the haughty clerk. It was clear to Brewster that vinegar was also useless. His attempt at incivility was also met with futility.

It was time to go to option three and to break open a nasty bottle of bile. Brewster said, "Now listen to me, you cross-eyed bitch. I can clearly see why a person like you would need to be on the horn all day long, as no respectable man I know would ever want to try and stick it to such a disgusting, syphilitic, nasty-ass skank like you. I have no doubt that you would readily transmit some form of an incurable, lethal, venereal disease that could not be easily treated by penicillin, or by any other form of antibiotic currently recognized in the universal pharmacopeia." The unit clerk dropped her jaw and was speechless at the lashing she had just received.

Brewster was devolving into a man who was capable of exercising option four, and he proceeded to threaten the ward clerk. "If you don't tell me what I need to know now right now, you useless sea hag, I'm going to climb over this desk, and you and I are going to dance together. Do you know how to do the Skate? How about the Shimmy? I happen to be quite fond of both the song and the dance called the Locomotion. That was a big hit by Little Eva, and it was released on the Dimension record label back in June of '62. Boy, was that a great song or what? Grand Funk covered it six years ago, but I think the original is still the best version. It was written by the song writing team of Carole King and Gerry Goffin, and it shot to the top of the charts. I loved the black girls from that musical era, don't you?"

The ward clerk was now alarmed and realized she had just set a lit match to a fast-burning fuse. "Slow down, okay?"

"Did you know that Little Eva was the babysitter for singer/ songwriter Carole King? Please tell me you remember the Locomotion," the medical student asked. "I must say, if I teach you how to do the Locomotion, it will grind you right through to the floorboards. Do you know what I mean? Trust me, if you and I dance together, two things will happen. First, you will end up as a patient here in this unit on a ventilator. Second, I'll be going to prison for attempted murder. My career is failing. At this point, I just don't give a shit anymore. Go ahead. Test my resolve. It's your call." Brewster was serious. Dead serious.

The clerk responded by finding a three-ring black binder that was the unit admission/discharge record. She slammed it on top of the counter above her desk and said, "It's in here. You know how to read, don't you? Look it up yourself, and then get the hell out of here."

Brewster recalled digesting a disturbing novel several years earlier that was called The Painted Bird. It was a story about a young orphan boy trapped in Eastern Europe during World War II. The main thematic undercurrent was that the ability for a human being to act like a Nazi was not aberrant behavior per se. It was just part of the broad spectrum of human capabilities, plain and simple. Perhaps under the right circumstances, everybody could act like a Nazi. That certainly seemed to be the case, at least for those who were associated with the Gulf Coast College of Medicine. In light of his abhorrent comments to the unit clerk, whether she was uncooperative or not, Brewster sadly realized that he was no exception. It was now quite evident that his very moral fibers were starting to erode.

—∘∘∘〉◎〈∘∘∘—

Upon finding that Ms. Segulla had been transferred to the surgical floor two hours earlier, Brewster threw the binder back at the unit clerk as if it was a pie plate. She dodged the binder and then shouted out to Brewster as he walked away. "That could have hit me, you bastard! I'm going to file a complaint against you."

As Brewster left the unit, he sarcastically replied with a wave and said, "Tootles!"

J. D. believed what the unit clerk had said was an idle threat. Nothing could have been further from the truth, because within two minutes of his departure, the unit clerk had written up a scathing report that had accused Brewster of creating a "hostile work environment." Once filed with administration, a report of this magnitude would have devastating consequences. Not only would it have ended Brewster's PhD training program, but it would have also resulted in his complete expulsion from medical school altogether!

When Dr. Cannon finished visiting one of his patients in the ICU, he was met in the hallway by an elderly black woman who had perfect white hair. She was dressed in an old-fashioned white nurse's dress. She approached Dr. Cannon and said, "Excuse me, Dr. Cannon, but I'm a floating nurse from the temp pool, and my name is Sister Buena. I overheard the argument you had with the unit clerk. I just wanted to let you know that she disregarded your order, and she never placed a call down to the transcription service as you requested. I took it upon myself to personally recover your dictated consult. I put the original on the patient's chart, and I have a copy here for you to review. I also took the liberty to call Dr. Reynolds to explain to him about the mishap that occurred. I just wanted to let you know that Dr. Reynolds was most relieved, and he canceled the second consultation order that he requested from a different internal medicine specialist."

Dr. Cannon was grateful and said, "Thank you, Sister Buena. I have never seen you before, but you are without a doubt the very best floating nurse I've ever met. Can I get you a donut from the break room?"

"Thank you, but no. I must be going as I'm on a very tight schedule."

"You've turned a very unpleasant morning into something quite beautiful. You've made my day," Dr. Cannon said. "God bless you!"

Sister Buena replied, "He does just that, and He does it every day!" With that, she disappeared down the hallway.

Dr. Cannon went down to the human resources department and found the director of nonmedical personnel. Dr. Cannon brought the director back up to the ICU, along with two hospital security guards. They confronted the unit clerk, and a formal charge of disobedience and insubordination was levied upon her. The clerk was summarily terminated on the spot and escorted out of the building by the security personnel. Upon her departure, the excoriating complaint she had written about Brewster miraculously disappeared, and it was never filed with administration. Once again, it would seem that J. D. Brewster had dodged a bullet.

When Brewster found Ms. Segulla on the surgical floor, there were two Houston Police Department detectives in her room reviewing mug shots of previously convicted violent felons with her. She could not speak as her jaw was wired shut and her face was heavily bandaged, but she was able to effectively communicate with the detectives by writing on a white board with an erasable black marker.

Although Ms. Segulla was no longer on ventilator support, she had humidified oxygen flow delivered across her tracheostomy site via a blue blow-by tube. She still had IV fluids administered, and she was receiving a thick white protein and carbohydrate suspension through a percutaneous gastrostomy tube.

"Hello, Irene," Brewster said. "I see that you're busy, so it is probably better for me to come back later. Dr. Beathard sends his regards." Ms. Segulla started waving at Brewster vigorously, and this caught the attention of one of the police detectives.

"Hold on there, young fellow. You're J. D. Brewster. We need to talk to you," one of the detectives said.

The two men identified themselves as detectives Culp and Watt with the HPD, and they showed Brewster their police badges. Each of the two men handed the student their business cards with their phone numbers on it. "Ms. Segulla wrote a message to us on her white board you were the last person with her before she was assaulted. We believe you may have seen what her alleged assailants looked like," Culp said.

"I'm happy to help if I can," Brewster said.

"Flip through this book," Detective Watt requested. "We would like to see what you think."

Within moments, Brewster selected two photographs, each revealing somewhat similar-appearing black men who were wearing dark jackets with turtleneck sweaters. In each photograph, the individual shown had a goatee mustache and was wearing wraparound sunglasses.

"Those are the men!" Brewster exclaimed. "They did it!"

The two detectives looked at each other and shook their heads. Detective Culp said, "I'm sorry, but I don't think you'll be able to help us after all. You just picked out old stock photos of Huey P. Newton and Eldridge Cleaver. These were photographs taken in Oakland, California, back in 1968. It was my idea to throw these two photos into the mix. These photos that you picked out so quickly were taken of the two founding members of the Black Panther Party."

Brewster did not follow what the two detectives were saying. He asked, "Do you really think that Ms. Segulla had been attacked by two of the founding members of the Black Panther Party? That doesn't make any sense to me."

Frustrated, Detective Watt said, "No, dumb ass! The perpetrators are smart. I put these photos in there to see if I could trip you up. Besides you and Ms. Segulla, there were five other witnesses, and *everybody* picked out these two photographs."

"Are you trying to tell me that white people think that all black people look like?" Brewster asked. "Frankly, that's absurd."

"No, pay attention; two of the witnesses happened to be black guys, and they still picked out the same photos," Watts said.

"What are you telling me?" Brewster asked.

"They wore disguises," Culp replied. "When we sent the dogs after them out into the park, the canines found two black jackets, mock turtleneck shirts, and paste-on goatees that the perpetrators had ditched while they were on the run. There were no prints on any of the items. I'm telling you, these guys may be evil, but they're not stupid."

Detective Watt added, "Ms. Segulla looked at several hundred photographs over the last two hours, and she has not been able to identify any of the known and previously convicted felons who may have been capable of doing this. We actually think that the perpetrators don't have any previous criminal records, and this is going to make it a lot harder for us to collar these bastards."

"I don't mind taking a longer look at more photographs if you would like," Brewster said. "In fact, I want to help."

"Fine," Culp said. "We'll have you officially come down to the station and look through some mug shots for us. You have our business cards. Give us a call, and we'll set up the visit for you. In addition, give either of us a call if you can think of anything else." With that, the two HPD detectives left the hospital.

Ms. Segulla tapped on the white board, indicating that she wanted to convey a message to Brewster. She crudely wrote, "Happy to see u. Glad I'm off vent, but long way to go."

Brewster replied, "Well, everybody is rooting for you, Irene."

Ms. Segulla erased the message that she had written and wrote a question to the student. "When u ask my niece Stella Link on date? Have u been doing breathing exercises like I told u? Ha, ha!"

Brewster blushed and replied, "You're not strong enough to play cupid yet, Ms. Segulla. I'm certain I'll meet Stella sooner or later. You rest now." Brewster kissed Ms. Segulla on the forehead, and then she nodded off to sleep. He left her hospital room and went back down to the basement.

When Brewster caught up with the research biologist in the lab, Rip Ford was obviously pensive about a having a meeting with the secondary investigator, Dr. Sassman, about the non-A, non-B hepatitis experimental study. Brewster asked, "Are you ready to do this?"

Ford replied, "Let's go before I lose my nerve." Ford replied, The two men wandered through the dark bowels of the basement hallway until they came upon the office of Dr. Sassman, which was adjacent to the animal laboratory.

When they reached the door, Brewster told Ford, "You knock and introduce us as you are the one who blew off the last meeting. If anybody is going to take the heat on this, it is going to be you."

Ford nodded his head in agreement and rapped his knuckles on the closed office door. "Dr. Sassman, Rip Ford and J. D. Brewster are here to see you. Per your request, we're here to discuss the pending inoculation experiments upon the great primates."

A voice from behind the door said, "Come on in and take a seat." As the two men entered the room, Dr. Sassman stood up and went to a mini-fridge located in the corner of his office. He pulled out two Mr. Pibb sodas and handed them to the men who sat across from him at the desk. Dr. Sassman's office was cluttered and dimly lit.

There was a peculiar ashtray in the middle of his desk that appeared to be a large, ancient pewter goblet that may have been the

Holy Grail for all Brewster had known. The stem of a mysterious pipe peaked over the rim of the goblet, but neither Ford nor Brewster could readily ascertain from their vantage point if the business-end of the pipe was merely a crude corncob or a finely carved Meerschaum bowl.

Dr. Sassman didn't waste any time. "Don't blow smoke up my ass. You need to be straight with me. I know both of you are reluctant to use the big primates in the next phase of this non-A, non-B virus study. It's okay, boys, and I get that. While Dr. Holcombe will be out of commission for these biopsies that he's going to get, you'll have only a three-day stay of execution. It'll be my job to desensitize you from the discomfort of working with the great apes." Sassman interlocked his fingers and put his hands behind his head as he leaned back in his chair.

"I know exactly where Mr. Ford stands on this issue. He told me he would much rather be doing experiments on human prisoners that are incarcerated on death row than on doing experiments on the big primates. Now, of course, that will never happen at least as long as we have the likes of Jimmy Carter in the White House." Denny paused after he made this inappropriate comment and added, "I'm sorry, I'm only joking on that matter. Don't repeat that, or else the Secret Service will probably be paying me a visit! Tell me, Brew, is that how you feel also?"

"If you had asked me that question a few weeks back," Brewster replied, "I would have said no. I must be honest with you, however. In light of what happened to Ms. Segulla out on the employee parking lot, I now take a fresh new stance on the matter. I have come to the conclusion that God has backed the wrong primate. He must have put His money on the wrong monkey. At this point, I don't think human beings deserve to have a soul. He should have given a spirit to the orangutan. You don't see these gentle and noble beings going about and beating each other to death with lead pipes. I believe that God now looks upon His human subjects as abject failures that are no longer redeemable. He's no doubt wandered off to some other part of His universe to tinker with some other project that He may find more meaningful and fulfilling."

Ford turned toward Brewster to dispute his colleague's fatalistic cynicism. "God doesn't think like that. I was having a cold beer with God just the other day, and He told me, quite frankly, that you're full of shit."

Brewster countered the research biologist's critique when he raised his hand and replied, "Genesis, chapter six: 'And God saw that the wickedness of man was great in the earth, and that every imagination of the thoughts of his heart was only evil continually. The Lord regretted that he had made human beings on the earth, and his heart was deeply troubled.' Put that in your pipe, Rip Ford!"

Ford, as usual, became annoyed with Brewster's theological edicts. "So sad to think that at one time you called yourself a Christian. Spare me! The cornerstone of faith should be redemption and perhaps even salvation." While pointing his thumb and index finger at Brewster as if he were a man holding gun, Rip Ford looked at Professor Sassman and said, "Don't pay attention to this heretic. He can go on like this for hours."

Sassman half-jokingly rebuked Ford and said, "Silence, you godless Philistine! We have a prophet in our midst." Sassman pivoted at his desk to face Brewster. He made a fist and pounded the top of his desk three times. "We have heard a voice crying in the wilderness. Heed not the heathens that whisper into your ear. Remember—even Jesus was rejected in His own homeland! Listen to me, boys. The only thing you have to do is to keep an eye on the ball. Success will be ours, and we will all triumph in this endeavor."

Dr. Sassman turned back to Ford and concluded, "I'll be awarded a department chair, you and Zip Talbot will get to keep your jobs, and in addition, I suspect you'll get a fat promotion out of this whole ordeal. As for the goofy medical student sitting directly across from my desk, he'll no doubt earn the MD/PhD degrees, which he so dearly covets!'

"Am I goofy?" Brewster asked, "Say, it ain't so, Rip!"

A hirsute brute at six four and 260 pounds, Dr. Sassman's nickname of "Dr. Sasquatch" was well deserved. He had rings of black hair that completely covered his ears. With a bushy beard and eyebrows to match, Dr. Sassman was invariably delighted to wear a black patch over his left eye and dress up like a pirate on Halloween. He had been awarded a PhD degree in primatology from Dick Dowling University back in 1970. Four years later, he matriculated from the El Paso Osteopathic School of Medicine when he got his DO degree in 1974. Although he had never engaged in any type of a postgraduate residency or fellowship training program, he nonetheless had been able to secure a tenured faculty position at the Gulf Coast College of Medicine for the last six years. Deeply entrenched in research, he was now the secondary scientific investigator under Dr. Hank Holcombe, who had been vigorously toiling on the non-A, non-B hepatitis study for the past year.

To break the thick layer of ice that was already accumulating in his office, he decided to chat up the two men to try and win them over. Dr. Sassman had a notorious reputation for distrusting anybody who was not a bona fide Texan. The further back a person's lineage could be traced into the remote history of the Lone Star state was a terribly important matter to Dr. Sassman. After all, if he was going to be working closely with these two young men on the non-A, non-B hepatitis project, Dr. Sassman had to be able to trust them. To trust them, he had to be able to vet them. "Brewster, I've been told that you are a historian and a mutigenerational Texan. How long have your people been here?

Brewster replied, "I am a Texan through the grace of my father's side of the family. My paternal ancestors came here when Texas was still a republic in 1840. They started a small ranch west of Navasota. My mother, though, is a first-generation paisan. My great-great paternal grandpa was a lieutenant with Wahl's Brigade from Brenham during the Lost Cause. He was captured at Vicksburg and never came home."

"I assume he died as a prisoner of war?" Sassman asked.

"Family tradition holds that he was a verbose man with an acerbic tongue," Brewster replied. "He was apparently not particularly fond of the company of other people. Legend states that he could generate long-winded, degrading, and inflammatory insults. I romantically surmise that he made an off-color critique about some blue-belly's mother who was engaged in some type of unspeakable prolific and illicit bestial porcine or equine sexual acts. No doubt, the times being what they were, a comment like that would have probably cost my great-great-grandpa a bullet to the brain!"

"Well, the apple certainly didn't fall too far from the tree," Ford correctly observed.

Dr. Sassman turned to ask Ford about his ancestry. As he was adopted, Rip Ford replied that he was uncertain about his lineage.

Sassman and Brewster must have been cut from the same bolt of fabric. Just like Denny Sassman, J. D. Brewster had a notorious reputation for distrusting anybody who was not a bona fide Texan. The further back a person's lineage could be traced into the remote history of the Lone Star state was a terribly important matter to the medical student. After all, if he was going to be working closely with Dr. Sassman on the non-A, non-B hepatitis project, the medical student had to be able to trust him. To trust him, he had to be able to vet him. "How far back does your family go in the state of Texas, Dr. Sassman?"

Sassman smiled and went to the office wall. He pulled down a framed reproduction of an old photo and handed it to his two guests. The picture was of five men who were dressed as Old West desperados, and each man was heavily armed.

"My great-grandfather was the man second to the left in this photograph. This was taken after the Battle of Palmetto Ranch in May 1865. This was the last land battle of the American Civil War.

Ironically, it was a major Confederate victory, but neither the Union nor the rebel forces knew that the Civil War had already ended a month before in April. My great-grandfather was a cowboy on the King Ranch, and he signed up with the Confederate cavalry at the outbreak of the conflict."

Brewster looked at the picture and was amazed at the accouterments and some of the weapons the cavalry members possessed when the photograph had been taken. Except for having similar slouch hats that had been adorned with a single star, none of the men in the photograph were wearing anything that looked like a Confederate uniform.

Brewster noted, "Three of the long arms in this photograph clearly appear to be breech-loaded Sharp carbines. The man on the far right is holding a five-shot 1855 edition Colt revolver carbine. Every man in the picture had two revolvers. They look like gunslingers, not soldiers. What I don't recognize is the type of carbine your great-grandfather was holding in this old photograph. What kind of gun was that? I've never seen anything like that before."

Sassman proudly replied, "That, my young friend, happens to be a rare LeMat revolver carbine. It was originally designed in New Orleans by a surgeon who tinkered as a gunsmith. Before the Crescent City fell to the Union forces, the factory was broken down and shipped off to England and France. Carbines and revolver pistols were made overseas and then sent back to the South on blockade runners. Throughout the remainder of the war, it was the only rapid-fire long arm that was made exclusively for the Confederacy. To my knowledge, only five or six examples are still extant."

Brewster replied, "That's simply amazing! I studied the Civil War extensively while I was in college, and I never had even seen a picture of one of these weapons before now. Is this gun still in your family possession?"

Dr. Sassman answered, "Sadly, the answer is no. In the early 1950s, my grandmother became demented, and she gave all of my great-grandfather's mementos from the Civil War away to other people. These irreplaceable and priceless historical artifacts were not sold to other people, mind you. They were simply given away to complete strangers. To this very day, I still have a burr up my ass about that humiliating fact. I swear, Brewster, I would give away my left testicle to have those military heirlooms back in my family's possession. Do you know what I mean?"

"Yes, Brewster replied, "I understand exactly what you mean, and far more than you could ever know."

Sassman continued, "The only thing left that I have in my possession is a remnant of the Union flag from the Thirty-Fourth Indiana Volunteer Infantry that my great-granddad had personally captured at the Battle of Palmetto Ranch. This was the last flag of the United States that was been captured on the battlefield up until the fall of Corregidor. It is framed and hanging on the wall here in my office. Go ahead and take a look at it."

Ford and Brewster respectfully observed the historical artifact that was behind Dr. Sassman's desk. It was only a remnant strip, and some of the stars had been cut out of the blue field, no doubt to be given away as souvenirs to some of the other cavalry troopers who fought in the battle.

Brewster asked, "How much do you want for it?" Dr. Sassman laughed and didn't even give the student an answer. At least by that time, the medical student and the professor had developed a considerable amount of mutual respect for each other.

As the two men returned to their seats, Ford took another look at the Civil War–era photograph and asked Dr. Sassman, "Did they have disco dancing back in the 1860s? I'm looking at the chaps that your great-grandfather was wearing, and I must admit that they appear to be quite stylish."

"No, dumb ass," Dr. Sassman replied. "Those chaps were made from the pelt of a jaguar. The last wild jaguar that was killed in the state of Texas was about thirty years ago or so in the north-central part of the state around the town of Brownwood. Okay, Mr. Ford, you are a biologist. I want to show you something. This is a plaster of Paris cast of a footprint that I took in East Texas about two years ago, in the year 1978. I took it to Texas A&M to be analyzed. I was informed that it was, without a doubt, the footprint of a jaguar. I swear to God, those Aggies are relentless. They have hounded me ever since to try and find out where in the forest I took that casting, but I won't give up the secret."

Brewster asked, "Why not? This could be a major scientific discovery if this great cat is making its way back across the Rio Grande."

The professor answered, "The reason is quite simple. I have never seen a jaguar in the wild, and I probably never will. I suspect that the species is trying to make a comeback in the semitropical forests east of Houston. I am a Texan, and I know very well the basic nature of some of my fellow Texans. Some idiot would likely take a gun and try to find the poor creature, if it is indeed still out there, and then blow it into smithereens just to have a pelt to put in front of a fireplace somewhere."

"You're probably right," Brewster conceded.

"So Ford," Sassman continued, "I have to ask you a question. If there are university-based, scientific analytics that confirm that this casting that you are now holding in your hand had been created from a paw print made by a jaguar, what is the probability that it is a casting of a paw print made by a jaguar?"

Ford thought it was an odd question but replied, "One hundred percent guaranteed, and without a doubt."

Dr. Sassman was pleased and said, "Very good. That was the correct answer. As I stand here right now, gentleman, I assure you that there are many strange things out in the forests of East Texas that you could not possibly imagine. Now, my job is to desensitize you gentleman from working on the great apes. I am going to show you something that I rarely share with other people. It is my PhD thesis from the Dick Dowling University."

With that, the professor stood up and went over to his bookcase. He pulled out a large binder and passed it over for Brewster and Ford to look at. The document was entitled "The Existence of a Previously Unrecognized Bipedal Primate in East Texas."

Ford and Brewster looked at the each other in disbelief, and then they opened the document to take a look.

Inside the binder were three remarkable photographs showing what appeared to be, for all intents and purposes, a Sasquatch. The first photograph in the series had the sharpest resolution, and it showed a Bigfoot standing at the base of an oil pump jack in the forest. It appeared it was looking up to the sky as it stretched out its hands upon the sill, and it had crossed its right foot behind its left. The photograph was taken of the dorsal aspect of the animal.

Brewster scoffed at the picture and said, "Frankly, this is nonsense. I can't believe that my alma mater bestowed a PhD upon you in the field of primatology based on a man in a monkey suit. If you think this hocus-pocus is going to somehow get us on the bandwagon where either Ford or I would be willing to inoculate and sacrifice the big primates that are now in the lockdown kennel, it's not going to happen, Dr. Sassman."

Undeterred, Denny Sassman opened up the bottom drawer of his desk and pulled out a plaster of Paris casting of an enormous footprint that was eighteen inches long and six inches wide at the ball of the foot. Sassman remarked, "This is a plaster of Paris casting of just one the six footprints that was made by the creature in the photograph. It indicates that the animal that made this footprint had vertical dermal ridges on the sole of its foot. Human beings do not have eighteen-inch footprints with vertical dermal ridges on the sole."

Brewster failed to grasp the meaning of the atypical marks found in the casting. "Please repeat what you just said. I'm not following you. Now, what exactly is the significance of finding vertical dermal ridges in these castings that you made?"

"Pay attention; it confirms that these footprints were not made by a primate taxonomically categorized within the realm of Homo sapiens. I can't say it any plainer than that," Dr. Sassman answered with confidence. "The dermatoglyphic anomalies were carefully analyzed under magnification at my alma mater, Dick Dowling University, and also at Texas A&M. It was determined that these footprints were genuine. This particular casting that you are now holding was compared to the other footprint castings that I took, and the toes were dynamic from one casting to another. The official analytical report confirmed that the casting had been made from a footprint of an 'unknown primate, nonhuman, not otherwise specified.' Is this all starting to sink in yet?"

Brewster remained skeptical and said, "Sorry. I'm not buying any of it."

Dr. Sassman paid absolutely no heed to what Brewster had said. Instead, he focused his attention on the research biologist, who likely had a better grasp of the circumstances. "Now, Mr. Ford, I need to ask you another question as you are the biologist among this august body of scholars who are sitting around this desk. If there are university-based scientific analytics that confirm that this casting that you are now holding in your hand had been created from a footprint made by an 'unknown primate, nonhuman, not otherwise specified,' what is the probability that it is a casting of a foot print made by an 'unknown primate, nonhuman, not otherwise specified?"

Ford stared at the professor and could not answer the question. In fact, he was so stunned that could not even blink his eyes at that point in time. Dr. Sassman raised both of his arms triumphantly into the air as if he were a referee at a football game who had just signaled a touchdown. "Your Honor, and also ladies and gentlemen of the jury," Dr. Sassman crowed with pride, "the prosecution rests!"

14

FIELD TRIP

Intrigued, Brewster stood up and went to look at the college diplomas hanging on Denny Sassman's office wall. Brewster said, "I find this odd. You got your undergraduate degree at Dick Dowling in petroleum engineering in 1966. It looks like you completely shifted gears in life and went back to Dick Dowling and got a PhD in primate biology. What's wrong with this picture?"

Dr. Sassman answered the student's question with another question. "Do you recognize the name Tom Slick? He was a renaissance man and an absolute genius. He had his fingers in a lot of different pies—construction, engineering, oil and gas production, espionage, cryptobiology. Look—you went to Dick Dowling University. Did you live on campus?"

"I lived at the J. B. Hood dormitory for two years, and I was the dorm mother there my last year of college."

"Then you surely should recognize the name Tom Slick," Sassman noted. "Years ago, Slick's firm developed an innovative construction technique called lift slab technology. In multi-floored buildings, each floor was made at the ground level as a steel-reinforced concrete slab. Then the slab would be jacked up on steel beams and secured into place. This saved a considerable amount of money compared to the usual technique of pouring concrete floors at each building rise."

"I'm ashamed to say that I was not aware that," Brewster confessed.

"Both Dick Dowling University and Trinity University in San Antonio had a lot of buildings on their respective college campuses constructed in this fashion," the professor explained. "My father was a structural engineer who worked for Slick, and he helped design the lift slab technology with other engineers. Back in 1961, Tom Slick sent my father deep into the swamps south east of Dayton. Mr. Slick found oil in the area and wanted to drill a well. After he struck oil, a Christmas tree wellhead assembly was dropped in, but a pump jack in the swamps was required to develop the well site into a true production zone."

"What did your father have to do with that project?" Rip Ford asked.

"Slick sent my father out into the forest on a scouting trip to figure out a way how to put concrete footings in the swamp land that would be strong enough to support a heavy pump jack. The wellhead was named Fertile Myrtle Number Four. Well, as it turned out, my father actually had a life-changing experience during this expedition. While he was out in the woods, he had an up-close encounter with what could have only have been described as a Bigfoot that forever altered the way that he looked at the universe. For years, my mother and I refused to believe the story that my father told, but Mr. Tom Slick certainly believed that Dad's encounter was a real event."

Rip Ford remained incredulous. "What did your father's experience in the woods have to do with your PhD thesis that you generated many years later? You said you didn't believe what he had to say at the time about his Bigfoot encounter."

"That's a good question," Dr. Sassman replied, "but as it turned out, it had everything to do with what has happened in my life. Tom Slick previously had funded a cryptozoological expedition to California to look for Bigfoot. He also had funded the infamous adventure undertaken by Peter Byrne to the Himalayas in the late 1950s. The solitary objective of the expedition was to steal a mummified hand of a Yeti from a Buddhist monastery. I'm certain you wouldn't know anything about any of this, as the event up until now has been kept largely a secret. Most of the perpetrators involved are still very much alive at this time, and I am not sure as to when the statute of limitations would run out for the crime of stealing an archaeological artifact. The great American actor and World War II hero Jimmy Stewart was involved. So was his wife. For the few of us who are aware of the caper, it has become known as the Panboche Affair."

Brewster responded, "This is absurd. I have never heard of such a thing."

Dr. Sassman replied, "Look, I couldn't make up a story that's this wild in a million years. The wife of Jimmy Stewart smuggled the amputated hand from Nepal to India. From there, it made its way to London, and it fell into the possession of the world's most famous primatologist at the time, Professor William O. Hill. I actually spoke to Hill before he died in 1975. He told me that nascent DNA assay technology confirmed that the Panboche hand came from an 'unknown primate, nonhuman, not otherwise specified.' Think about that for a moment."

Brewster would one day learn that what Dr. Sassman told the young scientists was indeed the truth. It was many years later when the actor Jimmy Stewart revealed his nefarious part in the theft of the Panboche Yeti hand. Unfortunately, after Professor Hill passed away, the priceless artifact had disappeared, and its current whereabouts remain unknown. Some cryptozoologists have speculated it is now in the possession of a private collector. Although a reproduction of the hand was manufactured and returned to the monks in Nepal, the whole unpleasant adventure will likely deter any future cooperation between the Nepalese and potentially unscrupulous Occidentals. Are there other additional Yeti artifacts that may still be hidden somewhere in the Himalayas?

—∞∘⟩◈⟨∘∞—

"Well, after my father had his Bigfoot sighting," Sassman continued, "he and Tom Slick became good friends. My father went on a hunting trip with Tom Slick to Montana in the fall of 1962. Actually, those in the know confirmed to my mother and me many years later that this was probably another Sasquatch expedition. On October 6, 1962, the plane that ferried my father and Tom Slick out into the woods crashed. There were no survivors. Tom Slick was, and still is, one of the most famous people to have ever come out of the Alamo City. He was a larger-than-life human being, and I'm most grateful that his estate was very generous to my family after my father died."

"How so?" Brewster asked.

"To avoid wrongful death litigation, Fertile Myrtle Number Four was directly conveyed to my family. I'm talking about the real estate deed, mineral rights, the pump jack, and all the goodies including the above-ground tank battery. Oil and saltwater flow out of the wellhead into a receiving vessel called a separator. This is where the oil and saltwater are forced to separate before being sent to their respective separate giant two-hundred-barrel-capacity storage tanks. My family had been awarded all of this stuff, lock, stock, and, forgive the pun, barrel."

"As the old saying goes, every black cloud has a silver lining," Ford opined.

"Well, in my case at least, that may indeed be true. For the last eighteen years, this little gem has cranked out five barrels of oil from the ground every single day. Unfortunately, it looks like production is starting to slow, and I'm beginning to pull out more saltwater from the wellhead now. However, it may still very well produce some amount oil for the rest of my life. That's the precise reason I became a petroleum engineer. If I could learn how to operate and maintain the well site by myself, it would cut down on overhead, and it would improve the bottom line. My hope was to eventually acquire additional production sites and set up a little modest oil company for myself and my family."

"I guess your life jumped the rails after you took those three photographs that you just now showed us," Ford surmised.

Denny Sassman confirmed Ford's speculation. "Take a look at the dates on the Polaroids. May 18, 1966. Over the last fourteen years, I have found large footprints encircling the pump jack a total of four times, and I have always discovered them between the months of March and June. The alleged sighting that my father had back in 1961 took place in March also. I hypothesize that these creatures are migratory and come through East Texas in the spring. I just don't think they are here all of the time. In any event, I had just graduated from Dick Dowling, and I had gone out to the wellhead to try and take care of some problems."

"Like what?" Brewster probed.

"Even though the jack is located in a very remote location, some rascals found Fertile Myrtle and had stolen oil from the on-site storage tank," Sassman elaborated. "Now, this is a big, above-ground tank battery that is sixteen feet high, and it's capable of holding an enormous amount of crude. I was going out to the site to measure the perimeter and to try and figure out the cost of the materials that would be needed to build a secured chain link fence. I just had to try and keep those scalawags from stealing any more oil."

"Is that when you had, for lack of better phrase, a pump jack epiphany?" Brewster asked.

"Precisely," Sassman answered. "As the place was very swampy when I went out there on that day in May, I had to park my truck about a hundred or so yards from the pump jack and proceeded to hump in the rest of the way on foot. That's when I saw the creature.

Its back was to me, and it actually appeared as if it was examining the pump jack for some unknown reason. I crept up behind a bull rush and snapped these pictures. I was only about fifty feet away from the creature when it realized I was present."

"Why do you think it was looking at the pump jack?" Brewster inquired.

"How in hell would I know, J. D.?" Dr. Sassman replied. "Perhaps it was just curious about the steady and repetitive mechanical movement of the jack. Perhaps it was trying to comprehend if the 40,000-pound pump jack assembly could actually generate the 228,000-inch pounds of torque that was needed to be exerted upon the 54-inch-long polished rod with each cyclical rise of the horse's head."

"Lay into him, Doc!" Ford enthusiastically commanded.

"If so," Sassman continued, "was that actually enough force to draw out liquefied hydrocarbon fossil fuel that was over a thousand feet deep in the ground, complicated by saltwater contamination that was infiltrating into the top of the formation? Don't be a dumb ass."

"Don't pay attention to Brewster," Ford said. "What happened then?"

"At first, the creature glanced over its shoulder when it saw me." The professor continued. "Its initial reaction appeared to be one of misrecognition. I swear to God, I thought for a moment that it must have believed I was one of its own kind. It actually smiled at me briefly. I can't make this up. It smiled at me as if it had human traits. When it must have realized I was one of those potentially dangerous hairless apes, it let out a low-pitched chortle as it pooped like a wild man. I must have scared the shit out of it. He let it rip in a ninety-degree-arc. The copious spray of hot, steaming stool made the creature look like it was a Marine who was using a flame-thrower that was charging up Mount Suribachi during the Battle of Iwo Jima. The second photograph I captured with the Polaroid showed a side profile of the beast after it had evacuated its lower colonic track onto the base of the pump jack. I actually was able to collect some of this stool specimen for analysis, and you can see the report in my thesis." Dr. Sassman's recollection was disgusting but nonetheless compelling.

"Did the creature charge at you?" Ford asked.

"No, but that's another good question," Denny replied. "As you might know, a chimp is five times stronger than a human being. A silverback is likely to be seven times stronger than a human being. By extrapolating out from what we know about the strength of the great primates, I would have to estimate that this being was ten times stronger than a human. It was strange. Perhaps the creature was bashful."

"I'm sorry, but if there's an unknown primate out there that's ten times stronger than an average human being, I can't possibly imagine how it could be bashful, as you report," Brewster surmised.

"Check this out," Sassman elaborated. "There was an old TV show from the mid-1960s that was called *Lost in Space*. Do you remember the robot that belonged to the character they called Mr. Smith? Whenever that little redheaded bastard on the television show got into trouble, the robot would flap his arms around like a bird. He would shout out in his mechanical voice, 'Danger, Will Robinson, danger!' That always cracked me up. Well, I tell you, it was just like that!"

Déjà vu. Was it possible that Denny Sassman was somehow a medium for the evil prisoner, E. Rockholder? Perhaps God or the universe picked up a lead pipe and hit Brewster over the head with it. For a transient moment, Brewster acutely lost vision in his left eye. He rose from his chair and covered the afflicted eye with the palm of his left hand.

"Brew, are you okay?" Rip Ford asked with obvious concern. "Fine, fine, fine," Brester answered. "I must have experienced an annoying ocular floater that caused a transient disruption of my visual field. I'm okay, now. Please continue, Dr. Sassman. Don't let me your interrupt your story."

"You better not keel over on me with a premature stroke, Brew,"

Sassman warned. "If you croak, I'll just haul your carcass out to a dumpster so your earthly remains will end up as solid waste to be dumped in a land fill lot somewhere off Holmes Road. Look at the bright side; if you're lucky enough, maybe you could be re-cycled into fossil fuel eons from now."

"Not funny," Brewster protested.

"It wasn't meant to be!" After Dr. Sassman gave the medical student a cursory once-over glance, Brewster's peculiar symptoms spontaneously regressed as quickly as they had originally appeared. The professor proceeded to expound on the photographic evidence he had presented in his doctoral thesis. "In the third picture, the creature had, in one step, cleared a sluice adjacent to the jack. It was easily fifteen feet across. It peeled off into the forest, flapping its arms about. To this day, I believe that the creature was a male specimen. Go ahead, gentleman—take another peek at this picture."

Brewster took another look, and it appeared as if it had both of its arms extended high over its head, as if it was making a "reach for the sky" gesture during a Wild West stagecoach holdup from an old movie.

"It appeared as if the beast was carved out of a block of oak," Sassman noted. "It looked like it had no neck. It was as if its head was bolted directly onto the torso. In the first photograph in the binder, you can see that it had a broad, flat plantar aspect to its foot. The muscular definitions of the calf muscles and deltoids were readily apparent. I know these photographs were taken with black-and-white film, but the color of the creature was slightly reddish. It was not like an orangutan but more like the color of a cinnamon Chow-Chow dog. It's likely that these creatures, if they do indeed exist, have the same range of hair color expressed in human beings."

Dr. Sassman thought for a brief moment and then added, "Well, that might not be completely true. Before my grandmother died from dementia, she had silver-blue hair that was all spooled-up like cotton candy. Her hair matched the fjord blue color that can be found on

Dr. Reed's old BMW 3.0 C.S. automobile. I think it's highly unlikely that any self-respecting mammal would ever choose to have a color that looked quite like that. In any event, after I had this encounter, my life was forever changed. I took plaster of Paris castings of six of the footprints and gathered hair samples and fecal samples as well. I then enrolled into the PhD program at Dick Dowling. In four years, I was able to step up to the plate and defend this thesis you now hold in your hands."

"I find all of this quite incredulous. You based year PhD thesis on a man who may have been dressed up in a monkey suit," Brewster protested. "I was told by Dr. Reed that my alma mater was a second-rate institution. I'm wondering now if that's indeed the case."

Sassman scowled at Brewster and asked, "Does a monkey suit from a costume shop come with a built-in bung hole for a poop chute? I don't think so, Brew. Like the plaster cast of the footprints, experts at Dick Dowling and also at Texas A&M confirmed that the medullary structure of the shafts of hair specimens I recovered was from an 'unknown primate, non-human, not otherwise specified.' Is this starting to sink in yet?"

"What was found in the stool analysis?" Rip Ford queried. Sassman replied, "It was all quite interesting; leaves, berries, whole pecans with the outer shells and all, bone fragments from carp fish, grass, June bugs, grasshoppers, fur and bone fragments from squirrels and armadillos, undigested dog kibble, and bird seeds. Lots and lots of bird seeds. The last two items noted from this creature's epicurean extravaganza would indicate that it had likely made nocturnal residential neighborhood backyard visits. The creature was clearly an omnivore."

"So are bears," Brewster scoffed. "Maybe it was a misidentified black bear running around on it back legs. I would bet my last dollar that the items you described that were found the scat are also items that can be found in bear poop."

"Maybe so," Sassman responded. "I thought about that, but there has been no official black bear sighting in Texas since before the war. No bear tracks have been seen either. In Texas, the black bear has been hunted to extinction. By your theological pontifications, Mr. Brewster, perhaps this is another reason why human beings do not deserve to have a soul. We are at the top of the food chain pyramid, and it would appear that human beings are compelled to either kill or shit upon everything and anything that is below us on the pyramid. Unfortunately, I'm just is guilty as anybody else. Nice, huh?"

Neither Brewster nor anybody else, for that matter, had any idea that black bears would eventually make their way back into the Lone Star state by the mid-1980s. However, at the time that Dr. Sassman took the three photographs of the mysterious creature in question, it was the mid-1960s. Brewster would have to reluctantly concede that whatever creature Sassman had captured in his photographs, it was certainly not a bear.

"What you have shown me seems more compelling than the original Patterson-Gimlin film that was taken at Bluff Creek back in 1967," Rip Ford duly noted. "Why hasn't any of this been openly published or put into a television documentary?"

"I can't lie about this," Sassman reported. "It's all about monetary aspirations. As you may know, the local television star Alonzo Santa Cruz announced that he would give one million dollars to the first person who bags a Sasquatch. He announced it on his TV show, *Live, on Alonzo!*"

"Who is this guy?" Ford querried.

Dr. Sassman was a bit surprised that Ford was apparently ignorant of popular culture. "He's the egotistical, pompous dickhead from Costa Rica with the fat sideburns, leather pants, and hair swept up into a greasy pompadour. I envision that one day he will be handing me a million-dollar check on his TV show. That's why I refused to allow Dick Dowling to have my original thesis editorialized and then published in the *Scientific Texan,* as they insisted. If this ever got out, every yahoo with a gun will be tromping through East Texas, and somebody will bag the beast before I do."

"That scumbag Alonzo doesn't have a million dollars or even a pot to piss in!" Brewster objected. "He's usually doing interviews with homophobic transsexual Catholic priests that used to be celibate lesbian nuns, or maybe misogynistic satyrs with no less than four florescent testicles, or perhaps three-legged, alien mutant midgets from Mars. Let's not forget about the telepathic unicorn sex slaves, feral freaks raised by furry ferrets, card-carrying members of the Democratic Party, and other kinds of retarded and kinky-kind of shit like that."

"Well, maybe so," Denny Sassman considered. "If that's the case, there will still be book deals, movie deals, appearances on talk shows with Johnny Carson, commercial endorsements for a four-wheel-drive off-road type of vehicle, and who knows what else? If I hit the big time, I am even thinking about starting a company that would make different flavors of beef jerky. I'd call it Bigfoot Beef. I could even make silly television commercials showing comical interactions between human beings and a Sasquatch out in the forest to help sell the product."

"Yes indeed," Ford said, laughing. "You, good sir, have the makings to become a bona fide marketing genius."

"For your sake, Mr. Ford, I hope that you're not being sarcastic," Dr. Sassman said as he eyed the biologist with suspicion. "By now, you should be warming up to the idea that chimps, gorillas, orangutans, and maybe even this thing called the Sasquatch are genetic relatives, but they're *animals*. Animals, I tell you. Nothing more and nothing less. At this point, there should be no moral dilemma for you boys to perform medical experiments on animals. Am I clear about this? You have to accept this fact if we are going to move forward on this experimental project!"

"No offense with you being the secondary investigator on this project and all, Dr. Sassman, but I think you're a lunatic. Don't get me wrong, I get along quite well with crazy people," Ford confessed. "Just ask Brewster. Now, this Bigfoot may or may not be a living creature, but nonetheless, your views are a bit odd. I like it, though. In fact, I like it a lot. Hey, Brew; do want to go on a field trip to try and bag a Bigfoot?"

"Why not?" J. D. asked. "I certainly can't see how it would have any bearing on my decision as to whether I would want to proceed with performing inoculations on the big apes. However, I might find a visit into the swamps rather interesting. Although I've lived in Houston all of my life, I'm ashamed to say I've never been out there. I'll go out into the forest with you, Ford, just as long as you promise me that we won't get lost out in the boonies. I wouldn't want to end up as prey to a bunch of rabid Texas Aggies that might be out there lurking in the woods."

"You're on, sport. I'm driving," Ford said enthusiastically. "Why don't you give us a map on how we can find the Fertile Myrtle Number Four wellhead?" Brewster asked Dr. Sassman. "We'll check it out for ourselves."

"No way, José," Denny Sassman cautioned. "Unless you have DNR tattooed on your forehead, you can't go out there by yourselves. You're going to need a native guide. It's beaucoup nasty out there—corals, cottonmouths, copperheads, quicksand, oil-field desperados, and giant 'skeeters that will swoop down and latch on hard. They won't break off until they suck out a quart. They can do it quickly before you even know what happened. There's a sluice of gradeaux with gators, feral hogs straight out of the University of Arkansas that will gore you, Gigantopithecus giganteus, you name it. If we're really unlucky, we might even run into Texas Aggies. As Brewster has already intonated, those are probably the most dangerous and scary wild beasts that a civilized human might encounter in the forest."

Brewster interrupted Denny Sassman and asked, "Back up, back up, back up! I know what a sluice is, but what is gradeaux? I have never heard of such a word."

"It's like grunge, but only slimy." Though he was a bit reticent to infuse any new words into the vocabulary of a medical student he already found to be a bit verbose, Dr. Sassman in the end didn't shy away from what he thought would be a teaching moment. "You will generally find that gradeaux stinks more than grunge. The word can be readily found in the Trans-Pecos lexicon."

"Good God in heaven!" Brewster exclaimed. "You've been hanging around Uncle Hank way too long. There has obviously been a trans-cultural exchange that has no doubt been detrimental to both the people from East Texas and West Texas. I'm indeed fearful that the Republic of Texas is being degraded to the level of a third-world country!"

"Put a sock in it!" Denny Sassman admonished the student. "If you boys insist on going out on a field trip, then it's time for a field trip. I'm going to hit the head and then grab a couple of fryers and some ice-cold beverages that I have hidden away in the lab fridge. Then we'll be off like a herd of turtles. Or perhaps a turd of hurdles depending on how well my Bronco is running today. Before we leave, I want you boys to perform a mental exercise that will cleanse you from any guilty feelings that you may have about performing medical experiments on the big primates. Repeat this sentence after me: 'I'm just following orders.' Say it!"

Brewster and Ford glanced at each other before saying in unison, "I'm just following orders."

"There, now. Are you boys feeling any better about all of this?" It occurred to J. D. that the words he had spoken with Ford happened to be the verbatim ineffectual line of defense that failed to spare the convicted Nazi mass murderer named Adolph Eichmann from swinging at the end of a rope ...

When Sassman returned from the food-stock refrigerator in the animal kennel, he toted a plastic grocery bag with two whole-packaged frozen chickens and a six pack of beverages that he had previously purchased from a local supermarket. He spun his car keys around his right index finger as if he were a gunslinger spinning a .44 Colt. "Follow me, boys. Our little expedition will be about a four-hour round-trip."

In the staff parking lot, Denny's old, two-door, light blue Ford Bronco four-wheel-drive vehicle was discovered to be as nasty as any totaled wreck found at the Holmes Road East-Side Salvage Yard. Gasoline receipts were scattered among a half-dozen empty cans of beer and dirty napkins. There was a petrified, half-eaten taco that was welded to the middle of the dashboard.

"Forgive the unkempt appearance of my humble chariot," Dr. Sassman petitioned, "but I got too busy to take Baby Blue to the carwash when it was scheduled."

Ford poked Brewster in the ribs and asked, "What wash schedule could that possibly be—every other leap year? It appears as if this filthy beast has not been washed since Saul of Tarsus developed an acute case of bilateral cataracts on the Road to Damascus. Come to think, old Saul was probably driving this broken-down shit-box when it happened."

Brewster smiled broadly and said, "Dr. Sassman, I just want you to know how much Ford and I are looking forward to taking a ride in your chariot."

"Smart-ass ..." Dr. Sassman laughed as he glanced over his shoulder.

Within thirty minutes, three men piled into an old Ford Bronco were peeling off the 610 Loop and heading East on Interstate 10 into the dark, deep swamp lands and primordial forests of East Texas. Unbeknownst to Brewster and Ford, the cold beverages Dr. Sassman had brought along for the ride happened to be a six pack of cold beer. Sadly, the professor appeared to have no qualms about the consumption of alcohol while he was driving the big Bronco on the open interstate.

"I'm getting a little twitchy watching you slam down one beer after another while you're driving this vehicle," Ford complained. "Maybe I should take the wheel right about now."

As he tossed another empty beer can over his shoulder onto the floorboard where Brewster was sitting, Dr. Sassman casually disregarded any concerns that Ford expressed about the dangers of driving while under the influence of alcohol. "Tell me something, Brewster; I weigh a hundred twenty kilograms. For a man my size, how much alcohol can be readily metabolized in an hour?"

"With normal hepatic reserve, a seventy-kilogram man could theoretically metabolize the equivalent of one ounce of eighty-proof distilled spirits into inert organic byproducts over the course of about an hour or so. As for a man your size, however, I'm not altogether certain. In any event, I would surmise that it would be at a somewhat quicker pace," Brewster answered.

"Well, there you have it," the professor said with a belch. "You boys are perfectly safe with little old me as the commander of this battle wagon."

"I don't think so," Brewster replied. "By my count, you slammed down a six pack of beer in about ninety minutes."

Ford reached over from the passenger seat, gently tapped the top rim of the steering wheel, and said, "Why don't you pull over and let me drive, Doctor Sassman? It would be the right thing to do."

Dr. Sassman took his fist and slammed Ford's hand against the top rim of the steering wheel. As Ford recoiled in pain, the professor uttered a warning. "I'll break every bone in your hand if you think I'm about to let you take over." Dr. Sassman was now inebriated, and dangerously so. J. D. was also quick to realize that the professor was indeed a nasty individual when he was drunk. There was no apparent recourse at that point for the medical student, or even Rip Ford for that matter, than to simply hope for the best.

"Fortunately, that was the last of the beer," Ford said to his colleague, who was sitting in the back seat.

In the back storage area of the old Bronco, there was a camouflaged rifle case. Brewster pointed to it with his thumb over his shoulder and asked, "Is that the heavy artillery you plan to use to bag the Bigfoot?"

Denny smiled and replied, "Go ahead and laugh, you impudent infidel. It's a twelve-gauge pump, and there are a lot of reasons I need to be armed out there. Snakes, gators, feral hogs, and even a Bigfoot are not too much of a concern. The biggest things I'm worried about are oil field vandals and thieves. After the scalawags stole our oil from the storage tank back in '66, I put in a chain link fence topped with concertina wire. As it turned out, that was about as useless as pissing in the ocean. It barely put a dent in slowing down these rascals. A few years ago, I found a guy who was dead out there. I shit you not."

Alarmed, Brewster and Ford simultaneously asked, "What happened?"

"The guy drove through the chain link fence with a pickup truck," Sassman explained. "That bastard tried to steal the electric motor that powers the pump jack. It's an expensive electric motor, and it's powered by a 480-volt electrical current. It would seem that it didn't occur to him to flip off the power lever in the fuse box before he tried to steal the motor. He got fried. His body was probably out there for six or seven weeks before I found what was left of him."

"Do you have any idea who the thief was?" Brewster wondered.

"I have no idea, not even to this very today," Sassman said with slurred diction. "After he died, something ate most of his carcass. When the DPS arrived, I was severely scolded for not having physically secured the pump jack perimeter. They noted that there was a big breech in the chain link fence. The police said if there was not a big hole in the fence, the guy would have been kept out of danger. It was really weird."

"How so?" Brewster asked in an attempt to keep Dr. Sassman verbally engaged, thinking it would help prevent the professor from getting sleepy behind the wheel.

"I tried to explain to the DPS that it was the would-be thief who had punched a hole in the fence with his pickup truck, but they just didn't see it that way. I can't make this stuff up. Some dumb-ass yahoo breaks into my property to steal my wellhead equipment, and it ends up being my fault when the rascal electrocutes himself," Sassman explained.

"That's a perfect example of how our society is turning upside down," Ford added. "I'm surprised that the family members of the perpetrator didn't try to sue you because you didn't have a sign on the fence that said, 'Danger: Attempting to steal equipment from this site could be hazardous to your health.' That, after all, is the new societal norm."

"Well, that probably would have happened to me," mused Dr. Sassman, "but the truck that was found at the site had been previously stolen. Predation and decomposition had reduced the trespasser to a state that was unidentifiable."

"Sounds to me that whatever happened served the guy right, in my humble opinion. If this was my property and something like that happened to me, Denny, I don't think I would have called the cops," Ford proclaimed. "I would have gone into a Vlad the Vampire mode, cut the dude's head off, and then jammed his skull onto a pike. In the end, I'd spike the damned skull at the entry way into my property at the crossroads. After all, you can always find the Devil at the crossroads. I'd do it just to serve as a deterrent to other trespassers. That's the ticket. After all, this is the state of Texas, and we should be able to get away with shit like that."

"Wait! Wait! Wait!" Denny said, remembering. "Things got a lot worse. Two weeks after I found the dead guy, I came back out with sacks of concrete, a post-hole digger, and new uprights to fix the chain link fence. Guess what I found when I got back out there?"

"A Sasquatch?" Brewster asked.

"No, dumb ass!" Sassman said. "Oil field thieves were back at the site! Two guys in an old pickup truck rolled in with four fifty-five-gallon oil drums, and these bastards were helping themselves to the contents of the storage tank. It looked like they had filled up two barrels by the time I arrived at the pump jack. I broke out my shotgun, but both of these guys had revolvers."

"I hope you were able to scare them away," Ford said.

"No! No, I wasn't," Sassman exclaimed. "Jesus—I was in a Mexican standoff! One of the thieves said, 'I don't think somebody should die today over a couple of barrels of oil. If you promise not to shoot us, we'll unload these barrels and we'll be on our way.' If they had done what they had promised, I would have called it a no-harm, no-foul event. Unfortunately, there's no honor amongst thieves apparently, and it turned out to be a very bad day."

Sassman took a break from telling his story while he tried to extricate the taco that was plastered to the top of his dashboard. After he determined that the fast food item was probably toxic, he heaved it out of the window of the Bronco as it sped down Interstate 10.

"Boys, I have to pee," Sassman proclaimed, "but I don't want to stop. Listen, Ford, you take the wheel of the car and aim it straight. Keep your foot on the accelerator and hold it steady. I'm going to take a leak right out my driver's side window." Ford nervously obliged as Sassman kneeled on the driver's seat of the Bronco to relieve himself.

Brewster anxiously submitted a vociferous formal protest. "You're under the influence of six beers, Professor! Don't do this! You're going to get us all killed."

Sassman replied, "This is one of the benefits of external male plumbing. When I cut loose, I just have to aim at the driver's side mirror. The venturi hydrodynamic effect will kick in, and it will draw the stream of urine away from Baby Blue and into the adjacent lane of traffic. It works beautifully."

Brewster repeated his previous plea, "You're drunk, Denny! Don't do this! What if the people in the other lane don't want to get a golden shower?"

Sassman answered, "That's why the windshield wiper was invented."

For any human endowed with external plumbing who has ever tried to pee out of the driver's side window of a moving vehicle at seventy miles per hour, he would immediately recognize that Dr. Sassman's invocation of the hydro-dynamic Venturi effect was not quite correct. A man should not aim his urine stream directly at the outside mirror. The target ring is actually 3.5 cm lateral to the mirror. If the stream of urine is aimed directly at the mirror, a nasty blowback will occur. J. D., who was sitting in the back seat, was about to get an unpleasant lesson in the laws of physics. He should have moved over to sit behind Ford, who was occupying the front passenger seat. Brewster made a grave error by sitting directly behind Dr. Sassman. When Denny's detrusor urinae bladder muscle had contracted, Brewster was treated to an unpleasant facial mist of aerosolized nitrogenous waste.

After draining his bladder, Dr. Sassman tucked away his plumbing and commenced to zip up his fly. Denny reassumed control of the Bronco from the copilot, Rip Ford, who scolded the professor. "If you do that again, I'll have Brewster take out that scatter gun and draw down on you!"

Brewster was, well, for a lack of a better word, pissed. "You just blasted me with a spray of urine. I swear to God, I'm going to kill you someday. You won't see it coming when it happens." Brewster found a crusty napkin in the back seat and started to dry the mist of urine off his face.

Sassman feigned alarmed and said, "No, no, no! Don't use that napkin! I dropped a load on that."

Brewster's eyes enlarged to the size of dinner plates. "Are you telling me that you ejaculated into this napkin? I just wiped my face with it! What in the hell is the matter with you, Denny?"

Dr. Sassman replied, "Sometimes when there's heavy and dangerous traffic on the loop, I get anxious. Usually, I'll just chug down a beer to take the edge off things. Occasionally, I'll break out the old one-eyed weasel and work it up into a thick lather. It helps to reduce a lot of stress if I'm not able to drink while I'm driving."

Brewster believed he had just been marked with not only urine from his superior but semen as well. It was as if the student had just become the property of Dr. Sassman through some bizarre scatological ritual.

"Did you just get whizzed on?" Ford asked.

At that point, J. D. snapped. "You're right as yellow rain, Rip. Let me get that gun!" Brewster reached back to get the zipped camo bag, and he was about to pull out the twelve-gauge shotgun. "Keep your head down, Ford!" Brewster, however, was thwarted by the trigger lock that had rendered the shotgun inert.

"Relax, Brewster it was just a joke, you idiot!" Dr. Sassman explained in a nonchalant manner. "For heaven's sake, are you really that gullible? Those napkins might be a bit crusty from dried-out mayo, but nothing more and nothing less. Take it easy! The key to the shotgun trigger lock is dangling on my car key ring. Since I'm not about to give it to you, I suggest that you calm the hell down. I have plenty of old gasoline receipts scattered about the interior of this vehicle. You are welcome to tidy up with those if you truly have concerns about the sanitary status, or lack thereof, concerning any old napkins that you might find on the Bronco's floorboard."

Rip Ford looked over his shoulder and tried to assuage his agitated colleague. "It's over Brew. I suggest that you chill out." Brewster realized that Rip Ford's recommendation would be the best course of action. After all, his medical school training was turning out to be one surrealistic hurdle after another. Why should this field trip out into the swamps be any different?

Dr. Sassman began to sober up a bit and correctly thought the best way to defuse the agitated student would be to finish the story about the dangerous encounter with the armed oil field thieves. "Where did I leave off? Oh, yeah. Let me make a long story short. The rascals who were trying to steal the oil from my storage tank had a gate lift on their pickup truck. The fellow in the bed of the truck was a huge, hairy man. He was bigger than me, and I'm not a small fellow."

"You should have blasted the guy then and there," Ford said.

"In retrospect, maybe I should have," Dr. Sassman surmised.

"He muscled one of the barrels onto the truck's hydraulic gate lift and then hit the toggle switch to lower the barrel. Once done, he gently eased the oil drum off the gate lift and inched it onto the ground. I thought he was about to do the same with the second barrel of oil that he had stolen from the storage tank, but that was not to be the case. Both men unloaded their revolvers right at me and then they began to speed away!"

"You see, Denny?! No good deed goes unpunished." Brewster said. "You should've seen that coming."

"It's often said that hindsight is always twenty/twenty or better," Dr. Sassman reflected. "I took two shots at the truck with my shotgun and blew out the back window. I know that I hit the big fellow in the bed of the truck because he grabbed his shoulder and went down like a load of bricks. I also know I hit the driver because I heard him scream. Dig this, boys; I saw blood splattered against the inside of the windshield. I don't think that I killed either guy as the truck was able to speed away. I was too shocked or stupid to get the license plate of the truck as it booked out of the swamp."

"Did the DPS ever catch these guys?" Ford asked.

Sassman didn't answer this most pertinent question.

"Look, Dr. Sassman, I'm not kidding now. I previously said that I wouldn't call the cops under similar circumstances, but what I told you earlier was just a line of bull," Ford now proclaimed with sincerity. "Well, tell me; did they ever catch these guys, or are they still out there somewhere?"

"I never did report this to the police," Sassman finally replied. "Maybe that was wrong, but I just shut up about it. Just two weeks earlier, the DPS had given me a serious rash of shit when they actually implied that it was my fault when a guy got electrocuted while he tried to steal the electric motor that operated my pump jack."

"Well," Brewster asked, "what of it? It sounds like self-defense to me."

"I was afraid," the professor explained. "What would the authorities do to me if I told them about the shootout that I had? Would I be charged with the illegal discharge of a weapon in a dangerous manner? I didn't catch the license plate number, and I couldn't tell you even to this day anything about their pickup truck except that it was old and white."

"This is a bad situation for you, Dr. Sassman," Brewster correctly surmised. "You should've told the cops. I wouldn't be surprised if these two fellows come back and hunt you down someday. If you ever come back out here and simply disappear someday, it will be a fair guess as to your fate. I'm sorry to say that you might not have heard the last from these assholes. After all, revenge is a powerful motive. From my own perspective, revenge is a *very* powerful motive indeed."

Dr. Sassman seemed obviously nervous when he replied, "Yes, I know, Brew, I know. That's the situation I now find myself. I'm very aware that they may come back someday to try and extract their pound of flesh. That's why I have to be especially careful whenever I come out here."

Sassman pulled off the interstate past Dayton and meandered in a southeast direction until he finally came upon an unmarked dirt road. The professor directed the Bronco down that muddy path toward the Fertile Myrtle Number Four wellhead.

A reflective Denny Sassman asked, "Do any of you boys believe in miracles? To this day, I can't understand how those fellows unloaded a total of twelve rounds from their revolvers and missed me completely. I was totally unscathed, and I was only standing twenty-five or thirty feet away from them."

"You must have been lucky that day, Professor," Ford said.

"Well, maybe luck didn't have anything to do with. How could that have happened?" Sassman asked. "I remember that I went to church that Sunday and got down on my knees to thank God that I was still alive. I know that you're a spiritual man, Brewster, or at least you used to be. I wish that you were there, just to have witnessed the miracle that occurred. If you had, you could testify as to what happened."

Brewster noted, "Miracles do happen, but you never know who has been chosen to be the witness. I guess I just wasn't supposed to see this one."

"We're almost there," Denny said. "In another two minutes, we'll be at the wellhead. If the road stays fairly dry like this, we'll be able to drive up the entire way. At a great expense, my family and I added sections of drill pipe set in concrete at four-feet intervals that come up at a forty-five-degree angle. Do you see? These barriers are like a tank trap and they would impale any car or truck that tried to break into the site. There's a ten-foot gap at one spot in between the barriers that is secured by the fattest galvanized chain on the planet Earth. This was put in to allow service trucks to get into the site."

Sassman appeared to be cautious as he looked out the car window and through the rearview mirror to ascertain if there may have been any danger lurking about. When he was absolutely convinced that no unwelcome visitors were hiding in the vicinity, he felt that it was safe to proceed. "Okay, it looks like we're here. Let's go, boys."

The three men climbed out of the Bronco and started to walk up to the pump jack. Sassman said, "Ford, I'm an idiot. I always forget to take the keys out of the ignition of my vehicle. Please be a good lad and fetch them. I don't know what I was thinking, but I also forgot to get the shotgun. Grab the weapon and the metal tape measure that are in the back of the Bronco as well."

While Ford obliged, Brewster noted something unusual on the heavy galvanized chain that helped to secure the site. On one of the chain links, there was an obvious deep V cut that had caught Brewster's attention. "Hey, Dr. Sassman, take a look at this. It appears somebody tried to cut through this chain."

Denny Sassman mumbled an expletive and noted, "Well, some varmint came in here with a bolt cutter, but it was obviously not big enough to get through this chain. Good God, when will this ever end?"

The three men walked directly up to the pump jack, and it was curious to both Ford and Brewster that a large area of about ten thousand square feet that surrounded the pump jack was totally devoid of any vegetation.

Ford dipped his fingers into the moist mud and held it up to his nostrils. It had the odor of an old, dirty oil filter that had been spun off from a V8 engine and then discarded in a back alley.

Brewster asked, "What's wrong with this picture?"

"In oil field parlance," the professor explained, "most production operators refer to these barren regions as the spoil area, although I do recall that an oiler who once worked for me referred to the contaminated ground as the spill zone. In any event, I must confess that it never should be this big, and one would hope that a spoil area never extends much further beyond the footprints of the pump jack and storage tanks. I'm sorry to admit that this relatively large contaminated area is all of my own doing. I readily confess that I'm guilty of the crime of dumping the BSW tank sludge here."

"BSW?" Ford asked. "What does that mean?"

"That stands for base sediment and water," Sassman explained. "Suffice it to say, this nasty, toxic waste fluid is certainly not compatible with carbon-based biological life-forms. The Texas Railroad Commission has jurisdiction over oil production in the state of Texas. I'm not really sure how that came to pass, but I suspect that when the first drop of oil was sucked out of the ground in Texas, the Railroad Commission was comprised of the technicians and engineers that had some kind of expertise to possibly oversee this new enterprise."

"Well," Brewster asked, "what happened that caused all of this damage to the soil around here? Don't tell me the contaminated BSW was accidentally spilled on the ground, Dr. Sassman."

"Well, it was no accident," Dr. Sassman expressed with a big sigh when he took the toe of his shoe and kicked away the oil-impregnated topsoil under his feet. "By law, I'm supposed to hire somebody to haul off the dirty tank sludge and have the waste pumped down into a registered and non-productive wellhead somewhere to prevent environmental pollution and contamination."

"That certainly sounds like a reasonable course of action," Brewster said. "After all, we live on this damned third rock from the sun. Are we not compelled to be good stewards to this home of ours called, the Earth? After all, it's our very one and only confirmed planet 'A' contingency. Last time I checked, we don't have a planet 'B' option to fall back on!"

"What a crock of crap," the professor answered. "I'm not about to hire somebody to haul off saltwater and dirty sludge. That would eat into my profits. I do have a separation tank, but when it gets filled with contaminated, oily saltwater, I just dump it onto the ground. When I have an accumulation of tank sludge, I just dump that onto the ground also. I'm out in the middle of nowhere. Who would know?"

At that point in time, Brewster still had a few residual operative moral fibers. He said, "Dr. Sassman, you just can't do this. That's flat-out wrong. You're going to irreparably damage the environment if you keep this up!"

Dr. Sassman clicked his tongue three times and shook his head as he said, "Listen to me, grasshopper. There are more than twelve million acres of forest in East Texas. There's more forest in East Texas than in the entire state of Oregon. So what if I made a small bald spot? In the big picture, this will *never* matter. I want you boys to follow me now."

Sassman pulled the shotgun out of the camo bag, unlocked the trigger guard, and tucked the weapon under his right arm. He picked up the plastic grocery sack that held the two now partially thawed chickens, and he walked toward the sluice of gradeaux adjacent to the Fertile Myrtle Number Four wellhead. Sassman drew his two companions toward the edge of a nasty, algae-filled, stagnant body of water that was anywhere from fifteen to twenty feet wide at any given location. The body of water trailed off deep into the thicket. Sassman said, "Don't fall in there. That stinky slime is so thick that I suspect if anybody falls in, they will likely drown."

The three men were suddenly bombarded by voracious mosquitoes. In addition, large horseflies would land and immediately inflict painful, sharp bites on any exposed area. The huge, black, flying marauders had enormous, iridescent eyeballs that were the size of marbles. These flying terrors were actually much more annoying than the thick cloud of blood-sucking mosquitoes. Brewster and Ford began to dance about as if they have been dashed with a spritz of Tabasco sauce on their tally wackers.

Sassman apologized. "I forgot to have you boys grab the canister of bug spray that I had in the Bronco. I wanted to show you that this was the place where the Sasquatch jumped over the sluice in just one stride. Now Ford, you must be very careful about where you're standing right now. Six feet to your right is a pit of quicksand. I accidentally got my right leg caught in it up to the calf. It was like stepping into wet concrete. I dislocated my right ankle, and it took all of my strength to free myself from the dangerous muck. I have no idea how deep the pit goes, but if anything stumbles into it accidentally, it would be like a wooly mammoth falling into the La Brea Tar Pits."

What happened next seemed truly unbelievable. Dr. Sassman pulled the two fryers out of the plastic bag and yelled out, "Come here, Popeye! Come here, Bluto!" When Dr. Sassman repeated the call a second time, two alligators appeared in the gradeaux and slowly approached the three men who were standing on the edge of the foul body of water. To avoid becoming Scooby Snacks, the anxious Ford and Brewster backed away from the edge of the sluice.

"That's probably a good idea," Dr. Sassman observed. "These prehistoric reptiles can outrun a human being for a distance of about ten meters or so. Exerting a force of hundreds of pounds per square inch in their bite, they could dispatch with any of us in no time at all. These creatures know me, but they don't know you. Here, Ford, you take the shotgun. There's already a shell in the chamber and three more in the tube. I've got the safety in the off position. If one of these beasts bites me and tries to drag me into the sluice, just blast away. I don't trust Brewster right now with a loaded weapon!"

The two alligators had slowly climbed up the bank of the sluice and patiently remained side-by-side with their gaping maws wide open.

"The eight-foot beast is Popeye. He's my favorite 'gator," Sassman proclaimed. "I gave him that name because he must have been violently assaulted by another 'gator and lost the vision in its left eye. The ten-footer is Bluto."

Dr. Sassman presented a chicken to each of the alligators, and they gently and politely took the offering into their mouths as if they were parishioners receiving the Eucharist at a Sunday Mass. After gulping down their snacks, each of the alligators extended their necks while their semiopaque nictitating membranes snapped closed to cover their eyeballs.

Dr. Sassman sat down between both of the prehistoric monsters and started to vigorously rub their necks right below their massive mandibles. Each alligator was making a low rumbling sound while Dr. Sassman stroked the predators. He spoke to them as if they were dogs. "Who's a good boy? Why, Mr. Popeye is a very good boy! Who's a good boy? Why, Mr. Bluto is a very, very good boy! I love you guys. Okay, I'll see you later."

It seemed undeniable that the alligators appeared to enjoy having a relationship with a human being, if such a thing was actually possible. Once dismissed, each of the giant dinosaurs slowly pivoted and disappeared into the sluice. Brewster was the first of the young scientists to offer an editorial. "Ford was right about you. In fact, the word *odd* fails to capture the gravity of what I just witnessed. I'm sorry, but as far as I know, an alligator has a brain that's about the size of a walnut. You can't domesticate such a creature. You are nothing but grub to an alligator. How about we take the time and trouble to get you fitted out for a hook that you can strap onto a right arm stump?"

"You're mistaken, Brewster," Dr. Sassman replied. "These gators are like pets to me."

"I have an idea," Brewster elaborated. "We should get you a goldplated hook covered with rhinestones. That way, when you get fired from the Gulf Coast College of Medicine for being a dumb ass after a gator bites your arm off at the elbow, you can start right away with your new job as a pimp."

"You'd be a rather imposing pimp at that," Ford added. "I doubt that any John would be stupid enough to try to welsh out on paying for a trick."

"I can see you now driving around in a purple 1972 Cadillac El Dorado, complete with curb feelers and white walls," Brewster said. "Let's not forget the boomerang-styled TV antennae attached to the trunk lid. I'll contact John Phillips from the Mamas and the Papas, and I'll have him send over an ermine hat."

"Silence, knave!" Sassman commanded.

"You'll probably need spats like Babar the cartoon elephant. Oh baby, baby, baby—I can see it now!" J. D. predicted. "You can jam about five or six fat, sweaty, chicks into the back seat of your ride, and you can farm them out for hire by the hour."

Annoyed, Dr. Sassman asked, "Are you finished yet? I'll have you know that these alligators understand who I am. I have a close, warm, and personal relationship with them."

Unbeknownst to J. D. Brewster at that moment, Dr. Sassman would mysteriously disappear from the face of the Earth one day in the not-too-distant future. Perhaps the professor should have heeded the dire warnings the medical student had proclaimed.

Decades later, J. D. would hear a story about a hippy surfer who was known as the Grizzly Man. This character was imbued with the grandiose ideation that he was spiritually connected to grizzly bears that were living in the wild. This deluded individual would go out into the wilderness and get within just a few feet of these dangerous beasts, as he actually believed he was one with the bears.

Well, an incident occurred when the Grizzly Man did indeed become one with a bear. After he and his misfortunate girlfriend were eaten by a grizzly, the bear's digestive system broke down the Grizzly Man and his girlfriend into basic fats, carbohydrates, and amino acids. These raw materials were incorporated into the very being of the grizzly bear that had consumed the two humans.

Any indigestible part that was deemed worthless (i.e., the brains of the "Grizzly Man") was quickly flushed out of the south end of the bear's colonic system. Do bears shit in the woods? Why, most certainly. If the alligators one day deemed that Dr. Sassman was grub as Brewster had warned, the next question to be logically considered is as follows: Do alligators shit in a sluice of gradeaux? Why, most certainly.

Sassman said, "Okay, ladies. It is now time for biology lesson 101. Follow me." Sassman led them back toward the pump jack. He showed them a rusted piece of rebar that had been hammered into the ground. "This is the exact site where I took the photographs of the Sasquatch. From this piece of rebar that has been here now for fourteen years, it is exactly fifty-one feet and eight inches to the base of the pump jack."

"Your orders, Captain?" Brewster inquired.

"Now, Brewster, I want you to go over to the base of the pump jack, and I want you to take this steel retractable measuring tape and start running up the tape from the ground until Rip tells you to stop," the professor instructed. "I want you to place the end of the tape measure nineteen inches from the left side of the fourth-angle iron on the sill of the pump jack. Ford and I will stand here by the grounded rebar, and we'll look at the first photograph as a point of reference when you start to extend the measuring tape. Don't worry, just extend the tape slowly. Listen up; when Rip says stop, I'll ask you to push up the red lock on the measuring tape."

Brewster complied with the instructions, and when he heard Rip Ford shout, "Stop!" he pushed the red lock on the steel measuring tape.

Dr. Sassman asked, "What is the length of the measuring tape where you hit the lock button?"

"I'm at seven feet and seven and a half inches," Brewster replied.

"You boys did pretty well," Sassman indicated. "The optical team that I brought out here to get precise measurements came up with a measurement of seven feet and eight and a quarter inches."

"What's next?" J. D. asked.

"Pay attention, Brewster. Now, I want you to measure the height of the angle iron that supports the walk-around railing on the sill of the pump jack." Brewster again complied and found that the measurement was exactly forty-eight inches.

Dr. Sassman then asked Brewster to rejoin him and Ford at the steel shank of rebar that was embedded in the ground. "Now that we know that the uprights on the walk-around railing at the base of the pump jack are exactly forty-eight inches tall, we can use this information as a point of reference to estimate the creature's wingspan, as both of his arms are outstretched away from his body on the sill of the pump jack," Sassman explained. "You boys need to take a look and give me an estimate of the creature's wingspan."

Both Brewster and Ford agreed that the creature's wingspan was more than eleven feet.

"That's correct," the professor agreed, "and that does not even account for the length of its fingers, which cannot be clearly seen in the photograph. That means the length of its arms comes down almost to its knees. Is that a proportional measurement to the upper extremities of primates designated as Homo Sapiens?"

When Brewster and Ford could not answer the question, Professor Sassman concluded his lecture. "Look, I know you guys think that

I'm a full of shit. I want to prove to you that I'm on the square. No, that was an understatement. I *need* to prove to you that I'm on the square. After all, if you don't believe the story about my encounter, then you're certainly not going to believe anything else I tell you from here on out. If you don't trust me, then the three of us will never get to the finish line on our research project."

"It is not a matter of trust," Brewster said. "The issue is that there's nothing that you've said that makes a convincing argument that you weren't simply looking at a fellow human being that was merely misidentified. I didn't come out here for a religious conversion. I just thought it would be a nice break for me to get out into the forest for a short while. To be honest with you, my trip out here today has certainly been anything but enjoyable."

Brewster would soon come to realize that Dr. Sassman did not just have a conviction that a North American primate actually existed. Instead, the professor's peculiar belief had become an all-consuming, self-destructive obsession. For the medical student, he found that fact to be far more frightening than any possible mythical uncategorized North American primate hiding in the shadows.

"So, the figure in the photograph is possibly a picture of a fellow human being. Is that what you think? I don't give a damn that the creature was over seven feet tall. Maybe one in two hundred fifty thousand to three hundred thousand human beings will grow to be greater than seven feet tall. That's fine by me," Dr. Sassman said. "Maybe a lot of these guys are already playing in the NBA. Even a human being who reaches eight feet tall might not be all that weird. Perhaps only one person in fifty million human beings will grow up to have a height of eight feet, and believe it or not, that's perfectly okay with me."

"Get to the bottom line, Dr. Sassman," Rip Ford said. "By all indications, everything you have just reported falls within the parameters of possible human proportions."

"Well, not quite," the professor replied. "Here's what I have problem with. For my thesis, I did research to see if there was any data concerning the number of human beings who had an eleven-plusfoot wingspan, and I couldn't find anything. I'm serious. In fact, I'm dead serious. Nada. Zippo. Nothing. The Sasquatch, if it indeed exists, is not human."

"Okay, okay, okay!" Brewster said. "I'm not going to argue with you about any of this. Frankly, at this time, I don't give two shits if this animal exists or not. Whether it does or not has no bearing on the primates we have in the lockdown kennel, however. This little field trip today was an excursion into the swamps where I got attacked by flies and mosquitoes. Nothing more and nothing less."

"You and Ford wanted to come out here and see this place for yourselves. I didn't drag you out here," Dr. Sassman said defensively.

"I just thought that maybe this animal that you allegedly encountered in the remote past would give me some perspective on the animals we have locked up in the primate kennel," Brewster replied.

"Just listen to what you said!" Professor Sassman exclaimed. "It has everything to do with it! In your own words, you stated that the Bigfoot, if it indeed exists, is an *animal.* Those were your words! I just heard you say them. Don't you see? That's the whole point! I want you boys to repeat this word after me: animal. Say it!"

Brewster and Ford looked at each other and then said in unison, "Animal."

"If you boys are expecting an epiphany to be bestowed upon you by yours truly, here it is: The gorilla is an animal. The chimpanzee is an animal. The orangutan is an animal. Neither of you guys should ever have any qualms whatsoever of doing any experimental studies on animals. Look around, gentleman. As I previously told you, human beings are on the top of the pyramid. Anything downstream to us really doesn't matter, now does it? Although it's an animal; I'll admit it's a noble beast. It's shy and capable of physical restraint even when frightened, unlike homo sapiens. Perhaps God ended up backing the wrong primate, but who am I to cast judgement?"

Brewster was appalled by Dr. Sassman's lack of insight that everything in the universe was connected somehow. What the professor had actually professed was nothing less than blasphemy, as far as Brewster was concerned. This was a golden opportunity for Brewster to speak out and vehemently object to the vile hubris and arrogance of the Gulf Coast's secondary investigator, ostensibly trying to isolate a mysterious virus. "All right, Dr. Sassman; Let's just suppose you're correct regarding your opinion about primates…"

"You're darned right!" Sassman crowed. "We can take Dr. Hank Holcombe's vision and press on with our hepatitis study and start to inoculate these great apes. We'll be the first to discover this damned virus, and we'll become rich and famous. Let's get back to the Bronco and head down to Houston. This place is creepy when it gets dark. Brewster, I promise I won't piss on you this time."

Brewster replied, "I need you to promise not to shit or spooge on me either. If you don't pinky swear on it, I'm walking."

—∘∘◦❈◦∘∘—

Brewster wondered how it was possible for an extant six hundred-pound bipedal North American primate to avoid being killed or captured. Perhaps if they were smart, stealthy, and little in number, it would be within the realm of plausibility. That was certainly the argument that Dr. Sassman had made in his PhD thesis. Dr. Sassman had hypothesized that if the ratio of the black bear in North America to the Sasquatch was at a ratio of one hundred to one, the mysterious primate would have a breeding population, but it would rarely be seen. What about bone or carcass artifacts? Sassman had actually done an experiment where he had taken a dead deer and staked it out in the forest in East Texas. He used time lapse photography to document the disintegration of the corpse. Within a month, scavengers had assured that the dead deer had completely disappeared.

What did all of this matter? After all, there couldn't possibly be any new primates that are left out there that still remain to be discovered on this planet, Brewster thought. Although for years, Brewster would launch off on pointless expeditions into the forests of East Texas to ascertain if there was any veracity to the claims that a nonhuman, bipedal primate existed in North America, he felt foolish in doing so. At least he felt that way until the first month of the seventeenth year of the twenty-first century. At that time, a great new scientific discovery occurred when the previously unrecognized Skywalker Hoolock primate walked out of the Myanmar forest...

Over a decade after his field trip to the Fertile Myrtle Number Four wellhead, J. D. Brewster's brother Bill told him a disturbing story. Bill left the Tenneco oil company in the early '90s to strike out on his own. Brother Bill had gone off into the deep East Texas woods with a petrologist to look for possible areas that could be exploited for oil and gas production. Bill had met a fellow who was living in a broken-down travel trailer, and he had been off the grid since the end of the Vietnam War. Bill Brewster was only the second or maybe third human contact that this recluse had encountered in eighteen years. The hermit was happily living out his life of solitude without electricity or running water, and he was nearly naked. He lived his life as a hunter, gatherer, and fisherman. The recluse used a bow, and he learned how to trap with a snare. Eighteen years with encountering only two or three other human beings in that time period was quite a remarkable feat, as the fellow was literally hiding out in plain sight.

The recluse told Bill Brewster that there was a clan of separatists that had been living further east, near the Louisiana border. Except for the recluse, this small clan also had no outside human contact since the end of the war. The Civil War! If human beings can completely disappear into the forest, what else is out there?

15

PRIMATES

When Brewster arrived at Blomeo Colima's apartment clubhouse for band practice, he was met at the door by Zip Talbot, who already had his bass guitar slung over his back. As far as how Colima's apartment complex community clubhouse ranked in the subjective hierarchy of ambiance, this facility was, at best, subpar. As it was only a 450-square-foot facility, it was sadly about the size of a standard two-car garage. As such, the clubhouse really had little if any utility to the residents of Blomeo's apartment complex. The kitchenette only had a mini-refrigerator, and unfortunately, it was in a perpetual state of disrepair.

"How was your field trip?" Talbot asked. "I trust it was most illuminating. Dr. Sassman can give quite a pep talk. He also had to give one to me about six years ago out at his pump jack site. When the first shipment of the big primates came in to the medical school back in '74, I thought about resigning from the job. Now it all makes sense to me. I got used to working with the great apes many years ago."

Zip Talbot was a contemporary of Rip Ford, as they were both hired on at the medical school during the same year. Originally from Marble Falls, Zip was a graduate of Baylor University in the early '70s. Zip was a dropout from the South Texas College of

Veterinary Medicine, but his BS degree in biochemistry afforded him the opportunity to join the Gulf Coast College of Medicine research department. Like Ford and Brewster, Zip was single, but he had a well-deserved reputation of burning through girlfriends like a nicotine addict would burn through a pack of cancer sticks. Tall and slender with a pointy proboscis, he was a good tennis player, and he carefully followed the professional career of his idol, Bjorn Borg. His sandy blond hair gave Talbot a striking appearance, and the research scientist had a profile that many would consider was on the threshold of being handsome.

Brewster was surprised to see that Rip Ford had made a guest appearance at Blomeo's clubhouse, and this was a pleasant albeit unexpected surprise. "Rip, I thought that you didn't particularly care for rock-and-roll music. To my recollection, I don't think you've ever heard DNR perform in the past. Aren't you more of a country and western kind of a guy?"

"Talbot invited me to come," Ford replied, "and I thought that my presence would class up the joint of bit. I brought cold beer, and that got me through the front door."

"From my standpoint, having cold beer is like holding a firstclass ticket to the front of the bus," Talbot opined as he addressed J. D. and Rip. "When it comes to the business of primate research, you boys need to be not only on board but also at the front of the bus with me. I look forward to working with you guys, and I hope you're now converts too. Come down to the primate lockdown kennel tomorrow and meet the big boys we've got caged down there. You're both behind schedule. You need to show me the work you've done on calculating the inoculation timeline. Are you gentlemen good to go?" Rip Ford shrugged his shoulders while Brewster nodded his head in an ambiguous counterclockwise circular pattern.

"Where's our drummer?" Brewster asked.

"Dr. Bryan is on the way, and he should be here in five or ten," Talbot answered. "I guess his E.R. shift ended late for some reason, and since Rip used to play drums in high school, I took the liberty to have him set up the drum set now so we'll be ready to go when Dr. Bryan finally gets here. It's sad to think that DNR is going to have its very last gig coming up on the Fourth of July. I'm truly going to miss all of this."

"What's to miss—the flat, piss-warm beer fortified with dead cigar butts?" Brewster asked sarcastically. "After all, that generally constitutes the compensation we receive after each performance."

"You don't get it, do you?" Talbot asked in earnest. "We're not doing this for any reason but to try and sustain an international movement of peace, harmony, and the freedom to engage in antiestablishment personal expression. I believe these aspirations are now on the brink of extinction. If the few people that are in the audience enjoy what we do, that's just fine and dandy. None of that really matters, though. What's important is that we pay homage to the greatest era of recorded music in history."

"Wow, Talbot," J. D. said with mild surprise. "That was actually quite profound. As for me, I just want really cold beer and for it to have at least a modest amount of residual carbonation when I slam it down."

"You made my day, Zip," Ford said, applauding. "I never knew there was somebody walking around on the face of this planet that was full of more BS than Brewster over here."

Blomeo walked up to Brewster to greet him and said, "Hello, brainiac. How's it shakin'?"

"I'm happy as a clam," Brewster replied." Now, I'm not certain how a person is able to discern the emotional status of a brainless, bivalve mollusk. However, if such a humble bottom feeder could be of good cheer, then that would also fit the bill for me. What's up, Blow?"

"You know, I've been thinking," Dr. Colima replied. "Perhaps it's time that you get a field promotion before I finish my fellowship training. I sure as hell will never see any of you guys again after July 4, and I think it's the very least that I can do for you, Brew. You truly are a dumb ass, but at least you try to do good work once in a while. More importantly, you strike me as a man who's always trying to do the right thing, even when you're doing something wrong."

"Thanks, I think," Brewster replied, not exactly knowing where the conversation was headed.

"I have no doubt however that you'll get over your basic decent nature and that you'll become jaded and corrupted before your medical school training is over. As for the time being, you are a good guy and it's time for you to be promoted to the rank of stud status. You need to relegate your rank of being a brainiac into the rearview mirror as of right this minute!"

There was a specific hierarchy at the Gulf Coast College of Medicine, and medical students were ranked according to their clinical prowess. Except for the "brainiacs" enrolled in the MD/ PhD dual-training program, all of the other medical students held the base rank of mushroom at the end of their first two years of classroom education. The mushroom, after all, is but a lowly fungus that's kept in the dark and buried in a copious load of fresh manure.

Once a student finally enters the following two years of clerkship training where direct patient contact occurs, he or she suddenly becomes eligible to be promoted to the higher rank of scut puppy. For a medical student to be promoted to scut puppy status, at least a modest amount of proficient clinical skills had to be demonstrated at that point. The job of the scut puppy is to do scut work—run errands, track down missing laboratory reports, mind-numbing library research assignments to find obscure and esoteric clinical publications, and the like. A scut puppy is a trench grunt and is generally thought of as little more than a dull tool.

The highest rank that a medical student could obtain prior to graduation was the rank of stud. This is a prestigious rank that generally most students would not be awarded until well into their fourth year of clerkship training. This was a rank that allowed the specific privilege of unfettered access to the student lounge, where complimentary beverages and snacks could be found.

Promotions were usually only allotted at the end of a clinical rotation, and the only physicians who had the authority to promote a medical student to a higher rank was either a physician completing fellowship specialty training or an actual attending. When a promotion would occur on rare occasions outside of the parameters of the completion of a clerkship rotation, this abrupt change in a student's rank was considered to be a field promotion, and this certainly gave any medical student bestowed such a rank a pocket full of considerable bragging rights.

Once a student received a promotion, it was the responsibility of either the attending or fellow who authorized the change in status to hand the student a three-by-five-inch index card indicating the student's new rank. To avoid any forgeries or chicanery, a rank card had to be signed and dated by not only the student but by also the physician who issued the promotion. It was imperative for the students to carry their rank card with them whenever they were in training on their clerkship rotations. Needless to say, a student could be busted down a rank if he or she made an egregious clinical error, or perhaps just pissed off the fellow or attending physician one time too many.

⸺◦◦◦❦◦◦◦⸺

"Hey, I just promoted Brewster to the rank of stud, everybody!" Dr. Colima proudly proclaimed. "It was a field promotion, to boot. Let's give Brew a warm round of applause."

"Can you do that, Blow?" Talbot shot back. "I didn't know a student could jump a rank from being a brainiac all the way to becoming a stud. Is that even possible? I've never heard of a medical student completely bypassing the rank of scut puppy like that."

Brewster was shocked. A field promotion given by a fellow was not only rare, but it was also quite an honor. Talbot's question was certainly pertinent, however. After all, was it even possible to leapfrog over an entire rank?

Being a brainiac was okay at best, but it was just one step ahead of being consigned to the rank of being a mushroom, where one is perpetually shrouded in ignorance and fed a lot of dung. On this rare auspicious occasion, Brewster decided not to look at a gift horse in the mouth.

Dr. Colima said, "Come with me. There's a cold beer in the ice chest with your name on it. Talbot has already seen my new toy, but I want to show it to you also."

After Brew grabbed a brew, Blomeo brought the student over to the counter and opened a new guitar case to show him something wonderful. The newly commissioned stud remarked, "There it is in all its glory. A twelve-string electric Ric 360. May I strap it on and plug it in?"

"No!" Blomeo anthropomorphically insinuated that the new guitar had been greatly insulted by the medical student. "That would be like trying to grab the reproductive unit of a stranger standing beside you at a public urinal in the Astrodome. There are some things that you just don't do. Besides, it is not an *electric* twelve-string guitar, you knave. It's way beyond that. It's an *atomic* twelve-string guitar!"

"How proficient are you at playing this thing?" Brewster asked.

"Well, not very," Blomeo honestly replied. "I knew how to play the banjo before I ever learned how to play the guitar, so I already know how to use a pick on the thumb, index, and middle finger. It'll just take a lot more practice."

"So, what's the big secret that you've been keeping?" Brewster wanted to know.

Colima was coy and just smiled back at the student.

"I have to know." Brewster pressed the GI fellow for an answer. "What's the final song in the last set going to be before you ride off into the sunset like Alan Ladd did in the movie *Shane*?"

Before Dr. Colima could answer the question, Dr. Bryan arrived, and it was quite clear that the physician was filled with great mirth. Dr. Bryan was an emergency room attendant in his mid-thirties, and he joined the Gulf Coast College of Medicine soon after completing his residency training. No longer able to exercise because of the long emergency room shifts that he endured, the former college wrestler was starting to develop a mildly protuberant abdominal girth. He had wiry brown hair that was as stiff as a steel wool scouring pad. Although he was not above playing pranks upon others, he was frequently annoyed when his colleagues would rub their knuckles on his sharp and wiry hair as a good luck gesture.

"Well, was it a good day at the salt mines, Doc?" Zip Talbot asked.

"Holy cow! This was actually the best day that I've had in quite some time," Dr. Bryan replied. "I have some great news, boys. I was just informed that Frank Barber was found alive in Nuevo Laredo, and he just made it back to our side of the border!"

"Where in hell had he been all of this time? Has he risen from the dead?" Talbot asked.

"Well, let's just say that what was once lost has now been found. He's coming back up to Houston as we speak," Dr. Bryan reported. "For all of those years, he was being held prisoner by a drug cartel called the Calle Vampiro. This is apparently a new organization that's a branch of one of the Colombian cartels. Brewster, tell me something; were you here in February of '77 when Dr. Barber went missing?"

"No, I wasn't. I came on board in July of that year," Brewster answered. "However, I do know a little about the story, though. It was still all the buzz around the medical school campus when I got here, even though Dr. Barber had disappeared half a year earlier prior to my arrival at the Gulf Coast."

"Here's the setup," Dr. Bryan explained. "Barber and his wife went to San Antonio for a weekend trip. His wife, Nancy, was not from Texas, and she wanted to see the old missions around the Alamo City. They checked in at the Palacio on the Riverwalk and apparently went down to El Mercado to have lunch. That was the last time that anybody saw them. Frank and his wife paid the restaurant bill, and then they just disappeared."

"I remember," Colima added. "It was as if the ground had opened up and just swallowed them whole."

"Precisely. His car keys were found in the ignition of his abandoned car at the restaurant, but for the last three and a half years, there's not been any sign of Nancy or Frank. With blood discovered on the steering wheel, the authorities obviously realized that Frank and his wife were the victims of foul play," Dr. Bryan explained. "It was thought that they'd been kidnapped for money, but that was apparently not the case. Nobody ever requested any kind of a monetary compensation for their safe return."

"Why would a drug cartel want to kidnap Dr. Barber and his wife if it wasn't for money?" Ford asked.

Dr. Bryan was surprised to see that Ford made a guest appearance and was going to listen in on the band's practice session. "Well, look who dropped in from outer space! I guess you're here to critique our noise. It's about time you came out to hear us play. It is good to see you, Rip," Bryan said.

"Thanks," Rip replied, "but what in hell would make Dr. Barber such a valuable commodity?"

"Think about it: Frank probably mentioned what he did for a living to the wrong person at the wrong time while he and his wife were dining out at the restaurant," the ER doctor surmised. "A board-certified emergency room doctor would be a valuable commodity for a drug cartel. Frank became a slave, and they forced him to patch up the injured mules and coyotes that smuggled contraband across the border."

"Are any of us truly safe in this life?" Brewster asked.

"It certainly gives one pause to ponder," Bryan said. "After all, it's indeed a bad world out there. Anyhow, our effete State Department likely knew about the location of Dr. Barber for quite some time, but they didn't want to offend the sensibilities of the Mexican government, which likely is now strongly influenced by the cartels."

"How did he manage to escape from down there?" Colima wondered.

"From what Barber told me on the phone, some gringo went south of the border to engage in illicit recreational activities, and he overheard that an American doctor from the Gulf Coast College of Medicine was being held against his will in Nuevo. Word got back across the border, and it reached Barber's family. Since the State Department under the current Carter administration is useless, Barber's mom and dad sold their house in Dallas and liquidated their own retirement funds to raise two hundred fifty thousand dollars."

"That's a lot of scratch. If that's the case, Barber's going to be paying back his parents for the rest of his life!" Talbot said.

"No doubt about that," Dr. Bryan agreed. "Through logistical planning provided by the philanthropist H. Ross Perot, Frank's family in Dallas hired four mercenaries and a private detective. Apparently these fellows had done similar work on behalf of Mr. Perot in the past. In any event, those five guys went down there to Mexico and rescued him. Just like that. Barber told me over the telephone that the rescue team came in with guns blazing, and they killed everybody at the drug house where he was being held hostage. Barber called me as soon as he got across the border safely and back into Texas. That was less than forty minutes ago. Hallelujah! I've already contacted administration about this good news. There is going to be a press release, and a huge barbecue will be thrown in his honor."

"What about his wife, Nancy? Were they able to find her?" Brewster asked.

Dr. Bryan remained silent for moment and then spoke. "I asked Frank what happened to Nancy. He said when they were first kidnapped, they were separated from each other. He said his captors told him that she was alive and well and that she would stay that way as long as he worked for the cartel, but he never saw his wife ever again. Do I have to spell it out for you? You boys can do the math."

The five men stared down at the floor while the gravity of the situation began to sink in.

Brewster broke the tension when he said, "Let's take a beer and hoist a toast to Frank and Nancy Barber."

Afterward, Colima said, "Let's get to work. DNR will have its last gig on the Fourth of July at the Guaiac Dick Club in Bellaire. As usual, we will open the first set with 'I Fought the Law.' I would like to keep set one and two exactly the same except for one change. 'Who'll Stop the Rain?' will not be the last song in the second set. I want to add a new final song."

"Wait!" Dr. Bryan protested. "I have always liked it when we take the rose petals and throw them out on the audience during the last refrain of the CCR song. It has always been our signature closure now for the last six months."

"Consider this to be a going away present for me, now that I have a twelve-string atomic Ric 360," Colima replied with great resolve.

"I knew it!" Zip Talbot happily exclaimed. "It's about time we're finally able to do something by the Roger McGuinn and the Byrds. About *damned* time, if you ask me. I already know the bass line to 'Mr.Tambourine Man,' so let's crank it out."

"No, I want to do 'My Back Pages.' It's still a folk-rock tune, so you should be happy, Zipper," Colima explained. "Brewster, I'm sure you know the lyrics, so let's give it a try."

"I can't do that song," Brewster said defiantly.

The other three members of the band stood frozen in their tracks and stared at Brewster in shocked silence as their collective jaws dropped. J. D. Brewster was a man who could recall every song, every record label, every release date, and every lyric of every hit tune recorded in the 1960s. Brewster was an idiot savant when it came to rock-and-roll trivia. To be honest, his voice had limited range, but he was a band member only because of his extraordinary encyclopedic memory about rock-and-roll music. His fellow members could never stump him on any record. Surely, he must have remembered this famous song by the Byrds. After all, it was the last hit song the original members of the band, less Gene Clark, ever recorded together.

Talbot spoke first. "Oh my God! Could this be true? We finally found a song that Brewster doesn't know. I'm completely stunned. What's the matter with you, Brewski? Don't you like the Byrds?"

"England had the Beatles," J. D. noted, "but America had the Byrds. In my humble opinion, when it comes to the Byrds, this band of five musicians was without a doubt the most important rock group this country has ever produced. They are completely responsible for three entire subgenres of rock and roll. They were totally the driving force for electric folk rock, and also psychedelic rock."

"Everything you've said so far is a testament as to exactly *why* we should close with this song," Colima said.

"No, that's not it," Brewster elaborated. "After David Crosby was fired from the group, they brought in Graham Parsons, and they produced the magnificent, groundbreaking album in 1968 called Sweetheart of the Rodeo. In light of that fact, they're also clearly responsible for creating what is now known as country rock. No, Blomeo, I love the Byrds. I played the record Mr. Tambourine Man until I wore it out. That was a song that was touched by the hand of God. I would give my left testicle to meet Roger McGuinn. Wait a minute—I don't have a left testicle. Maybe I would be willing to give up my autographed picture of Otis Redding."

"So, if that's the case, how could it be that you don't know anything about the song, 'My Back Pages'?" Dr. Colima asked.

Brewster let out a big sigh of exasperation. It looked like he was going to have to humble his fellow band members yet again. "'My

Back Pages' was originally penned by Robert A. Zimmerman, a.k.a. Bob Dylan. The song first appeared on the album Another Side of Bob Dylan, recorded in the style of classic early to mid-1960s folk music on the Columbia label. It was released in August of 1964, and it had six full verses. Thank God for the Byrds and Manfred Mann. If it was not for those two groups, the interesting lyrics of any of Bob Dylan's songs would have likely never seen the light of day. Dylan couldn't sing worth a shit on a shingle. To me, his voice is reminiscent of the cries emanating from a man who just had a concrete cinder block shoved up his ass sideways. I don't even think that Dylan likes the song 'My Back Pages,' and he was the one that wrote the lyrics. The first time he ever performed it in public was only two years ago."

"If we pull this off, I promise you we'll do it in the style of the Byrds, not Dylan," Talbot said, thinking that Dylan's style of singing was anathema to Brewster's sensibilities.

"I appreciate the offer, Zip," Brewster said, "but there's much more to my feelings about this song above and beyond Bob Dylan's ability to carry a tune, or lack thereof as the case may be. When the Byrds finally came along, they were able to put those lyrics to music. Real music. Not that nasty caterwauling snot that spewed from the perpetually congested sinuses of the singer/songwriter known as Bob Dylan. Although the song was recorded by the Byrds in December 1966, it was not heard by the public until it appeared on the album Younger than Yesterday that Columbia finally released in February, '67. The version by the Byrds had only four verses. After the third verse, McGuinn broke into a signature banjo roll on the twelve-string electric Ric 360."

"Damn it to hell, Brew! For the last time…it's an *atomic* twelve string guitar, stud," Colima professed, "not *electric!*"

"I stand corrected. It was beautiful in any event. It sounded like a zither to my ears. To really appreciate the song in stereo, all rock-and-roll aficionados need to turn the bass way down low and crank the treble up as far as it will go until their ears bleed. I happen to know all six verses of the song as originally written by Dylan. In retrospect, I guess you are correct in your assessment, Dr. Colima. Perhaps I really don't know *anything* about 'My Back Pages', now do I?" Brewster's smugly asked.

As usual, whenever Brewster was able to pull a piece of rock-and-roll trivia out of his ear and expound upon it ad nauseam, the other band members would clap in reverent admiration. Bryan just had to ask, "Tell me then—what kind of problem do you have with the damned song?"

"The song is a downer," Brewster replied. "Of course, lyrics are always open to interpretation. As I see it though, it's a song about a flawed man who toiled at a life squandered in a morass of moral ambiguity while burdened by self-inflicted, unfulfilled potential. If I tell you guys a secret, I want it to stay within the confines of the four walls of this clubhouse. I must confess that every time I sing this song, I break down into tears during the last verse. I'm not kidding."

Dr. Colima needed clarity. "Let me get this straight. Do you actually cry as if on cue when you sing this particular song?"

"Like a baby," Brewster confessed.

"This is fabulous news, boys!" Dr. Bryan proclaimed. "The post-liberated, modern type of woman now digs a man who has an alleged sensitive side. You, Mr. Brewster, appear to have a very sensitive side. That's very hot. I know, I know. I can scarcely believe in such an unmitigated load of horse manure myself, but it must have an element of truth to it. If you can pull this off and actually cry during the last song of our very last set together, something really good is going to happen to us that night!"

"Oh, yeah?" Brewster asked. Failing to see the big picture, he requested Bryan to expound on his obvious enthusiasm about some unforeseen beneficial happenstance. "What would that be?"

Dr. Bryan answered what was already obvious to everybody in the band except Brewster. "We're all going to get laid that night, you moron! Even a dumb ass such as you might accidently find some nookie, just like when a blind hog stumbles upon an acorn! I'm happy for you, stud. I truly am. You are going to be the new love monkey at the Gulf Coast. Life is short. Enjoy it while you can."

"Now, wait just one minute. I don't want to be somebody's sex toy. Men are sensitive creatures, and we're all looking for longterm, meaningful relationships," Brewster responded sarcastically. "I don't want to just pop into the sack with somebody, only to get kicked to the curb in the morning. If I behaved that way, you boys would think that I was just a tramp. A tart. A harlot. A greasy whore on a rollin' dance floor. You know, I'm jail-house bound. Thirty days in the hole. That's what they'll give me now. Thirty days in the hole!"

"Don't you want a snuggle buddy?" Rip asked.

"I'm just saving myself for the right woman!" Brewster professed.

"Hey, Brewster, do you remember the song 'Angel of the Morning' by Merrilee Rush and the Turnabouts from '68?" Ford asked.

"That was actually a cover of the original recorded by Evie Sands on the now-defunct Cameo-Parkway label from 1967," Brewster reported in a nonchalant manner. "The song was written by Chip Taylor, who is, of course the brother of the famous actor Jon Voigt, but I'm certain everybody already knows that fact. In any event, both Evie and Merilee are, to this very day, drop-dead gorgeous. I would gladly let them tie me up and hurt me. Hurt me badly, as a matter of fact!"

"Brew, you're such a freakazoid!" Blomeo said. "I don't know how you could possibly know any of that trivial nonsense. You scare me sometimes! I have a question that's even more pertinent: how can you even possibly stand yourself? You have no idea just how annoying you really are as a human being."

J. D. blushed with embarrassment as everybody howled with laughter. Brewster belted out "Angel of the Morning" and sang it acapella.

After the medical student completed his solo performance of the well-known song about unrequited love, Rip Ford went home.

Fortunately, he left the band with a stocked ice chest of adult beverages. The four band mates worked feverishly until two o'clock in the morning to polish their new song. They also made a point to freshen up the old tunes that were already in their well-rehearsed sets. They wanted to put on a good performance for the very last gig they would ever do together. The spit and polish that enhanced their modest craft would turn out to be an effort worth taking. After all, Brewster had no idea that the upcoming July 4 holiday in 1980 would be a turning point in his life.

The following morning, Brewster and Ford wandered through the dark and foreboding hallways of the research department in the basement of the Gulf Coast College of Medicine until they showed up at the animal kennel adjacent to Denny Sassman's office. "I hope I never get lost down here in this dark, dank shit-hole," Ford mentioned to Brewster. "If I died down here, it would probably be years before somebody would stumble upon my skeleton."

"Don't worry about it, Ford," Brewster replied. "If you ever croaked down here, I assure you that no one would ever come looking for your carcass."

A standard door key was required to gain access into the main animal laboratory. The fifteen-hundred-square-foot experimental animal repository was divided up into three separate sections. The main body of the lab held rows of white mice, standard albino Fischer three forty-four lab rats, rabbits, and the like. These creatures were waiting in the queue to be subjected to a variety of experimental protocols evaluating an array of different human diseases, from cancer to cardiovascular disease, and everything in between.

A second section of the laboratory, known only as the restricted lab was a laminar flow isolation room that could only be reached by going through an air lock. This was the section of the animal lab where misfortunate creatures were inoculated with infectious disease entities to evaluate the natural history of such illnesses in the test subjects, and experimental management thereof. It was mandatory to keep these creatures in isolation to prevent the half dozen or more lab workers who were usually present from contracting some horrid and potentially lethal infectious disease.

At the far end of the lab, there was another security door that was the entryway into the primate lockdown unit, where six large primates including chimps, orangutans, and gorillas, were caged. Although this area was truly more of a prison, it was euphemistically referred to as the "Primate Hotel."

They were met at the entryway into the main kennel by the veterinarian, Dr. Paul Caleb. The khaki jumpsuit that Caleb invariably wore made him look more like a zookeeper than a veterinarian. A bald man with a slight frame who wore glasses, Dr. Caleb was already in his mid-forties when he was invited to come to Houston. Previously the head veterinarian at Emory, Paul Caleb got a big raise to jump ship when he joined the faculty at the Gulf Coast.

Caleb said, "Welcome, gents. It's about time you had an introduction to the great apes. Talbot is already back there. Well, this is a big day. Are you guys ready?"

Exhausted from sleep deprivation, Brewster replied, "Frankly no, but I just keep telling myself that I'm only following orders." Rip Ford frowned and remained silent.

The veterinarian director motioned for the two men to follow him down to the Primate Hotel. This special section of the laboratory kennel had a double-lock system. The primate section not only had a different electronic pad at the entry door, but it also required a standard key to allow entrance into the secured site.

Dr. Caleb said, "Let me introduce you to the specimens we have inside. Before we go in, I would strongly discourage you from giving any of them names for obvious reasons. It's the same reason chicken farmers won't give a name to any of the chicks that hatch at his ranch, no matter how cute they are."

As they entered the Primate Hotel, Zip Talbot was waiting for them. "You look tired, Brew. You really need to try to get more sleep. Okay, boys, before we get started I need to take a look at the inoculation timeline and protocol that you've come up with. It has to be approved by me, Dr. Caleb, and also Denny Sassman. It goes without saying that Hank Holcombe will aso need to relinquish his endorsement before we'll be able to move forward on this phase of the project."

"Well," Brewster interjected, "that final crtierion is of course predicated on whether or not Uncle Hank will actually be our present tense, *active,* or past tense, *erstwhile,* director of this viral isolation study, wouldn't you say?"

"Were you born a pessimist?" Zip Talbot asked. "Have faith, Brother Brew–Dr. Holcombe *will* get back in the saddle at some point."

"That remains to be seen," Ford said as he handed Talbot a manila folder that contained the requested documents that outlined the proposed primate inoculation sequence. The plan was to infect the great apes with the non-A, non-B hepatitis entity in an effort to isolate and identify this mysterious infectious disease.

"What's with the security?" Brewster asked. "It's like Fort Knox around here."

"Better than Fort Knox," Paul Caleb responded. "Each animal is caged in an eight-by-eight-foot iron bar jail cell that is bolted directly to the concrete floor. There is an open drain in the middle of each cell. The pressure hose on the wall is used to flush any waste right down into the floor drain."

"Well, I'm not particularly impressed with the overall hygienic status of this kennel area," Brewster observed. "The ambiance of this Primate Hotel is frankly, less than inviting. It stinks like urine, musk, and body odor in here. Maybe you need to slap a little underarm deodorant on these apes."

"You boys will get used to this stench sooner or later. To be honest, I don't even notice it any longer. In any event, you obviously noted the strict security around here. There's one main reason why security is so high here in the primate section; it's is to keep out the eco-freaks," Caleb explained.

"Eco-what?" Ford asked.

"Terrorists, really. Bunch of nutbar activists that want to put an end to animal research altogether. Last year in Austin, there was a veterinarian who was working for an upstart biopharmaceutical company who got wounded by a sniper. While the scientist was getting into his car after he had left the laboratory to go home from work, some environmental terrorist blew out his left lung with a two seventy-three."

"Wait just a moment," Ford said with alarm. "Are you telling me that some psycho killer with a burr up his or her crazy ass might take a pot shot at me?"

"The Gulf Coast College of Medicine has done a really good job in keeping this primate laboratory a secret. When you start to work with the primates today, it will be necessary for both of you gentleman to sign a nondisclosure agreement. There might be other people within the confines of the Texas Medical Center who know about this place, but for obvious reasons, we certainly don't advertise what we do down here," Talbot explained.

"Okay, Zip–I'll zip it and lose the key," Brewster said.

"That was really funny!" Zip exclaimed with a laugh.

"The radical leftist group known as ALL was thought to have been responsible for the assassination attempt on the veterinarian from Austin," Dr. Caleb reported. "However, no organization ever stepped up to the plate and claimed credit for that particular foul deed. There have been no arrests or convictions on the matter. Nonetheless, while the animal experimentalist was sprawled out and seriously wounded on the pavement beside his automobile and gasping for air, a masked individual approached him with a can of spray paint and left a message on his car. It said, 'Free the Animals.' Do you see what I mean? Eco-freaks…"

"Nice," Rip said. "This just gives me another reason to never go out on a date with a vegetarian. I could end up in a world of hurt and never see it coming."

"That's what we're up against," the veterinarian confirmed. "The Gulf Coast College of Medicine tries to keep the fact that we are doing primate research here at the Texas Medical Center on the QT. If you have any personal concepts of self-preservation, I suggest you do the same."

"Why would a group of patients with acute lymphoblastic leukemia try to assassinate this particular veterinarian?" Brewster asked, although he was obviously confused about the acronym.

"Brewster, you're such a dumb ass," Dr. Caleb responded. "I'm not talking about that kind of ALL, you moron! I am talking about the organization that calls itself the Animal Liberation League. They're a hardcore, violent offshoot of SETA."

"Wait a moment," Brewster said. "Why would the folks looking for extraterrestrial intelligence give a tinker's damn as to what's going on down here on this planet?"

"For shit sake, Brewster," Dr. Caleb exclaimed with frustration, "take a Q-tip and get the wax out of your ears! I didn't say SETI. I said SETA. That's the acronym for the Society for the Ethical Treatment of Animals. It's widely believed that ALL is the para-military arm of SETA. They try to break into labs and free the test-subject animals into the general population. Many of these critters that get liberated are often contaminated with infectious transmissible diseases!"

"I actually know about these characters," Ford confessed, "but I certainly don't think that they're prone to violent acts."

"Oh, really? Are you sure about that?" Dr. Caleb asked with considerable incredulity.

"My roomie from grad school flirted with a member of this society," Rip explained. "I even met the woman on one prior occasion.

I don't remember her real name, but her friends called her Ramrod. She seemed nice enough, though."

"So, you met one member from SETA, and now you're a self-ordained apologist for these yahoos. Are you that naïve? If they *were* a benign organization in the past, they're not now. It would seem that SETA's subgroup organization, ALL, has indeed upped the ante," Paul Caleb said. "They're trying to assassinate laboratory and research personnel involved with animal test-subject specimens."

Without hard evidence, this proclamation was purely conjecture on the part of the lab's chief veterinarian. Nonetheless, he held this conviction to be true. "It's almost a religion to the people who are involved with these types of organizations. I know for a fact that the foundation charter for SETA states that animals should not be exploited for food, clothing, or research. All human beings should be vegans."

"Would part of their fervent mission also include trying to convert lions, tigers, and great white sharks into becoming vegans also?" Brewster wondered. "I'm just sayin'. I'd pay good money to watch them try and do just that. I'll bring my first-aid kit along for good measure."

"You told us the first reason for the ultra-high security. What's the second reason?" Ford asked.

"Rip Ford, do you have a PhD?" the veterinarian asked.

"No, just a master's degree."

"Well, you're nonetheless a bright fellow," Caleb said. "Take a look at these six stinky monsters that we have locked up in these cages, and then *you* tell me why. All three of these species are abundantly stronger than Homo sapiens, by far. If any of them got loose, they might be pissed off at the laboratory personnel that have been keeping them prisoners against their own will. They might go grape ape on us. No, it would be worse than that. They might go purple monkey shit on us, and it wouldn't be pretty."

"That was a rather gonzo hilarious comment you just made there, Bossman," Zip said, "and you didn't even know it!"

"Oh, yeah Dr. Caleb asked. "What's so damned funny?"

"Sorry, Dr. Caleb, but purple monkey shit is the colloquial name for a local strain of a *very* potent Indica that flourishes along the coast," Talbot explained. "Although I don't have any personal knowledge regarding these matters, I understand that it's popular among the legion of cannabinoid aficionados that live here in Texas."

"Do I need to get you drug tested, Mr. Talbot?" Caleb asked.

"No, but thanks for asking, Dr. Caleb. I'm fine right now," Zip cheerfully answered, as if he was politely turning down an offer for a doughnut and a hot cup of coffee.

"Hang on," Brewster objected. "I thought the orangutans are gentle creatures."

It was Talbot's turn to continue the dissertation. "Okay, let's consider the orangutans. Here in the lab, we call them the o-rings. They do seem to be quite docile and amiable; however they're amazing escape artists that could easily shame Harry Houdini in a sleight-of-hand showdown. They study you. They watch you like a hawk. One of them had figured out that there was a press-button, coded electronic lock to get into and out of the primate zone. I remember two years ago one of the brainiacs was working on a MAI bacterial infection project. He was that tall, skinny black fellow that had sickle cell disease. I don't remember his name, but he's already graduated from this program."

"His name was Booker Marshall," Dr. Caleb interjected. "The last I heard was that he was doing research now in Santa Fe, New Mexico, at the St. Francis College of Medicine. He was a funny guy, although he seemed to be in severe pain most of the time. If being stoic is a virtue, Booker had it in spades. Sadly, as far as I know, Booker Marshall's not in good health now. I've been told by the folks in Santa Fe that's he's virtually living on borrowed time."

"That's right! His name was Booker," Talbot remembered. "Well, one night when Booker left the lab, he erroneously thought everything was buttoned-down before he split the scene. You're not going to believe this shit, but one of the orangutans had stuffed a piece of celery into the latch receiver of his cell to jam up the cage's door lock mechanism. After that, the o-ring gently stole the door lock key out of Booker's lab jacket pocket. Booker didn't realize until the following day that he was the target of a master primate pickpocket artist!"

"I hope you're not about to tell us that one of the orangutans escaped from this unit," Brewster interrupted.

"That's exactly what happened, cupcake," Zip confirmed. "After Booker left the lab, the orangutan popped through his own cage and pressed the electronic code into the padlock. It seems that it had learned the code sequence by simply watching Booker and other lab personnel performing the same repetitive motion over and over."

"Believe it or not, this is a true story," Caleb confirmed.

"Wait, it gets a lot better!" Talbot exclaimed. "This crafty beast had slipped the key into the lock by trial and error, and he managed to figure out how to get the door open. I can't make this up. This entire fiasco was captured on the security tape films. Anyhow, instead of trying to make it out of the main laboratory door, guess what he did next?"

As a wild guess, Brewster proffered a highly improbable, yet nonetheless sympathetic scenario. "Did the o-ring try to free the other primates in the lock-down unit?"

"You're darned right!" Talbot replied. "Good guess! That's exactly what it tried to do. Once it found out that it couldn't open up the other cages, what it did next was also amazing. We never really figured out its motivation either. Instead of trying to flee the lab completely, the ape goes over to one of the white rabbits that had been caged up in the general kennel section. It takes the rabbit out of its enclosure and carries it back to the o-ring cage in the primate area. The hairy orange monster then proceeds to cuddle up with the rabbit all night long. Very strange indeed, if you think about it."

"Not really," Rip surmised. "The o-ring wanted a snuggle buddy. "After all, if you can't be with the one you love, love the one you're with."

"I wouldn't think that an o-ring would be familiar with any rock and roll songs recorded by CSN&Y," Talbot said, missing the big picture. "The security tapes indicated that it just held the rabbit closely. For whatever reason, the rabbit didn't appear to mind at all. Why in the world would the orangutan do something like that is anybody's guess, but we couldn't put up with that kind of monkey business. No, sir! We moved that animal up into the queue for the study on the MAI bacterial infections and made sure that the big beast got sacrificed soon after that."

With a strong penchant for sarcasm, Brewster stroked his beard as he stared at the ceiling. "Why would the o-ring do that? Well, that's a tough question, Zip. The answer must be *way* beyond my pay grade, buddy boy. We human beings are unlikely to ever conjure a tenable theory that could account for such inexplicable, evil, and abhorrent behavior specifically displayed by this miscreant primate in question. After all, as these noble creatures only share about 97% of our genomic complement, it would be absolutely impossible for us as Homo sapiens to ever conceptualize the motivational forces that compelled such wretched demonstrable behavior from our closest extant relatives on this planet. Can you postulate any ideas about this intellectually challenging conundrum, Ford?"

"Beats the shit out of me," Ford replied with a shrug.

"Well, there you have it." Brewster was clearly annoyed by Talbot's lack of perception. The student sharply swiveled his head and looked at Dr. Caleb. J. D. tried to ascertain if the veterinarian was also struck by how truly callous Talbot appeared at that moment. The director of the kennel, however, was completely unfazed by Talbot's recollection.

It was clear to Brewster that Dr. Caleb was just a company man, devoid of compassion.

Ford directed his attention to the gorillas and asked, "What do we need to know about these big boys? I have to learn more about the other primates and their idiosyncrasies."

"Now the gorillas here are powerful," Talbot replied as he pointed to the largest specimen. "They might make a charge and rough you up a bit. They'll likely swing away with their big arms, and they might even try to bite. I was charged by this beast in here a while back when I had to enter its cage. I was scared, but I wasn't hurt. I grappled with it, but the animal clearly showed restraint."

"Wait just a moment, Mr. Talbot," Dr. Caleb said, now quite perturbed. "Are you saying this gorilla bit you? This is the first time that I've heard about this event. You committed a laboratory safety violation for failing to report this incident. What in hell is the matter with you?"

"Well, the big male bit me on the calf after it knocked me down," the research assistant explained, "but it didn't break my skin. In retrospect, I actually think that it just wanted to roughhouse with me. Since that time, we've had mutual respect for each other. I know, Dr. Caleb, that's technically against the rules, but occasionally I'll go in there and wrestle with the beast. It even lets me win sometimes, as it'll play dead. Then the ape pops right up and starts to laugh."

"Are you kidding me?" Ford asked as he wagged his index finger at the largest of the incarcerated apes. "I'm sorry, Zipper, but if you get your arms ripped out of their sockets someday because you were jerking around with Magilla Gorilla over there, that's on you."

"Relax, gentleman," Talbot continued. "Do you know gorillas can laugh? It is a deep basso profundo, rapid rumble. It doesn't sound like the laugh of human beings, but I know laughter when I hear it. The smaller gorilla watches with great interest when I wrestle with the big guy. When I get after it, the younger and smaller ape makes the same deep rumble sound, and it seems to be quite entertained by the spectacle. A while back, I decided to take on both gorillas at the same time. It was a real hoot."

"Now I know what's going on back here when I hear the racket coming out of this lockdown kennel," Caleb suddenly realized. "Is there anything else you want to confess?"

"The big guy lets me pin him to the floor sometimes, and the younger and smaller fellow will gnaw on my arm," explained Bart, not fully realizing that he had just jumped into a pot of boiling water when he told his story. "The little guy will work away at my arm as if it's trying to eat corn on the cob. Of course it never hurts me, but it'll make that low-pitched rumble the entire time while I'm getting worked over."

"So, you regularly come in here and play with these animals?" Brewster asked in astonishment.

"As Dr. Caleb will attest, I'm not supposed to interact with these animals in such a fashion," Talbot explained. "Not only is there is safety issue, but both Dr. Holcombe and Sassman have expressed concern that I might become too fond of these creatures."

Ford and Brewster both looked at each other and then fixed their gaze back on Talbot. Brewster hoped that somehow Zip Talbot would indeed become too fond of these creatures. Maybe Talbot was potentially redeemable and he would again find the compassion that he once had for these noble primates.

"I swear, Mr. Talbot, if I hear about you wrestling with these gorillas again," Paul Caleb cautioned, "I'm going to flat-out stomp your sorry ass. Am I making myself clear?"

"Cut me some slack, Doc," Zip pleaded. "I promise I won't do it again."

"I've got administrative duties," Caleb reported as he walked toward the exit of the primate kennel. "Don't forget to tell them about the potential issues they might face with the dangerous chimps. When you are done, Mr. Talbot, you need to come over to my office for an official chat about your clandestine sophomoric activities."

"Go easy on him, Dr. Caleb," Brewster pleaded.

"As for you, Mr. Brewster, you have a reputation for being a screwball," Dr. Caleb interjected. "What happens to Talbot is none of your concern, but let this be a lesson to you: don't even think about engaging in any foolish monkey business down here, or else I'll make sure you get kicked out of the dual-training program. If that happens, you'll never get your PhD." Dr. Caleb issued a dire warning to the student that was clearly not just some hyperbolic threat.

"Straight up, boys; it looks like I'm in a sling. I've got nobody to blame but myself," Talbot realized. "Before I face a firing squad, I need to tell you that the animal that offers the greatest risk to your personal safety is the chimp. Down here in the nether world of the primate unit, we call them trogs. I have given them the nickname to honor the 1960s English proto-punk rock band of the same name. The college paid a lot of money for us to get our hands on these specimens specifically for Dr. Holcombe's hepatitis research. I couldn't begin to tell you how much liability insurance we have to pay to house the chimps down here."

"If I didn't know any better, it sounds to me that you're actually afraid of these trogs," Ford observed.

"I am indeed," Talbot admitted. "These chimps don't come from the wild. In fact, none of the primates that we have here were harvested from the forest. Every one of these animals came from breeding farms that explicitly produce specimens for medical or scientific experiments. It's believed that the chimp is our closest living relative from a genetic standpoint. Just like human beings, they are occasionally prone to profound acts of violence."

"Well, you said it," Brewster concurred. "Here in Houston, you can simply go out on the streets and find evil people who would kill or maim you for no apparent reason. Am I not correct?"

"So it would seem," Zip agreed. "Just go ask Irene Segulla that question. I'm certain she would tend to agree. The chimp is so much like a human being in its ability to reflect both our good and bad characteristics that it's actually quite disturbing. I have seen kindness and altruism that has been displayed among these animals, but they can turn on a dime."

Brewster was curious and needed to know more. "Give me an example of what you mean."

"We get our chimps shipped to us from a breeding facility in the port city of Libreville in Gabon," Zip explained. "Back in '75, a big adult male chimp that was being used for breeding purposes grew up to a stout two hundred eighteen pounds. It got loose in that facility, and in a matter of minutes, it killed one of the lab technicians. The story made the news wires in Western Africa and also in France, but for some reason the AP and UPI didn't find the story interesting enough for dissemination to the Western Hemisphere."

"Fill us in on what happened," Brewster requested.

Talbot extended his left hand dismissively, as if he was an elementary school crosswalk attendant attempting to stop approaching rush-hour traffic. "No, stud, you really don't want to know."

"To hell with that," Ford interjected. "If we're going to be working with these potentially dangerous creatures, I want to know exactly what happened to the lab tech in Africa. Fill in the blanks right now, and I want to hear all of the gory details."

"Okay, you asked for it," Talbot said. "Don't go a-runnin' home to yo' mama if you don't like what I'm about to tell you. The chimp attacked the lab tech's face, biting off his nose and jaw. You heard me correctly. The tech lost his jaw, tongue and all! If the guy had survived the attack, he would have looked like the character known as Mort from the old Bazooka Joe bubblegum cartoons. Do you remember him? He was the goofy character that would always wear a red turtleneck sweater that would cover the lower part of his face up to his eyeballs."

"Yeah, yeah, yeah," Brewster said impatiently, "but how long did this attack last?"

"From what I was told, it all went down very fast," Talbot replied. "When one of these trogs gets riled up, things can fly off the rails pretty quickly. In any event, after munching on the dude's face, the chimp went after the guy's genitalia. I can't make this up. He yanked the guy's trousers down to his ankles and then chowed down on the dude's external plumbing. No mustard. No relish. No bun. I'm saying it must have been a very bad day to have been an Oscar Meyer wiener."

Talbot began to digress. "Now, personally, I'm not a big fan of Rocky Mountain oysters. One of my crazy ex-girlfriends and I used to go to a restaurant over on Westheimer where they served exotic grub. This gal of mine would always order a plate of deep-fried Rocky Mountain oysters. I don't think she liked eating the rubbery gonads as much as she enjoyed trying to piss me off. As she smiled maliciously, she would just sit there and chew away on them as if she was working over a piece of Bazooka bubblegum. She would gnaw on each deep-fried testicle for twenty minutes. It was a horrible spectacle to behold."

"Stop right there, Zipper—tell us more about the chimp attack," Rip requested. "Where's this story of yours supposed to be taking us?"

By this time, Talbot was not about to get reeled back in. "I often wonder what someone like Sigmund Freud would have said about my ex-girlfriend's libido, or what opinion a shrink would have about her psychological mainframe in general. She used to make a rather disgusting sound when she chowed down on a plate of rubbery, deep fried bull balls. It was as if she was speaking Vietnamese. She would say, 'Nguyen! Nguyen! Nguyen!' She was nasty in more ways than one, but maybe I'm getting off track."

"I think you're so far off track that you are on another planet," Brewster said. "Finish your story about what happened to the lab tech when he got attacked by the angry chimp."

"Bear with me," Zip said. "I'm almost at the finish line. Well, the poor bastard was still alive at that point, and he tried to escape the hostile ape. However, his assailant was apparently not finished quite yet. As the lab tech tried to crawl away, the chimp grabbed him by his legs, and then it pulled the man's shoes off to keep him from escaping. However, the trouble was that the man's feet were still inside those shoes! The chimp ripped the dude's feet off right at the ankles. The chimp didn't bite off the man's feet; it just did it with brute strength!"

"That's terrifying," Ford said.

"Now do you see why these monkey sons of bitches scare the holy crap out of me? I'm not precisely sure how a trog could do something like that, and therefore I'm not exactly certain as to what specific technique was employed to rip the man's feet off from his lower extremities at his ankle joints. Perhaps the chimp just yanked them off, much like a man would pull a pine cone off a tree branch," Talbot speculated.

"Stop right there!" Brewster demanded. "Do you think that these two chimps in here are perhaps capable of doing something like that?"

"Hands down, Brew," Zip answered.

"Well, fuck me runnin'!" Brewster said. "I'm out of here."

"Don't go yet," Zip pleaded. "Let me share an alternative theory I have about what happened to the lab tech back in Africa. I'm inclined to think that the beast torqued the man's feet off like a person would spin the cap from a bottle of a tasty, cold wine cooler. Do you boys like wine coolers?" Talbot asked. "I like the ones that taste like margaritas. I know that the alcohol content is quite low. However, if you throw in a lime wedge, they can be quite refreshing on a hot day."

Both Ford and Brewster were irritated with Talbot at that point. "Focus, damn it!" Ford commanded.

"Will you just finish it?" Brewster clamored. "What in hell is the matter with you? Quit gargling with the bong water, Zip! Get back on track and fill us in about what happened next."

Talbot shrugged his shoulders and said, "Nothing. That's end of the story. The lab's security team breached the door, and they blasted away at King Kong with twelve-gauge pumps until the beast was cut in half. They hit it with alternating magnum rounds of lead slug and buckshot, as I was told. Happy now?"

"No," Brewster said, "I'm far short from being happy at this moment. You're a dirt bag, Talbot. You are too, Rip, if you're on board with *any* of this."

"I have to amble off and get some things done, and Dr. Caleb needs to rip me a new one." Zip was apparently resigned to his pending reprimand for unprofessional behavior. "I'll leave the door open, and you guys can stay in here for a while and get a bit more familiar with these big boys. However, for what it's worth, I wouldn't dick around with the trogs if I were you."

"Fair warning," Ford said.

"You simply have to close the door upon your departure. After you leave, I'll come back with my key and engage the second door lock," Zip added.

"How do we get back in here when we need to?" Brewster asked.

"Depending on whether or not my ass-end is still attached to my body after I see Dr. Caleb, I'll head over to maintenance and get Harper to cut you each a key so you can have free access to the Primate Hotel," Talbot explained. "The code for the primary electronic lock is simple to remember; it's one-two-three-four and then the pound sign. Press it in sequence, and don't screw it up, or else you'll engage an automatic lockout. Don't let the bedbugs bite."

When Zip Talbot finally vacated the kennel to receive a well-deserved tongue-lashing in Dr. Caleb's office, he left the two young medical research scientists alone with their future test subjects.

Upon Talbot's departure, Brewster walked over to look at the gorillas, and Ford went to the cage that held the biggest orangutan. "I've been here as long as Talbot, and I've known the guy for what seems to be an eternity," Ford said. "Despte that fact, I don't know what happened to him, but Zip's lost something."

"Yeah," Brewster readily agreed, "his mind! Talbot's a smart guy, Rip, but I think his head bolts are a bit loose now."

"He's actually a decent fellow," Ford said in the defense of his colleague. "I've oftentimes heard him wax poetic about peace, love, and rock and roll. Somehow, he's been brainwashed."

"Sadly, I believe you're spot-on in your clinical assessment," Brewster concurred.

"Talbot appears to be completely desensitized about performing medical experiments upon the great apes," Rip observed, "and I'm rightfully afraid that's what Denny Sassman is trying to do to us. It's as if the research department expects us to able to compartmentalize this job and sequester our own emotions somehow."

"Either that," Brewster said, "or leave us completely devoid of any emotions whatsoever. I do *not* want to end up like Dr. Caleb."

"Me neither. As far as I'm concerned," Rip concluded, "it would seem they want me to put my very soul into a jar and then tightly screw the lid down to keep it confined. That's not going to happen. If for one minute I would ever allow myself to forget about the reality of what I'm expected to do, that jar would soon be filled to the brim with moral decay."

"Perhaps it's quite possible to actually become disconnected from the internal moral compass that governs human behavior," Brewster postulated. "I believe it would be more likely to happen if we abide by Dr. Sassman's mantra of just following orders."

"Perish the thought!" Ford exclaimed.

"Allegedly, the evil Nazi doctor named Josef Mengele was reportedly a beloved family man," Brewster offered as an example. "Despite this admirable attribute, he was nonetheless able to butcher other human beings in cold blood during WWII. I'm not sure how something like that exactly happens, but it happens."

The big gorilla had no discernable facial expressions when it knuckle-walked over to J. D. and then turned its back toward him as it sat down. Then it pressed its back against the bars of the cage. "I guess this big boy doesn't like me very much," Brewster speculated. "I just got the brush-off."

"No, dumb ass," Ford replied. "It wants to be groomed. Scratch its back!"

While Brewster obliged the gorilla, the orangutan reached out its hand toward Ford. Rip cautiously put his index finger into the palm of the orange primate. What happened next was amazing. The amiable ape gently moistened Ford's index finger with its lips. It then took a piece of straw from the floor of its cage and began to gently clean the man's fingernail and groom his cuticle. A few tears began to run down Ford's face as a received his pro bono manicure.

"I'm not going to be able to do this, Brew," Ford said with apprehension. "I can't bring myself to inoculate these animals. I know you must feel the same way that I do. How are we supposed to handle this situation?"

Brewster walked over to visit the smaller gorilla, and as the medical student had approached the younger primate, it also plastered its back against the bars of its cage to eagerly await a back scratch. "I don't know, Rip. If and when Uncle Hank ever comes back to take charge of this crazy-ass place after getting his skin and lymph node biopsy procedures done, we're going to have to tell him something."

On the following day, a team member from the Department of Occupational Safety and Infection Control, Kristina Coffee, paid Brewster and Ford a visit at their workstation in the basement laboratory. "You boys are not going to like this, but we have some new regulations to contend with. These orders have come directly from the medical school and the hospital's joint task force that was formed to reduce the risk of occupational hazards. What I'm about to tell you about is an official edict directly issued by the Work Safety Commission. From this time forward, whenever you guys are going to be in direct contact with contaminated blood or body fluid, you will now be required to wear double gloves, a disposable yellow paper gown, and a full-face shield. In regard to wearing double gloves, the cuff of the first pair must be underneath the sleeve of the yellow gown, and the cuff of the second pair must be pulled over the *outside* of the sleeve."

"Okay," Brewster agreed, "but none of these new precautions will ever prevent us from getting an accidental needle stick someday. After all, that could still happen."

"You won't get any argument from me about that particular matter. Nonetheless, rules are rules," Mrs. Coffee explained.

"Is there anything else?" Brewster asked.

"There's one more safety issue that I need to specifically discuss with you specifically, Brewster," Mrs. Coffee said with a scowl. "The med-surg nurse Missy Brownwood informed me that she saw you recap a used needle before you dropped it into the red safety bucket for disposal. Have you lost your mind? If you're concerned about getting an accidental needle stick from infected material, that's exactly how it might happen. I swear, if you get infected with the non-A, non-B hepatitis entity from doing something stupid like recapping a used needle, I'm going to clobber you!"

"That was my mistake," Brewster admitted, "but I'll make sure it won't happen again. Anyhow, Missy Brownwood talks too much."

The occupational safety nurse pinched her lower lip between her thumb and index finger while she studied Brewster and Ford momentarily. "As a black American with African roots, I must honestly tell you that I have serious misgivings about the utilization of the great apes in your upcoming experimental project. I can't help but feel that this is just another exploitation of natural resources from parts of the world that will forever be condemned to nothing more than a perpetual third-world status."

Brewster was unable to maintain eye contact with Mrs. Coffee, as he felt embarrassed.

"By the same token, I personally believe it would be immoral to inoculate these animals with an infectious disease and then sacrifice them," Kristina Coffee professed. "I just couldn't do it, and frankly, I can't see how you boys could do it either."

Ford looked up from his workstation and reprised a comment that the occupational safety nurse had previously stated. "You won't get any argument from me about that particular matter …"

❖

Before Mrs. Coffee left the laboratory, a looming figure showed up in the doorway. It was none other than Dr. Denny Sassman. While the research scientist purposefully blocked the egress from the lab, he waved about the folder that contained the inoculation protocol previously outlined by Brewster and Ford. He brought the folder down to waist level and began to tap on top of the document with his index finger.

"Well, your proposal isn't bad," Sassman admitted, "but there's one obvious deficiency that Dr. Caleb and I found in this protocol that needs to be addressed. You gentleman neglected to consider that the non-A, non-B infectious agent may be transmitted by an enteral route. We don't know for sure one way or the other, but it's possible. Before anything else, that matter needs to be either ruled in or ruled out. As a matter of fact, this should be studied right off the bat. Think about it—this would be the easiest subset of our experimental study to actually get completed, and we can knock this out much sooner than later."

"Wouldn't the investigation into the possibility of an unlikely oral route of infection absolutely mandate that an extra round of test subject sacrifices will need to be performed?" Brewster asked with concern.

"Hang on, Brew," Dr. Sassman said. "Let me lay it out for you."

"Ford and I already considered expanding this experimental study to include the investigation of a possible oral route of infection, but we shit-canned the idea. That's why I don't like your suggestion. Frankly, I don't like your suggestion one bit," Brewster said defiantly.

"Hear me out, grasshopper," Dr. Sassman implored. "As long as you boys follow up with the necessary lab work to evaluate hepatic parameters during the post-inoculation incubation period, I'd venture that we should be able to get these six apes to the finish line. If you play your cards right, we won't need to bring in any additional primate test subjects down the road. Tell me this—do you boys have a handle on what the incubation period might be for this infection?"

Brewster and Ford glanced at each other and then looked back to Professor Sassman without being able to answer a question that should have been addressed long ago. If Brewster had simply paid more attention to the medical history of the numerous patients who had passed through both the infectious disease clinic and also the hepatology service over the past year, he should have readily ascertained the answer. A more thorough observation of the natural history of the onset of this disease in the known patients who were infected with it should have offered a clue.

"Oh, for the love of Jesus! You guys have already been on this project for an entire year, and you can't answer this one, fundamental keystone question?" Dr. Sassman asked with expressed disappointment. "Stop what you're doing! Stop right now. You boys need to go back to the drawing board and get this issue sorted out properly."

It was late in the afternoon when Brewster realized that Irene Segulla was still expecting him to come by her room on the med-surg unit to pay a visit. For Brewster, these daily visitations to the hospitalized patient had become much more than a professional obligation. He had truly grown quite fond of the nurse, and his obvious concern for her well-being had only grown exponentially from the time she had been critically injured. Although she was restricted in her abilities to communicate to him through an erasable marker and a white board that she kept on the Mayo table beside her bed, Brewster was nonetheless quite pleased that Irene's feelings toward him were mutual. After all, Irene would invariably beam at the young student whenever he entered her room.

"Well, Irene, I'm still waiting to meet your niece, Stella," Brewster joked as he entered the room. "To be honest, I went by the Psychiatry Department where she works to pay her a visit. I stuck my head into the office of Dr. Corka Sorass to introduce myself to her, but she was away from her desk at the time. It's really a shame, because it took me all day to build up enough courage to actually have a face-to-face meeting with her. As you suggested, I entered a physical training program to improve my stamina. No less than four times a day, I practice by holding my breath as long as I can, and I also use an incentive spirometer device to enhance my pulmonary reserve. I believe that I'm now ready to take Stella out on our first date together!"

Something was wrong. Brewster realized that Irene had a look of terror on her face. She pointed up to the plastic bag of liquid nutrition that was being fed into her percutaneous gastrostomy feeding tube and made a quick motion with her hand across the anterior aspect of her neck, which indicated to Brewster that she wanted him to discontinue the tube feeding immediately. The student pulled back the sheet covering Irene, and it was obvious that her abdomen was markedly distended and also tender to palpation. Brewster placed his stethoscope upon the epigastric area of the patient, and he did not detect any bowel sounds.

Brewster realized that Irene Segulla was on the threshold of a catastrophic event. She had developed either a small bowel ileus or an acute episode of gastroparesis. Regardless, none of the liquid nutrition that was being gravity fed through the percutaneous gastrostomy feeding tube at that moment was moving downstream. All of the nutrition that was being poured into her was dammed up in the stomach with no place to go! Brewster realized that the gastric contents of Irene had to be evacuated, and it had to be done immediately.

Brewster clamped off the feeding bag and disconnected the line that was connected to the indwelling, large-bore gastrostomy tube. He needed a big irrigation syringe to suck out the contents of Irene's stomach, but there was none to be found in the patient's room. Brewster flipped on the emergency call light to get somebody's attention, but his plea for help remained unheeded. He opened the door, stuck his head into the hallway, and called out for assistance. "I need help in room three sixteen. I need it now!"

The nurse Missy Brownwood showed up and said, "Irene's nurse is in the can. What's going on, Brewster?"

"No bowel sounds! I turned off the feeding tube, but her abdomen is really distended. We need to get her stomach emptied out right now. Her mouth is wired shut. If she pukes right now, she's going to be in a world of hurt!"

Missy immediately understood the peril Irene faced. "Oh shit, oh dear!" Missy Brownwood looked at Brewster and said, "We had this trouble with Irene once before, and this is why her gastrostomy feedings should have been carefully monitored. Her feedings should have only been administered with a small volume syringe utilizing a bolus technique! Somebody screwed the pooch here!"

Nurse Brownwood turned back to her colleague and said, "Hang in there, Irene! For God's sake, don't vomit. Do you hear me? I'll be right back!" Irene clenched her eyes tightly as she sweated profusely and tried to stave off the overwhelming urge to regurgitate.

Missy Brownwood returned immediately with a long, firm plastic tube and a big irrigation syringe. Missy hooked up one end of the plastic tube to the wall suction device and the other end to the percutaneous gastrostomy feeding tube. Sadly, when she turned on the wall suction vacuum machine, nothing happened.

Brewster began to panic. "What in hell is wrong with that goddamned thing, Missy?"

"I don't know! It is not working. Use the irrigation syringe, Brewster. Hurry!" the nurse instructed.

Brewster immediately began to suction out Irene's gastric contents as fast as he could manually operate the irrigation syringe, but then disaster struck. Irene began to vomit! As her mouth was wired shut, the hapless patient was incapable of parting company with the now acidic and caustic material that was previously occupying the space in her upper gastrointestinal tract. Following the path of least resistance, the vomitus poured into the patient's lungs as if a dam had burst. As her eyes rolled to the back of her head, Irene Segulla quit breathing.

Within seconds, the voice over the PA system cried out a plaintive call for help that was repeated over and over again: *"Code blue! Med-surg unit, room three sixteen. Code blue! Med-surg unit, room three sixteen!"*

To Be Continued

GLOSSARY OF TERMS

(MEDICAL OR OTHERWISE)

aerobic organism: An organism that cannot live or grow in the absence of air.

anaerobic organism: An organism that is able to live or grow in the absence of air.

anoscope: A transparent plastic tube that is utilized to visually inspect the rectal vault.

antigen: A foreign material that may be able to insight an immunological response.

atheromatous plaque: A fatty deposit within the interior lining of a vessel that can cause vascular narrowing.

big dirt nap: Dead and buried.

bilateral mastectomy: Surgical removal of both breasts.

bilirubin: Waste material found in bile that is formed from the biological breakdown of hemoglobin.

bowel perforation: A puncture in the bowel wall. If it occurs, it is a medical emergency.

BRCA1: An inheritable oncogene that may predispose a patient to acquire breast cancer.

BRCA2: Another recognized inheritable oncogene that may predispose a patient to acquire breast cancer.

choriocarcinoma: A subtype of cancer that may involve the testes.

cirrhosis: A disease of the liver characterized by scarring and fibrosis as a consequence to chronic inflammation caused by a variety of diseases, including viral infections, alcohol abuse, etc.

code blue: This is an announced hospital emergency requesting a full-court press to try to resuscitate a patient who has suffered a cardiopulmonary arrest.

code gray: This is an announced hospital emergency requesting security intervention to assist an individual who is being physically assaulted.

Cowden's syndrome: An autosomal-dominant inherited disorder characterized by an increased risk of certain forms of cancer.

creatinine: A component of nitrogenous waste. Levels of this material found in the blood reflect kidney function.

crab picker: Colloquial term for a medical oncology cancer specialist.

crab zapper: Colloquial term for a radiation oncology cancer specialist.

DNR: *Do not resuscitate.* This is a designated declaration indicating that a patient declines to receive any heroic revitalization attempts in the event of a pending cardiopulmonary arrest.

ECOG: Eastern Cooperative Oncology Group.

ECOG performance status: A standardized measurement of a patient's symptoms and ability to participate in life activities. An ECOG 4 indicates that a patient is bedridden and no longer capable of independent living.

EDTA: An abbreviation for ethylenediaminetetra-acetic acid; generally refers to a specialized blood-collecting tube to be utilized for clinical laboratory testing.

endorphins: Naturally occurring, self-generated analgesics.

epinephrine: Adrenaline. The primary acute stress hormone released during fight-or-flight situations. It is a hormone that is produced in the adrenal glands.

erythematous: An overt red discoloration.

estrogen: The primary biological female hormone.

eternal care unit: Heaven.

gamete: Either a male (sperm) or female (ovum) haploid cellular entity that is able to engage in conjugation with an opposite sex gamete to form a zygote in the act of biological reproduction.

Genesis 6:5–6: (King James Version, public domain): "And God saw that the wickedness of man was great in the earth, and that every imagination of the thoughts of his heart was only evil continually. The Lord regretted that he had made human beings on the earth, and his heart was deeply troubled." Cross reference to *Dr. Blow's Honeybun Diet* 6:5–6: "It looks like God backed the wrong primate."

gradeaux: A wet and slimy version of grunge.

GRID: Gay-related immunodeficiency syndrome. This was a disease that is now known as AIDS.

grunge: A drier version of gradeaux.

gyri: Convolutional contours of the brain.

halitosis: Butt breath. Bad breath that is even nastier than the ass end of a dead hippopotamus.

hematocrit: A measurement of the percentage of whole blood that is comprised of red cells.

hemoglobin: The oxygen-carrying respiratory protein found in red cells.

hepatitis B: A subset of an inflammatory infection of the liver caused by a specific DNA-type virus.

hepatocytes: Parenchymal cells of the liver.

hepatology: The discipline that involves the study of the liver.

hepatorenal syndrome: A life-threatening illness that results in the degradation of both the liver and kidneys.

HER-2/neu oncogene: An oncogene responsible for a tyrosine protein kinase component of an epidermal growth factor receptor. Amplification of this oncogene may result in the development and progression of an aggressive form of breast cancer.

HIPAA: The 1996 Health Care Insurance Portability and Accountability Act. Sadly, it was a HIPAA regulation that prevented John Q. Public from ever learning what type of multiple sexually transmitted diseases previously infected the serial sexual abuser known as William Jefferson Clinton. Although inquiring minds want to know, it is only a matter of speculation as to what caused his male plumbing to rot off at the curly cues.

homo-satchel: The Trans-Pecos dialect's pronunciation of the word homosexual

hysterectomy: Surgical removal of the female reproductive plumbing including the uterus and fallopian tubes

immunological seroconversion: A clinical situation that is tantamount to the recognition of an antigen by the immune system with the possible conveyance of immunity.

inflammatory breast cancer: A very aggressive form of breast cancer that presents with inflamed and erythematous skin overlying the malignant breast.

integument: Skin.

Kaposi's sarcoma: A cutaneous malignancy that generally appears as a violaceous plaque associated with AIDS. This is a cancer caused by herpes virus 8.

keloid: A firm, nodular, hyperplastic scar.

lyophilization: Cryodesiccation—a preservation technique utilizing freeze-dried methodology.

MAI: Mycobacterium avium intracellularae. An infectious bacterium.

Matthew 5:29 (King James Version, public domain): "And if thy right eye offends thee, pluck it out and cast it from thee."

mesenteric lymph nodes: Lymph nodes that are found within the intra-abdominal area.

metastases: The appearance of cancer that has spread far from its primary site of origin to other body areas via the lymphatic system or blood vessels.

mushroom: A lower fungal life-form utilized as a derisive nickname to describe an inexperienced medical student.

mycobacteria: A gram-positive, aerobic, acid-fast bacteria. Tuberculosis and MAI are two examples of infectious diseases caused by microorganisms that are designated as mycobacteria.

NCCN: National Cancer Coalition Network.

nephrotoxic: A substance that is potentially dangerous to the kidneys.

non-A, non-B hepatitis: An infectious entity that is now recognized as hepatitis C.

norepinephrine: A secondary acute stress hormone.

omentum: A rubbery membranous tissue found in the abdomen that acts as a shock absorber for the internal organs.

oncogene: A gene that when often mutated or amplified has the potential for cancer initiation and proliferation.

orchiectomy: Surgical removal of the testicles.

paracentesis: The removal of an abnormal accumulation of fluid within the abdomen.

paraplegic: Paralysis of the lower extremities.

perctaneous: The access of internal tissues directly through an invasive approach through the skin.

Port-A-Cath: A central venous access device that is surgically placed in the body to facilitate the administration of intravenous medications, including chemotherapy for the treatment of cancer.

proctoscope: A longer version of the anoscope.

progesterone: The secondary biological female hormone.

proptotic: Bug-eyed. As an example, go to Google and look up the late English comedian Marty Feldman.

psychogenic blindness: A stress-induced, psychiatric dissociative disorder manifested by self-limited unilateral or bilateral loss of visual acuity.

PTEN gene: An oncogene that drives the production of dephosphorylate proteins. Mutation and amplification of this gene can cause human cancers.

seminoma: A subtype of cancer that may involve the testes.

serosanguineous: A bodily fluid that is an admixture of blood and watery serum.

sulci: The normal grooves and fissures that are found on the surface of the brain.

tachycardia: Rapid heart rate.

transient ischemic attack: A completely reversible ministroke event

triple-negative breast cancer: A very aggressive and poor-prognosis form of breast cancer. The cancer cells in this particular subset of breast cancer lack estrogen receptors and progesterone receptors, and there is no amplification of the HER-2/neu oncogene.

vitreous intraocular material: The gelatinous material found in an eyeball.

vivisection: Dissecting an animal (or human being) while the subject is still alive.

yolk sac (tumor): A subtype of cancer that may involve the testes.

Z-track: The introduction of a needle into a body cavity that purposefully follows an irregular path to prevent a postprocedure fluid leak.

zygomatic arch: Part of the skull that protects the eyeball.